"If thou gaze long into an abyss, the abyss will also gaze into thee."   —*Nietzsche*

Abyss: The primeval chaos. The bottomless pit; hell. An unfathomable or immeasurable depth or void."
    —*The American Heritage Dictionary*

You're holding in your hands one of the first in a new line of books of dark fiction, called Abyss. Abyss is horror unlike anything you've ever read before. It's not about haunted houses or evil children or ancient Indian burial grounds. We've all read those books, and we all know their plots by heart.

Abyss is for the seeker of truth, no matter how disturbing or twisted it may be. It's about people, and the darkness we all carry within us. Abyss is the new horror from the dark frontier. And in that place, where we come face-to-face with terror, what we find is ourselves. The darkness illuminates us, revealing our flaws, our secret fears, our desires and ambitions, longing to break free. And we never see ourselves or our world the same way again.

PRAISE FOR
BRIAN HODGE'S BOOKS

Nightlife

BRIAN
HODGE

A DELL BOOK

Published by
Dell Publishing
a division of
Bantam Doubleday Dell Publishing Group, Inc.
666 Fifth Avenue
New York, New York 10103

ISBN: 0-440-20754-1

Printed in the United States of America

Published simultaneously in Canada

March 1991

10   9   8   7   6   5   4   3   2   1

OPM

For Clark Perry,
my Siamese twin
joined at the id;
and
for Dolly Nickel,
who showed me stars
and gave me ladders

ACKNOWLEDGMENTS

Yes, it's time to hack down a few extra trees to provide a well-deserved page of written applause to deserving souls.

Thanks go to Jeff Hamilton, R.N. C.E.N., Brad Strickland, and Randy Smith, for providing useful information on, respectively, the effects of hallucinogens, the effects of poisons, and every piranha's Achilles heel. Topics that make life more interesting, to be sure. Also, thanks to my editor, Jeanne Cavelos, for the usual faith and advice and new, improved suggestions.

Thanks to Karla Sanner and Kristin Leister of the Orlando Convention Bureau for pulling a few strings (You're still missed up north, Karla. Especially happy hours on Thursdays!), and to Glenda Gilmore's office at Busch Gardens, for the freebies.

And extraspecial thanks to Clark, Donna, Mike, Tim, Laura, and everybody else who makes Tampa what it is: dangerous for normal people to visit.

PART I

GREEN STUFF

1

THE RAId

The jungle grew shadows, and the shadows grew eyes.

Across the Western Hemisphere, dawn was coming simultaneously to tens of thousands of locations. Millions of souls arising for their days, stumbling sleepily for radios and coffee and morning editions—oblivious to anything going on in the world not covered by Bryant Gumbel and the rest of the mass-media pack.

Equally oblivious to the denizens of high-tech civilization were those who rose with the dawn in the equatorial jungles of southern Venezuela. They were the Yanomamö. They were the Fierce People.

Angus Finnegan watched as the brown-skinned warriors crept near to the low stockade wall surrounding the village of Iyakei-teri. The raiding party, numbering just over twenty, moved like predatory cats, jaguars silently stalking prey. They carried bows made of palm wood, so hard it deflected nails, that were as long as the Yanomamö were tall. The arrows alone were six feet long, built for interchangeable tips. This morning war tips were in place—bamboo lanceolate coated with sticky brown curare.

Angus made a curious sight among the raiding party. Better than a full head taller than the tribe's tallest man, he stood a hulking six foot five. His long, unkempt hair and beard had gone white several years before, giving him a look of some Old Testament prophet sun-blasted toward madness in an unforgiving desert. He wore dirty khakis instead of robes, but the allusion wasn't far off. And at sixty years old, he looked to have the power of a man twenty years younger.

Kneeling beside a thicket of brush and ferns, Angus scanned through the gloom toward the village. Weak shafts of sunlight cut through at a slant, and the air was alive with the calls of birds. Macaws, parrots, others. Beneath the constant canopy of trees, the jungle was never very bright, and during the chill of dawn, visibility was murky at best.

But they had not come too late. The Colombians were still at the village; probably overnight. Their rowboat, powered by a large outboard motor, rested against the muddy bank of the stream near the village's main entrance. A few winding kilometers downstream, it linked with the larger Orinoco River. Odds were that the Orinoco would take them back to one of the more civilized areas with its own airstrip.

Before Angus even heard him coming, the headman of the raiding tribe, from Mabori-teri, was at his side. His name was Damowä, and like many of the raiders, he had painted his body black with the pigments they used in ceremonies and warfare.

"Are the enemy still here?" he asked in the native tongue.

Angus nodded.

The black paint ended just under Damowä's eyes; above the line, those eyes spoke a profound mixture of ferocity and fear. "Will they have the wasp-guns?"

Angus lowered his great shaggy head for a moment, then raised it. Inside, what the Yanomamö called his *buhii*— his inner self—was cold. Their expression for sadness.

"Yes," he said softly. "I think they will."

Damowä nodded once. "Then we will just have to kill them before they point them at us."

If only it were as simple as it sounded. As Damowä silently padded away on his callused feet, Angus bowed his head once more. And left it there.

"Father God," he prayed, whispering, this time in English, "there will be deaths this morning. But I see no other way. And so I ask You, if there is to be punishment for them, that You'll heap it upon my head, and not theirs. Because I'm the one who led them into this. Through the blood of Your Son, amen."

Some of the Yanomamö had long since accepted the presence of God. Or Dios, as they sometimes called Him, depending on the nationality of the missionaries who had first arrived to convert them. In many cases, their religion was a mixture of reverence to Dios and a tenacious clinging to the spirit world served by countless generations of their ancestors. Of the ten thousand or so Yanomamö in the rain forests of Venezuela and Brazil, many had been converted to some degree.

Angus wondered, not for the first time, how often it happened the other way around. That a missionary was converted by the Yanomamö. He was willing to bet that he was the first and only.

Angus lifted the shotgun he'd brought. He wasn't one to leave *all* the dirty work to his primitive charges. If they were going to be risking death at the hands of an enemy village, at his bidding, he could do no less than join in the fray. And in their eyes, it made him just that much closer to being Yanomamö—and therefore, human.

The cultural values running deepest in their souls were nearly a complete flip-flop of what Angus had known as a Scotch-Irish Catholic from Boston. Christianity taught meekness, forgiveness, turning the other cheek. The Yanomamö believed that ferocity and avenging all trespasses was the key to living. Theirs was a society of small villages, usually numbering seventy to eighty, never more than 250. A village grows too packed, and it becomes one giant pressure cooker, with feuds and fights constantly erupting over sins real or imagined. Stealing food, sorcery, trysting with one man's

wife while the husband's back was turned. Theirs was a society in which men beat their wives to show they cared, and a
wife without scars was considered unloved. Should she cheat
on her husband, he might go so far as to hack her ears off with
a machete as just punishment. Yanomamö country was indeed a man's world.

It was a society in which nearly every afternoon the men of
the village would load yard-long hollow tubes with *ebene,* a
pale green powder made from the inner bark of a particular
tree. They would squat and take turns blasting the *ebene* into
each other's nostrils with strong breaths. *Ebene* was halluci-
natory, putting the takers into a trance in which they met
with their personal demons. Experienced shamans could
sometimes even coax the demons into living within their
chests.

Naturally, men of God were appalled. And over the last
few decades they had attempted to dispense with the naked
pagans' filthy demons and bring them around to the ways of
Western society. American Evangelicals, various Catholics,
Spanish Salesians. Methodology and doctrine differed. The
results were invariably the same: the gradual erosion of a
culture that had heretofore remained pure for thousands of
years.

Angus Finnegan had spent nineteen years with the Yanomamö of Mabori-teri. The first fifteen trying to strip them
of their silly spirits. And the last four trying to repair the
damage.

For in their well-intentioned meddling, the missionaries
had managed to trip a row of dominos that would eventually
lead to the twentieth century bulldozing right over one of
the last sovereign Stone Age tribes in the world.

Missionaries led to mission posts. Posts led to airstrips. Airstrips led to increased contact with foreigners, including
tourists with a yen for the exotic. Which led to exposure to
diseases that the Indians had never encountered and, therefore, had no resistance or immunity to. A measles epidemic
could kill, and had. Trinkets of the West had wormed their
way into the Yanomamö way of life, even in the most remote
villages.

At first such trade goods were innocuous—machetes, aluminum pots, steel axes and knives. Later came boats with outboards, and clothing. And shotguns.

Once the Yanomamö roamed their homeland nearly naked. All the men wore was a narrow waistcord, to which they tied the foreskins of their penises to keep them from dangling. That the sight of a naked body stimulated thoughts of lust had never entered their minds until the missionaries insisted so. Increasingly the Indians felt ill at ease without some sort of covering. Swimming trunks, loincloths, even Fruit of the Loom Jockey shorts were often the rule rather than the exception now. Headman Damowä had come by a pair of which he was extremely proud—boasting drawings of a jubilant Mickey Mouse, whom he called "the happy rat."

But whereas clothing was harmless and sometimes even amusing, the arrival of shotguns was not. They were finding their way more and more into Yanomamö warfare. And where a quarter of adult male deaths were already due to warfare, an arms race was the *last* thing they needed.

A lot of the shotguns had even come from the missionaries themselves. Give them flashlights and shotguns, went the sentiments of some, and the Indians will be forever dependent on you for batteries and ammunition. Even the missionaries were not above petty squabbles over who would be first to reach uncontacted villages.

Angus was fully aware that violence and treachery were a part of daily Yanomamö life. Still, as bad as it could get, that seemed far preferable to hypocrisy. And hypocrisy was something the Yanomamö did not know.

It was learned by example.

Angus had long resided in *hushuo*— emotional turmoil. For he had come to know the Indians on a level that most of the missionaries never would. With dignity, nobility, wit, with a strength of kinship unsurpassed anywhere. *As fellow human beings.* While some of the missionaries outspokenly professed beliefs that the tribesmen were subhuman, on a par with animals.

Well then, let him who is without sin cast the first stone, Angus had thought at his breaking point four years ago. *As for me, I'll have no part in destroying their lives any longer.*

Not that they shouldn't come to know God. But God dwells

in unspoiled jungles as readily as in suburban tract homes. There had to be a happy medium.

But the die had been cast, and its path was downhill all the way. Change could not be stopped. Impeded, perhaps. Which meant knowing what to expect. It was only a matter of time, then, before they were contacted by traffickers in the drug trade. At least in Iyakei-teri.

Angus still kept a calendar, kept track of days and dates. This was April, tail end of the dry season, and that had been of enormous benefit to hopes of ending things here and now. Intervillage gossip ran rampant during the dry season. During the rainy season, the trails between villages became impassable swamps, isolating each tribe for the duration. Had the Colombians come between next month and September, he would never have heard the news. About men from the outside world coming to trade fabulous supplies for a magical powder recently cultivated by the Iyakei tribe. A powder called *hekura-teri*, which had made them the most feared tribe around.

May God have mercy should it reach the outside world.

The raiders could see thickening plumes of smoke rising from within the village. Newly awake, the Iyakei were stoking their dwindling fires with fresh wood. It wouldn't be long now.

The raiders nervously worked wads of green tobacco in their mouths. They were edgy. Mabori-teri was a three days' walk away. Their traveling food—the bananalike plantains, a dietary staple—was nearly gone. And last night they could have no fire, since it might have gotten them spotted. As a result they were cold and feared spirits that might have approached overnight. Raids were always like this.

They could hear voices now, steadily increasing chatter.

Yanomamö villages consisted of an oval-shaped succession of huts called a *shabono*. Each hut was built adjacent to its neighbor, until the oval was enclosed. An open plaza in the middle. A log stockade surrounding the huts. Periodic gaps in both for entrance and exit. Overnight, these were filled with brush, a first-defense burglar alarm.

Angus watched and listened as the Iyakei removed the deadbrush and a few emerged. Voices mostly announced intentions to defecate. Bodily functions were as ripe for talk as plans for later in the day.

The raiders, concealed in brush and gloom, were as silent as ghosts, notching arrows into their bowstrings. Ready. Meat-hungry for war. They waited patiently as the Iyakei, armed even during this commonplace activity, relieved bowels and bladders. Alert for any sign of discovery. Angus tensed as a taller man in bush pants came out to do his duty as well, fifteen feet away. Long hair; certainly not Yanomamö. They kept theirs trimmed by razor-grass into bowl-shaped cuts, men and women alike.

Colombian. Toting along a small machine pistol. What Damowä had called a wasp-gun, because the spray of automatic fire reminded him of an attacking swarm of angry wasps. No doubt these were their fundamental trade gifts for the *hekura-teri* powder. Keep the tribe full of incentive for continued cooperation. All they'd have to bring next time would be ammunition. If the missionaries could play that game, why not the drug exporters?

Fifteen minutes later, the same Colombian led two others out, armed as well. Couldn't be any more left inside. Three men and their load would be pushing it as it was, given the size of the boat. They stood guard and oversaw Iyakei tribesmen, who came out toting canvas bags to load into the boat. *Now or never.* Angus signaled.

Damowä was the first to let his arrow fly, and a second later some twenty more went streaking in. A Colombian was the first hit; he took Damowä's arrow in the throat, the war tip snapping off as the shaft fell to the ground. As one voice, the Mabori roared their savagery.

In answer, the wasp-guns roared back.

Angus unleashed his own war cry and erupted from his crouch. He let the shotgun do the talking from then on.

His first blast peppered the leg of another Colombian and sent him sprawling into the mud of the stream bank. He jacked another shell into the chamber and spun, an avenging angel with broken wings, and blasted a tribesman clumsily attempting to sight in on him with a machine gun.

Pandemonium had arisen from within the village. Screams from the women and children, enraged cries from other warriors who came out to join the battle. Arrows whizzed back and forth, bullets chewed up trees and foliage all around the Mabori. Twenty feet to Angus's left, the machine-gun fire nearly tore one of the raiders in half. Six guns were firing at once, two with the Colombians and four in the inexperienced hands of the Iyakei.

Experienced or not, it didn't matter as long as they pointed in your direction and squeezed the trigger. You were just as dead or wounded. And the casualties began to mount up on the raiders' side quicker than on the Iyakei's.

Angus fell to the ground as bullets chopped at a tree above his head, then took out one of the gunners with another shotgun blast. One of the Mabori, Kerebawa, took out another one with an arrow. The wound itself, in the thigh, would never be fatal. But the curare wasted no time in taking over, paralyzing him from the outside in.

The Mabori were pinned down behind their cover, with little recourse left but to fire blindly into the air and hope the arrows got lucky. Dumb luck and instinct. While the injured Colombian laid down covering fire from the ground, his long-haired partner and a tribesman crouched low to finish loading the boat.

Another gunner fell, after which a Mabori warrior loosed an arrow and sprinted closer. With a quick burst of fire, his head showered apart.

Another Mabori screamed for vengeance and charged from his cover, a machete held aloft. He actually managed to outrun the path of bullets sent after him, and Angus watched as he descended upon the hapless gunner and hacked him across the face. A moment later, the avenging Mabori was skewered by the sharpened end of a seven-foot club.

The one saving grace for the Mabori was the Iyakei's unfamiliarity with their guns. Ammunition was wasted, long bursts were fired instead of short ones. And once their clips were empty, the attempts to reload were clumsy, those who had extra clips to begin with. It was the only thing preventing Mabori extinction.

Still, the Iyakei had managed to buy enough time to finish loading the boat. Angus swore aloud and clenched his teeth firmly when he heard the outboard fire up. He rose again, heedless of the danger, an arrow nearly skinning off his nose. He unleashed two rapid shotgun blasts toward the boat. When the injured Colombian rose to return fire, he took an arrow in the belly.

But the third throttled the engine and kicked up a sudden wake as the boat took flight. Angus could have wept with frustration. Unless a wild arrow claimed him, and this seemed less and less likely the farther away he got . . .

. . . the entire massacre had been for nothing.

As he looked at fourteen bleeding bodies strewn across the forest floor, with more likely to fall, he could have ripped out his hair in great handfuls. Even greater than the sense of failure was the self-loathing over what he had done: he had torn apart the very men whose souls he had come to save. If a man like that was not condemned to Hell, who was? His *buhii* was so cold by now, it was a glacier, scraping his heart raw.

He was about ready to motion to Damowä that they might as well retreat when he heard it. When they *all* heard it. The entire jungle split with the sound, and it held its breath to listen in awe.

From within the village came as unearthly a shriek as any of them had ever heard. Angus had heard something similar twice before, this dry season, and had prayed never to hear it again. Now it was worse, though. Now he was going to get a chance to witness its source close up.

It wasn't quite human. It wasn't quite animal. It wasn't quite spirit. It was somehow the worst of all three, and then some.

Every warrior still alive on the battlefield froze as it tore the morning air to shreds. The upper canopy exploded with birds that hadn't even been driven off by the sound of gunfire taking flight. From deeper in the jungle, monkeys screeched in fear.

Fierceness as a way of life be damned. Two of the Mabori flat-out turned tail and made tracks back through the jungle.

While *it* came running from the main entrance of the *shabono.*

Angus recognized it only by the clothing. Whatever it was now, it had been their chief. The Iyakei headman had ended up with a change of oversize clothes that he had worn into filth-encrusted stiffness. Cotton pants, with the crotch cut out because the zipper was too bothersome to work. Ancient workshirt, unbuttoned and the sleeves rolled up. Apparently he had felt that clothes *do* make the man, and he had learned enough Spanish to call himself *capitán*. Yes, it was the headman's clothing.

But the face . . . His *face* . . . *His entire head.*

"*Iwä!*" screamed one of the Mabori. "*Iwä!*"

Alligator.

From his upper chest on up, the headman's flesh had thickened into knobby hide, brownish green in color. From within chunky folds of skin, a pair of slitted yellow eyes gleamed. His mouth and nose were no more, at least not in human terms. The entire cranial structure had become rearranged into a long, long snout, flattened across top and bottom. And lined with so very many teeth. Sharp teeth. Snapping.

"Don't kill him!" Angus cried to the rest of the Mabori. Without need. They'd already learned their lesson once before. The hard way.

The headman came charging past his own awestruck warriors, locking onto Angus's voice. The yellow eyes alive with hunger.

Instinct said to shoot. Wisdom prevented it. And altruism thought, in the second before the *iwä* pounced, that perhaps his own death might buy more time for the rest to flee.

He lifted the shotgun in both hands, like a quarterstaff, as the headman bore him down to the ground. He wedged it sideways between the thing's jaws; rows of teeth grated on metal, gouged out splinters of wood. He was bathed with the thing's foul breath, and as it sat atop him, it lunged relentlessly for his throat.

Claws. The man's hands had thickened into leathery reptilian feet, twisted claws instead of fingers. They flailed past the shotgun and ripped Angus's shoulder open to the bone. Blood soaked the ground beneath him.

The jaws, snapping, grinding through the shotgun . . .

The yellow eyes, inhuman, unblinking . . .

The face, mutated far past anything he'd ever dared believe existed this side of Hell . . .

There was no point in struggling. To give in to its jaws

would be the quickest way out. One brief moment of agony, then merciful oblivion.

But he couldn't. Life instinct was strong. Even as another swipe of the claws tattered his cheek. Even as yet another tore across his chest. Even as a claw worked its way between two ribs and punctured a lung.

He wheezed blood, swallowed it, coughed it.

A blur above him. *No, they should run. . . .*

One of the burliest of the Mabori, a man named Ariwari, had come hurtling to Angus's aid, leaping onto the back of the headman and pulling him free. They rolled across the ground, and when they came to a halt, Ariwari was beneath him. One arm was clenched around the headman's swollen throat, the other around his stomach. The headman, the *iwä*, thrashed and bellowed another unearthly cry.

Kerebawa was close on Ariwari's heels, while the remaining warriors fired arrows to cover them. And as Angus watched, bleeding profusely and barely able to move, Kerebawa knelt beside the thrashing headman and tenderly rubbed his stomach. Ignoring the slashing jaws, the flailing talons. Rubbing the belly.

Incredible.

The thrashing weakened, and quickly ended altogether. Scrabbling limbs stilled and relaxed. Of all defenses—sleep.

Angus had seen this before, rolling an alligator onto its back and rubbing its belly. Something about the sensation and the backflow of blood into the brain induced sleep. That it should work here, now—nothing short of a miracle.

Ariwari eased out from under the heavy body and scuttled away through the underbrush beneath a hail of arrows. Kerebawa reached beneath Angus's arms and locked his fingers to drag him away. Angus clenched his teeth against a feeble cry. The pain was almost beyond belief.

"I have you, Padre," Kerebawa murmured into his ear, and Angus watched his heels dig furrows on the jungle floor. "I have you."

Angus's head felt too heavy, a massive weight atop a fragile stalk. As Kerebawa pulled him backward, the remaining Mabori fell into position to retreat. Gradually falling back in teams to guard one another's escape.

And as Angus watched Iyakei-teri fade into the background, this savage green world turned gray. Then black. Then . . .

Nothing.

He came to later, and by the position of the sun, it looked to be midafternoon. Had they been home at Mabori-teri, the heat of midday would have driven most of them to their hammocks to rest.

As it was, they were resting now, ever alert for Iyakei warriors in pursuit. Or worse, the *iwä*.

Out of a raiding party of twenty-three men, they now numbered only fourteen. The bodies of the dead would remain, to be recovered later by the old women of Mabori-teri. Angus had always found it a strange double standard, that the young women were treated no better than chattel, but if they survived into old age, they were revered. Old women were often used as emissaries between warring tribes. Never harmed. Even when recovering the bodies of warriors who had slain the enemy.

Once home, the bodies would be burned. The remaining bones and ash ground into powder. The powder saved to be mixed with a soup of boiled plantains. And eaten.

Angus wondered if they would do the same with his bones. Burial by other missionaries? No. He didn't belong with them anymore. He belonged in Mabori-teri, in death as well as in life.

Kerebawa had tended the claw wounds as best he could, but they were gruesomely bad. If one of the shamans were here, he would chant a healing plea. Even so, it was not altogether unpleasant, feeling numbness overtaking his body as he stared into the canopy overhead. Teeming with life that had no idea men killed one another over powders.

"I am cold inside for you, Padre," Kerebawa said. He held one hand behind Angus's head so he could drink some water.

Angus choked on a little, got the rest down. He patted the hand that fed him, felt the stinging trickle of tears. For the friendship to be severed. He'd known Kerebawa nearly all the young man's life. Angus didn't know precisely how old he was; there were only three numbers known to the Yanomamö. One, two, and anything greater than two. But he had been a small child when Angus had arrived nineteen years ago.

The way he saw it, Kerebawa had the brains and courage to assume headman status someday. *If* the tribe remained intact that long. Survival depended on ones such as he, who could adapt.

Angus had singled out Kerebawa to introduce to the outside world. He had told him of lands near and far—England-teri. Mexico-teri. America-teri. It was easier to put the names into a form and context Kerebawa would find meaningful. The *-teri* suffix denoted "village of." Mabori-teri meant, simply, village of the Mabori people. America-teri, then, village of the American people.

Nowhere was it more poignant, though, than when Kerebawa and the others had finally grasped the concept of Heaven—God-teri.

The Yanomamö had no way of conceiving of the enormity of the outside world. In their minds, they were the center of the universe. In their imaginations, the Venezuelan city of Caracas was merely a large *shabono,* just another succession of huts.

So Angus had shown Kerebawa the reality, in hopes that he might understand. And when the time was right, convey to the rest just how large and diverse the world was out there. Forewarned was forearmed.

Kerebawa had seen Caracas. Later, Mexico City. Eventually they had ventured all the way to Miami. The culture shock didn't seem to be particularly painful, no doubt in part due to the young man's schooling. As a child, he had been educated with other Indian children in a mission school in Esmerelda, taught to read and write. He had learned to be marginally conversant in Spanish. Over the last four years, Angus had taught him a good deal of English as well.

A trilingual Yanomamö. Angus could have wept in bitter sorrow that such a rarity was needed. But better trilingual than extinct.

"Padre," said the headman Damowä, "today you became a true *waiteri.*" A fierce one. "We will tell our children of this day. We will not forget."

Angus closed his eyes and smiled. The numbness had left his arms and legs nearly paralyzed. But he could smile. For now he knew that his bones would end up in their bellies. Living with them, in a strange way, forever.

Kerebawa gazed down at his teacher, his mentor, tears in his eyes. He wiped away the flecks of blood that Angus coughed up.

"The *hekura-teri*," Angus whispered. "They still got away with it. Do you know what that means?"

Kerebawa didn't twitch a muscle, didn't even bat an eye. But he knew. Angus could feel it. The young warrior understood it all.

"You wish to avenge my death . . . don't you?" There, appeal to centuries of inbred honor. Angus felt horribly manipulative. "Then you'll have to follow the path of the *hekura-teri*. And stop it."

"The world is too big," Kerebawa said. "It will eat me."

"Maybe not." A spasm shook his body; he didn't have long at all now. "The Colombians will take it back home, to Medellín-teri. To Vasquez. From there?" He shook his head in surrender.

Kerebawa simply closed his eyes in resignation.

"In my hut, papers, maps. The names of the men who took us to see the outer world. Barrows and Matteson? Use them all."

The paralysis crept up his chest to seize his throat. But no matter. He had said all he needed. After death, he knew his name would never be spoken again among their tribe. Their way of showing respect. But they would remember. Always.

And in the midst of this massive green cathedral, Angus let go his spirit, and let it soar.

While around his body rose the sudden sound of mourning.

2
NEW HORIZONS

TWA flight 435 from St. Louis to Tampa, non-stop, took just over two hours. They had made good time, caught a tailwind, while Justin had caught a good buzz on airline vodka. He wondered if the stewardesses had posted an alert on him. Watch out for the guy in 19A, could be trouble. A human sponge. And he hardly says a word.

It's always the quiet types that flake out.

Couldn't much fault their concern. Not since the April 1989 flight into St. Louis from Tennessee. Some anthropoid drinks six bottles of airline hootch, disembarks, steals an electric cart for a joyride past the gates, ducks into a mysteriously unlocked maintenance room, and tries to hide in a trash chute. End of story. Said anthropoid winds up crushed to death in the trash compactor.

From obscurity to legend in less than an hour. All in all, there were worse ways to go out.

With his A-seat, he managed to spend a lot of time staring

out the window. Flight was a strange mix of illusions. While gazing out over nearby cirrocumulus clouds, it felt as if they were skimming low over vast polar regions and snow-drenched mountains.

The sight kept him isolated from his seatmate. Late thirties, gray suit and yellow power tie, receding hairline. Hunched over the drop-down tabletop, scribbling into arcane reports while his fingers danced on a calculator's keypad. What a horrible life it looked like from the outside. Justin would have preferred the trash compactor to ending up like that in ten years. He had come to learn its price. The hard way.

Sometimes life felt like a bad movie, moments of reality that seemed like anything but. Wondering if other people looked on him with the same benign loathing he felt toward his seatmate. Wondering if his life were indeed a movie being lensed for the enjoyment of some cosmic film buff with a penchant for tragicomedy. Wondering how the script read . . .

Fade in, interior, a TWA DC-10, economy class. In seat 19A sits Justin Gray, swilling his fifth screwdriver of this Monday morning. He stares out the window for answers and finds none, as he leaves behind the wreckage of his life in a desperate attempt to rebuild anew. Will he succeed? Only the Smirnoff distillery knows for sure.

He looked aisleward as a woman threaded back to the bathrooms. She had apparently boarded after, of all things, a trip to donate blood. Her blouse's collar still bore the little Red Cross sticker: *Be nice to me. I gave blood today.* Justin wondered what might be appropriate for his own sticker. *Be nice to me. I fucked up my life this year.*

They touched down in Tampa shortly after noon, taxied to the gate. Halt. Everyone clogged the aisles to retrieve overhead carry-ons. Justin wavered a bit as he left the plane for the gangway and imagined a collective sigh of relief from the stewardesses.

Freedom, then. Transplantation complete. Hopefully, salvation.

He scanned unfamiliar faces inside the terminal until the sole familiar one broke into a big smile. Hugs were next, big back-slapping bear hugs just so no one got the mistaken impression that these two rather artistic-looking fellows were reunited lovers. Public image is everything in a land of sun and water and misspent passions.

"Welcome to my con-tree," said Erik, counterfeit south-of-the-border accent flashing briefly. Then back to white-bread American: "How was the flight?"

"Crash free," Justin said. "That's all that counts, isn't it?"

The similarities between them were almost brotherly. Both tall, with similarly high cheekbones, the same purposeful stride. But Erik smiled more. He looked healthier; maybe the tan. And the eyes . . . Erik's wide baby blues tagged him as one of life's innocents, whereas Justin's chocolate browns seemed warier, too many laps around the fast-track. Maybe Erik's ambitions had not been quite as high, but he was *happy*. Without betraying the aesthetics and values truly important to him. Justin had traditionally been the better groomed, Erik the true artiste, just a touch scruffy, boyishly and endearingly so. But the gap was narrowing. Six weeks since Justin's last haircut, while shaving was now an every-other-day inconvenience; once upon a time, unthinkable.

Justin let Erik take the lead. Following airport hieroglyphics to locate baggage was now beyond him. They boarded a stand-only elevated tram that whisked them to another building, and out its windows Justin drank in the change of scenery. Palm trees, bluer sky than he had left behind, flat tarmac. It was May in Florida, and it didn't look any different than it did in October. He would adjust, gladly.

"My guess is that in-flight service was very very good to you." Erik tipped an imaginary bottle and made a *gluk-gluk* noise.

"Mother Russia's finest."

"That's a good start. I talked myself into some premature vacation time this week. So what we do is, you and I bag over our legal limit of fun and we slay brain cells left and right until we get you down to one cell. And then you start over from scratch. Sound good?"

Justin said that it did. Erik, bless him—planning strategies for overhauling the pieces of a life when he knew only the barest facts as to what had caused its kamikaze dive to begin with. Such was his way. You couldn't ask for a better partner in crime when you wanted to lop off a few brain cells and revert to prehistoric language. But he would still be there the next morning to make the hangover more bearable. And he was equally handy at the heart-to-hearts, as well. Erik Webber, last of the emotional Renaissance men.

"So what's this new job you've gotten?" Justin asked as they waited for the luggage from Flight 435 to find its way onto the carousels. Praying that the gods of airborne transportation hadn't sent it elsewhere. "I thought you'd be snapping pictures for the *Tribune* forever."

Erik grinned, pushing errant hair back from his forehead. It was sun-bleached a few degrees lighter than the shade of brown it had been when Justin had last seen him. Had it really been a year and a half? They had both been too lax about contact lately.

"You won't believe me if I just tell you. I better show you."

The feed hole in the carousel wall began to spit fresh luggage. Dozens of conversations halted in midstride, eyes flicked to inspect what was emerging next. It was like watching numbers come up in the lottery. Ah, a winner.

Justin plucked up his bags and they turned away, hoofing it toward the garage for Erik's car. Both of them sharing the burdens.

Justin couldn't wipe the perplexed grin off his face as he flipped through the rack. Nothing but lingerie. Sheer nighties, peekaboo teddies, lacy little inconsequentialities that exposed a lot and left the best to the imagination.

This didn't make sense. The place was a photo studio, sign outside saying NORTH LIGHT PHOTOGRAPHY. He'd seen customers elsewhere in the building awaiting portrait sittings, engagement shots.

Justin looked at Erik, found a more knowing grin than his own. As if it had gotten the joke minutes before.

"Boudoir photography," Erik said, somewhat sheepishly.

"Boudoir. Meaning?"

"Meaning I shoot tasteful cheesecake and make good money doing it." Erik shrugged, easygoing.

Justin pulled a hangered black lace thing from the rack, held it before his own torso. They both shook their heads, and he put it back.

"It's the latest thing. One of them, anyway." Erik motioned him to follow, led him past a jumble of studio gear. Lights, tripods, backdrops, ornate brass-rail bed with frilly coverlet. They left it behind for a side cubbyhole crammed with a desk and file cabinet. Erik flipped on the light. "Be it ever so humble, there's no place like the office."

"So what does this involve, if I may be so bold?"

Erik spoke while digging through a file drawer. "In a nutshell, women come in to have erotic pictures taken of themselves. No hard-core nudes, no couples, no guys, transvestites or otherwise. Very classy. The management is pretty strict on that." He plucked out a folder with a satisfied nod. "Yah. Here we go."

He handed a few proof sheets to Justin, who scanned the miniature images with wide eyes and a longing heart. Three different women, looked to be from midtwenties to late thirties. One per proof sheet. Obviously, they knew how to pose and Erik knew how to capture the moment.

"We're supposed to destroy the proofs after they place their orders." Erik made doubly sure they were alone. "But sometimes I fudge and tuck them away. The *really* good ones. An artiste's life has so few rewards, you know."

Justin handed them back, and away they went. "I hate you. I bet you make out like Don Juan in this job."

"Huh. Dream on. There was only once that the client-photographer relationship got a little heated." Erik sighed, settled in his desk chair. "I'd say at least ninety-nine percent of the women who come in are having them shot for someone else. They give them to husbands, boyfriends. So it's a lost cause. Or they're giving them to a girlfriend, in which case it's *really* a lost cause. You kind of have to be a real philosopher to not go crazy in this job."

Justin slid down to the floor, back to the wall. The vodka buzz was waning. Have to remedy that soon. Hung over by early afternoon was not the most ideal proposition.

"So why the switch from shooting news? I thought you loved that job."

"I did." Erik's eyes grew cloudy. He laced his fingers while gazing at the ceiling for inspiration. "But with some of the stuff I was shooting—man, it really takes a certain mind-set to not get to you. The drug wars, especially. I mean, this isn't Miami, but we're not immune here by any means. I was shooting pictures of these people—men, women, kids, everybody gets caught in the cross-fire sooner or later—and I was seeing some really hideous stuff. Shootings, knifings, beatings. Murder by automobile. One guy they found—one of his arms wasn't anything but bone from the elbow down. Coroner said somebody had stuck his arm in with a bunch of piranha, if you can believe that. So I'm seeing all this through my view-finder, and I find that it's not making much of a dent in my head anymore."

Justin nodded. "But you're supposed to bring a certain amount of objectivity with you."

"Objectivity is one thing. Not giving a damn anymore is another. I was burning out big-time. And I just didn't want to end up one of these grizzled old guys trading their worst murder stories over coffee and doughnuts every morning." Erik pulled up from his slump, rested his elbows on his knees. Smiled and upturned his palms. "So now . . . all this is mine."

"Lord of the thighs."

Erik wrinkled his nose. "Crass." He dug through the center desk drawer. He pulled out another sheet of photographic paper. Withheld the image for a moment. "I've got all kinds of stuff lined up for us to do the next few days, get you out and introduced to a few people."

Justin grinned. "So you're not stuck with me the whole time, right?"

"All for your own good, dear boy. We've got to get you circulating among single women again. You're probably out of practice." He handed the picture over. "Here's someone you'll be meeting tomorrow night. And don't drool on the picture."

This was no proof sheet, best served by a magnifying glass, but a full eight-by-ten glossy. The girl was mid- or late twenties. It wasn't a standard lace-teddy shot and was therefore all the more provocative. Faded ancient jeans, unsnapped and halfway unzipped. Blue denim shirt, completely unbuttoned as well, with only the inner swell of each breast showing. Bare feet, luxurious dark hair bunched messily around her shoulders. Her face looked vaguely exotic, as if she carried within a few drops of Oriental blood.

Yes, it could be love.

"That's April. April Kingston. She used to work at the paper too. In advertising. See, you already have something in common. I took that shot of her, oh, seven, eight months ago."

Justin pulled his eyes away, an effort. He looked at Erik with a sudden plummeting of his heart. "This is too good to be true. So what's the catch, what is she? Married, engaged, or a lesbian?"

A wide smile from Erik. "None of the above. Formerly engaged, if you must know. It broke off around Christmas. I don't know why, she never talked much about it. Best thing that could've happened, though. Her fiancé's name was Brad, but I used to call him Dickless. That should clue you in. He was about as exciting as a bowl of oat bran."

Justin perused the photo again. "He was probably too safe for her. A womanchild like this needs the kind of thrills that *my* roller-coaster life can provide."

"That's the spirit. Turn that checkered past to an advantage." Erik wiggled his fingers, and Justin reluctantly parted with the print. Back it went into the drawer. "Come on. Let's go start on those brain cells and play catch-up on the past few months."

They rose to leave, Erik killing the light. Justin threw one last longing glance at the desk drawer.

"Can't we bring her along?"

"You're smitten already, aren't you? I recognize that look. She stays put. Your first day in town, *I* get all your attention. I'm selfish that way."

They were halfway across the boudoir set before Erik spoke again.

"Besides, I've got another print like that at home."

Erik Webber lived in a section of Tampa called Davis Island. The "island" label made it sound more exotic than it really was. It was simply a bulbous little annex that barely missed extending to the southern edge of the city proper. You hardly knew you were forsaking the mainland when the highway bridged over a channel leading into the bay. Near the edge of the island, round timbers jutted a few feet above the water, and brown pelicans often perched there, a respite from scooping up fish that were probably contaminated by now anyway.

They made the island their final stop, ducking into the last of three bars on Erik's agenda. Knocked back a few more beers, played a few video games, and retired to Erik's Davis Boulevard apartment to whittle on his refrigerator stock and tune in to the VCR. Evening was well under way by now.

They watched a mutual favorite, *Barfly*. Generally heralded by critics but little known. See Mickey Rourke swagger about, full-time derelict and part-time literary genius. See Faye Dunaway match him drink for drink, understandably proud of her legs. See them revel in lowlife, for here is their life's true niche, and they know it.

"Why is it every time I watch this, I feel like I'm just that much closer to living it?" Justin asked. The credits were rolling beneath sleazy jazz organ by Booker T.

Erik shrugged. Legs dangling over one arm of the apartment's love seat, he aimed the VCR remote and zapped it into rewind mode. MTV came on as the video image disappeared.

Justin looked toward the row of windows. The apartment was third floor, a corner unit. The first two windows were nearly filled with an extreme close-up of the top of a palm tree. Wonderful view. Beyond lay the buildings of Davis Boulevard, a low skyline of apartments and commercial property. Darkening clouds beyond them.

He had always found dusk the most supremely dismal time of day. Never sure why, only knowing that the advent of night felt like a painful transition. The sun bleeding into the horizon. Nature's subtle reminder that death is inevitable, that the law of the jungle prevails even on asphalt.

He knew what was coming next. The moment was ripe for it.

"Storytime now, I think," Erik said. He remoted the TV volume to a whisper. "Okay?"

"I suppose there's no way around it."

Erik nodded. "I think I've showed enormous patience today. But hey, I do deserve a little more explanation about what went down in St. Louis. I get a phone call and my friend's telling me that the entire U.S. system of justice is coming down on his head, I tend to wonder why."

Justin pulled thoughtfully at his beer bottle. How to begin, how to begin. Erik knew the setup. . . .

College graduate Justin Gray, armed with his degree, a B.S. in advertising—never was there a more appropriately named degree. Returns home from the University of Illinois to St. Louis, lands an entry-level position with the agency Hamilton, Darren, and Stevens, annual billings in excess of twenty-four million. The creative department is good, allows business-world success without necessarily becoming a corporate clone. Wide-eyed Justin hopes he'll become the wunderkind of the midwestern advertising scene, perhaps use St. Louis, then Chicago, as stepping-stones to New York. He does okay, nothing spectacular. Respectable. Solid. He sows his wild oats, then marries well, a blond-haired blue-eyed fashion merchandiser named Paula. The archetypical upwardly mobile couple. This, Erik knew.

"Well," said Justin, "you know we've always been into better living through chemistry."

"Sure." Even now, Erik had a couple of joints rolling around on the coffee table. He hadn't offered any nasal powder, so Justin assumed there was none around.

"So. Couple years ago, I started dealing. I mean, it was a nice secondary income. I wanted things, Paula wanted things. This was just a quicker way to do it. I kept it strictly small time, though. Friends, acquaintances, people at the office—that sort of thing. I figure don't get greedy, keep it downscale, I won't get caught. No hassles with anybody, no rough stuff. A kinder, gentler drug dealer."

Erik had a hearty chuckle at that.

"And that's the way it was, too. Paula felt a little weird about it. It wasn't exactly approval, but it wasn't disapproval, either. It was like, 'This makes me nervous—but I sure do like these new toys we have to play with.' A boat, couple new cars.

"Then in November we went to this party, and a guy turns some friend of his on to me that wants to score some heroin. So I made a few calls, made a couple stops, and came back with it. No problem, right?

"Wrong." Justin felt the tears creep up to the backs of his eyes. He had reached the point where the threshold of memory and the threshold of pain were one and the same. "Some guy, some idiot . . . with an IQ about like his shoe size . . . he'd laced the junk with strychnine. Just to see what would happen, he said later. So I got to watch this eighteen-year-old nail up right in front of me and go into convulsions and die.

"All because I thought we had to have a better stereo system."

He gauged Erik for reactions, for the loathing he had become accustomed to feeling directed his way from endless sources. Thankfully, it wasn't there.

"So I got pinched that night. No way around that. A nice grueling four-hour interrogation. But. I was a little fish. They wanted big fish, and I was the bait. Cut a deal, and I could walk. So I turned state's evidence and led them to some guys they *really* had a hard-on for. It was either that or manslaughter charges, on top of the dealing and possession and all that. So I rolled over and squealed like a pig from *Deliverance.*"

They both smiled. Sometimes it seemed their lives were one constant string of cinematic references.

"Everything else—job, home life, everything—it kind of went over like a row of dominos. Pretty soon I didn't need a lawyer just for the bust, I needed him for divorce proceedings too." Justin ran his hands through his hair, left it sticking up from his head. Shock therapy. "I've got to get my proverbial shit together, Erik. The trials, the testimony—it was all over three days ago. My first stop after I left the courthouse was the travel agency."

Erik abandoned the love seat and wandered over to the couch. Sank in beside him, looped a brotherly arm around his shoulders.

"Tell you what. Stay here as long as you need, to get your head back together. When it feels right, we'll find you a new job. There's loads, this place is booming. And then I'll fly back up with you, and we can both load up your stuff and road-trip it down here. Sound good?"

Justin shook his head. "No need for that, man."

"I insist. It's the least I can do."

"When I say there's no need, there's *no need*." He hitched his thumb toward the corner, where the suitcases sat patiently. Still full. "That's it. That's my sum total of worldly possessions."

It could have been the evening's low point. The pit of despair. But for some reason, the thought of the quintessential yuppie reduced to traveling around like a gypsy caravan of one struck Justin as funny. He surrendered to laughter, and Erik quickly followed. It was like spitting into the eye of Fate. Gallows humor.

And Justin hoped, prayed, that he would be smart enough to keep lightning from striking twice in the same place.

3

PARTY ANIMALS

The name of the club was Apocalips, and the name said it all. Too many lights, too much glitz, too many speakers with too much wattage. An exercise in sensual overkill.

On the other hand, Justin loved it.

Given the turn of events in St. Louis, it had been a long time since he had tasted any sort of nightlife. He'd not realized how much he missed it, like someone whose hunger doesn't surface until the first crucial bite of food.

True to his word, Erik had managed a sizable turnout of friends to welcome Justin to Tampa. Most of them didn't seem to have needed much coaxing. There were nine or ten in all. Hard to keep track, though, with everybody on the move. Drinks, dancing, some of them taking trips to the johns to powder noses from the inside.

They had pulled a few tables together inside a chrome corral elevated above the dance floor, creating a home base of sorts. A core group of four or five stayed at the tables at any one time.

Names, faces—too many to pair together. He'd have Erik quiz him tomorrow until he had them down. A few stuck in mind, though. Angel, a blond tigress on the dance floor. She showed him her signature, a halo above the *A* and a devil's tail tipping the cursive *l*. Trent, perpetually wired and hyper and suffering from a self-induced runny nose, rarely still for three seconds at a time.

And then there was April, at once cool and animated, drinking margaritas at a pace of two per hour. She seemed much less the exotic goddess she had appeared in the photo, and for this Justin was grateful. Exotic goddesses lean toward the unapproachable.

"Ask her to dance, you weenie." Erik had to hover close to his ear to be heard over the music. "We've been here nearly three hours. You're disappointing me."

Justin, sucking from a Killian's Red bottle, nodded. "I'll get around to it."

"Not later. *Now.*"

Justin set his bottle on the mauve table. "Answer a question first."

"Sure."

Justin glanced sidelong at April. Her attention was elsewhere. Good. He hated discussing someone when he thought they knew it.

"She hardly seems like someone *you* wouldn't go for. Tell me the truth. Was there ever anything between the two of you?"

Erik bit a knuckle, frowning. "You perceptive little cuss, you. Well . . . yeah, sort of. For a couple weeks after she broke up with Dickless. But it just didn't feel right. We were friends first. By the time we tried lovers, we thought it made more sense not to risk killing the friendship." Erik played priest, made the sign of the cross. "You have my blessings, my son. Now move your ass."

So much for pep talks. April sat on the other side of the tables, three chairs down. Shouting across the distance seemed less than suave, so he stood. Mohammed must go to the mountain.

The floor thumped with basslines, swirling lights glinted off chrome and glass. Across the packed dance floor stood a wall of video monitors, thirty in all, each playing the same image. Like a fragmented worldview through multifaceted insect eyes in B-grade movies. INXS blared from the speakers; good dance music.

Distance crossed. Nerves steeled. Justin smiled down at her.

"Would you like to dance?"

She smiled back, nose crinkling a bit. "No thanks."

It shotgunned the smile right off his face. His eyes darted to Erik, who was talking with Angel. This was Erik's fault. *He's a dead man, I will kill him.* He started to grope for a graceful way out, knowing such dignity was hopeless.

"I've watched you out on the dance floor tonight," April said. She seemed friendly enough—what gave? "You don't *really* like to dance. Do you?"

"Sure I do. I wouldn't have . . . asked if—"

She grinned, hazel eyes sparkling. She was enjoying this torture! After Erik was dead, perhaps he'd turn on her.

"Don't lie," she gleefully warned. "Liars go to Hell."

He let his arms hang limp, palms out in surrender. Here stands a complete and utter fool. "No," he finally said. "I don't, really."

"Neither do I."

He was starting to catch on to her game. Perhaps this could be salvaged after all. "So would you like," he ventured, "to sit one out with me?"

"I'd love to." April motioned to the empty seat at her right, and he took it before they could slip back into retrograde progress. The conversation was anyone's ball game. He punted.

"So why the aversion to dancing?" he asked. "You look like you'd be good at it."

"I am, I guess. Oh, it's not dancing per se I don't like. I dance a lot at home, alone. I just don't like all the little games it entails in public. You know, a dance, then a drink, then . . ." She seemed too shy to blurt out the last one.

"Debauchery?" he tried. Words were his life. Used to be, anyway.

"Yeah! Close enough." She looked relieved.

April gazed out over the bodies clogging the dance floor, some graceful, some spastic, some exhibiting moments of both. Then the spectators and their glasses and bottles. Closer still to home base: Trent, a chair away, nervously tapping an empty coke vial against the tabletop.

"Did you ever think about the function a place like this serves?" she said. "Not the shallow surface stuff. Deeper, I mean."

"A marketing ploy for hangover remedies?"

She rolled her eyes. "You're not even close. But I have this theory—why society in general is so screwed up today."

"This should be good."

"It's because we don't have any more rituals. Sure, we have weddings, and baptisms, and funerals. But how many times a year do any of us go to something like that? I mean everyday rituals."

He nodded, if only to be polite. He had no idea what she was talking about. This was the most bizarre first-time conversation he could recall ever having had with anyone, male or female.

"Now look at primitive cultures," April continued. "They sing, they chant, they take hallucinogenic drugs, they have established dances for different occasions. And they're happy! You don't see *them* needing mental health centers."

This girl was a challenge of Alpine dimensions. He had a sense that she operated on a slightly different plane than most everyone else. And yet he was starting to grasp what she meant.

"Come to a place like this, and you'll see the exact same sort of behavior." April was really into this, had completely forgotten her drink. *"Exactly.* Only there's more desperation. We're so far removed from the primal part of ourselves that we mix it up with all this other stuff. Scoring on somebody, seeing who can drink the most or snort the most. Making someone jealous by dancing with someone else. Stupid stuff like that." She shook her head, smiled in summation. "We need to get reacquainted with our primitive sides."

Justin regarded her in close to dropjaw amazement. He had heard so many theories seeking to explain everything from discos to chemical dependencies that he was sick of them. Sick of the theorists who concocted them. And not a one of them had ever made this much sense or been this succinct.

"You sound like a sociologist," he told her.

"Nah. I took a few courses in anthropology when I was in college. Art major, anthropology minor, if you can believe that combination."

He told her that based on his first five minutes with her, he could believe anything. She took it as a roundabout compliment, and he supposed he'd meant it that way.

They made a game of zeroing in on different clubgoers and finding appropriate designations for them. Primitive terms, of course, as they were all natives in the global village. Here a fertility goddess expecting worship. There a predatory hunter. Elsewhere an electric shaman in passionate sync with the music.

And a bit later came the arrival of the obligatory medicine man.

Justin caught periodic glimpses of him over the next fifteen minutes. A brown-skinned guy with jet-black hair that shone under the lights. In long, gentle curls, it was pulled straight back and tied at the back of his head, with the loose ends trailing to his shoulders. He wore a black mesh shirt, and beneath it sleek muscle tone and a simple gold chain with a mounted shark's tooth. Pants of many pockets.

The guy seemed to know everyone as he gradually weaved through the club. Stopping now and then to talk, to kiss a girl on either mouth or cheek, dance a little. King of the night-time world, handsomely Hispanic. Good-time Carlos. Justin wasn't surprised when he eased over to Erik's friends. It seemed inevitable.

"Tony!" cried Trent, spirits buoyant. "Been waiting for you, man." He raised the empty little vial.

Tony flashed an easy smile, caught Trent's hand in a soul shake. Then he laughed and ran his finger along Trent's neckline, plucking at half a dozen gold chains. Erik had explained that Trent was a darkroom tech at North Light Photography. His presence had been unavoidable, though not urgently desired.

"What's with all this shit, man?" Tony rattled the chains. "You got enough gold there to give Mr. T a wet dream."

Justin turned a questioning glance to April. She seemed a little tighter all of a sudden, a little chillier. A whiff of bad karma hovered in the air.

"Tony Mendoza," she said. Flat, neutral.

That he was a dealer was without doubt. Justin had thought April might find all manner of anthropological observations to make about him. Maybe she didn't find the game quite as much fun when it fell too close to home. Which made him fear all the more her reaction to the moment she would inevitably learn about his own past.

He had to wonder in another direction, though, when Tony smiled down at her and pursed his lips for a quick airborne kiss. She shifted uncomfortably and pretended not to notice.

"Friend of yours, I take it," Justin said lightly. Anything to undercut the moment.

April faced him then, offering an unflinching look into her almond eyes. Lovely, dark, and deep. Clear and wide. And somewhere within, pained.

"Acquaintance," she said softly. Though he had the idea she didn't care if Tony heard or not. "Guys like that never really have friends."

How well he knew that. Even from his own tentative steps into the same waters. No friendship, no love in the world of white powder. Only alliances and loyalties subject to change. Profit takes precedence over all other matters, from the heart outward. One look into Tony's all-seeing eyes, and Justin knew why he'd never have survived even one foot deeper into the waters of the St. Louis trade. No heart for it. Or maybe that was backward: too much heart, and not enough stone.

He watched April rediscover her margarita, then saw that Tony was leading an expedition toward the bathroom. As he stepped down the little risers toward the main floor, another guy fell in step behind him. Come to think of it, the guy had usually been in the background wherever Tony had been. Big guy, also Hispanic. Close-cropped hair and beard, like one continual coat of dark wiry fuzz. Tiny eyes that looked as if they'd never been touched by a smile.

Trent was about to follow when he turned and grabbed Justin by the sleeve.

"Why don't you tag along, Jus?" he said. "Time to reload."

"Think I'll pass."

Trent would have none of that. "Oh, come on. Deviate that septum a little. New in town, you might even get a freebie."

Justin felt the will of resolve crumbling brick by brick. Had April not been beside him, he probably would already have been halfway there. He wanted to go. *Wanted* it. Hungered for the quick sniff, the icy hot surge of adrenals. Senses in perfect clarity. Nightlife hadn't been the only thing he'd not tasted in too long.

"Sure. Why not."

Justin checked April for reactions and got nothing discernible. Just another dive for her margarita. Screw it, he was worrying too much. A second later he was on his feet and making it a foursome.

Halfway down the steps, he recognized the touch on his shoulder even before he turned to face Erik. Erik leaned down closer.

"Just between you and me," he said, "it probably won't do you any good if the wrong people start connecting you with Mendoza. Might make a fresh start a little harder, if you know what I mean."

"Just gonna go take a leak is all."

Erik nodded, eyes slightly narrowing. "Whatever. Just . . . don't get lost." He returned to the tables.

Seconds later, the guilt hit, free-floating shame. Lying to Erik? Who was he trying to kid? Erik knew the score.

Justin fell in behind Trent again, bringing up the rear. The drinks hadn't seemed to be hitting him at the table, but now, on the move, was a different story. Colored lights whirled, reeled. Music pulsed with jackhammer intensity. As if it were all part of a master plan to thwart dignity in walking. He was already flying.

The noise level dropped considerably in the bathroom, but the overall environment wasn't much better. The place was a black-and-white checkerboard nightmare, a glossy assault on sensitized equilibriums with fluorescent firepower.

"Tony, here's a friend of mine I want you to meet," Trent

said. Happy as a lapdog greeting its master at day's end. "This is Justin Gray. He just came down from St. Louis."

Tony nodded, then grinned at Trent. "Trent probably told you I'd show you a taste of Tampa hospitality. Didn't he?"

"He gave me that idea."

"Yeah? Well, I think I can handle that." Tony eased across the tiles, pushed open a stall door. "Step into my office."

The old gang-toidy routine, he knew it well. Always looked funny from the outside, three or four pairs of shoes facing each other under the door. Replete with sniffing sounds. In this case, four was definitely a crowd. Given the size of Mendoza's companion, it was a tight fit.

"Where are my fucking manners?" Tony said. He proffered a hand toward the incredible hulk. "This is my friend, Lupo."

So he'd been wrong; Mendoza had a friend after all. They swapped good-to-meet-yous.

"Show him just how good a friend you are, Lupo."

The guy grinned, baring large white teeth through the beard, and tugged up his tight pastel muscle shirt. Across the cobblestone muscles of his abdomen was a veritable landing strip of paler scar tissue.

"Lupo took a can opener across the gut for me a couple years ago." Tony looked like a proud trainer inside a cage of obedient lions.

Justin tried to act nonplussed, knew it was an obvious sham. These guys were *serious* players. "It's hard to find good friends like that anymore," he managed to say.

Lupo pulled his shirt down into place. " 'To desire the same things and to reject the same things, constitutes true friendship.' Sallust, in *Catalina.*"

So. Not only did the giant have a softer voice than expected, he could also spout ancient Latin proverbs. Curiouser and curiouser.

"Got a new treat for you two, fresh in stock." Tony was already setting it up, cutting lines on the flat side of a cigarette case held in one hand. "Six keys, just in."

Both Justin and Trent did double takes. The powder was a first-time sight for them both. The stuff was a pale green.

"What the hell is *this*?" Trent asked.

"They're calling this shit skullflush. New strain of powder, just up from South America, my friends tell me." The lines were ready. "Maestro!"

Lupo pulled out a hundred-dollar bill, rolled it into a tube, tighter than a New York joint. He handed it to Trent.

"You like this," Tony said, "I can let it go for a grand an ounce, forty bucks a gram. That's a fucking steal, man. Bargain-basement opportunity."

Trent did a line through the rolled bill. Drew back sharply, eyes bulging. "Now I know why." He leaned back against the stall, shaking his head gently. "Whooooaa . . ."

Justin eyed him for a moment, wondering if this was quite as good an idea as it had seemed a moment ago. Thoughts were muddled, though, sobriety sacrificed in the name of fun and new beginnings. He looked at the waiting green lines. What the hell. Free was free.

He took the tube. Bent at the waist. Powered up a line into his right nostril.

Drew back even more sharply than Trent.

"What the hell do you have that cut with?" he snapped. "Ajax?"

It felt like someone had clubbed him across the lower back of his head. From the inside. The pain flared, then ebbed to a dull molten core running from nasal cavities to brain. His eyes watered.

"It does have a punch," Mendoza said. He held up the cigarette case another couple inches. Six more lines were waiting.

"No thanks," Justin muttered. Free or not, this stuff was bad news. "I've got a Killian's out there with my name on it. Thanks anyway."

His eyes flicked about, Tony to Lupo and back and forth again. Faces wavered. They seemed a little too attentive, scrutinized a bit too much. Eyes, eyes . . . leering in. Into flesh, *past* flesh, into soul. Or was it just imagination? Paranoia blues.

"You get used to it," Trent said, taking the tube back. "If it's all the same, Tony, I'll have his. No sense letting it go to waste, right?" He leaned over to hoover into his other nostril, then back again for the first, and back again.

I've gotta get out of here. . . .

Past Lupo, past the stall door. Black-and-white checkerboard, chess game come to horrifying life. There, by the door, a knight moving over two and up one. No. *No.* Just an ordinary guy, no chess piece come alive. Normal.

Glimpse into the mirror as Justin passed. A frightening caricature of his own face, while in the background Trent groaned ecstatic anguish. Frightened face, painted in fluorescent light. His nose starting to run. The mucus green, stained with the powder. Disgust at himself. Worried that April would see him like this, and disgust would be contagious. He furiously wiped it away, stumbled out into the club proper.

The ambience was at once screaming in his face and receding away. Lights had become kaleidoscopic patterns, the music a pair of cymbals clanging with his head in between.

"Tampa hospitality," he mumbled.

Justin was in the flow of bodies now, passing faces looming into peripheral vision with the swell and fade of images seen through a wide-angle lens. Liar, Mendoza was a liar. Whatever this stuff was, it sure wasn't cocaine. Justin made it to the chrome corral and hung on to the railing for dear life.

Motes of light flashed before his eyes. Strains of music soothed his ears, music that had nothing to do with what was blasting from the speakers. Stravinsky, possibly, the dark majesty of *The Firebird*. It had been years since Justin could recall hearing it, and now it was returning in perfect clarity . . . then gone again.

"Erik?" he muttered.

Thoughts were racing, mach speed, mental fiberoptics. He felt his nose gush anew, wiped it again. Breath was coming hotter, faster.

He glanced back at the bathroom door to see what had become of the others. A moment later, Mendoza and Lupo emerged, quick-stepping with precious little left of the cool they had entered with a half hour ago. Disappearing into the crowd, the night.

Trent. Where was Trent?

"Erik," he said again, louder.

The floor was a chasm, the chasm eternal. He clung to the chrome railing with sweating hands. Limbs, joints—everything was fire, and jelly.

Someone back at the table must have pointed him out. He saw the back of Erik's head suddenly become his face, and then Erik was moving down the steps, face pinched in sudden concern.

"What is it, man?" Erik said. "You look terrible."

"I don't feel so good. Get me out of here." His voice barely seemed his own anymore.

"Yeah, sure. Gimme a minute." Erik turned his back a moment.

"Now, Erik."

The feeling was coming in out of nowhere and feeding on itself, and he was helpless before it. A claustrophobic paranoia that could either turn him into a god or crush him beneath its heel.

Trent stumbled into view, staggering from the bathroom door. Stringers of green mucus dangled from his nose. He absently wiped them away after noticing someone look at him aghast and give him a wide berth. Trent was reeling, face a shell-shocked blank—and then it was overtaken by a sickened smile.

Justin tugged at Erik's sleeve. No good, still talking with Angel. April looked their way from the background, and he didn't want her to see him like this. He turned away.

Trent was dancing, his body electric at the edge of the dance floor. Prancing, preening. Seemingly inventing his own dance on the spot. He looked ridiculous.

"Erik, get me *out* of here."

Trent danced, faster and faster. With total abandon. *Faster.* For reasons beyond comprehension, Justin felt his own heart quicken, knew somehow that its rate synced with Trent's. His breath was close to hyperventilation. The claustrophobia deepened, and all at once he had the sensation of plummeting down an elevator shaft.

The dancing, faster still . . .

Falling, falling . . .

Toward . . . *something.* Something buried, forgotten for aeons.

Trent staggered into a pillar supporting a lighting arrangement. Looked Justin's way. Their eyes meeting.

And Trent's face rippled.

Justin stared dumbstruck as it happened. Trent's mouth opened as his cheeks stretched and sprouted downy fur. Trent's teeth, folding back into his mouth, blood weeping from the gums, then gushing as they split with the rows of emerging new teeth, sharp and carnivorous. Entire head, elongating slightly forward, nose flattening into an inverted pink triangle. Cupped ears standing out from his head. Ringed spots darkening across the lighter fur.

His eyes, staring, yellowing, nothing but huge irises, pupils.

The moment was a juggernaut, unstoppable. Within the unfolding labyrinth of Justin's mind and soul, he could feel the beating of a kindred heart. A longing to do the same, a desire that at once seduced and repelled. It felt like aeons of evolution regressed and done away with, then tipped with a burning fuse.

Ready to detonate.

I don't want this I DON'T WANT THIS—

Trent's hands had shortened and fattened into paws, claws curving outward, predatory tools ready for use. While the beat went on, while all around him the dancers rocked and rolled.

Justin's inner soulstorm, falling down the shaft toward primeval bottom.

Ready to detonate.

"Erik, if you don't get me out of here, I'm gonna die!"

Justin doubled over suddenly and retched everything into the floor, onto Erik's shoes, just as Trent whirled and disappeared into the heaving throng. The lights switched from pulsing colors to violently rapid strobes, and as Erik finally turned around to help, Justin rose to stare across the dance floor.

Rapid-fire images, intense flashcuts. Instants of frozen motion sandwiched between milliseconds of total darkness. He could see it all. An out-of-control Trent, whatever he was now, tearing through the crowd.

flash

A throat laid wide open, arcs of blood splattering a girl.

flash

A wide-eyed head, toppling from its shoulders while blood geysered upward, too too red in the drenching white light.

"Son of a bitch, Justin." Erik, angry. Oblivious. "Look at this mess you've made."

flash

Jaguar jaws clamping down on a splintering arm.

flash

Jaguar claws, tearing open a belly like a gaudy Christmas package and letting the ropy delights within spill out.

flash

Terrified dancers scrambling all over each other to get out of the path of whatever was in their midst. Screaming with sufficient volume to drown out the music.

flash

Stampede.

The strobes were killed and the pulsing colors resumed, and the music pumped onward. Justin hung on to Erik's shoulder as they both staggered away. Only now did Erik notice the carnage strewn across the dance floor. Only now did he realize there was a lot more to worry about than his shoes. Beneath his tan he went white, and he firmed himself up under Justin's deadweight.

"Oh, shit. Oh, shit. Let's get you out of here," he said, and Justin bobbed his head in complete agreement. "You don't need to be around for the aftermath of *this* scene."

And he dragged them both for the nearest exit.

4

WATERWORKS

Tony Mendoza didn't normally like to rise much before ten or eleven in the morning. Today, though—the morning after the serious weirdness at the Apocalips—he was willing to make an exception. This morning he was a regular newshound, tuning in local radio and TV to get the official version.

Tony stretched in the breezes sweeping across the balcony of his condo. *Condo.* He hated that word. Sounded like one of those little raincoats for your pecker. He much preferred the term *luxury penthouse.* It was a lot easier to look down on people from the balcony of a penthouse than from some wimpy condo.

A fine Wednesday morning. Balcony, orange juice, and bran muffins. The sun and wind on his bare skin, obstructed only by his bikini undies. Hair loose and blowing about his shoulders. His boom box tuned to local news, back and forth, getting all the updates. He was alone. Lupo was out in the

Lincoln, on an errand. At a pet store, picking up a couple dozen white mice.

Witnesses' accounts of what had happened last night varied wildly. This was understandable. Four hundred people, toked up, coked up, drunked up, or in combination—you bet there'd be a lack of concurrence. Not to mention that it was bizarre to begin with.

Some people swore that a wild animal had been brought into the club. Leopard, jaguar—something. Others swore that it was some loony wearing a mask. Others claimed it was something in between those two. Maybe Lon Chaney's grandkids were out running amok. Whatever. But more than one person had mentioned Trent Pollard's name to the police, claiming they'd seen him acting funny right before the slaughter. A few said that from the back, it had looked like him tearing through the crowd.

Apocalips had been a meat market, once figuratively, now literally. Four people were dead, very messily so. Several others with bite marks and scratches. Doctors indicated that the wounds were consistent with animal teeth and claws.

Trent Pollard might have been able to explain, but he was no longer talking. Dead men tell no tales. He'd been found dangling from the business end of a noose by his employers when they came to open up the photo studio where he worked this morning. Leaving the police with a prime suspect of *some* sort, but no motive and no definitive explanations. Which was all for the better, really.

But what the hell *was* that green shit he'd snorted?

So far as Tony knew, Trent was the first around to sample any. It was a new product and all, and Tony himself most definitely did not touch any of the stuff he handled. Such was the general rule among the Colombians. They were businessmen, not party boys. Let the *norteamericanos* wipe themselves out one line at a time. Such was their destiny, not Colombia's.

The green powder, skullflush, had come up through the usual channels. Six kilos, out of a refinery owned by the Vasquez family of Medellín, Colombia. Flown north to Cuba's Varadero military airbase, a routine stopping point. Transferred to a boat and brought into the United States through the Florida Keys. Up to Miami under the wing of Luis Escobar, regional godfather in the Colombian mafia. Then transported northwest to Tampa. Mysteriously bypassing Tony's frequent connection and superior in the Tampa–St. Petersburg area, Rafael Agualar.

Tony had been happy enough to wet his Speedos in excitement upon learning that Escobar was running an end-sweep around Agualar. It could only mean good news for Tony. Everybody knew that Agualar was getting soft and fat, sticking his nose into his product far too much for his own good. Tony knew he wasn't anywhere near next in line among the *Agualares,* but nobody could deny he was an up-and-comer. A promising one at that.

That Escobar dealt with him directly boded well for the future. Maybe he was being groomed for takeover, seeing how well he handled the new product. Bigger deals, bigger shipments, bigger profits. Or so he had thought until last night.

Not knowing exactly what skullflush was, Tony had wanted to try it out on a guinea pig. That's where Trent had come in. Irritating numbnuts that he was. A good customer from the past, from Tony's lower-echelon days of street dealing, but a real weaseldick when it came to paying. Should it turn out to be poison, he was expendable.

Just what *had* it done to him?

In the bathroom at Apocalips, Trent had really weirded out. Strutting around like a peacock, singing gibberish. All the while, his nose running like a faucet. From what Tony could tell after he and Lupo had beat a hasty retreat, things had only gotten worse.

Whacked him out like PCP? Maybe. Turned him into some kind of werewolf? No way. But still, you had to wonder. Because nobody was in agreement on what had gone down.

Now that Trent was dead, it was no big shakes. Except, of course, the little hitch in the plan. Trent's friend. Justin? Yeah. Justin Gray, who had partaken of the green as well. An out-of-town rube, he was expendable too. Only nothing seemed to have happened to him. Last he saw, the guy was hanging on to a railing looking like it was all he could do to stand up. Of course, he'd hoovered only one line to Trent's seven. Could have made a big difference.

At any rate, he was a loose end that might have to be tidied up should things even remotely appear messy. Have to put Lupo on finding out where he was staying. Trent's apartment? Maybe.

All of which would take care of itself.

Tony stood, stretched. Gazed with appreciation at the beauties on beach towels at poolside, four floors down. Sighed and ducked back through the double balcony doors. Life was grand.

He plucked up the wireless phone from its cradle and whipped up the aerial. Time to do a little business. It was getting to be about that time, in between class periods. He punched out a number that triggered a quick pulse in a beeper a few miles away. Hung on to the receiver to await the return call.

Tony wandered into a side room, his favorite in the entire sprawling penthouse. His sanctum sanctorum. Flipped on the light and smiled at his babies. The room was ranked on all four sides by nothing but aquariums.

He had small ones, for fish like gouramis and cichlids. Larger ones, fifty-five and 110 gallons each, for larger, more aggressive fish such as his oscars and Jack Dempseys. And then his prize, on the far wall, a three-hundred-gallon job stocked with piranha.

Tony had divided the room into fresh- and saltwater sides. Of course, the saltwater tanks held fish far more vivid than the fresh, as vivid as anything seen by Jacques Cousteau on a coral reef. Absolutely stunning yellows and blues and reds and blacks and whites. Sometimes it took the breath away, that something so beautiful existed in the world. By comparison, the freshwater fish were bland. Dowdy stepsisters paling beside Cinderella's beauty. But he loved them too, like a commoner ascending to royalty refusing to forget his roots.

The room never failed in therapeutic value. He could leave the rest of the world outside the door whenever he wanted. Just ease back into the recliner—the sole furniture in here—and stare at whichever tank he wished. Letting the music of gurgling water and humming filters lull him into something like a dream state. Aquatic heaven.

Every important lesson of life that he needed to know was right here in these tanks. When to go for the prize, when to lie low. The powerful eat the weak, the large eat the small. Nowhere was it any more apparent than in the piranha tank. The pit bulls of the underwater world. He owned an even dozen of the little wonders.

He gently tapped the thick glass wall of their home. A couple turned toward the noise in their sluggish way that could be oh so deceiving. Mouths slightly open, jutting lower jaws rimmed with sharp ridges of teeth. Muscular sides silvery and scaly, as if bejeweled.

"Morning, babies," he said to them.

At last the phone gave its shrill electronic chirp. He let it chirp a couple more times, let the kid on the other end sweat a bit. Tony flipped it on and answered, finally.

"What took you so long?" With a grin.

Listened a moment to the thin piping voice on the other end.

"Got something heading your way today. One-thirty. Same spot as last week. Rice Krispies for lunch!" His own slang term for another substance. Snap *crack*le pop. The kiddies got a kick out of it sometimes. And at ten to twenty bucks a chunk, it was a rock that every kid could afford to get a piece of.

Listened to the kid whine.

"Hey, you think I give a fuck you got a big math test this afternoon? What are you now, twelve years old? Man, you gotta start getting some priorities straight, own up to your responsibilities. You blow this meet, I can get somebody else to cover that junior high action just like *that*." He snapped his fingers by the mouthpiece.

Listened. Now the kid was singing a more agreeable tune. Standing there in a junior high office, using the phone between classes on the pretense of calling a parent about a doctor's appointment or some other good one.

They signed off and Tony compressed the aerial back down. A minute later he heard the front door open, close. Heavy footsteps.

"In here," he called out. Lupo joined him, carrying a couple of boxes that looked as if they might hold reams of paper, were it not for the airholes punched around the sides.

"Good news," Lupo said. "They had plenty of white ones this time." He set the boxes on the floor and opened the first. A dozen furry little white mice squirmed inside, pink feet scurrying, pink tails flicking about.

"Ah, bless you, Lupo. You know how to brighten a day, don't you."

Lupo shrugged modestly. He looked very fit and resplendent this morning. He was far more the morning person than Tony. The guy didn't need but four, five hours of sleep a night. Tops.

Tony reached in to pluck up a mouse at random. Held him aloft by the tail, watching his four legs flail like nobody's business. All that energy, wasted. And for what? Futility.

Tony dropped him into the piranha tank, watched the nearest fish home in on the splash and make short work of little albino Mickey. A few quick chomps, and a wet cloudburst of red. He dropped another, this one squeaking, into the tank's opposite end. Zap. Two more flashes of chomping silver, and it became an underwater tug of war. The rest of the piranha were beginning to get the idea. They were used to this game. Among others.

Tony held two by the tails this time, one in each hand. Looked back at the smiling Lupo, who got just as big a kick out of this as did Tony.

"Just like feeding popcorn to pigeons," Tony said.

And let the mice fall.

5
hawkwinds

⟡ The Venezuelan savannah burned under a sun that seemed to grow hotter with every passing day. Coarse grasses wavered in breezes too pitiful to offer much relief. On the crude but serviceable airstrip at Esmerelda, an equally crude but serviceable cargo plane rumbled down the runway, tentatively cleared ground, then seemed to gain confidence and pulled up into the sky.

In its belly, Kerebawa white-knuckled the safety harness that strapped him into his seat along the inner fuselage. The vibrations were nothing short of terrifying, like the convulsions of a sickened animal readying to lose a recent meal.

He still wasn't comfortable with the idea of flight, even though the late Angus Finnegan had tried to allay his fears once by referring to a plane as a canoe with wings. That helped, and once in the air things were usually fine, although turbulence still gave him fits. Not so long ago, though, the mere thought of flight was enough to chill the spine of an otherwise brave warrior.

"What if we crash into the *hedu kä misi*?" he had asked Angus on that very first flight, to Caracas. He was referring to the next layer of the Yanomamö cosmos, hovering overhead at some undetermined altitude.

"The *hedu kä misi* is too high," Angus had told him. "We could never reach it. No man could."

Kerebawa had nodded. Then, "What if we crash into God-teri?"

Angus had frowned, looking puzzled. At last he had answered, "We'll not crash there unless God calls us to."

Two years ago, that had been. In comparison with that younger Kerebawa, he was quite the world traveler by now.

The cargo plane, now as then, was piloted by a man named Barrows. An old friend of Padre Angus, immense of belly and bald of head. His copilot, Matteson, was almost a complete opposite—tall and lean with his hair pulled into a graying ponytail. They ran a helter-skelter circuit between Miami and numerous cities across northernmost South America. They frequently touched down in Esmerelda, bringing supplies to the missionaries working among the Yanomamö. In turn, they bought plantains and other fruit and sold them to produce wholesalers in the cities. Both had been dismayed over Angus Finnegan's demise. And reluctantly agreeable to aiding Kerebawa as he sought to continue Angus's work.

They had already proven their worth as allies. For so much had already happened to get Kerebawa this far.

Medellín is Colombia's second largest city, founded in 1616 by Spanish Basques settling in the New World. It's nestled in a lush valley between two stretches of the Andes Mountains, five thousand feet above sea level and only six degrees north of the equator. Such logistics give it spring-perfect weather all year long. Medellín is world-renowned for the beauty of its orchids, and it is one of Colombia's chief industrial cities. It has more than a few parallels with American cities—a juxtaposition of mirrored-glass office buildings with working-class ghettos struggling against poverty.

In the past ten to twelve years, it has rapidly become to the cocaine trade what Sicily is to the Mafia. A criminal mecca, center of a worldwide network. The Cartel. Exporters who found it far more profitable to work in cooperation rather than as independent rivals.

Standing on a sloping mountainside above the city, invisible within dense foliage, Kerebawa could smell the city's fear. Hundreds of thousands of innocent people who never knew if death by gun or knife was moments away. You don't ascend to the top of the coke heap without a cheap price on human life.

Angus Finnegan had never been here, but he understood it. That much Kerebawa had been able to divine while poring over the Padre's papers after his death. A wealth of sometimes incomprehensible information obtained by trading medical supplies to a network of leftist guerrillas fiercely opposed to the Cartel. And who sometimes worked in clandestine fashion with the American Drug Enforcement Administration. Angus had been a man possessed about compiling the information once word spread that "traders" from the west were visiting Iyakei-teri.

As the hawk flies, Medellín lies better than eight hundred miles from Esmerelda. Once Kerebawa understood the enormity of the distance, after studying Angus's maps, he felt the shame of disgrace rising within. The distance was too vast. He would fail to avenge his friend's death.

Then he remembered the sky-men, who soared close to God-teri. Barrows and Matteson. And recognized a name on the map he had heard them talking about.

Bogotá.

They had told him he was crazy, a rain-forest savage wanting to fly with them all the way to Bogotá so he could disappear into the jungle bordering the runway. Kerebawa knew he had to be crafty about travel, for he had no Padre to explain the complexities of civilization, and no pockets for the papers civilized men always demanded to see. *Crazy.* But it wasn't any skin off the pilots' noses if his mind was made up.

He traveled light, carrying a machete, his bow and arrows, and a bamboo quiver of arrow tips. A cloth roll for his tobacco and *ebene* powder and maps and pictures and a few other odds and ends.

Angus had taught him the way white men measured time. When Barrows told him they would be back in Bogotá in two weeks, he knew precisely how long they meant. And that he had enough to keep him busy in the meantime.

Kerebawa felt quite the adventurer when leaving a remote stretch of the airport for the mountain jungles. Relieved, too, for they felt a lot more like home than the belly of the flying canoe. As well, he thought himself quite clever. He'd just reduced his distance to travel solo to 150 miles or so. With two weeks to cover the distance to Medellín, find Vasquez and the *hekura-teri*, then return to Bogotá to wait for the sky-men.

Kerebawa descended the slope outside of Bogotá, and walked until the miles took him to the north-flowing Magdalena River. At its banks, he fashioned a disposable canoe out of tree bark and made the traveling a lot easier by letting the river carry him better than half the journey.

He traveled over mountains, through jungles, across dense valleys, past immense trees stretching up like the legs of some great antediluvian beast. And through it all he felt the pull growing stronger. You lived in the jungle, thrived there, by becoming a part of it. Feeling its rhythms inside bones and soul. Bending to its will rather than fighting it. And in turn, it would open up its mysteries and let you see and hear and smell and taste all the things an outsider would never notice.

The *hekura-teri* had been born of jungle. And he could sense its path across the face of the sky.

Kerebawa would daily perform, alone, the same rituals that went on back home in Mabori-teri. He had no one to blow the *ebene* through a tube for him, so he sniffed it from his fingertips until he had enough to open his eyes to even deeper mysteries. The mysteries of the *noreshi*, his soul. And the spirit animal to which his soul was aligned. *Noreshi* referred to either as well as both, for the two were inseparable. The fate of one was the fate of the other.

And during his *ebene* trances, he would sing and chant and dance, then look to the sky to see a large hawk, his spirit animal, circling aloft in the distance, in the direction of the next day's travel. The hawk was far wiser than he, with keener senses. No doubt the bird could *see* the trail left by the passage of the *hekura-teri.* And guide him.

It reminded Kerebawa of one of his favorite Bible stories Angus had taught him. The man called Moses, leading his people out of slavery into a new land. Following signs in the sky. Cloud by day, fire by night.

He followed the hawk for five days, until it hovered in circles over a sprawling home of white stucco and red-tiled roof. Far down the mountainside. In the distance, Medellín-teri lay like a scattering of enormous jewels. But they were poison. The stink of fear was like morning mist that winds could never blow away and sun could never burn off.

So long a journey, now ended. While the hard part was just beginning.

He eased his way down the mountain, at one with the jungle. Ferns, vines, creepers, palms, underbrush. The chattering of monkeys and the calls of birds. Keeping soft, silent. Stripped to the skin as his forefathers would have been, before the white men taught them shame. Wearing only his waistcord.

Kerebawa came within scant feet of the edge of the jungle and the start of a clearing. He shook his head. All these hard-looking *shabonos* looked alike. He dug through his cloth roll and found a picture of the home of Hernando Vasquez. Compared the picture with real thing. At least they *seemed* to match.

Ebene time. For once he dispensed with the noisier aspects of the ritual. When he looked skyward, he saw the departing hawk, and that cinched it for him. Here the traders would learn the true wrath of the Fierce People.

Kerebawa stole about to various vantage points. He scaled trees, pulling with callused hands and pushing with callused feet, until he had better views of the area. Wise warriors always know the lay of the land before a raid.

And this place did not look good.

The house, with perhaps a hundred yards between it and the jungle at the clearing's broadest point, was guarded by six men. Four in back, two in front. With wasp-guns.

They were the *sicarios,* assassins employed by Vasquez and men like him. As guards, as hit-men. Like the Yanomamö,

they too learned savagery at a young age. Most were anywhere from early teens to around twenty years old. The
young were more dangerous, always thought they were immortal. And gave less thought to pulling a trigger.

Kerebawa knew none of this, only that they were many to
his one. Arrows would be of limited value against this enemy.
He'd have to resort to a variation of the *nomohoni,* massacre
by treachery.

And for that, a wise warrior is patient. To plan carefully.

For two days he watched their routines. Noting by the
position of the sun when they came and went. He moved like
a wraith through the surrounding jungle to watch the house
from back, front, both sides. A few times he caught sight of an
older man who moved among his inferiors with the authority
of a headman. Kerebawa consulted his pictures. Hernando
Vasquez. The back of the photo was stamped with the phrase,
DEA SURVEILLANCE PHOTO.

The first night he even ventured, long after most of the
compound had retired for the day, down onto their grounds.
Painted black with his pigments, hugging the shadows of the
house and trees and a couple of smaller outbuildings. One he
even dared to enter, and he found a garrison of sorts for the
soldiers. He passed a pair of men sleeping on cots. So easy to
slit their throats in their sleep—but no, now wasn't the time.
Predominant in this block building was a kitchen. Mealtime
had looked to be their primary moment of vulnerability,
when a fat cook would bring a bowl of food to each *sicario* on
duty.

When Kerebawa returned to his hidden stash of supplies
back up the mountainside, he was satisfied. And slept. Tried
to, at least. He dared not build a fire this close, and it left him
cold inside and out. He thought of the fire burning low back
in his own *shabono* so far away, of sharing its warmth with his
wife and son. This was a trying time back home. Mating with
Kashimi was taboo now, as their son was but a year old and
she still nursed him. It left him plenty *beshi.* Angus had
taught him a funny English word for that one—horny, Padre
had called it. It was enough to make a man want to load up on
ebene and become a shaman.

Kerebawa watched the routines of the guards all the next

day. They were lazy men, he could tell, used to doing little or nothing. By late afternoon, when the men of Mabori-teri would have been sniffing *ebene* and chanting to their demons, Kerebawa was engaged in an activity of a far more lethal nature. Luckily, he'd come prepared.

The Yanomamö and other equatorial Indians bake a bread called cassava, the flour derived from two varieties of the manioc root. Americans know the root as tapioca. And the Indians know that the bitter manioc root is violently poisonous. Kerebawa had brought several roots along, just in case.

A wise warrior plans ahead.

He peeled the roots, soaked and squeezed them in water to leach out the toxins. Normally the water was then boiled; the heat gradually destroyed the poisons while the liquid thickened into a tasty syrup. But Kerebawa merely stored the water, perhaps a half quart, in a gourd container.

There was more than one way to stage a massacre.

Kerebawa painted himself black again, then descended the mountain. First with the water, ever so carefully, to stow it near the kitchen. He notched it in some tree roots so it wouldn't topple over. He returned for his weapons, then positioned himself in foliage, concealed and still able to peer through the outbuilding's windows, as the cook prepared the evening meal.

An hour later, while the sun waned, the cook left the building long enough to take two bowls to the guards out front. Kerebawa padded silently out of the forest, across open ground, then into the kitchen. Gourd in one hand, machete in the other. He peeked inside first, found it empty. Just cabinets, boxes of supplies, a stove built up from red bricks. Countertops and a refrigerator. How could human beings eat food processed by these contraptions? It seemed the food would lose all flavor and value.

On a countertop stood a large pot; beside it, several bowls and spoons. He dipped a finger into the pot. Cold, somewhat greasy. He licked his finger clean, one eye on the door. A tart taste—gazpacho soup. Good. It would help mask the bitter water. He dumped the water from gourd to pot, then clumsily rattled a wooden ladle around to mix it. He returned to the lip of the forest to wait. And watch, as the cook waddled back and forth to distribute the bowls to the rear guards.

Shortly after returning from the final trip, the cook remained in the building. Kerebawa heard running water, the clang of pots and pans. Wait a bit more, time to make himself hot and meat-hungry, ready for war. And time for the poison to take effect.

Kerebawa had mixed it strong, and it would take from fifteen to thirty minutes for the onset of symptoms, the poison entering the bloodstream from the stomach. Once that happened, the men had but three to five minutes. Symptoms progressed quickly. Tingling in the extremities, increasing tunnel vision, sweating, then unconsciousness. And death.

After the guards had been eating awhile, Kerebawa returned to the kitchen. An ebony shadow, machete in hand, he was through the doorway in an eyeblink. The fat cook, glancing up from his sink full of dirty cookware, barely managed to squeak out a cry before Kerebawa split his wide forehead with the machete. Kerebawa caught his heavy body before it fell, extracted the blade by wiggling it back and forth. Stowed the body behind several crates as the head leaked onto the floor.

Back to the forest's edge, crouching. He retrieved his bow and arrows. He had earlier fixed war tips onto the arrow shafts, sharpened bamboo points with barbs made of monkey bone. Coated with curare.

When the first of the disoriented guards out back fell, Kerebawa sprinted low and parallel with the jungle's edge to the front of the house. No poison to do his work up here, unfortunately. The far guard was near a small barricade beside the drive leading up to the house. Kerebawa aimed and drew his bow, let the arrow fly. It slammed into the guard's back, barbed tip breaking off just under his shoulder. He went down with a grunt, and Kerebawa was already loading and aiming the second. Before the other guard, nearer the house, could make sense of his fallen comrade, the next arrow had sunk into the soft flesh just below the breastbone. The curare made short work of them both, rapidly relaxing muscles past the point of any movement. First the limbs, then inward until the lungs and heart themselves were stilled.

Kerebawa rushed the house, acutely feeling the exhilaration of bloodshed, born into his blood and spirit. He tried a side door, recessed into a covered little walkway, but it was locked. He used the stained machete blade to slice an opening into a nearby screened window and slid through. Dropped to a crouch, looking furtively about.

The house smelled of too much wasted space and idle hands. The machete he carried aloft, ready to swing. Around his neck hung the bamboo quiver. The bow and arrows themselves were too cumbersome for inside.

He was in a small bedroom and padded out to the hallway. The walls were the color of bone, and he stood out against them like a man risen from a tar pit. South American artwork of both Spanish and Indian origins hung on the walls. Kerebawa crept deeper into the house, ears pricked for alarm raised by the discovery of the fallen guards.

Up a flight of four steps, a wider central hallway. Footsteps, shoes on the polished wooden floor.

"Qué tal?" he heard a man gasp upon looking out a window overlooking the back.

Kerebawa pressed in close to the wall as the man rushed around the corner. Surely no older than himself, wearing a black shirt with a gun suspended in a leather shoulder rig. His hand was just closing on the gun when he rounded the corner and saw Kerebawa. His eyes widened even as the machete chopped straight across them and the bridge of his nose. Bone splintered into brain, and he was dead on his feet, and Kerebawa eased him to the floor.

Another guard was on the second floor, his back in view as Kerebawa crept up the stairs. Oblivious to everything going on around him. Kerebawa came up behind him and clamped one hand over his mouth and reached around to drive a bamboo arrow point up into his heart with the other. He waited until the man quit spasming beneath his hand, then laid him to one side.

What tales he would have to tell when he got back to Mabori-teri! Tales that would be told to children and grandchildren of the village for generations to come. Kerebawa, a true Fierce One, creeping into a strange enemy's *shabono* even before nightfall and spilling the blood of many a foe.

He would be legend. And Angus would be avenged.

He found no more guards on the rest of his silent trek through the dark of the house. But he found the big man himself at the opposite end. Hernando Vasquez, in his bedroom. The man was older than he had appeared at a distance, hair rapidly graying, his face tight and leathery, with jowls just beginning to turn heavy. Droopy eyes. He was almost grandfatherly. Vasquez wore a silk robe and was with a woman less than half his age. She saw the intruder first, the stalking dark shadow, and gave a startled cry. Dropped a champagne glass to shatter on the floor.

Kerebawa, knowing the advantage of surprise was gone, charged in with the machete high, cocked, and ready to swing.

"Carlos! Diego!" Vasquez yelled. He had twitchy eyes. A rat's eyes. After a beat he called for them again.

"Muertos," Kerebawa said. Might as well let him know that he could scream his lungs out and help would not come.

That a man should live in such splendor and unused space was repugnant. As if Vasquez had to surround himself with trinkets and baubles to distract himself from how empty his life truly was. Such a man was impossible to understand. Truly foreign. Which made Kerebawa wonder: How much more foreign did he seem to Vasquez? How much a part of another world? Probably far more so than Vasquez seemed to him. Which was where the man's true fear lived.

Kerebawa backed them across the room until the woman stood beside a canopy bed and Vasquez by a large desk. Kerebawa made a show of stepping aside and looked the woman straight on. Beneath reddish-brown hair, her dusky face was flushed, her lips trembled.

"Vete a freír monos," he told her. In short—get lost.

She took a tentative step forward, then another, eyeing him the whole time. Apparently felt no great loyalty toward her man. As she passed by, Kerebawa lashed out to give her a solid whack across the temple with the machete's flat side. Certainly not a killing blow, but it would keep her trouble-free for a while. Her lacy gown billowing, she half spun and crumpled to the floor.

Vasquez looked considerably paler than he had a moment

before. A man of bluff and bluster, it seemed. Strip him of his support, and the true coward would be revealed.

"Dónde está el hekura-teri?" Kerebawa asked the sweating man.

Vasquez looked at him, confusion pinching his face. *"No comprendo."* His voice quavered.

Of course. How could he know its true name?

"Dónde está el polvo verde"—green powder—*"de Venezuela?"*

Vasquez made a relieved face, nodding and smiling broadly. As if he had nothing whatsoever to worry about. Laughing, even. Kerebawa was immediately suspicious.

"Ah, es no problema! Está en la gaveta." He eagerly pointed to a desk drawer. Slowly moved his hand for the knob.

Impossible. Large as the drawer was, the load of powder taken by the traders couldn't fit in there. Ignorant man, taking him for a brainless fool.

Vasquez slid his hand inside the drawer, barely open wide enough to accommodate it. Kerebawa brought the machete around and down in a vicious arc that severed the hand at the wrist with a meaty crunch. Vasquez's mouth dropped open as he watched the hand jitter atop the butt of an automatic pistol, then fall still. While gouting blood sprayed across papers and books strewn over the desktop. A moment later he shrieked, lifting the stumpy wrist in disbelief. He cradled it to his chest, a huge stain spreading across the silk robe.

Kerebawa recognized the glazing eyes. The man, even were the bleeding to stop, wasn't going to be of much use for very long. Shock was setting in.

"Dónde está el polvo verde?" he asked again, this time threatening with the machete.

Vasquez was past tricks. And when he sputtered the powder's destination, Kerebawa's heart took a high plunge. He pushed paper and pen across the blood-dewed desktop and had Vasquez write down as much pertinent information as he could.

And when he was done, Kerebawa accomplished something that neither the DEA nor the leftist guerrillas nor the rival cocaine exporters in the nearby city of Cali had managed.

He effectively removed the head of the Vasquez family.

And now, a couple of weeks later, here he was in the belly of the flying canoe once again. Ready to resume the trail of the *hekura-teri* in an even stranger land, a land he'd visited but once.

Miami-teri.

He looked at its name, written on a crumpled, dirty sheet of paper, stained with brownish splotches of dried blood. And the name of another man to seek out: Luis Escobar. Plus the word *Estrella*.

Miami.

He was dressed for it; gone was the nudity of the jungle. He wore fresh clothes from Angus's hut, garments the Padre had given him on their previous trips but that had gone unused since. Pale brown shirt, olive pants, purple socks. Horribly confining shoes with the mysterious word *Keds* on the sides. The clothing was all cotton and smelled of mildew.

Kerebawa dared to look out the window; maybe he could see God. But no, only the sun-splashed water below, coarse and silvery gray. And the skimming shadow of the plane itself.

He looked back into the plane when he heard the cockpit door latch. Barrows was wandering back to him, bald head sunburned and big belly loosely hidden behind an untucked shirt. A couple of days of beard darkened his face.

"If you don't beat all," Barrows said, and dropped down a few seats away. He looked at Kerebawa and shook his head. "You know, I could get in all kinds of trouble hauling you into the country like this. Won't be using that passport Angus got you. No visa. No customs clearance."

Kerebawa frowned with confusion. This was mostly gibberish.

"Papers," Barrows said, and that got the point across. "An illegal alien, that's what you'll be."

"I will disappear before anyone can ask me for them."

"Yeah, I believe that much. Lucky for you, we're flying into a smaller airport outside the city. Miami International, you'd probably never make it out of that place alive."

Kerebawa said nothing.

"Why are you doing this?" Barrows asked, eyes narrowing. "What does this have to do with Angus dying?"

"I must find something for him. I promised."

Barrows grinned wryly, shook his head. "Promise to a dead man. Don't that beat all. He was really a good friend to you, wasn't he?"

Kerebawa smiled, gazed up into the plane's roof. "He came when I was a child. The elders say he was funny then. They say he was . . . very foolish. They could talk him into giving away all his valuable goods for no trade in return. But he learned to speak like us. And then to think like us. I wish I remembered him then."

Barrows smiled and nodded along. "He was a good guy. A little crazy toward the end, but a good man." The fat pilot dug one hand into his pants pocket, produced a wad of green paper.

The people of Mabori-teri thought of such things as decorated leaves. But Kerebawa knew better. It was the white man's method of trade. And Barrows gave it to him.

"Maybe you can run around the jungle in Colombia without that green stuff. But you can't get by in America very long without it. Do you know how it works?"

Kerebawa flipped through the bills. Some with *twenty* written across them, some with *ten*, several fives, a few ones. He nodded, uncertain.

"I learned how to count in the mission school."

Barrows nodded. "Just take your time with it, it won't go that far. Don't spend any more than you have to. And remember, just because they're all the same size don't mean they're all the same value."

"I know *that*." Exasperated, Kerebawa grinned at the pilot, bared one eyeball by pulling down the lower lid.

Barrows laughed and returned the American equivalent: an upraised middle finger. He stood, moved for the cockpit door.

"Won't be long now," he said.

"Could you find me something when we get there?"

"What do you need?"

"A map of Miami?"

"That can be arranged," Barrows said, and shut the door behind him.

More tales to tell his children and grandchildren.

Kerebawa looked at the money in his hands. Green, so green. He understood that men killed each other over it. Just as he had seen them kill for the green powder. Men, acting as savage and violent as could the *hekura*. Or using Angus's word, demons.

He wondered if they knew their name had been affixed to a powder that did far more than show visions. And if they did, if they were angered, or flattered.

Hekura-teri . . .

Village of the demons.

6
WATChiNG THE
Tide Roll AWAY

Justin's morning after the slaughter at Apocalips was considerably less gleeful than Tony Mendoza's. While Tony and Lupo were making sure the piranha got their Recommended Daily Allowance of white mice, Justin was finding that awakening was even more fitful than sleep.

The bathroom mirror showed bloodshot eyes. The inside of his nose burned like a freshly paved road. His muscles were out of kink from sleeping on Erik's couch. A queasy stomach was the least of his worries. The price of fun—he'd paid it often.

Erik had risen fifteen minutes earlier and was fixing breakfast in the kitchen. Wearing rumpled gym shorts, Justin shuffled in and joined him.

"It's days like this I wish my mom had had me aborted," he said.

Erik tilted a skillet. "Want me to fix you some too?"

Justin peered toward the stove. French toast, bacon, OJ at the side. His stomach roiled at the sight, the very idea. "No thanks." He found a beer in the refrigerator, cracked it open, and slumped at the table. Let George Killian's settle his stomach. Hair of the wildebeest.

"I don't think I've started the morning with beer since college," Erik said.

"You're a wise lad." Justin's mouth felt leathery and dry, eluding control. "Paula used to tell me I belonged in AA."

Erik flipped his toast. Sizzle. "Was she right?"

"I don't know. Don't care." Justin leaned heavily, elbows on table, looking at his bare arms. Too pale, severe deficiency of Florida sun. "Mornings-after like this, sometimes I'll concede she might have had a point." A long pause, while thoughts cleared and a mental spotlight shone on last night. Highlighting memories he hoped were bad dreams but feared were not. "Was I blown out of my mind last night—or did some people get killed?"

"You're right on both counts."

Justin stared morosely into his bottle while Erik recounted what had been publicly broadcast. The body count, the eye-witness reports. The uneasy consensus that someone had turned a wild cat loose within the club. It didn't entirely correlate with all the witness claims, but a roomful of eyes yields at best inconsistencies, while forensics results don't lie.

"Did you see anything last night, what happened?" Justin asked.

"Not until it was pretty much all over."

Justin tried to reconcile the truths released for public consumption with his own distorted memories. A poor match. Although Mendoza had undoubtedly fed him some sort of hallucinogen. That *had* to be the culprit in the way he remembered things. Geeks just don't stumble out of bathrooms and go lycanthrope on dance floors.

Still, the sensations remained vivid. That feeling of plummeting toward a pit of primordial ooze from which anything could have evolved and crawled forth.

It wasn't until Erik was carrying his plate of food to the table that he told Justin about a call from work earlier in the morning. About Trent having hanged himself.

"Oh, man . . . I'm sorry." Justin reached across the table, touched Erik's arm for a moment.

Erik shrugged. "Yeah. He wasn't exactly a friend. Nice enough guy, I suppose, but—well, forget it. Shouldn't speak ill of the dead." He frowned. "I keep thinking I should feel worse about it. It's like I think, 'Gee, that's too bad, that's awful.' And then I go on about my business. Sometimes I think *I'm* dead inside."

"If there's no love lost, you can't pretend. If it had been me, you'd feel lousy then, wouldn't you?"

Erik nodded vigorously, mouth full of French toast. Swallowed hard. "You *know* I would."

"Okay then. Case closed." He leaned across to rap knuckles on Erik's chest, over his heart. "It still works in there."

Watching Erik eat, he drank the ale, rolling the bottle between his palms. A minute later he groaned. Mortal anguish, wounds deep in the soul.

"I bet I really blew it last night with April. Shit, I hope she didn't see me blow chow like that."

Erik rattled his fork against the plate. "Please? I'm not quite done here?"

"I didn't even say good-bye."

"Under the circumstances, I'm sure she'll understand. She's kind of bohemian, real easygoing." Erik mopped up the last of the syrup, downed the final bite. "Give her a call today, ask her out."

"Mm. Maybe."

Erik tossed his dishes into the sink, sprayed them with water. "Knock it off with the bashful-puppy routine, okay? Look at it from this perspective: How long have you been celibate?"

"Too long." Justin chucked his empty bottle into the trash. "I passed this construction site last week. Even the knotholes in the fence looked pretty good."

"Oh, mayday, mayday! You're in the danger zone, spud man."

Justin agreed, and the conversation roamed onward as they moved from kitchen to living room. Justin stared out the windows, past the palm tree, down at the traffic on Davis Boulevard. Wondering who was in the cars, where they were going. If any would die soon. How their lives were progressing, satisfactorily or otherwise.

The airflow from bedroom to living-room windows brought warming winds from outside, a clammy trickle of humidity. Justin shut his eyes, letting it work its way inside him to fight the residual chill left by this long, cold winter. And that was when the phone rang.

It jangled once before Erik's machine caught it. He left it on continually to screen his calls, weed out siding sales pitches and personae non gratae and the like. The speaker broadcast the outgoing message, Erik's rhythmically breathless voice apologizing for his unavailability. In the background was the sound of squeaking bedsprings and moaning sighs that could have come from any of several hundred porn films. Then the beep.

"Cute, cute. That's a new one, isn't it?" At April's voice they both perked up. "Does she have all of her permanent teeth yet?"

"You want to catch that?" Erik rose, rapidly backing toward the hallway and bathroom beyond. Grinning. "Emergency! Gotta take a power-dump."

Justin cursed him as April went on.

"I just wanted to make sure you guys got home okay. You've probably heard all the news by now. And about Trent? Wow—"

Justin had heard enough. This didn't sound like a girl who thought *too* ill of him, and he killed the machine and cut in. They talked for a few minutes, mostly about the previous night, what the media had to say on the subject. He felt comfortable, no pressure. Was she bohemian? He couldn't tell. Easygoing? Definitely. Fabulous. Lately he wasn't feeling up to the challenge of icy walls of poise, unbreachable to all but the most self-assured.

"I'm sorry we cut out last night, left you there," he said. "That was my fault, a hundred percent."

"Come on, no apologies. You *did* look pretty bad all of a sudden."

Ever the manipulator, Erik decided to make his presence felt. "Oh Juuus-tiiin!" he called, his voice sing-song. "Don't forget that feee-eeence, those knooot-hoooles!"

Justin clamped his hand over the mouthpiece, but it was too late. Barn door open, horse already escaped.

"*What* did he say?" she asked.

"Who knows." Maybe the floor would open up and swallow him, phone and all. "I think he's trying to serenade me from the shower. His mind and libido work in strange ways."

April said she agreed completely, and he decided to dive right in and ask her out. Get it over with before Erik blurted out something even more embarrassing to nudge him along. And in the end he was rather grateful for Erik's persistence.

Especially since April said yes.

April had graciously offered to drive, since Justin was without wheels. She picked him up late that afternoon. He'd stayed sober all day, a minor triumph, and felt much improved over the ghoul he had been upon awakening. Clean, shaved, comfortable, wearing baggy blue slacks with a drawstring and a simple white shirt. All-purpose, hard to go wrong. The only thing he knew to expect was that they definitely wouldn't be going dancing.

They decided to eat Cajun, and she wheeled to what she said was one of her favorite restaurants, in a quieter stretch of Tampa. The restaurant's little microcosm felt more like New Orleans. Stately two-story red-brick building with white wooden trim. Surrounding willow trees dripping Spanish moss. They ate at a black wrought-iron sidewalk table while down-south jazz wafted out from a piano inside.

April taught him the finer points of eating boiled crayfish as they shared a plateful for an appetizer. They looked like a mound of tiny lobsters, red of shell and beady of eyes. Ready to swarm across the table and mount a counteroffensive. That the menu informed him of their colloquial name, mudbugs, was of limited charm.

"Nothing to it," she told him, delighted either to introduce him to something new or inflict subtle tortures. "Just break off the tail, suck the juice out of the head, and peel the meat out of the tail." She demonstrated, then laughed as he massacred one with his first attempt.

They *were* good, once initial aversions were overcome. By

the time the plate was empty he was a seasoned pro, and he found that he liked this April Kingston very much.

Main courses were next. Blackened redfish for him, barbecued shrimp for her, sides of red beans and rice. By the time these were gone he felt he had a better fix on her.

April was almost a Tampa native. She'd grown up across the Old Bay in St. Pete. The dusting of Oriental influence in her features wasn't imagination. She had a Japanese grandmother, who had fallen in love with a GI while stuck in an internment camp in California during World War II. Grandpa had married her, despite lots of resentment and downright nasty hatred directed his way. Very romantic stuff; she seemed to enjoy the story a lot.

She was self-employed as a commercial artist, working out of a portion of her loft apartment. April had gone free-lance after doing a few years of dues-paying and contact-making at the *Tribune*'s ad department. It was better than the creative department of an ad agency because she didn't feel compelled to accept anything that might jar sensibilities. A bit less stable a career move, perhaps, but a lot of businesses preferred to get their advertising services on an à la carte basis rather than put an entire agency on a fat retainer. She had kissed the *Tribune* good-bye eighteen months before Erik.

"How do you know him?" she asked. "I know you're not, but you almost look like you could be brothers."

"People have said that. And I'm the fairer-skinned, darker-haired twin." He pushed his plate away across the wrought iron. Feeling, for the first time in a long while, that people just might be looking at him with envy. This was nirvana—fed and sober and happy to be in the company of a lovely female who wasn't dragging him through ugly litigation. "We used to say we were supposed to be brothers, but biology and genetics conspired against us. And that fate won out in the end."

April smiled. "That's kind of sweet."

"We met in college, at the University of Illinois. Almost eleven years ago, first week there as freshmen. We both started off trying the fraternity route—different houses—and we both hated it. With me, it was like, four days in and I *knew*

I wasn't cut from that cloth. We both walked out of our houses the same morning with our bags packed and threw ourselves on the mercy of the university housing system. We ended up assigned to the same temporary housing room."

"Neither one of you strikes me as the Greek type."

"Thank you." He drained his water glass, and someone was there to refill in moments. "Temp housing was bizarre. It was this double-size room that was supposed to be used as a lounge. They crammed five of us in there. Makeshift bunk beds, freestanding clothes racks, desks everywhere there wasn't a bed. Sardines go to college. The rest of the guys on the floor called it the Refugee Camp."

She laughed. "Grandma would sympathize."

"I guess it gave Erik and me a pretty strong common bond. Because our backgrounds were pretty different. I came from St. Louis, and he was from some tiny little place in Ohio. We ended up rooming together until we graduated. Apartments after that first year."

April was leaning in, chin atop laced fingers. "I love happy endings."

He whipped out his almighty MasterCard Gold to take care of dinner. Had to smile at the imagined horror of the First National Bank of Wilmington should he apply for one under his present circumstances. After dinner they grabbed a bottle of cheap sangria. She drove back to Davis Island but bypassed Erik's building, kept going to the south rim. Left a winding two-lane drive and veered onto a broad expanse of lawn overlooking Hillsborough Bay. She stopped a few yards from the abrupt shoreline, where a layer of chunky rock was land's last bastion before sea.

They got out, strolled to the edge, sangria in hand. The day had cooled down to the low seventies, and salt breezes skimmed off the water. Behind them was the small Peter Knight Airport. Angled across the bay was some sort of shipyard, a huge freighter docked. Farther out on the horizon, there came another one, its guttural basso horn rolling across the water. Sailboats and catamarans milked what they could from the dying sunlight and waning winds, wedges of brilliant color flashing to and fro.

Justin and April sat on the grass. It was as close to paradise as he'd found recently.

Justin unscrewed the top of the sangria bottle. "Want to sniff the bottlecap?"

"I'll trust your selection."

He took a pull from the bottle. Chilled, fruity; the original wine cooler. He passed it to her. "We should've thought to get cups."

She drank, smiled. "I don't mind your germs if you don't mind mine."

"Deal."

The bottle was on its third go-around when she drew her knees up beneath her chin and gazed out over the water. A pair of miniature speedboats were playing cat and mouse.

"You don't talk much about yourself, do you," she said.

"Not much lately." He felt them heading out over thin ice. "Did Erik say much about me? Why I was moving down here and all?"

"Not a lot, no." She laughed. "He said *he* wasn't going to defame your character, he was going to leave that up to you."

"Always thoughtful, that Erik. I love him a lot, you know."

April was silent. Waiting, he supposed, for him to fill in some blanks regarding his life. At no point this evening had she seemed judgmental about anything, so maybe the revelations wouldn't be as disastrous as he had feared. Maybe the ice would bear up under the weight of his guilt after all.

So he spilled it, without resorting to sugar coating, without whining that it wasn't really his fault. Facts only. Here sits a stupid guy who made a very stupid mistake and paid dearly for it and *still* realized he'd gotten off exceedingly lucky.

"So that's it," he said in conclusion. "If you feel like driving off and leaving me sitting here, I'll understand."

April leaned in to knock shoulders with him. A very tender, subtle way of telling him he was still accepted. It went far deeper than words. You don't touch someone whom you revile, not like that.

"I admire you, in a way," she finally said.

This was a real shocker. *"Why?"*

April looked his way, head slightly atilt. Such depth in the almond eyes. "It must have taken a lot of courage to pull together what you had left, instead of just sinking lower and lower. Picking up and moving somewhere to make a fresh start. That takes guts."

"It was a necessity."

"It still took guts. Sometimes I wish I had the guts to do the same thing, just pack up and find somewhere else. Someplace where I don't know anyone and nobody knows me. That would make us even."

Justin wondered why, what emotional dirty laundry she could be toting around. Maybe the rift with her former fiancé, Brad. So what if people called him Dickless; the ties may have been strong indeed. From the outside, no one else can truly know how deep your rivers run.

So he wondered, but got no answers. He would not press, not dig. If it was important, meant to be shared, she would offer it freely. As he had.

After he got the sangria back, he held it up to the west, let the sinking sun play through the reddish-purple. Half gone. Not half full, he realized. Pessimism still reigns.

"You may have noticed last night, I'm not exactly without faults. I do too much of this sort of thing, for one."

She nodded. "I wondered about that."

"After everything started falling apart, my ex-wife told me I could drink all I wanted but I was never going to be able to forget."

"Maybe she had you all wrong. Maybe you don't drink to forget at all."

"To numb it, then. Same thing."

"Maybe. Or maybe you do it to remember."

He smiled, relishing the ease of the conversation. No accusations, no reproachments. Almost as if they were discussing someone else. He looked curiously at her.

"What would I be trying to remember?"

"Your true self," she said softly.

He played it over in his mind. "I don't even know what my true self is anymore."

"There you go, then." April resumed her vigil over the water. "I hardly know you, but it seems like you've spent a lot of time trying to shoehorn yourself into places that don't really fit you, deep inside. Like the fraternity. And whether you realize it or not, you sound pretty relieved to be out of the agency game. And that whole upwardly mobile track that burns people out and eats ulcers into them before they're thirty." A long pause. "I'm sorry. I don't have any right to try and figure you out like that."

Justin told her not to apologize, that she was probably more on target about him than he'd managed to be about himself in quite some time. Maybe that was it. And maybe it was just the easy way she laid it out. As a friend, instead of someone doing some coldly analytical dissection.

"So maybe you drink to breach those walls inside and get back to yourself," she went on. Confidence renewed. "Kind of the same principle I was talking about last night at the club. Substance abuse as a way of returning to the forgotten. The things buried so deep in your unconscious that they might never see daylight again."

He grinned into the sangria as he drank. "I get the feeling that the Betty Ford Clinic will never call to hire your services."

"And if they did, I'd turn them down."

Justin mulled her theorizing over, testing its merits, probing its weaknesses. He had no reason to believe the latter outweighed the former. Not at all; it held water surprisingly well. *I drink, therefore I am. Can you see the real me?* Couched in April's terminology, it sounded almost romantic. Reality was likely far more mundane. Firewater simply anesthetized sensibilities offended by his backstabbing belief that happiness was a component of more than material acquisitions, status, and employer perks. He'd known who he was all along—had just tried to live some other yuppie's life-style.

The sangria was gone by the time the sun gave up and sank into the bay. Taking with it more of the day's warmth, stealing the rest of their light. Scrubbing clean the unflinching stare of day in favor of the guarded cloak of night.

For better or for worse, he felt different now. Unburdened. Justified. Even if things went no further between them, he would always thank her for that.

A bit later, April told him she had to make an early night of it. Had to be up early in the morning, meetings with a couple of clients were scheduled. That was okay. He didn't mind.

The evening had already given him far more than he had expected.

7
HOUSE CALL

The Lincoln was smoky gray, always washed, always waxed, and as it glided through the night, Tony thought the Town Car felt like a shark. The streets were their seas, the other, lesser cars fleeing before this king of predators. The tinted windows, opaque from the outside, hinted of no mercy. Traffic lights were merely suggestions. Cruising, cool and confident. Waiting for the proper trigger to snap hunger and need beyond containment.

Not just anyone would do, however. There had been a couple of promising possibilities earlier in the eve, but these had gone belly-up. Friends had been in the vicinity, witnesses who might remember.

Shortly after they had turned onto East Seventh, Lady Luck did an abrupt U-turn. There, up ahead, outside Masquerade—

"Pull over here," he told Lupo, and the car slowed and veered, smooth as butter. "Looky what we got here."

"Sasha, as I live and breathe," said Lupo, à la W. C. Fields, "heavily."

"And all alone too. *Pobrecita,*" Tony murmured, pursing his lips. Poor little thing.

Masquerade was a dance rock club, part metal, part punk, all gloom. The predominant philosophy was nihilism, the predominant sartorial color black. Music at nuclear-holocaust sound levels. He should have thought to check here first. All these gothics and gloom rockers, sounded just like Sasha's kind of magnet. Little blond chippy, she had few reservations about professing to anybody who'd listen that death was just about the most romantically sensual thing she could conceive of.

Sasha was leaning up against an ebony Jag outside the club, wearing a short leather skirt, black fishnets, and lace glovelets. Hair teased into a mane. Red, red lips.

Tony, riding shotgun, hit the electric window, and it whirred down just as Lupo eased the Town Car to a halt beside her. She broke into a broad smile when she saw who it was.

"Waiting for me, baby?" he said.

Sasha puckered up and blew him a kiss across the four feet separating them. "Just waiting."

"Hot lady like you, all alone? Crying shame. You tied to this place tonight? Or can you come out and play?"

She looked back toward the club's entrance. Rockers, both headslammers and morbids, hither, thither, and yon. "I had plans." Sasha adjusted the tiny purse riding one hip, hung from a shoulder by a long, thin strap. She looked him straight on with a wet red grin. "But, like, maybe they've changed."

Mendoza stepped from the car as Lupo punched another button to unlock the back doors. Tony opened the door for her, ever the gentleman. She told him he looked sharp himself, and wasn't it the absolute truth. He was dressed to the nines tonight. White silk suit and tie, pale blue shirt. Definite inspiration for respect. He got in after her and had one hand exploring the upper limits of her fishnets by the time Lupo was back in traffic.

"Where are we going?" She teased a red fingernail along the zipper of his slacks.

"No limits tonight. Wherever you want." He leaned in, helped himself to a taste of that ripe mouth. Mm-mm-mm. "I got some business to take care of down here around Ybor first. Wanna tag along?"

Her eyes lit up, Nordic blue. "Do I get party favors?"

"Hey, you know me. I'll take good care of you."

Sasha sighed and leaned back into the Lincoln's upholstery, shutting her eyes a moment as he twirled a finger inside her. Opened them again, rolled her head to gaze blissfully out the window. At life, lowlife, and neon.

"I wish night could go on forever." Her longing was almost childlike. "I hate daylight."

Tony pulled his fingers free, tweaked one down her lips. Give her a taste of herself. "The trick," he said, "is to never open your eyes."

Ybor City is a Spanish district in southeastern Tampa, mostly Cuban and Colombian. Lots of quaint, historically relevant renovations in the globe-lit cobblestoned Latin Quarter. Mere blocks away, however, were slums that no tourist brochure ever pictured. It was here that Tony Mendoza had grown up and come of age, learning the ins and outs of the real world. Learning that nothing much in life means jack shit unless backed up with cold cash. The green stuff.

Whenever he came back to the old neighborhoods, he felt like a conquering hero returning from the Crusades. Local boy makes good, discovers truth, free enterprise, and Keynesian economics beyond the dusty narrow streets.

Lupo glided the Lincoln to park near one of Tony's cash cows, a two-story house of scabrous brick and grime. Not much to look at, but the patrons were less concerned with appearances than results. Same principle as the corner tavern. Just like *Cheers*, only more potent. The phrase *crack house* seemed so accusatory.

Tony reaped its profits on a daily basis but was rarely here himself. Always sent trusted runners, usually driven by Lupo. Kids, mostly. Eleven, twelve, thirteen at most. Minimize the danger, maximize the buffer zone between himself and illegalities. A kid gets pinched by the law, they can't do a whole lot but ask some futile questions and let him go. The kids knew the score. Knew that a job well done now meant better work and pay as they got older. Also knew that screw-ups were very costly. In terms of fingers. Toes. Lives. Never let it be said that Tony Mendoza wasn't investing in the future of youth. Let Nancy Reagan come suck on that one awhile.

Tony and Sasha got out, left Lupo behind to guard the car.

"It *stinks* here, Tony." Sasha was clinging close to his side. You had to appreciate the humor—suburban baby *way* out of her element. "Are we gonna be here long?"

He took a deep breath. A gaseous mix of urine, feces, smoke, sweat, despair. He didn't mind it. "That's the smell of money in the making. Don't bitch."

As they paced up the house's walk, a gaggle of very young kids swarmed around their legs. They chattered excitedly. White suits got them every time. Tony dug into a pocket and flipped them a handful of loose change, and they scattered like beggars in India. Being a role model was such a burden sometimes.

An older boy sat beside the door on the stoop, unreadable behind his wraparounds. He idly flipped a butterfly knife through its various permutations. He was better security than he looked. Kid had already killed four times by age fifteen—that anybody knew about.

The heady smell thickened inside the house until it was almost solid. In dim light, smokers lined the walls and what furniture was left. A pretty docile crowd, for the most part, many of them lean to the point of emaciation. Somebody in another room had a boom box with Hendrix ripping at full volume.

Tony sought out the homeboy that managed the place, a scarecrow of a guy named Freddy. His wife hung behind him, face sunken and a baby at her chest sucking on one wrung-out tit.

Tony leaned in close to Freddy. "You got everybody out of the basement?"

Freddy nodded. "Cleaned it out this afternoon. I been making sure it stays that way." He smiled hopefully, teeth scummy and gray.

"Good man." Tony peeled out a fifty and stuffed it into one of Freddy's pockets.

He looked back at Sasha. She was down on her knees in front of some other homeboy sitting in a corner, and he was pawing at her. She kept pushing his hands away but didn't seem to mind. She was leaning into the guy's face and asking him what it felt like to be rotting from the inside out. No answers, just mindless groping. Autopilot.

"Hands off the lady," Tony said. He chopped his foot across loverboy's face, driving him back into the wall. The guy was so far gone, he thought it was funny that his nose bled into his vacant smile.

"Come on." Tony grabbed Sasha by the wrist and started pulling her along, deeper into the house. "One quick stop downstairs and then we're out of here."

"There's no hurry," she pouted.

Glad you feel that way.

Tony led her to a back stairway that took them to the basement. It was far cooler down here, much fresher than upstairs but compensated with a musty odor. Brick walls wept moisture, and somewhere in the darkness a pipe dripped into a puddle with cavernous plinks. Tony flipped on a light bulb dangling from a cord. Little good it did; forty watts at best.

He led her into a side room, its heavy iron door hanging open like the entrance to a meat locker. He switched on another weak bulb. Made a show of checking some nonexistent merchandise in some scrap crates in a corner. Muttered meaningless satisfaction to himself and stood up to rejoin her.

"I could live here," she whispered, looking around with those baby blues. "It's like—a dungeon." She stretched her hands open, ran them down her sides, her thighs. What a kick. This pesthole was actually getting her hot.

Better strike while the moment was prime.

Tony pulled her to him, grabbed another taste of her mouth. She breathed into him, mounting passion. He let his hands burn across her thin shoulders, down her back, around to her belly. Sasha was ready to melt. He pulled back from her suction-cup mouth and grinned and baited the hook:

"You wanna do some lines?"

She nodded, eyes wide. Eager. He was more than happy to oblige. He brought out the gold cigarette case and let her roll a crisp bill while he dumped out some skullflush and cut it into sharp lines. As dim as the light was, she didn't even notice that it was pale green instead of white.

Ever since last night's Apocaliptic slaughterhouse and this morning's news updates, he'd been thinking it might be wise to hang on to this particular product for a bit longer. Long enough, at least, to find out more about it, run another test or two. On the proper subject, under more controlled circumstances.

She coughed after she did the first line, fanned her nose like someone who had eaten too hot a bite of food.

"That's not coke," she said.

He smiled placatingly. "It's a new kind. Little cruder, yeah, but it's gonna be cheap as hell. You gotta do more to get the same kick, but it's worth it." He held it up, and she dived in for more. Lies were easy when someone wanted so much to believe in you.

Sasha's eyes were watering after the fourth line. "Don't you want some?"

"You know me, I don't touch it. It's just for special friends."

Happy to be one of the anointed few, she bent over to hoover the last two lines. Straightened up. Staggered on her high heels. Her nose gushed, and she wiped at it with her palm. She stared at the residue staining her hand, then looked at him. Blank-faced.

"Tony?" she whispered. *"Tony?"* Slivers of fear were starting to emerge as her nose flowed away. *"What did you give me?"*

He didn't answer, only peered intently at her growing panic. Her revulsion at just how badly she was messing herself. Sasha lurched backward into a wall, slid down, and left a trail in the clinging slime. Pleading up at him with her eyes.

There wasn't the euphoria that Trent had experienced, or had seemed to. Of course, Trent had been in a party mood to begin with. But Sasha just looked plain frightened. Disoriented. Like her eyes were trying to keep pace with a spinning room and losing. She scrabbled away from him across the floor.

"What did you give me?"

"What's it feel like?" he asked. "What does it *feel like*?"

She spluttered mucus; it streaked her hands, her blouse, her hair. Could she even see him anymore? He couldn't tell.

"Feels like . . . like . . . falling," she quavered. Then her head tilted up as if sensations had overtaken her, spirited her from the room. "I'm back—back in the womb . . ."

Man, this *was* some heavy-duty stuff.

". . . This is before I was born. . . ."

Tony felt like Carl Sagan discovering a new universe. Fascinating stuff. He watched as she groaned, writhed, wept. Slimed herself with mildew from the brick walls and concrete floor. Not exactly what he'd want to bury his bone in anymore, but hey, anybody could function in that capacity. This was a rare diversion.

And then something else entirely started to take over.

This was the sort of thing that popped your eyes right out of their sockets. The sort of thing where, if there was the slightest doubt that your faculties were operating at full capacity, you surrendered and said no way. Because this just didn't happen.

But there it was, and he was straight as a priest—*she was changing.*

Her whimpering cries grew throatier, deeper. And as he stared, facial bone structure crackled and flesh rippled and stretched, then sprouted fur. Pale blond, like her hair. Her nose and mouth started to merge into a conical snout that pushed out from her face, while tufted ears eased out from between locks of teased hair. Her hands, still clutching at the wall, compressed in on themselves. The black lacy fingerless gloves she wore pulled apart at the seams, then ripped as blond-furred paws replaced her hands.

Face, hands . . . That was it, no more.

Holy fuck, but what *was* this stuff?

When she started to rise from the floor, still on two good feminine legs, delicate ankles and spiked pumps, Tony decided he had seen quite enough. He turned tail and vacated the room as fast as he could. Slammed the iron door as if he were closing a prison cell.

And in essence, that was precisely what it was. No inside handle, just a small opening at head level for peep-checks. Installed a couple years ago for situations where somebody might need a bit of isolation. Reevaluate some priorities, maybe.

He had no idea it would ever double as a *zoo*.

But such was the case, and as what looked like some blue-eyed, blond-pelted Nordic she-wolf hit the door from the other side, he wondered what to do next. Go out, bring Lupo and his beloved MAC-10 along, and blow her apart? Terminate the experiment right now?

No. No. There were still a few unanswered questions. Give it time. After all, Trent hadn't been found wearing the head of a jaguar. He had come down; so would she.

A few moments later, Tony had to wonder if perhaps gold didn't come in shades of green, as well.

Justin, drifting somewhere in the vicinity of the threshold of sleep, thought that Erik could stand a more comfortable couch.

He'd come home a few hours ago, fresh from the truncated evening with April, and taken Erik by surprise by doing a Fred Astaire through the doorway and whistling happy tunes. It felt delightfully spontaneous. Such was probably the biggest difference between them. Erik could turn anything into a game, no advance notice required; Justin felt as if he'd been slave-bound to deliberation, even in the dumber things attempted. Erik applauded, needing no further cues that the all-important Real Date Number One had gone well. Justin Gray's life really was returning back to the upswing. Minor celebration was in order.

They split a six-pack and let the VCR assume the responsibility of entertainment. Erik had a sizable collection of video-cassettes. Legitimate, self-dubbed bootlegs, films taped off cable TV—somewhere around five hundred titles. They watched a couple, and Erik bowed out to go to bed.

Justin, meanwhile, stayed the course.

Back in St. Louis, insomnia had become a way of life. He didn't know why. Stress, maybe. Or perhaps residuals from various self-prescribed chemicals still chugging through his bloodstream, thwarting sleep in hopes of invitation to another party. He was every bit the videophile Erik was, and back in the days when all his material acquisitions were still intact, he consumed three, four, sometimes five films a night. He used to lie with Paula until she fell asleep, then grimly retire to the living room as an alternative to the slow torture of waiting for sleep that never came. After there was no Paula, there was no need of going to bed at all.

And after Erik had bid him goodnight, well, old habits die hard.

Crocodile Dundee ended happily, lovers affirmed, and credits rolled. End of film, but not end of tape. Gentle white static pulsed as it wound itself out, and Justin lingered pleasantly on that brink that was neither sleep nor wakefulness. When strange trapdoors spring open in the imagination and shortcuts develop between previously unrelated thoughts. When the self-censorship of rationality is repealed as unconstitutional.

When, if you were lucky, entire worlds could be unlocked.

Just like the poster on the wall near Erik's bookshelf. A shirtless Jim Morrison, before his own obsessions did him in. With his springboard William Blake quotation printed beside him: *When the doors of perception are cleansed man will see things as they truly are, infinite.*

He lingered, trying to remain poised there. Such a narrow ledge, really.

Justin thought of April, letting her drift through the layers of his mind. Weaving her into the fabric of his being. Emotionally, intellectually, sexually. It was the most satisfying sort of fantasy he knew of. If only she could knowingly participate in the process.

When his thoughts veered wildly off course, he didn't know where the new ones came from. But he went with them anyway. The expanding of consciousness is not something to impose barriers upon.

Even when it feels to be dragging you through a waking nightmare.

Justin knew something was different about this when the edges of his field of vision seemed to go green. Fuzzy green, pale green. He knew immediately where he'd seen that hue before, that it had mostly disappeared into Trent's nostrils.

And his own, as well.

It's still in my system. . . .

He echoed a memory of Trent at the club, on the dance floor. Wildly exultant, savagely so.

Transcendent.

Breaking through between known and unknown.

Justin felt as if he were leaving his body behind him on the couch, abandoning it while his mind soared to commingle with another. Linked, perhaps. But not perfectly. It was like forcing two gears to work together that meshed only on every fifth or sixth revolution. Windows of passage to glimpse through, doors of perception to traverse.

Infinity.

It was sensation, snippets of emotion, fragments of thought.

. . . pain . . .

. . . betrayal . . .

. . . fingers sliding down wet filmy wall, brick . . .

. . . *Help me, somebody nobody will* . . .

It felt as if he were being pulled against his will. He knew he could sever contact if he wanted; it wasn't that strong. Whoever it was—she, it was a she—was likely unaware of what she was doing. Just as he too was an innocent, receiving, as it were, via an open channel in his consciousness.

He knew her pain. Her fear. As only one who has already experienced them was able. Only she was going *so* much farther in. And he was along for the ride, with no safety bar.

. . . freely running nose . . .

. . . burning in the muscles, liquid flames . . .

. . . silhouette of a man in a white suit . . .

. . . with a familiar face . . .

. . . *"What did you give me?"* . . .

. . . high-tensile bones rearranging . . .

He clung to the roller coaster of her being, slung this way, then that. She was turmoil, and together they tumbled, toward the darkness at the center of the past, aeons hurtled in moments.

Walls of confinement loomed in, the prisons of flesh and brick maddening. He hung with it as long as he could, even when her thoughts dwindled to mere lightspecks of rationality and coherence, displaced by impulses that could only be described as instinctive.

To run.

To howl.

To mate.

To feed.

And then he was ready to lift his voice with hers, when all at once the unrecorded tape in the VCR ran out. The machine kicked off *play* and onto automatic *rewind*, and the overridden channel beneath roared through screen and speaker alike. Jarring. It blew him right out of the spectator's seat, leaving him to fall away while the ride went on, and on, and on. . . .

Without him.

Justin sat up, rubbed a mild headache at his temples into submission. Checked his peripheral vision. No green.

There was relief, though. And at the same time, sorrow.

Who had she been? Despite the oppressive feeling that bad news was befalling someone, somewhere, and that he knew precisely whom to blame for it, it was still the most exhilarating high he had ever known.

PART II

powderkeg

8
THE DARK
CONTINENT

The next day, Justin and Erik heeded the call of the tourist wild and went to Busch Gardens in northeastern Tampa. Three hundred acres of theme park, Disney World meets Africa. An interesting experiment in transworld hybrid capitalism.

The place was doing boffo business, and they were just two more splotches of roaming color amid the rest of the gawkers, rubberneckers, and sandals-with-black-socks crowd. Erik fixated on a parrot perched amiably near a palmetto. The bird's colors were almost too bright to be real, red merging to yellow to blue to draping red tailfeathers. Erik tried to teach it dirty words, and when a blue-haired woman chastised him, Erik tried to teach it to say, "Geritol causes cancer."

They watched a snake charmer along a stretch simulating a Moroccan street bazaar, nestled in between low blocky buildings the color of desert earth. Shortly thereafter, they were treated to a quartet of belly dancers and got to fantasize about what wonders those undulating tummy muscles could perform under more intimate circumstances. Then they strolled onward.

"Do you think Morocco really looks like this?" Justin asked.

"Maybe if you squint," Erik said. "Somehow I doubt Morocco has janitors patrolling with those little lever-action contraptions to sweep up the cigarette butts."

"Point," said Justin, and then an enormously obese behemoth passed before them, sunburned and greased with sunscreen and wearing plaid Bermudas. He was sucking down an ice-cream cone, and all remaining Moroccan integrity died in his wake.

They boarded the Trans-Veldt Railroad, and it took them across the Busch Serengeti Plain. Watch the wild animals roaming freely in their natural habitat. Somehow Justin doubted that their natural habitat was within easy view of Skyride cable cars and a monorail. Zebras, giraffes, gazelles, camels. He liked the white tigers best, though, lazing about their island in a pit in the park's northwestern corner. They looked otherworldly, as if despite captivity in these bizarre surroundings, they were *still* in charge.

Late afternoon saw them at the Hospitality House. Seven sides, almost an octagon. They got beers—no shortage of Anheuser-Busch products here—and settled onto the outer patio. The enormous peaked eaves on this side made the house look like a huge origami sculpture. They lucked into grabbing a small table along the railing overlooking the pond. The best of both worlds: they could watch waterfowl or halter-topped girls passing by on the patio, alternating at their leisure.

"What do you know about that Tony Mendoza guy?" Justin asked out of the blue.

Erik looked momentarily taken aback. "I don't know. Not much. Why him?"

Good question. Justin didn't really know why. Just a strange compulsion to get a handle on the guy, for whatever elusive reasons it seemed important. He tried to explain that the best he could.

"I don't think I could tell you much more than what you could figure out just by looking at him." Erik stretched in his seat and let his gaze get sidetracked by a well-modeled pair of cutoffs. "Just some midlevel coke distributor. From what I hear, he's decently connected around here." Erik pulled his eyes back, let his face wilt into concern. "Man, you're not thinking about getting back into things like you were in St. Louis—"

"Noooo. No way." Justin frowned. "But something's been bugging me about him. If he's doing midlevel deals—say ten, twenty keys at a time—what's he doing piddling around with tiny individual portions in bathroom-stall deals?"

"I didn't know he was."

"Sure. Two nights ago, at Apocalips. Right there in the john he was quoting Trent a price on some of that stuff we sampled. By the ounce. The gram, even. A guy like that shouldn't be dorking with penny-ante bathroom deals. If he passes out a little for party dust, I can understand that, but—"

"Maybe he does it as a favor to some people. 'Cause he used to be lower level, selling on a more one-to-one basis. He's not a stupid guy, he's pretty sharp, I think. I guess he parlayed his way on up into bigger time. I used to buy every now and then from him, like, four years ago or so. That's when most all of us know him from." Erik drank some more, wet his mouth. "From what I hear, he was trying to diversify his interests a while back, couple years, maybe. Porno's pretty profitable. And fun, if you don't mind AIDS roulette. I hear he sunk some money into that. If you want my views on the guy, I think he just likes to play big shot and spread some dust here and there to have his fun. You know, meet someone with more boobs than brains and lead her around by the nose for the night, have his fun, then cut her loose in the morning. If he's paid wholesale on the stuff, his cost is pretty negligible."

"Charming guy," Justin said.

"Oh yeah. Real old-world gentlemanly sort, isn't he?" Erik shook his head. "I meant what I said Tuesday night. Just stay clear of him. I have the feeling he wouldn't be healthy for your future."

"Hey. Don't have to club me in the head twice." Justin drained his first beer, looked sorrowfully at the empty. "Wish I knew what it was he gave us in the john. That was weird stuff."

"Just let it go."

"I think I had a flashback from it last night."

This one grabbed Erik's attention. Forgotten was a busty girl with a clinging damp T-shirt, probably fresh from the rapids on one of the river rides.

"Flashback? You're sounding like sixties vintage now."

"Don't I, though? You'd think I'd dropped acid. Don't know why I'd get a flashback out of this stuff."

Erik hunched closer to the table, lowered his voice. "You ever hear what causes flashbacks?"

"No."

"I learned this from a guy who used to work at the *Trib*. You want to talk sixties vintage, now *this* guy was a relic. We used to call him Quivering Bob. I think the sixties frazzed his nerves for good. But he told me that hallucinogens get dissolved into your system, and some gets absorbed into body fats. It can lie there dormant for a long long time. And then, bam, if a little bit of the fat gets broken down by the body, the stuff gets squirted right back into your system. Instant trip on the leftovers."

"Just like a time-release cold capsule."

Erik nodded. "But scarier. So what happened to you last night?"

Justin puffed a sigh. Trying to bring it all back as clearly as possible. Sensations. Thoughts. Emotions. Was it live or Memorex? He was no longer sure. He ran it by Erik. A second opinion was always valued. . . .

"Hell, I don't know what to make of *that*."

. . . Sometimes.

"A lot of help you are."

"Sorry. But it just doesn't sound like a typical flashback. I never heard of a flashback ending because a noise startled you." Erik cocked an eyebrow, playful skepticism. "Sounds more like you got awakened from a dream. Are you sure that's not what happened?"

"Positive." Justin steepled his fingers together, watched them for inspiration. Flex, back and forth. "I sleep so little anymore, you can bet I know when I do and when I don't." Watched his fingers until he grew bored by them. Didn't take long. "Of course, there's another option, but it sounds *really* out to lunch."

"Yeah? Try me."

"Say Mendoza gave some to somebody else—and somehow it linked us. A shared-consciousness kind of thing. But a real shaky one."

"My my. We *are* talking Twilight Zone here, aren't we."

"But do you think it's possible?"

"Anything's *possible.*" Erik scratched his head, classic heavy-thought poise. "It's just when you start looking at *probable* that a lot of things break down."

Justin kept reaching for his empty beer cup, then having to remind himself it was empty. Hope springs eternal for the spontaneous refill. An alcoholic's wet dream.

"Look at it this way," Justin said quietly. "It was a drug, a hallucinogen, I think we're safe in saying. And they do some pretty freaky things to the mind and the consciousness. Now, suppose whatever skullflush is, it's natural. Not synthetic. A lot of natural hallucinogens provoke a similar reaction in people." He gave a big smile, he was on a roll. "Like mescaline. A lot of people who take that report seeing a vision of the same figure: Mescalito, the demon of mescaline. They give the same description of the ugly spud and everything. It's a time-honored vision, man. And it stays consistent."

"Okay, okay." Erik lifted his hands in surrender. "You've overwhelmed me with your vastly superior intellect and powers of persuasion." He looked askance for a moment, got a dreamy cast to his face. "Wow."

"What?"

"A shared consciousness. I'm just trying to think of all the sexual applications in this."

"Degenerate."

"It's a way of life." Erik stood, motioned Justin to do likewise. "Come on, let's bail. Look for more parrots we can corrupt."

It sounded good. Appalling a blue-hair now and then was good for the soul, kept you young.

But questions remained, unanswered, uneasy. Who had

been last night's damsel in distress? How'd she figure in with Mendoza? He tried to tell himself he was better off not knowing.

Curiosity killed a lot more than cats.

9

CARETAKER

After a night of baby-sitting Sasha with her brand-new look, Tony had started to wonder if it hadn't actually been boredom that did in Marlin Perkins. All that waiting for something to happen in the Wild Kingdom. After she'd hit the door, as if to eat through the narrow peep-slot, she had backed off. Paced around the room a bit. Settled into a corner. Bayed mournfully at the naked light bulb every now and then. Mostly just whimpered softly.

Incredible. OD on some powder, and instead of going permanent schizo or keeling over from heart failure, the mythical beast within takes over. Just incredible.

Tony was dressed for waiting now. He'd had Lupo swing by the penthouse to grab him a change of clothes, back to combat pants and black mesh. This leaky basement was no place for a two-grand suit. Slimy stinkhole, the more he stayed down here, the more he disliked the place.

It reminded him of a sewer-level sub-basement he'd once

been in in New Orleans. Just your basic business trip mixed with enough pleasure to make it look legit. Some guys were developing a trans–Gulf of Mexico conduit from Florida's west coast—Tampa, natch—to the Big Easy. The guys had also turned up among their ranks one who had been into serious profit-skimming.

They had taken him to the catacombs beneath a French Quarter nightclub, a veritable dungeon down there, and let their displeasure be known. Turned the guy's balls into a pincushion for a packet of four-inch needles, then used a .22 automatic to widen his nasal cavities. Then dumped his body into an underground stream that carried it into the Missis-sippi, and from there it could sail all the way to the gulf and beyond. A very efficient system.

Tony was thinking about that place when Lupo came back in midmorning. Always had to keep the business rolling, no matter what, keep those runners trotting and get those con-nections made.

"What are we going to do with her?" Lupo asked.

"Not sure yet." Tony was kicked back into a chair scrounged from upstairs. Better than sitting on the damp floor.

Sasha had come back to herself, as it were, a bit over an hour before. No snout, no fur, no claws. No she-wolf, just a frightened little mussed-up death groupie sleeping the expe-rience off like a bad hangover.

Lupo reached beneath an untucked shirt, big and loose and all the better to conceal behind, and pulled out his MAC-10. Nice little submachine gun not much bigger than the aver-age pistol. A real favorite among the players. Accuracy wasn't for shit at long ranges, but you didn't need marksmanship quality to blow apart some bozo trying to jack with you on a face-to-face deal.

"Want me to do her?" Lupo asked quietly. "She *has* served her purpose."

"Put it away," he muttered, and Lupo did as asked. "That's too messy for here anyway. Same for your straight razor."

"I could just break her neck."

Tony shook his head. "Nah. 'Cause sure, I got a few ques-tions answered, but for every one, seems like ten more have popped up." He grinned. "Lupo, man, you should've seen that shit work! I couldn't believe it—just like Lon Chaney, I swear. You know? We got a gold mine here if we figure out what to do with the stuff."

Lupo nodded, strolled a bit closer, hunkered down on his haunches. "You can't just turn it loose like coke."

"Huh, don't I know *that.* Do that, we'll end up with a lot of scenes like what happened at the Apocalips. Which means patterns. Which means the police'll have something concrete to dig for. Which means somebody'll eventually point their little finger right back at me." He shook his head. "Fuck a duck, man. I'm sitting on six keys of blow that I can't move. Nearly a hundred grand that I'm not gonna get dime one back on. I could choke that fucking Escobar if I didn't have a feeling there's some way to get a return on this."

He slumped in the chair, pursed his lips in thought. Time to run through a few facts and speculations. Look at this rationally.

Origins? South American rain forest, that's all he knew. Probably some sort of Indian drug. Wouldn't be like the Bolivian and Peruvian farmers raising coca. So Indian, then, their version of North American Indians' mescaline and magic mushrooms. Except, obviously, a whole lot more potent. Who knew *what* the Stone Age folks down there believed in, what they practiced. And what actually went on in the jungles. Their magic. Tony had a not-quite-skeptic's healthy respect for such things.

Potency? Again, obviously strong. As he understood it, these six keys of skullflush, as he himself had so cleverly coined it, were what was left after the raw stuff had been refined. Get rid of the impurities, just like distilling corn mash into white lightning that's maybe ninety-five percent pure alcohol. Same principle. A dose of this would be stronger than an equivalent amount of raw powder. There was another influencing factor here as well: the stuff hadn't been cut. Normally, cocaine was cut at nearly every stage of the game, from wholesalers to midlevel distributors to the lowliest of dealers. With manitol, lidocaine, benzocaine, lactose, sucrose—the possibilities were legion. Dilute the purity and expand the powder base, and an already considerable profit margin is broadened even further. By the time it hit the street, the typical toot-head wasn't buying but maybe fifteen percent coke, the rest filler. Skullflush, however, hadn't been cut, and it would be a lot more difficult to do so unobtrusively, to come up with a mixer that same milky green color.

How did it work? He hadn't the foggiest. But at least he had an inside track as to what it felt like in the interim. A lovely lass who had gone through a trial by fire and lived to see the next day.

Be a bit jumpy to get rid of her this soon.

"Go get her some breakfast," he told Lupo finally. He stood, stretched his muscles. He'd been in that chair a long time. Felt like an expectant father or something.

"Breakfast?" Lupo clearly hadn't expected this.

"Breakfast, yeah. Anything. Egg McMuffins, I don't care. Just get her some breakfast." He peeled a five from the wad in his pocket and passed it over.

"Breakfast," Lupo muttered, and left up the stairs.

Tony crossed over to the big iron door, rapped on it a couple of times, opened up. Stepped inside. Curled up in one corner, on her side, Sasha opened her eyes and looked curiously at him. Sleepily. As if she were waking up in his bed instead of some damp cellar floor in a room where day from night had little meaning. She groaned and sat up.

"You feeling okay?" he asked. Ever the concerned gentleman.

"I have a headache." Very quiet, very soft.

She rubbed her skull. Girl was a mess. Clothes twisted around, hair snarled. Slicked with grimy moisture, spotted with dried green snot.

Tony squatted beside her, playing up his concerned eyes, touched the back of his hand to her forehead. Papa taking care of his wayward little girl. She didn't jerk her head back, and he took that as a good sign.

"I don't suppose that's ever happened to you before," he said, then snickered. Then pulled on a suitably worried face.

"What did that stuff do to me? What did *you* do to me?"

"It was a big surprise to me too, baby. You scared the hell out of me. I didn't know what was going on any more than you." He cocked an eyebrow. "You *do* remember. Don't you?"

Sasha looked at her soiled hands, felt her face. Expressed a certain relief that all was normal again. "Yeah." Her voice was foggy, faraway. "I remember . . . changing. Tony, what *was* that stuff?"

He shook his head. "I just don't know, hon. I swear I thought it was some new kind of coke. You know I'd never have done anything I thought might hurt you." Tony wished he could see his own face. Felt like he dripped with the sincerity of Pat Boone. "I'm sorry. Once it started happening, I figured it was better to keep you in here so you didn't hurt anybody, or yourself."

She nodded weakly. Smiled up at him. Trustingly. This girl was too much. He had her eating out of his hand.

"I got Lupo out getting you some breakfast. Feel like eating?"

She pushed up to sit a little higher against the wall. She looked like a rag doll left out in the rain. "I'm a little hungry."

"Good girl." A reassuring smile. "So what was it like when you were tripping? Did you know what was going on? Did you know who you were the whole time?"

Her eyes narrowed as she dredged mind and memory. Upstairs, somebody cranked the ghetto blaster. Basslines thumped through, no melody. Happy hour started early in the crack house. She didn't seem to notice.

"Did I really change?" she whispered. "Or was it all in my mind?"

"You really did. I saw it."

Her eyes glowed, awestruck. "Intense." A strange smile. "I knew who I was, all along. I just felt . . . different. Stronger. Almost like I was immortal. It didn't really hurt *too* bad at first, or feel uncomfortable, so much as it was just scary 'cause I didn't know what was going on at first. I think I had presence of mind, enough to know what I was doing. But it wasn't like I was thinking like *me* anymore either. I was, and I wasn't. Does that make sense?"

He nodded. "As much as anything does."

Sasha looked at her hands, the torn lace glovelet hanging

from one. The other lay on the floor a few feet away. She flexed her fingers, where once there had been claws.

"I liked it," she said after a while. "Once I knew I wasn't going to lose my mind. I thought I might die at first, but that was okay. It was like I kept going back, and back."

"Back where?"

"Through time. Through evolution." She looked him straight-on, head atilt. Weird smile. "People could do that, hundreds of thousands of years ago. Some of them could, at least. *Change.* You understand that while you're in there."

Tony felt prickles of excitement running through him as he listened. *What have I stumbled onto here?*

"Everything was so much more vivid too. I could smell you. Smell your fear. Smell the smoke upstairs. I could hear better. Tony, when can I have some more?"

"I don't know, babe. Gotta be safe first. This isn't the kind of thing you can do just anywhere, you know."

She nodded. "This stuff had something to do with what happened at the Apocalips. Didn't it?"

How much should he tell her? No more than needed. The experience hadn't freaked her, and this was good. No need to worry about her running into the long arms of the law, crying about how Tony Mendoza had turned her into the big bad wolf. Still, no reason to get loose-lipped. Tell her only enough to keep her interested.

"I think maybe it did. I was there that night, gave some to a guy. Didn't know that had anything to do with it, though."

"But you saw me. And now you know."

"Yeah."

Tony watched her grow increasingly self-conscious over the state she was in. She wiped at the grime, the snot.

And now I know. But what, exactly? That he had something the free white world had in all likelihood never experienced before? Something like that. With only a very few people privy to the secret. Knowledge is power, if you know how to use it.

And he was sitting on a virtual powderkeg.

Except there was still one untidy loose end that was looking better off trimmed. Justin Gray. Guy had sniffed enough to give him a taste of this stuff. Maybe he hadn't gone all the way in, but it had probably been enough to give him a notion as to just how powerful the stuff was. The look on his face Tuesday night, as he hung on to that railing, had said it all.

Justin was going to have to revert from present to past tense.

Sasha reached up to lightly clutch his arm. He fought down the urge to yank himself out of her grasp.

"There's another thing," she said. "I almost forgot about this. When it was happening . . . it's like I was aware of all these things I'd never have noticed if I wasn't tripping. And it was like I felt somebody watching me."

He rolled his eyes. "*I* was watching you."

"Not you. Somebody else. But just at first. Somebody else was in there with me." Sasha looked away again, seeking answers through mists and distances. "And then he went away."

"He?" Tony was all ears, sharp focus.

"Yeah. I don't remember much, I just felt him. He was worried about me. Worried. Isn't that just fucking precious?"

Precious indeed. You had to wonder, had to have your suspicions. Had she somehow yanked Justin along on her trip back through time? More strange side-effects of the drug? Maybe, maybe not. But better to assume the worst and plan for it.

Knowledge is power, and Justin knew too much. Even if he wasn't aware of it. Dead man, for sure.

Tony stood, held his disgust in check, and pulled Sasha up with him. He'd never been so anxious to see somebody get cleaned up in his life. Have to throw a dropcloth across the Lincoln's upholstery.

"Come on, let's get you out of here." He started to lead her out of the room, back to the outer world. "Feel like hanging with me for a while? Play Queen for a Day or something?"

Her eyes gleamed from her smudged face. And she nodded.

"Good. We're gonna be busy the next few days."

They ascended the stairs, and already the ideas were starting to formulate.

10
F-words

The rest of that day and most of the next had seen precious little turning up in terms of Justin Gray. Trent's apartment was vacant. Discreet inquiries turned up nothing helpful. No new phone listings for the guy, as Tony thought he might possibly have moved here. The way Trent had introduced them, this had been unclear. If it was just a visit, maybe the guy had gone back home to the Midwest after Trent's death. Which would reduce the worry factor considerably, but would mean that the loose thread would be forever dangling, waiting to catch on something.

With no better alternatives, they went back to Apocalips the second evening. Early yet, so the crowd wasn't wall to wall, as it had been the past nights. The ghoul contingent, hungry for cheap thrills, packing in to see where people had died. Sasha was getting off on the ambience of the place. Dancing by herself out on the floor, swaying to the amplified

Peter Gabriel's "Sledgehammer," lost in her own world. Head tilted up, arms wrapped around her thin shoulders.

You didn't have to worry much about her running off with other guys while she was left unattended. True, she was a looker, especially now that she was once again cleaned up. And that pouty little mouth was the stuff of which fantasies are born. But most guys got close enough, saw her dancing like that, saw eyes that looked into a slightly different dimension than they were used to—and they went off seeking better fortunes elsewhere.

Tony and Lupo patrolled the crowd, eyes peeled. Who knew, maybe if the guy was still around, he might come back to haunt the scene of the crime.

Luck turned around when they saw one of his crowd from the other night. At a corner table in another of the chrome corrals. Angel, she of the interesting good-'n'-evil signature. Looking hot tonight as usual, faintly steamy from a stint on the dance floor. He and Lupo invited themselves over.

They small-talked a bit. Shot the bull. Win that easy confidence. And then, without her even catching wise, he sunk the vital hook.

"Hey, I'm trying to find somebody, if he's still around," Tony said. "Met him Tuesday night in here, black-haired guy, friend of Trent's—God rest his soul." Tony crossed himself, a nice touch. "Justin Gray. Remember him?"

Angel nodded, took a sip of her drink. "Sure, but—"

"Guy didn't know who to trust to sell him some good blow. I told him I'd fix him up. Can't find him now."

Angel was still nodding. "But he wasn't Trent's friend, you got that all wrong."

Tony tried not to act too surprised. "No kidding?"

"Justin came down here to stay with Erik Webber until he gets a place of his own. Erik says they're old friends from way back."

Tony grinned big and broad, and every flashing tooth was genuine. "Well, fuck me! I been looking in all the wrong places." He rose to leave, and Lupo followed suit. "Thanks a lot. I owe you."

"Hope you find him. And tell him I said hi."

"Oh, I'll do that, for sure." Smile and nod.

They collected Sasha from the dance floor and left the pulsing lights and gilt-edged reflections for the street. Dusk was perhaps a half hour away. On the roll, they used the Lincoln's cellular to call GTE information, and that's all it took to get Erik Webber's address.

Next they switched cars, trading the Lincoln for an innocuous Olds that was sometimes used when they didn't want to drive anything traceable back to the Mendoza name. The plates, paperwork, title—everything was a dead-end street. Next stop, Davis Island.

They had no trouble finding Erik's building. A four-story place, tan stucco, Art Deco gone Minimalist. Lupo parked the Olds in the side lot, and they got Erik's apartment number from the lobby mailbox after leaving Sasha in the car. Third floor. No elevator, so they hoofed it.

No answer at his door. Disappointing. Ceilings were high in the building, with transoms over the doors, but they'd been opaqued over so there was no point in Lupo's boosting him to try peering in. They returned to the car. Defeat was unthinkable. This was merely a momentary setback.

"Can we go back to the club now?" Sasha said.

"Shut up," Tony told her.

"Wait?" Lupo asked.

Tony nodded; no other alternative. He thought for a moment.

Smiled as he played with the shark's tooth necklace.

Looked at Sasha. Crotchbait.

And he leaned over to pop the latch for the Olds's hood.

Justin and April had spent part of the early evening walking along Bayshore Boulevard. Downtown to the immediate west; bay to the immediate east, just beyond an endless concrete balustrade whose columns looked vaguely Grecian. She told him that this was the longest stretch of uninterrupted sidewalk in the world, and he was suitably impressed. For a moment he thought of the top of the Great Wall of China, but no, that probably didn't qualify as a sidewalk. Anyway, this place was better. It would remain historic to him as the site of their first hand-in-hand contact.

They were within walking distance of a raw bar called

Pearl's and sat at the bar itself while behind them, in the window, the place's name shone in a script of pink neon. They quaffed bottles of Sol beer from Mexico, very light and fresh, and ate raw oysters and clams on the half shell, and peel-and-eat shrimp.

"I need to start job-hunting next week," he said. This after a half-dozen oysters had gone down the hatch.

"What do you want to do?"

He shrugged. "I'd probably better stick with advertising."

She perked up. "Agency, still?"

"Yeah. If one would have me."

"I could make some calls on Monday." April poked the lime wedge down through the neck of a fresh bottle. "I do some free-lance work farmed out from a couple of agencies. Connections are everything, you know."

"Or we could form our own. I write the copy, you do the layouts and artwork. Gray and Kingston, Limited. What do you think?"

She frowned, threatened him with her tiny oyster fork. "I think Kingston and Gray has a better rhythm."

He nodded, had to concede.

"Did you ever do anything notable?" she asked. "I mean, any print or broadcast on a national level?"

Justin thought for a moment, speared oyster number seven free of its shell. "Well, I did most of the introductory campaign for Longhorn Beans."

It had been one of his favorite accounts, a new brand of beans catering to the Tex-Mex craze. All the spicy stuff—chili powder, onion, garlic, green peppers, brown sugar—already mixed in.

"I was really proud of that, especially that first commercial where—"

"Where the surly cowboys shoot the pot of plain old pork and beans!" she finished, excited. "I loved that! That was *yours*?"

He nodded, beaming.

"And that magazine ad, where the Longhorn can is standing on the grave, and the tombstone says 'Pork N. Beans'— those were fantastic!" April pressed palms together and bowed slightly from the waist; Japanese heritage coming through. "I truly am in the presence of greatness."

He grinned shyly. It had been a long time since he'd heard much in the way of praise.

"You know, if I didn't think you were kidding, I really would like to work with you."

"Do you have room in your office for another setup?"

She nodded eagerly. "Oh, sure. That's the great thing about lofts. There's always room for something else." Her face seemed lit up brighter than the neon *Pearl's* in the window. "Are you really serious about this?"

He told her he was, halfway. Something to think about, at least. Maybe he could work some part-time job for a guaranteed income while giving the partnership a shot. They clinked bottles, toasting the beginning of a potential co-op effort in the making. A few minutes later, though, her eyes darkened.

"I wasn't going to ask you about this, because it's your business." April frowned, hesitated. "But yesterday Tony Mendoza came by asking about you. Where to find you. Um, he said you might be wanting to buy some coke from him or something."

Justin felt a cold pick stab his heart. Unease, seeds of fear. Mendoza's interest seemed wrong. He was almost afraid for her to continue.

"He thought you were Trent's friend."

"What did you tell him?"

"I lied. I don't know why, but I just didn't trust him. I told him I didn't know anything about you. And I didn't set him straight about you and Erik. The less said, the better, as far as he's concerned."

"Thank you." Justin hunched down a few degrees on his barstool. "Because I never made any kind of arrangement with him. At all."

"Just forget about him." April dismissed all with a flip of her hand. "He's a sleaze, and I don't want him ruining this evening. Okay?"

Justin nodded. She was intensely resolute about this. No love lost between her and Mendoza, that was blatantly obvious.

"I've got an idea. Why don't we pull an all-nighter to-night?"

He paused in middrink. Eyed her a second over the bottle. An all-nighter? He wondered if oysters perked up female sexuality the way they were supposed to perk up male.

"Sure," he said. Ever cautious. You don't want to pursue one supposed meaning when the lady's intent is altogether different.

"I was thinking we could hit some blues clubs until they all close down, then go to my place and fix some kind of picnic breakfast, and then go to the Davis Island beach to watch the sunrise. Doesn't that sound like fun?"

He nodded. That it did. A lot better than vegetating on the couch, watching endless videos unspooling while waiting to catch a couple hours of fitful sleep before morning. Oysters or not, he was happy to take her up on it.

A few minutes later, Justin took a trip to the rest rooms, designated, rather than MEN and WOMEN, SPEARFISH and CLAMS. A public phone hung on the wall between the two doors, and he fed it a quarter. Dialed Erik's number. Suffered through the twenty seconds of outgoing message before leaving his own.

"Hi, sweetie, it's your freeloading roommate. Don't wait up for me. Sorry to disappoint, but I got a better offer. April's going to show me some more of the area's natural wonders, and it looks like it'll take all night. See you in the morning."

He hung up, turned away smiling as a couple of obvious newcomers to Pearl's suspiciously eyed the cryptic rest-room doors. He thought of the sunrise, of sitting on a beach and sharing it with April.

The dawn of a new day that he was actually looking forward to. A day whose light showed that life was really worth living again.

Erik was two blocks from home when Justin left his message, speaking to an empty apartment. Dusk was quickly cloaking Davis Island when he wheeled his car into the lot. Uh-oh, looked like somebody had car trouble. Nice big Olds, sitting there with its hood at half-mast. You had to chuckle.

He drove a lowly little Lynx, and it had never given him a single breakdown.

Erik parked near the back of the lot, along a border of pines and the pair of dumpsters servicing the building. He got out, carrying videocassettes freshly rented from his main outlet, Mind's Eye Video. More entertainment for Jus—and himself if he managed to stay awake for the entire duration. Three titles, about as broad a range as there was to choose from. John Boorman's *Hope and Glory*, Academy Award quality. For laughs then, a Monty Python epic. And for the bargain-basement sleaze they so dearly loved, *Hollywood Chainsaw Hookers*. A well-rounded lineup.

He felt good. Useful. Justin's reintegration with the world was showing definite promise. It had looked touch and go awhile, the first couple of days. Very iffy. Okay now, though. And to have made a difference in the guy's life left one warm glow within. Maybe Justin had been right—he wasn't dead inside after all.

"Excuse me? Do you know much about cars?"

Erik was passing behind the stranded Olds on his way to the front entrance when he heard the voice. Looked in its direction. Some girl was leaning out from behind the wheel. Had he looked away in the first place, he'd have had to do a double take. Her image, the car's image—an incongruous fit. She looked part punk, part metal, the rest vague gypsy longings for something she probably didn't even know yet herself. He'd seen the latter plenty of times.

"I know how to call a tow truck," he said.

"Could you take a look? Please?"

So naïve, so innocent in a way. How could he refuse? Erik moved alongside the car, stepped before the hood. Looked into the engine compartment. He set the three tapes on the fender. An errant breeze caught his membership card from Mind's Eye, flipped it behind him and at the base of the building's wall. He almost went for it, figured it would be safe for the moment.

Erik planted fists against hips, tried to look competent. Wished he had a tractor cap to spin around, bill to the back of his head. All the great mechanics did that. Right away he dismissed with the obvious. No ripped-out fistfuls of wires, no conspicuously missing parts. Like the engine. So much for visual inspection.

"Looks okay to me." This was embarrassing. Why was anyone with testicles automatically assumed a mechanical genius?

"What about these red lights on the dash?" she called out. "Do they mean anything?"

Erik rolled his eyes. He had thought such helplessness in young women was a thing of antiquity. A red warning light marked TEMP or OIL did not require a doctorate for interpretation.

He crossed around the driver's-side fender to lean in and give the dashboard a peek. She stepped out to give him room. She was a skinny little thing, smiling shyly at him, all blond hair and black clothing. He leaned forward from the waist, poked his head inside.

And the dashboard looked as unlit as a Christmas tree in June.

Erik frowned. Something did not feel kosher. Felt very, very wrong, in fact.

He started to pull out when he saw a dim shadow fall past his shoulder onto the driver's seat. Legs like tree trunks.

And then something dark and sleek arced in to slam behind his ear, and its eruption within his skull was loud and brilliant white. He felt, at the farthest reaches of painful awareness, large hands shoving him back inside the car. As he sprawled across the seat, other hands were reaching over the back, rising from the floorboard to pull him farther in, and doors were opening closing engines starting and his head raw thunder while white went black.

When Erik awoke, it was with a headache the size of the national debt. Mostly radiating out from behind his right ear. It seemed to sync with music pounding from elsewhere in the room. He'd seen enough movies to realize he had probably been popped with a sap, hard rubber on the outside, lead on the inside. Had he been able to get his hands up that high, no doubt there would be a lump the size of a grade-A small egg beneath his fingers.

But his hands were very limited in range. A tight rope

circled his waist a few coils, and to it, each wrist was tied independently of the other. He had just enough freedom to flex his fingers and scratch the upper sides of each thigh. His ankles were lashed together as well.

He blinked, let his eyes get used to the light. He was in someone's home. Light pastel walls, with furniture that was angular and very modern and equally soulless. He was on one of those shiny, leathery sofas that shuddered beneath you like enormous wind breakages if you weren't careful when you moved. Glossy black, in this case. Canted into one corner, Erik straightened, shook his head to clear the sludge.

The blond girl, his siren, was watching him from the other end. She didn't seem quite so innocent now, and perched atop her head was a World War II Nazi SS officer's black hat. She watched with clinical fascination.

Onward, try to make sense of things. . . .

The music, loud and painfully aggressive. Guns N' Roses, he realized, blasting from a large stereo housed on a glossy black fiber-glass shelf network. Against a nearby wall, the big guy who had probably sapped him was upside down, doing push-ups off his head. Up and down, steady as a piston. This was all very strange, like waking up in a Fellini movie. At this angle, the guy's face was hard to distinguish. Erik peered closer. *Oh, hell*— Lupo, associate and manservant and whatever else of Tony Mendoza.

His host.

"Hey. Sleepyhead! Let's talk." Tony's voice was irritatingly cheerful. He rose from a chair in the far corner, strolled across the living room.

Erik grimaced, tried to focus. Blurry Tony.

"You like music? I do. Couldn't live happy without it. Gotta listen to it *loud* sometimes too." Tony plucked a remote-control unit from the glass coffee table. Aimed across the room at the stereo. The volume swelled, and with it came more pain. Every bass thud, every slashing guitar riff were more spikes in his brain.

"You like that? Listen to that clarity! No distortion at all!" Tony was clearly proud of his toys, jammed his fist to the beat. *"Man, you just can't beat compact discs!"*

Erik shut his eyes against the sonic assault; his groan went unheard outside his own head. Fellini had quickly given way to Brian De Palma at his most perverse. Every beat underscored that this was no nightmare from which to soon gratefully awaken.

At last Tony remoted the volume back down to tolerable, to where he didn't have to shout to be heard. He carefully set the unit back on the table. Pulled a folding director's chair closer and sat atop it, looking down at Erik. The superiority in height was without doubt intentional.

"Neighbors don't hear a thing when it's that loud either." He smiled, inspected fingernails. "Soundproofing in the walls. Comes in handy. I like my music loud. Noisy sex too. Sasha, show him how loud you screamed last night."

The girl at the opposite end of the couch performed as if on cue. She moaned a couple of times, gearing up, then let loose a shrill scream. Could've been passion, could've been pain. From the looks of her, one might just as eagerly be the other.

Tony laughed. Blew her a kiss, then looked back at Erik. "You know what all that means?"

Slowly, Erik nodded. He could scream his lungs out, and no one beyond these walls would ever get wise. A very distressing point to have demonstrated.

"Sure," Tony said. "I knew you were smart."

Over at the wall, Lupo finished out his set of pushups, rolled down to his knees, then stood. Didn't pay Erik so much as a single glance as he moved to Tony's former chair and settled. He picked up a book and began to read. Erik squinted, unaccountably curious to see the title. A moment's distraction from the waking nightmare. Couldn't believe it. Guy was reading Betty Friedan's *The Feminine Mystique.*

"Now, since you're obviously so smart," Tony continued, "I know you're going to want to cooperate with me. Right?"

"We'll see," said Erik.

"No no no no no. This is not an option, understand. This is mandatory. You're a college graduate, so you know what I mean when I say this is a required course."

Erik said nothing. Unable to see much cooperation inspired by this beginning.

"I need to know where to find your friend from St. Louis. Justin."

Erik shut his eyes a moment, let the despair sink in. All at once, having told Jus to let go of Tuesday night's scene at the Apocalips seemed the most foolhardy of advice. It was the only connection between them all. Dead dancers, dead Trent. Next? He watched his chances for ever seeing things beyond these walls plummet, like mercury in a thermometer during a sudden cold front.

"So. Where is he?"

"I don't know."

Tony shook his head, frowning. "That's not good enough. That's not even the truth. Again: Where is he?"

"He got his own apartment, I forget where."

Tony sighed and left the director's chair. Stood before Erik and swatted him a good backhand across the face. Sasha wet her lips, and Lupo didn't even look up from the book. Erik tasted a thread of blood stringing from his lip.

"Don't make me repeat the question."

Erik glared up at him. Shook his head.

Two more backhands. When he tried to tuck his head down toward his chest, seeking what little protection that might provide, Tony boxed an ear. Every rise in pulse, in blood pressure, was that much more throbbing agony in the knot from the sap.

"Man, don't be a fucking idiot," said Tony. "We can do this as long as it takes. I'm self-employed, I set my own hours."

"Yeah?" Erik said. "I'm on vacation. I'm one up on you."

From behind his book, Lupo chuckled. Nice to know he was at least tuning in.

And so it went for a while, Tony hammering down with open fists and backhands. Erik weaving his head one way, then another, seeking shelter that was not to be found. Then, as it wore on, trying to reel in self-awareness to the point that he might no longer sense the pain, self-prescribed autism, until Tony was simply pounding on unfeeling meat. It was only marginally successful.

Finally Tony let up and stepped back, breathing hard. Erik raised his head, swallowed blood. His face felt like tenderized steak. Life's regrets began to creep up, and he wondered if that meant they were going to take him out and kill him soon. He wished he'd watched a few less movies, spent a bit more time with friends. Wished he'd visited his Ohio-bound parents more often. Wished he'd proposed marriage to a girl last year instead of breaking it off when things got to looking too serious.

Wished he'd hugged Justin before the guy had left with April this evening. For that matter, wished he'd hugged April too. That little moment, laughing by the door, all three of them. Nice couple, those two made. He'd been a tad jealous. Who'd have guessed it was good-bye.

Forever.

"Change your mind?" Tony asked.

Erik peered up, sweat dampening his hair, beading his face. "Go fuck yourself."

Tony breathed a weary sigh. "Lupo, this just isn't working." It came out a childish whine.

The Feminine Mystique was tabled, and Lupo crossed the room in long strides. Frowned down at Erik. Lupo had a very no-nonsense look about him when he wanted. Picture Roberto Duran on steroids.

"Time for Operation Aquaman," said Tony.

"Oh, definitely," Lupo agreed.

"Sasha, you maybe wanna make yourself scarce awhile."

She rose up in indignation at her end of the sofa, the Nazi hat's brim tipped low over her eyes. Thing was too big for her. "I'm in on this too, don't worry about me."

"Suit yourself."

Lupo reached down and seized Erik by the rope around his waist and pulled. "Arise and hop, my son."

Erik had no choice but to follow, bunny-hopping as Tony led them down a short hallway and opened a door to a windowless room. Dark within, but alive with the sounds of gently bubbling water and the hum of motors. Oddly soothing, given the inner turmoil he felt on the rise.

Tony flipped a wall switch, and nearly two dozen fluorescent lights flickered to life, housed in aquarium hoods. Erik looked around the room and ceased his feeble struggles. Outside of well-stocked pet shops, he'd never seen this many aquariums in one room in his life. The room was full of them. Fresh water, tropical salt water.

An oddly austere room it was, too. Like a shrine. Pastel-blue walls, white tile floor, ceiling of squares of white acoustic tile. Leather recliner in the center. And the aquariums, all lit up.

Except for one on the far side. A *big* one, biggest of all.

He wanted to cry. Refused to let himself, just let the urge burn at the back of his throat.

"You like this room?" Tony asked. "This place is my pride and joy, man. The outside world just does. Not. Exist when I'm in here."

Erik felt close to hyperventilation. Would not cry, not cry. Lazy gray shapes swam in the large tank across the room. He figured they would hold him aloft and repeatedly dunk his head, pull it out just as he was on the verge of losing his air. A time-honored interrogation method, since at least the days of witchfinder generals. He tried to calm his breathing, conserve precious air.

Lupo pulled him across the room, held him before the tank by a fistful of collar. Tony stood proudly beside the tank. Behind them, Sasha plopped into the recliner, a child at the movies.

Lupo withdrew a straight razor, opened it. Held it before Erik's face with a gentle grin. It looked very shiny, very sharp. He snugged it against the side of Erik's throat.

"Don't move," he whispered into Erik's ear, and Erik needed every ounce of control not to shake uncontrollably as Tony untied his left arm.

"You know, you can stop this any time," Tony said.

"You already know my answer."

Tony chuckled. "You're not sounding so tough anymore. Got that little wiggle in your voice."

It seemed oddly poetic, disastrously so, that he would be paying for Justin's new lease on life with his own. The final bill, coming due. He wouldn't betray Jus, couldn't, no matter what they did to him.

He had always known that he and Justin would wind up living in the same place. Had entertained this future dream that, once the nightlife and sowing of wild oats had lost their appeal, the two of them would settle down into pleasant, hopelessly conventional suburbia. Wives, monogamy, homes, mortgages, the whole bit. And each other, friends through the decades. Drinking beer in a backyard while watching their collective brood of children playing with one another. Growing old and gray together, hopefully not bald.

So, Justin, man, looks like you'll have to find somebody else for that scene. But before you do, I hope you figure out what's happened here—and put these fuckers in the ground.

Tony wrestled his one free arm into cockeyed rigidity, held it over the tank. Lupo reached out with the straight razor and flicked a pair of quick cuts before he even realized what was happening. One on the heel of his thumb, another midway up on his inner forearm. Cold slices, already weeping red by the time the pain set in.

Erik watched the lines of blood fill, then trickle down his hand, his arm. Watched the drops plink to the water. Saw a blur of silvery-gray, heard a splash as something briefly broke water. This wasn't going as he'd thought, and somehow that seemed worse.

Tony clicked on the lights over this last giant aquarium.

And Erik couldn't help but scream when he got his first real look at just what lived there. Pride be damned. He wept. There was no shame.

"Last chance," Tony said. "Then it's fish food."

Erik spat into Tony's face and received a brutal backhand for it. He desperately remembered telling Justin about his reasons for quitting the *Tribune*, enumerating the atrocities he had seen the aftermath of. Including the corpse whose arm had been chewed by piranhas. Never dreaming the killer had been under his nose all along.

He wrestled, he struggled mightily, but they had him outpowered. The temptation was there, the clutching at straws. Give them what they wanted. But it would do no good. He could spew out Justin's name, employment history, and Social Security number, and it would not change a thing.

Cause I'm fucked no matter what.

They plunged in his arm up to the elbow, and the blood awoke the hunger of the tank. A dozen ridged mouths, razor sharp, attacked. Set about their horribly efficient task of stripping flesh to bone.

Erik shrieked. Long and loud. So long as he could scream, he could keep secrets.

Fucked —a strange word. It could either denote, crudely so, that most intimate of unions, or the direst of circumstances. The f-word.

And as he watched the water boil white foam, then red, a couple more f-words came to mind. . . .

Feeding frenzy.

11
WRECKAGE

Justin had never known a day that had so quickly swung from one polar extreme to the other. Not even last fall, when the world in St. Louis had come crashing down about his shoulders. And that was a picnic in the country by comparison.

Saturday afternoon, slumped silent and motionless into a chair in some featureless little room, each hand cupping the opposite elbow. The stale reek of old cigarettes clung to the walls, and he was a guest of the Tampa Police Department. Alone for the moment, but knowing they'd be back. Knowing that he was likely being watched by eyes on the other side of a two-way mirror.

When had it started, when had the flip-flop occurred? He couldn't think straight. Was afraid that if he could, then the hurt and the grief would punch through the numb cocoon surrounding him. The deadening of sensation that set upon him as soon as he'd been sledgehammered in the heart and balls with the news that Erik was dead.

The turnaround—when? He remembered the blues clubs. April cruising him to St. Pete to show him her parents' house. He remembered the sunrise breakfast on the beach. Going back to April's, punchy from lack of sleep, howling with laughter at cartoons. She had run him back home around noon, and yes, that was when the happiest morning he'd known in months had begun turning inside out to reveal the nightmare. Yes. The police cars, patrol cruisers and unmarked, were parked before and beside the building. He remembered kissing April good-bye, knowing the cars couldn't have anything to do with him. Watching her leave in her Fiero. Feeling a chilly racing of his heart that had nothing to do with exertion as he climbed the stairs and didn't yet see where the cops had been called to. First floor, second floor, clear. *Third floor . . .*

No, he had thought, *not here.*

He had stood in the doorway, walking in on the middle of what appeared to be a very thorough search. Stammered out a few answers to questions. Identity, reason for being here. Listening to a cop tell another that his voice sounded like the one from the message on the answering machine.

Shortly thereafter—still in the dark as to everything—he'd been the recipient of a chauffeur-driven trip to the cop shop. And thus had Saturday taken its irrevocable U-turn. Decline and fall of a picture-perfect day.

He didn't smoke, never had. Figured if he did, by now he would have chained his way through at least three packs.

The door opened, and in walked a pair with whom he had already gotten better acquainted than he wanted. Homicide detectives Harris and Espinoza. Harris looked like a high school jock trying desperately to hold on to a physique from twenty years ago and losing, with receding black hair and close-set eyes. Espinoza was small, dark, black shoulder-length hair. Easy on the eyes. *Any* woman would be, with Harris in the room. Justin spent most of the time looking in her direction.

"Your story checks out with Miss Kingston," Espinoza quietly told him. Voice neutral. He wondered how many rooms

away April was, how long they'd grilled her to see if there
were any cracks in his account.

"But let's go over everything else again anyway, okay,
sport?" Harris swung a chair around, threw his leg over it to
straddle it backward.

"We've already been over it," Justin murmured, then
shook his head wearily. Raised his voice. "Tony Mendoza.
Tony Mendoza. What, I have to spell this guy's name out to
you? Go haul him in."

It was like dealing with the deaf. Go over it again and
again. He'd told them the unadulterated truth, beginning
with the night at Apocalips. The only part he had omitted
was seeing Trent's dance-floor metamorphosis. Mendoza,
Lupo, the whole bathroom episode? He had no compulsion to
keep them a secret. Trent he covered by saying the guy had
flipped out, violent PCP style. And now Mendoza was nosing
around, asking about Justin, his whereabouts.

Implication and inference scored big. Logical minds could
fill in the blanks regarding Mendoza and Erik.

But when he heard himself speak, only then did he realize
how thin it truly sounded. Judges and other bastions of justice
were rarely swayed by mere inference. Annoyingly, they
demanded evidence.

"Look, Justin." Espinoza, this time, gentler of voice, demeanor. "We appreciate your candor. You're being very upfront with us. But there's not a hell of a lot we can do because
a guy's asking around about where you live."

"Maybe he just likes your pretty face," Harris cracked.

Espinoza ignored that. "Mendoza's a slime, no arguments
there. Nobody'd like anything more than to see him fall down
a hole and watch the sides cave in. But guys like him—there's
a revolving door they go through down here. They can afford
the lawyers that scream the loudest. We bring him in on no
more than what you've said, all we'll accomplish is tying up
maybe an hour of his time."

Justin felt like tearing his hair out. "What about the Apocalips thing? You got me, I'm a witness to that, I saw him
supply Trent."

Espinoza stepped up to the table, flipped through a file that
lay closed. "We've got some problems there too. Um . . .

you're not the only one that gave us Trent Pollard's name."
She peered at a report of some kind, then looked up. "The
M.E. ran a gas chromotography on him, and there *were* traces
of a hallucinogen in his system. But forensics on the bodies at
the club don't lie. Those were animal wounds."

Best not to mention that the two weren't necessarily in-
compatible theories. Watch all credibility die a quick death.
"So—so you can't do anything about Mendoza? *At all?*"

"We can talk to him."

"Talk to him," Justin echoed dully. "And you know he'll
pull out a fat cushy alibi for last night."

No answer. Justin sat, wanting to die, melt away into nothing. No memory of this life, nor recollections of the pains of
the flesh. And the feeling doubled once Harris started in on
him again.

"We did some checking up on you, Justin. You're not exactly unknown to the St. Louis narc squad, are you?" Harris
leered in with a satisfied smirk that dared him to be dumb
enough to try knocking it off. "Well? Are you?"

He stiffened. "We had a working relationship."

Harris leaned back, barked a humorless laugh. "Working
relationship. I love it." Leaned forward. "So tell me. What
kind of working relationships were you starting up down
here?"

Justin frowned. Wishing he could be anyplace else besides
this chair, this room. "I don't follow you."

"No? Then why don't I lay it out for you the way I see it."
Harris leaned back again. Like watching a rocking horse.
"You fuck up big time in St. Louis. You're out of a job, your
wife decides she'd rather ball somebody else besides some
penny-ante dope dealer. But you still get lucky, don't you.
You cut a deal and walk away clean as the day you were born.
But you know nobody's gonna trust you again in that town, so
you figure, hey, why not waltz down to Florida, plenty of
opportunities for a dumb young man."

Justin flashed a look at Espinoza. She was watching de-
tachedly, leaning against a wall. *Jump back in here anytime,
why don't you.* he willed her. *Save me from this guy.*

"So you're down here, and I don't know how, but you make
some quick connections and start to set yourself up in busi-

ness, and somehow the deal goes sour. And now your good-buddypal Erik is lying in the morgue. Pissed off the wrong people or something." Harris crossed his arms. "So. How'd I do? Sound familiar?"

Justin couldn't believe this. Could *not*. Except for the one who'd done that to Erik in the first place, Harris was just about the cruelest human being on earth.

"You figured that out all by yourself?" Justin asked.

"I have that knack."

"You're not even close enough to be funny."

Harris rolled his eyes.

"Can I have a cigarette?" Justin asked.

Espinoza reached into her purse and withdrew a pack of Benson & Hedges. Gave him one. Justin tapped the filter on the tabletop a couple of times, then left it sitting in front of him. Untouched.

"Um . . . and a glass of water, too, please?"

She exchanged a look with Harris, and it seemed to translate *Sure, why not*. Harris looked disgusted for the half minute she was gone. She brought in a plastic tumbler. Not glass, so he couldn't smash it and cut their throats and escape. So much for Plan A. He set it beside the cigarette. Without drinking.

"You need a light for that?" she asked.

"I'm fine." He shook his head.

"You know what kind of shape your friend was in?" Harris said. "Some boaters found him floating just south of the Gandy Bridge this morning. A patrol boat gets him pulled out, and the guy's nothing but *bone* from the elbow down on his left arm. Now, not only had he been chewed up before he got dumped, looks like, but all these other little nibblers out there in the Bay had gotten to him too. *And* it looks like he'd been worked over pretty good about the head and shoulders too. Well, yech, I could go on and on—"

Justin surged to his feet. "Listen, that's my best friend you're talking about, *and I don't want to* hear *all this!*"

Harris was up on his feet too, shouting. Face-to-face. And in a moment Espinoza was stepping forward, a hand on each's shoulder, a referee breaking up a clinch. Justin was shaking, wanted to punch the guy so badly he could taste it.

"Just sit down. Sit. Both of you." Her voice conciliatory. "And knock off with the visuals, okay, Nate? He doesn't need those."

They backed off from one another, and she settled into a chair at the end of the table. Peacemaker, arbitrator.

"Nobody's accusing you of anything here," she said.

"Could've fooled me." Justin glared at Harris.

Espinoza's dark eyes sought his own. Hinting toward warmth. "Was Erik a drug user?"

He fully knew the game they were running on him. Nice cop, mean cop. He knew, as well, that he was falling for it. Hook, line, and sinker. Anything so as not to have to talk to Harris.

"You guys searched the apartment, didn't you?" To Harris: "What did you find? Two whole joints, right?"

"Yeah," he grumbled. "That was it."

"Wooo, impressive. Bet you'll make captain on that one, for sure." The sarcasm was irresistible, and Harris's scowl was its own reward. Back to Espinoza. "He smoked a joint now and then. But that's the extent of it."

"He never sold?" she asked.

"Never. Not his style. And I've sworn off it for good, ever since last fall. I don't know how many times I've got to say this before it sinks in, but I came down here to rebuild. Period. My whole life. There was *never* any intention of getting back into dealing. I screwed up, yeah, I admit that. If I could change that, I would. But I'm not going to make the same mistake again, come on."

Justin wiped a wrist across his forehead. Slick, oily. He felt as awful outside as in. Maybe the worst was knowing that chances were nil that he could escape this even in sleep.

"Could you answer a couple of questions?" he said to her.

"If I can."

"How did you get him ID'd so quickly? Was his wallet on him?"

She dug for a cigarette of her own, lit up. Looked curiously at the one he had requested and had hitherto ignored. "No, it wasn't. But his—um—remaining hand was fingerprinted, and he was on file. Two years ago he was picked up for a DUI."

I didn't know that. A minor shock to the system. So Erik had had his own little secrets. "Has anybody made the positive ID of his body yet? Or . . . do I have to do that?"

Espinoza shook her head. "It's been done. His boss, from the photo studio."

Justin nodded, felt himself wilting. The night without sleep, however fitful, taking its toll, compounded by loss and sorrow, topped off with Harris's absurd insinuations. A potent concoction.

"Look. My best friend is dead." Very low, very even. Very tired. "And I loved him a lot. I came down here because he was the only person I knew I could count on to help me get things back on track." He shut his eyes, rubbed them. Opened. They felt as red as a stoplight. "Now. Unless you plan on charging me with something, I just want to leave. Erik's gone. And nobody's even given me enough time to cry about it yet. And that's all I want to do now."

He stood. They stood.

"Any objections?"

Espinoza shook her head. "Where can we get in touch with you, if we need?"

He gave them April's name. Tried to reconstruct her address and phone number from memory. At least he hoped he could stay there. No way could he stay alone at Erik's now. For more reasons than one.

"Might be a good idea if you don't haul stakes and leave town suddenly. Okay, sport?" Harris again.

Justin frowned. "Erik'll probably be buried in Ohio this week. I'm not going to miss that. But I'll be back." He glanced down to the tabletop, the pristine cigarette and water glass. Looked back up to Harris. "I don't know what you think I am. Right now, I don't much care." Pause. "I don't smoke, and I'm not thirsty. Get it? Appearances can be deceiving. I was in advertising, so I know that as well as anybody. So thanks for *all* your concern." He submerged the cigarette into the water, pushed the glass before Harris. "Drink up."

Harris merely glared, and Justin thought he caught the faintest tic of a smile in one corner of Espinoza's mouth. She produced a business-style card and handed it to him. In case he came up with something more concrete regarding Mendoza. He pocketed it and was out the door. Into the hallway.

And a few paces later, in April's arms.

They said nothing, just stood in the corridor as cops and civilians alike traveled in sporadic currents around them. He felt her body shaking within his arms, warmth and wetness from her face dampening the collar of the now-sour shirt he wore. Questions, nothing but tears and questions. And the hurt, oh, the hurt.

Justin knew he couldn't hold on until they got to her car. And so let the floodgates fall.

Rene Espinoza watched Justin leave the interrogation room and briefly considered instincts.

She was thirty-four, had spent twelve years with the Tampa Police, the last four in homicide. Woman on a traditionally male turf, complete with the accompanying resentment from various sources. She held her own, gave no quarter.

Male or female, cops develop instincts to serve when facts are lacking. Honing them like surgical steel with the abrasion of years of experience.

Right now, instinct was telling her that Justin had laid it all on the table for them, hoping for the best. And they were sending him off with less than a Band-Aid's worth of hope.

Instinct said he was in *way* over his head.

"I hated that," she said, barely a whisper. "I hated every minute of that."

She watched Justin walk away, arm around a dark-haired girl who had gotten a head start on the tears. Misery loves company.

"At least you didn't have to play the *real* bastard." At the moment, Nate Harris looked a good decade older.

Fifteen minutes later, they were both standing in the office of their immediate superior. Lieutenant Chadwick was a slender, half-bald man, born to lead from behind a desk. She thought he had forgotten what it was like to look into the eyes of the constituency they'd sworn to protect and serve, only to regurgitate excuses. Excuses that, real or fabricated, boiled down to one thing: *No. I'm sorry. I can't help you.*

"I was watching through the mirror," Chadwick said. "That was good work in there."

Rene fixed him with a narrow gaze. A chilly voice. "We just hung that guy out to dry."

"I don't like sacrifices any better than you do." Chadwick sighed. "But the captain was breathing down my neck about this thing even before the uniforms had that Gray character in the building." Shook his head; he put on a good show. "The dope squad has spent the last fourteen months getting a guy into Rafael Agualar's stable. Agualar is *this close* to trusting him—and when he does, that ugly warthog's going down for good. It's the kind of payoff that casts political careers in solid gold. But Agualar's about as stable as a bottle of nitro. We start rousting somebody down on Mendoza's level, for no more than Gray could cough up, and Agualar's liable to clench his asshole and put a freeze on anything new."

She concentrated on breathing evenly. It would be too easy to lose her temper, say the wrong things. Improper form for a team player. "Was it necessary to send him out of here feeling like *he* was the guilty one?"

Chadwick strolled to his window, overlooking a vast parking lot. He laced his fingers behind his back, rocked on his heels.

"C'mon, Rene, please," Harris said.

"No, no. She's right, in a way." Still staring, as if all below were his toy cars. "But the more he's convinced we think he's in bed with people like Mendoza, the less likely he is to get self-righteous on us. We don't need a crusader. Especially if he would think of going to the press, saying we weren't doing our jobs. The dead friend—Webber, was it? He used to work for the *Trib*. So did the girl."

"So do we even talk to Mendoza at all?"

Chadwick turned, stared evenly across the office. "What would be the point?"

Fists clenched at her sides. "I hope you take it this well when that guy turns up as a floater too."

She left the office then, storming toward the bathroom. They had done it figuratively, now she might as well make it literal—

Washing her hands.

* * *

April ran the two of them back to Davis Island, late afternoon by now. The clear sky and sunshine of morning had given way to premature duskfall and a cloud cover that wouldn't quit. Gray, everywhere you looked. Fitting. It held in humidity like a wet, steaming blanket.

The police were long gone from the apartment, and it felt as empty and lifeless as a crypt when they entered. Treading up those stairs had been one of the hardest things he had ever done.

"At least they didn't leave too big a mess behind," April said. Her voice tight and forced. It matched her face, red and blotchy.

Justin nodded, crossed the hardwood to sit on the edge of the couch. Longing to look up and see Erik draped into the love seat, wielding omnipotence with his remote control. April followed, rested a hand on his shoulder. He covered it with his own. Not up to packing his things yet. How final that would feel, dirt on a coffin lid.

"Maybe we should clean some things up," he finally said. "For whenever his family comes down to get his stuff." Justin pointed at the scattering of empty beer bottles on the coffee table. Elsewhere there should be a package of rolling papers. "Know what I mean?"

"Maybe we should."

He sighed and got up, retrieved the trash can from the kitchen. They both pitched in empty bottles, and he found the rolling papers. April dampened a dishcloth and wiped up tabletop rings and places where his dusting had been lax. On bookshelves made from concrete blocks and boards, Justin found a few issues of *Penthouse* and scrapped them too. Mothers never understood such things, healthy boys' curiosities. Folded onto a bedroom closet shelf was a silky pink teddy, still exuding whiffs of perfume. He wondered whose. In the kitchen, he readied the remaining Killian's for transport to April's, threw out the stuff that was likely to spoil before his parents' arrival.

Justin lingered at the answering machine. Played the tape to see if any messages had come in lately. Only his own. Played Erik's outgoing message, almost cried at the sound of his voice. April paused while dusting to listen. He couldn't look at her, not right then. When it finished, he popped both tapes from the machine to keep. His last contact with Erik's voice.

They had the place in reasonable shape in a half hour, cleansed of benignly incriminating stuff his parents didn't really need to deal with. Let him retain *some* privacy in his life. They likely thought him an angel, so let it stay that way, without taint.

Justin cinched the trash bag, hauled it down and out of the building. Across the lot to the dumpster to pitch it in. Shut his eyes at the metallic thud. He'd heard that some people found intense cleaning after a death to be therapeutic. Not so here. He felt like a vulture, mopping up selective traces of Erik's existence.

My fault. My fault. This entire ghastly chain of events had been forged the moment he had decided to follow Mendoza at Apocalips. If only he'd just stayed put, kept his ass in that chair like someone with brains. If only, if only. The burden was immense, Atlas shouldering the globe.

On the way back, he lingered beside Erik's car. The mighty Lynx. Laid a hand on the hood, remembering when Erik had gotten it several years back.

It had been just before a vacation from the *Tribune,* and Erik had driven it up to St. Louis. That first night of his in town, they had taken it everywhere they went. Eventually grabbing some road beer and wheeling north, no destinations in mind. Justin had already decided to call in sick to the agency in the morning, and this was before spousal curfews. They had wound up on some bluffs overlooking the Mississippi, and there they had stayed. Talking the night away. Some Phil Collins tape cycling endlessly thanks to the auto-reverse of the in-dash player. Drinking until dawn, looking at life fore and aft. Discussing lost loves and lost causes.

Put it away, he decided. For now.

On the way back to the building's entrance, he hung close by the building. Passing the nose-ends of cars. Halfway along, he stopped. Peripheral vision; he stooped. On the ground, a familiar yellow rectangle the size of a business card, blown against the building's foundation.

Erik's membership card from Mind's Eye Video. He feared he knew how it got there.

Justin pocketed the card. Keepsake. One more connection to Erik, product of a shared obsession. And fuel for the fires of a debt he could not let go unpaid.

April's apartment was at a west central location, on Magnolia, south of Kennedy. Not too far from the University of Tampa, and maybe a twenty-minute walk from downtown proper. She had the second, and top, floor's northern half of her building; somebody else had the southern. It still seemed vast to Justin, as it had earlier when they'd come to fix the picnic breakfast, then later after the sun was up. The rent was undoubtedly high, but since it doubled as office space, she took out a chunk of that as well as utilities every spring for tax deductions.

Except for the east end, into which had been built a separate bathroom and a pair of large walk-in closets, the rest was essentially one long room. Areas subdivided according to use. Her office at the west end, which merged into bedroom, which merged into living and dining areas, which merged into kitchen. Rattan partitions helped perpetuate the illusion of rooms, as did a spaced pair of brick support pillars. One-inch Levolor blinds hung over the bank of north-wall windows, and across the street was some trash-chic bar and diner with reddish-orange neon. She left the lights off as they entered, and the neon glow filtered through the blinds like slatted fog.

The rain had started by the time they arrived, gusts of wind rippled the blinds. A place this big, she had little use for air-conditioning. Watch the electric bill skyrocket. Live with it; she was a native. He wasn't. Suffer.

He left his luggage sitting beside the couch, just sank into it. Tired, so tired. Conversation seemed as dead as the Latin language. He unbuttoned his shirt, left the short tail hanging out over his jeans. Sweat tickled along his breastbone.

"I don't suppose you're very hungry either," she said.

"No."

April nodded. "If you change your mind—" She pointed to the kitchen. "Help yourself."

She followed the direction of her own finger and then disappeared into one of the closets. Emerged in different clothes, shorts and a large T-shirt cut down to size. Sleeves, neckline hem, bottom few inches, all amputated. Beneath it, her body looked more fragile than before. Her hair was pinned loosely at the back of her head.

"Want something to drink, at least?" She paused in the kitchen.

He nodded. "Want to go for the Killians?"

"Yeah."

She harvested two from the refrigerator. They'd been transplanted there all of five minutes. When she opened the door, steam rolled out into the humid air, pooled at her feet, and dissipated.

He wondered where he would sleep tonight. Couch, probably. Considering they hadn't even kissed until last night, things didn't quite seem advanced enough to expect an invitation to her bed, even if all they did was collapse into exhausted slumber.

April put on music then, a CD. Someone he'd never heard of before named Giles Reaves. No vocals, just eerie open synthesizers, thick and warm and droning. Music for mists and distances.

She joined him on the couch. Held both bottles against her face before relinquishing his. The moisture beaded her cheeks.

"I never thought there'd be a time in my life when Erik wasn't around," he said after several moments.

She scooted closer. Touched his leg with one foot. He looked at her, and she tried one of those smiles that are meant to look consoling but just end up looking heartbroken. All that was felt, all that was intuitive, all that had been— words could only trivialize. How do you eulogize a world that has just come to an abrupt, violent end?

They did not try. Just shared mutual silence, the soft melancholy of the music. Shared interlocking fingers. And the heat. It meant so very much more than words. Strange. As someone who had earned his living manipulating words, he felt they were vastly overrated at times.

The rain fell. The sky deepened. The neon glow from across the street grew bolder.

Finally, then, she couldn't hold back.

"I don't guess anything came out of your talk with the police?"

"As far as I'm concerned, no."

She tilted her head. "What does that mean?"

He took a deep breath. Steady. "It means that no matter what I said, absolutely nothing got accomplished. Not a damned thing."

She leaned closer in, and he could almost see her eyes growing. "What's all this about, Justin? I mean, *why?* Why Erik?"

Justin hunched his shoulders, let them fall. "It's got to have something to do with Tuesday night at Apocalips, and whatever Tony Mendoza gave Trent and me to snort. Beyond that, I don't know. But that has to be it. You say Tony was looking for me—well, I figure he finally found out where I was, or who I was close to, something like that, and got to Erik first."

"Didn't you tell them that this afternoon?"

"Over and over."

April swung closer still, drew her legs beneath her until she was on her knees. "So why won't they *do* something?" More frantic now.

"Where's the proof? that's their argument. It's all conjecture on my part. Our part. It's not illegal to go around asking where I live. Sure, they can haul him in for some questions, but that's it. That is *it.*" He let the ale wash his throat; it felt very dry all of a sudden. "I sound like I'm defending them." He shook his head. "I shouldn't even be here. If he connects you to me, then we both might be in a real bind."

"Don't say that, don't worry about me." Although April looked as if something inside had just wilted. "Question him, that's the most they can do?" Fighting against dying hope.

"Hell, they turned the whole thing around onto *me.* They think I came down here to deal too! I felt lucky just walking out of there without handcuffs."

She leaned back again, spent. Held the sweaty bottle against her cheeks.

"I'm totally alone in this. So I guess I've got to deal with Mendoza by myself. It's their call."

"You're *not* alone." She stiffened. "And don't say the rest of that. Not even as a joke."

He simply stared. Not a joking matter.

"You can't take him on. Justin, please, think straight. That could get you killed."

"I think that's what he wants anyway. Look, I'm not talking *High Noon* here. I just mean there's got to be some way to trip him up. Set him up, something. Just so he catches the cops' attention."

"Yeah? *Yeah?*" April had wrapped her arms around herself. Skeptical. "How?"

"I don't know. But it's better than sitting around waiting."

It wasn't the answer she wanted to hear. Then again, he didn't think anything would have appeased her. April swung her feet to the floor, sat on the edge of the couch. Arms still clamped around herself, straitjacket-snug. Her head was lowered.

"I don't suppose I've known you long enough for my feelings to make any difference to you."

He was about to tell her they did, couldn't quite wrest it out. She got up, paced into the kitchen. Sweat trickled along her neck, forearms. Glistened at the backs of her knees. The cut-down T-shirt clung damply.

April leaned against the fridge door a moment. She reached out to grab a spindly chair from the dining table and dragged it over. When she opened the fridge door, the light was brilliant white in the dim apartment, unearthly so. Contrasted with the muted neon filtering through. Steam oozed out in tendrils, puffy wisps. She plunked herself down in the chair before it, fanned cool relief onto her face, body. Leaned elbows onto knees, as miserable as a rag doll destined for the furnace.

Thunder rumbled in the sky, delicate and eternal. Rain spattered.

Justin fumbled through some of the things he had brought from Erik's. Found what he wanted, carried it to her. Showed her, standing in the netherlight and cool steam. The picture

Erik had taken for her fiancé. When she looked up, her lower lip was quivering.

"It makes a difference," he said softly. "It has ever since my first day when Erik showed me his studio. And showed me this picture. It's made a difference ever since that moment."

April stared at the picture a long while. Then took him by the hand.

Maybe it was dirty pool. Showing her the portrait, scraping afresh the wounds caused by the breakup with her fiancé. But he hadn't meant it as such, only wanted to make a point. A picture is worth a thousand words.

Dirty pool?

Yeah. Definitely. And he probably *had* meant it that way. He knew he wasn't above it, wasn't above much of anything sometimes, it seemed. Maybe he just had trouble admitting it to himself.

But at least he hadn't consciously meant to be cruel. Some excuse. He hoped there was nobility there, somewhere beneath the crud. The knight in tarnished armor.

April was crying. Not so you'd notice. You might carelessly think them droplets of sweat. But he knew better. She held his hand, and with her other let the picture slip to the floor.

He bent down to kiss tears from her cheeks, felt her release a hot, wavering breath along his ear. Groping, she seized a fistful of shirt to hold him in place while moving her mouth to his. Her face, his own, their mouths . . . already so wet.

She rose from the chair, and they were a clashing symphony of twining arms, tongues, moistened hair. He felt the need, the yearning, rising within him. Past the point of no return now.

April parted his already-open shirt, lowered her face to skim across his slickened chest. Kissing here, nipping there. Lowering to stomach, tongue dancing across the fine hairs. Rose up to his mouth a moment, plunged down again. Crying, still. She fumbled to undo his jeans.

It was the trigger, and he joined the ballet of seduction. The give and take, stripping away barriers one at a time, alternating one to another. Too too rapid, no patience. Her damp T-shirt hung draped from one narrow shoulder. His shirt made it no further, gaping across chest and torso. Her shorts and panties she kicked skyward, and they came down to ripple the Levolor blinds, and the filtered neon undulated with them. Steam caressed them, music soothed them, blind urgency propelled them.

It was no longer a simple matter of release. No longer merely hunger for flesh. It was a quest across misty landscapes. Searching for something, anything, that was real. Stable. Reliable. Something that could not die in the moment, and be taken from them. A holocaust could not stop them.

He fell back into her chair, scooting down a bit to give her room. And she straddled him, taut legs an inverted V silhouetted by white light, red light. She lowered herself, trusting him to guide her with hands on her hips. And all gears meshed, perfect synchronization.

April wrapped one arm around his shoulders, clasped the top of the chairback with her other hand. Bent at the knees. Repeatedly. Justin reached up across the smooth arc of her back to impel her downward. They sought rhythms, found them, slid moistened bodies across each other, delicious wet friction. He too was crying by now, his face nuzzled desperately against her breasts. They accepted his tears like an offering, and her hair swung down to claim them as its own.

They rode. And rode. And when journey's end came, the neon sunset, her chair was no longer enough. They tumbled to the floor. Rolled. Struggled. Held fast. It was hard to tell which were cries of ecstasy, and which were cries of sorrow. In some ways, both the same. *La petite mort*, the French call it. The little death.

And he felt that they were bound now, for better or for worse.

Joined by death—until it might do them part.

12

ESTRELLA

This was a land of great beauty and great ugliness. And Kerebawa surprised even himself in how well he managed to blend in.

He looked a little ragtag, and this had concerned him even before Barrows and Matteson had flown him out of Venezuela. But after arrival, and slipping away along the airstrip and finally finding himself in hardcore civilization, such worries evaporated.

He knew it wouldn't do to carry around his large bow, at least in its usual form. So he unstrung it and tightly coiled the fibrous bowstring, pocketed that. Now all he had was a long, gently bent stick. Kerebawa used twine to bind it with the six bamboo arrow shafts he had brought, into one solid bundle. The arrow point quiver he hung down inside his shirt, and he did the same with his machete. His cloth bundle he carried as usual, and he resembled just one more denizen of the street, homeless, possibly eccentric, with a more than adequate walking stick.

Miami was a vast and confusing land, but the map Barrows had scrounged for him helped make sense of it. Once he had studied it top to bottom, he walked east. Always east. Toward the sea. And another name on that bloodstained paper written by Hernando Vasquez—*Estrella.*

Miami. He liked the white towers that were usually in sight, *shabonos* reaching up to the sky. They reminded him of seashells he had seen once in Caracas. He liked the way he could look up to see the sky from almost anywhere, without it being obscured by a canopy of foliage. And after more than a day's walk, he liked the ocean, the beaches. He liked the palms, a reminder of home.

But the noise, the smell, the vehicles careening about, the endless hot rock covering their ground—these were horrors. The white man's world was plagued by its own races of demons. Far more frightening and overt than those of the jungle.

As before, on his previous trip with Padre, the people amazed him. So many, so diverse. How patient they must all be, how kind, to live so closely. To think of that many Yanomamö living together was laughable; there would be so many feuds and fights that they would wipe themselves out within a month. And the women! They walked freely about, often alone, with no fear of being stolen.

Food was his main bother. It wasn't like Mabori-teri, where your garden was mere steps away, or where you could stalk a wild pig or harvest what grew wild. No. You had to trade the paper for it. The money from Barrows might as well have been a gift left by ancestors.

He went hungry the first night, Wednesday. The next day, in south Miami, he found a Spanish grocery and bought bananas—they looked almost like plantains—and other fruit. The next day he was drawn into something called a 7-Eleven; people were leaving with food, so that was a good sign. There was no fruit inside though. Just ugly plastic food. He wandered the aisles, plucking up packages that looked promising. Bread. Honey. A packet of ham, Padre's word for pig meat. He also grabbed a box that he wasn't sure about, but the woman on the front looked very happy, as if recently well fed, so he went for it too. Outside he was disappointed to find within it inedible rectangles of spongy paper. With pictures showing how to put them into your underclothes. Whatever Kotex Pads were, he sure wasn't going to waste any more of his money on them.

On Friday he came across a great shrine in the sky, atop a pole. He puzzled over the name several times, yellow letters on red background, knowing it to be familiar. Then he could have danced for joy. Here it was, a place heard about even in the mission school of Esmerelda. Mythical. Wondrous, by all accounts. *McDonald's.* No doubt the spirits had led him here.

He entered, hoped he was reverent enough. Watched from the doorway for several moments. The people lining up at a silver altar, leaving one at a time with trade goods. He could handle this easily. He got in line. Read the menu, overwhelmed. So many cryptic choices. He frowned warily at the figures of Hamburglar and Grimace and Ronald. Probably demons who inhabited the back dwellings. He placed his order by parroting the man directly before him.

Kerebawa carried his Big Mac, large fries, and medium orange to an empty table, uncomfortably wedged himself in one of the little seats. He withdrew the wad of green tobacco from his mouth, oblivious to the disgust of others when he rested it beside his meal. He watched those around him, quickly caught on to the latch mechanism of the Styrofoam box. And found within the most slimy, repugnant pile of food he'd ever seen. If he didn't know better, he'd have thought the meat a fresh kill. Probably during the act of procreation, given the amount of white ejaculate it dripped.

Appearances were deceiving, though. He liked it. Liked the fries. Loved the orange soda. The sole thing he found mystifying were the two grubs in the bottom of the bag, or whatever they were. Tough little creatures, like wide, flat worms. Kerebawa tried to eat one whole, found it unappealingly tasteless. He fought it, and finally his teeth pierced its hide, and ketchup squirted across his cheek. Disgusting. He wiped away the blood of this vile creature and left the other one alone.

He slept where he could, trying for optimal safety. In an

alley the first night, surrounded by bushes the next. On a
deserted stretch of beach the next. Once a grizzled man tried
to sneak up and steal his cloth bundle, but he awoke and
seized a rock he'd laid at hand and smashed it across the
man's jaw. He found blood and a tooth left behind the next
morning. Each night he yearned for the sounds of home—the
crackle of his family's fire, the frequent banter within the
village before everyone fell asleep. Good-natured insults
sometimes, long-winded dissertations on how the Yanomamö
were the center of the universe other nights. He missed the
cries of animals in the jungle darkness, night predators and
their prey. Instead, all he had were auto horns, near and far,
and frequent bursts of what passed for music in this world.
And predators of another sort.

But mostly, he just walked. Up and down the coastline,
miles and miles and miles. Looking for the giant canoe called
Estrella.

Whenever he came across a possible marina, he wandered
along its docks, eyes scanning each boat. The smaller ones,
with the cloth sails, he paid little attention to. According to
Hernando Vasquez, *Estrella* was a monster, docked at a bay-
side marina.

Perhaps the most distressing of all, though, was the ineffec-
tiveness in his use of the *ebene* powder. While it had tranced
him into knowing the proper directions for travel in the
forests and jungles of Colombia, he no longer saw his spirit
hawk circling the skies. Try as he might, it had deserted him
in this land. Kerebawa couldn't so much articulate why as
know it intuitively. He was too far from the jungle, and its
mysteries were not nearly so much a part of this world. This
world had forgotten much.

Which left him to rely on his own senses.

Estrella.

He had combed the marinas, looking at the names painted
on the huge boats, ever since reaching the bayfront on Thursday afternoon. They looked much alike, white vessels,
mostly, occasionally pale yellow or gray or blue or brown.
Moored beside the docks stretching out into the gentle sea.
The sky overhead a tiny secondary city of rigging and masts.
Prosperous-looking people coming and going, who either ig-

nored him completely or looked at him with undisguised disdain. Knowing he was not one of them.

Kerebawa didn't know how many miles he had covered by Saturday morning. Despite the shoes, his feet ached as though having traveled over rugged jungle terrain, pierced by thorns. And with the white seashell towers in the distance behind him, he felt cold over not having found his own prey.

Perhaps he had come upon its home at the wrong time, perhaps its owner had taken it on a voyage and would return. So he turned around, ready to trudge back the way he had come. And walk this course up and down as many times as it would take.

Kerebawa found his quarry on Saturday evening, not long before the sun turned red and bloody in surrender from the sky.

Estrella was moored at a marina in Coconut Grove, one hundred and ten feet of gleaming white luxury yacht. Sleek, streamlined. A smaller upper level and the larger deck-level structures were windowed with dark wraparound glass that defied any attempt to see inside. It looked to be all backswept lines and sterile planes, with red and black trim. *Estrella*—Star.

Logistically, its location was prime. For his purposes, at least. At this particular marina, the crafts were large and their spacing ample. Privilege breeds privacy. It was moored parallel to a long dock, thirty yards out from shore. Shoreline itself was a long paved stretch with a low wall running its length, plenty of room for cars to be parked. Further inland was open ground, lush green grass and stands of palms, a darkened bone-white building. He faded back to the trees, glad to feel a bit of nature underfoot.

A warrior's resolve and patience had won out once more. But as before, the battle was just beginning. Now he had to open himself to understanding the lay of the land. And the enemy.

Within a stand of palms, he set up a fireless camp, taking cover behind a fat clump of bushes. Tomorrow would be long, tense. The nerves before the raid.

And as night fell deeper over Miami, he leaned back

against a tree. Peeled off shoes and socks, dug his feet into cool grass, and eased his eyes shut in relief. He ate a leftover banana quickly going brown in the peel. Next, Oreo cookies.

Nightfall, time to think. Kerebawa still felt unclean from the lives he had taken back in Medellín. Ten men's blood on his hands, and upon returning to Mabori-teri, he had not had time to go through the ceremony of *unokaimou,* the ritual of purification for having killed.

A Yanomamö with blood on his hands, upon returning from a raid, would be cloistered within a *shabono,* sealed off from the rest for a week by palm leaves. He would use a pair of sticks to scratch his body. Food would be brought to him, but he could not touch it with his fingers to eat. Instead he would have to bring the food to his mouth with more sticks. Once the confinement was over, the purified killer would take his hammock used during the raid and his scratching sticks, carry them out of the village, and tie them to a tree. And here would hang his sins, now separate from the sinner.

The way things looked, he would remain impure for a long time to come. But a wise warrior doesn't waste time fretting over what he cannot change.

Instead he leaned back to gaze up at the moon. Like all Yanomamö, Kerebawa felt a special kinship with it. A kinship that uneasily remained even though the Bible stories and lessons from Angus had taken root.

The moon was an ancestor of sorts. Periboriwä, the Spirit of the Moon, was one of the first beings on earth. No one knew where the first beings had come from; they were simply *there,* at the beginning of time. Periboriwä had been a meat-hungry being, with the annoying practice of descending from the sky to eat the souls of children. Once, an irate pair of brothers retaliated by firing at him with bamboo arrows, one of which found its mark, hit his belly. And much blood spilled to earth, growing into men as it hit the ground. Most of the Yanomamö of today were descended from the blood. And with this blood as their birthright, they had no choice but to be fierce and make war.

Did it look down upon him, notice him? Think him a worthy successor to the heritage? He often wondered these things.

Once Angus had pointed into the night sky, pointed at the moon. Told him of men from America-teri who had sailed far past the earth and landed on the moon, even walked across its face. This was hard to conceive of, but he believed the Padre. And ever since he had to wonder about the abilities of white men. If they had the power to walk across the face of your ancestor, what did that make them? Sometimes this was an infuriating thought. Other times, terrifying.

Sometimes it bothered him, knowing he had no choice but to live up to the dictates of the past, of the blood running inside him. Such a conflict with the lessons he had learned from Angus and the other missionaries at the school in Esmerelda.

Thou shalt not kill, they had all taught.

But was it his fault, then, if his blood made him do it? Angus would never come right out and answer that. Kerebawa thought he had his answer weeks ago, during the raid on Iyakei-teri. After all, even Angus had joined in the killing, though he took no glory in it. The others, even headman Damowä, had praised him for it. But in those moments when Angus had spoken his last, a true Fierce One in their eyes, Kerebawa had felt coldness within. An additional sorrow that had had nothing to do with his dying.

For he had found no pleasure in watching Angus kill. Even when you cannot completely agree with a friend's ways and thoughts, there is something very sad about seeing him betray his own beliefs. As if a part of him had died long before his heart ceased to beat.

Enough. Wise warriors didn't concern themselves with doubts, not when they needed all their courage.

So he lay upon his side and curled slightly, one hand resting beneath his cheek. And he whispered a litany of the night, taught him by Angus when he was a child.

" 'Now I lay me down to sleep, I pray the Lord my soul to keep. . . .' "

Sunday.

Kerebawa rose just before the dawn, and at this hour of the lazy May morning, he was just about the only thing moving close by.

It was to be a day of silence, of stillness. Watching. He didn't find it wise to sit out in the open and do so. As long as he had kept on the move, when searching for the yacht in the first place, it hadn't really mattered. Now, though, while stationary, it seemed a good idea to remain hidden. Lest uninvited trouble come along. And in the bushes, the view of *Estrella* was poor indeed.

No problem, though. Not when he could go up.

Kerebawa relieved bladder and bowels in the bushes, then prepared himself. Tied his cloth bundle with twine to hang from a shoulder. Lashed shoelaces together and tossed them over the other shoulder. Looped his quiver and machete around his neck. The bundle of arrow shafts and the bow itself would have to stay behind; too cumbersome. He stowed them beneath brush, out of sight.

The trees he was within were Chilean Wine Palms, very robust and bushy at the top. He scaled one's seventy feet with the agility of a monkey, pulling with callused hands, pushing with callused feet. Even if the fronds didn't completely conceal him, the risk was low. Few people ever looked much more than a foot or two above their own eyes.

Kerebawa balanced himself at the top, stabilizing by planting his feet on either side of the crown, at the juncture of the fronds with the trunk. He plucked free a few leaves, tucked them in shirt openings to better conceal himself, and even so, he still had a splendid view of the marina in general and *Estrella* in particular.

He shared the palm top with a myriad of other living things. Beetles, roaches, spiders, centipedes, more. Few people realized how much lived in the top of a palm. Occasionally he felt something scuttle over him or even inside his clothes, but it was of little concern. A Yanomamö was used to such things. The leaves thatching the roof of a *shabono* generally grew infested with such things over time. Occasionally it would be so bad that the constant scurrying was like the rustling of leaves in the wind. Movement from below—say, getting out of a hammock—would startle them, and in their scurrying to safety, a shower of vermin would fall on the unsuspecting Yanomamö. That was why *shabonos* had to be rebuilt every couple of years—sometimes even burning out the old one first to kill the infestation.

Dawn became morning. Morning brightened into day, and the sun beat down, arced across the sky. Before him, overhead, behind him. Boats departed, docked. People traveled far below, wisps of conversations drifting up to him. And through it all, he shifted to remain as comfortable as he could.

And he watched.

Keeping tabs on the *Estrella* was far less interesting than had been his watch over the home of Hernando Vasquez. Much less to actually pay attention to.

Still, there were occasional comings and goings. At midday, a couple of women emerged onto the rear deck, nearly naked, drinks in hand, and lay beneath the sun in long chairs. Their skin glistened as if wet. He noticed four different men throughout the day, two of whom left for a while in a car, then returned with sacks. Food, perhaps, and Kerebawa's stomach rumbled in envy. He ate more Oreos, and that helped. For the most part, they were faceless as well as nameless. He kept them apart only by the colors of their clothes.

Nevertheless, as had been the case in Medellín, it was easy enough to tell the headman from the warriors. Luis Escobar's identity was obvious. He moved differently from the other three, he ordered them about. He carried his authority like a crown.

From here, at least, Escobar looked substantially younger than Vasquez had been. He was a dark-skinned man, with very black hair. Most of the time he was visible, he wore blue slacks, no shirt. No shoes. For a time, he dragged out his own long chair and lay between the two women on the rear deck.

Like the tides, the day moved on, and afternoon became evening, and evening deepened toward night. Shortly after dusk, Kerebawa removed his palm-leaf disguise, strapped his belongings on again, and descended the tree. Safely within his fortress of bushes, he removed his clothes and shook out the bugs that had nestled within them, swept them from his body. He stretched cramped muscles, massaged out a day's worth of kinks. Then lay in the cool grass and let it tickle his body, leaching out the heat he had absorbed through the day.

He urinated, having managed to do so only once since dawn, and that cautiously down the side of the palm.

And once again on the ground, he waited for the dead of night. Catnapping to feel refreshed.

Well past midnight, Kerebawa stole out from his hideaway. Eyes and ears alert. Close by, at least, the marina was quiet.

He readied for war. Restrung his palmwood bow. Lashed three war tips to arrow shafts. These he would have to make count. Given that he was about to turn amphibious, he couldn't carry everything. Not only that, the water would wash away the coating of curare on the tips. While dried, curare could remain potent for twenty, even thirty, years. Take it swimming though, and that was that. So tonight, accuracy was more important than ever. Last, he slung his machete around his neck.

Again he stripped, peeling down to his waistcord.

And he was off.

Kerebawa ducked to lower his silhouette, padded north a bit, keeping to darkness and shadows as best he could. A silent predator such as Miami-teri had never seen. North, until he was nearly two hundred yards up from the *Estrella*. Didn't want to enter too close to where it was moored. Even if they weren't visible, Escobar would surely leave a guard or two on duty.

He placed a coiled length of twine in his mouth, then stole across the open distance and slipped over the retaining wall and into the sea. The water was bracing, refreshing. Holding his bow and arrows in one hand, he sidestroked a lazy path from shore, leaving only his head above water as often as he could. He had entered between two yachts, slipped back south along the first one, then onto a second, and so on. Letting the currents help pull him along. Entering to the north was far easier than impossibly fighting the current had he entered to the south.

Kerebawa took it slow, quiet. A murky shadow on the water as it rippled, dappled by splashing moonlight. In the approaching distance, the *Estrella* was a ghostly white galleon.

When he reached it, Kerebawa braced himself against the starboard side, opposite the dock. Palm on hull, he treaded water and slipped around aft. Beneath the rear deck, past the opening for the inboard engines. On around to port. Here, on the yacht's left side, was where it was moored, drifting gently alongside the dock. Intermittent lines tying it secure.

He looked down its length, and from this water-level vantage point, the craft looked enormous. No gangway left in place to link it to the dock. As he had expected.

He kicked south a few feet to the pier, heavy pillars thrusting up from the sea, crisscrossed with support beams. Here he lingered, braced against a beam. Had to be careful with his bare feet. Beneath the water, the beams felt alternately slick and slimy, then hard and crusty enough to cut. Barnacles.

Kerebawa slung his bow down over his head, letting the string cross his chest from right shoulder to left hip. He spat the twine into his hand and uncoiled it. Looped it around his middle and used it to bind the arrows, now poisonless, to his back. There. He was as secure as he was apt to be.

And then he looked up. No palm tree had ever looked this tricky.

He inched himself up on one of the pier's diagonal crossbeams. Moving slowly, letting the water slide gently from his body instead of splashing. His body was like a compressed spring with tension. He tried to keep most of his contact with the barnacles to his hands and feet, but even now, his calluses had been softened by the water. He felt tiny cuts in a few places, stinging salt water. Once he was above the barnacles, he removed the machete from around his neck and held it in both hands. Rocking the blade into the beam to give him a cross-strut to hold to and pull himself along. Progress was agonizingly slow, but silent.

Finally. A few feet above the water, and now within reach of one of the mooring lines. For a craft this size, they were heavy, a nylon cable over an inch in diameter. He grasped it, gave an experimental tug, found it held fast. At both ends.

Holding tightly to the rope, he held his breath in anticipation and pushed free of the dock. Legs drawn up so as not to splash down into the water. He dangled for a moment, waiting until momentum died. Then pulled himself hand over hand up and across to the side of the *Estrella*. Once he was nearly adjacent to it, he planted his feet against the hull and pulled himself the rest of the way toward the deck like a mountaineer scaling a cliff face.

He pulled up and over, crouched just inside the railing of the rear deck. Watchful, listening. Nothing. Yet more tales of daring to tell his children and grandchildren.

Kerebawa untied his arrows, rubbing where the twine had creased the flesh. He unslung his bow. Decided to hold the machete in his teeth. Too much to carry at once, but no telling which he might need.

The fore end of this rear deck was bordered with a series of sliding glass doors, curtained from the inside. Disaster to try entering from here. On either side, a rubber-stripped stairway led to the upper deck, half open and half enclosed by the dark-glassed cabin. Again, risky, but he was betting that if guards were up and around, they would likely be watching the front to see if anyone should come from shore along the docks.

He crouched up the starboard stairway to the upper deck. Empty, save for the reclining chairs the women had used earlier, a cooler full of melted ice. The cabin sat like eyes behind dark sunglasses, not hinting if they were open, and if they were, where they gazed.

He could creep along no longer. Now the *real* risks would begin.

Kerebawa sprinted along the right side, crossed the upper deck. Launched himself to plant feet on the gunwale just behind the upper cabin. Pushed off to land on the roof, cushioning the landing with flexing knees to reduce the noise to a soft slap of his feet.

He froze. Waiting for any possible alarm to be raised. One minute, two. Still as a stalking panther. Nothing.

He crept around the perimeter of the cabin roof, perhaps twenty feet wide by twenty-five long, and curved at the front. It was like a giant platter. Unobstructed except for a sprouting of antennas and horns and such near the front, and a back-tilted flagpole with an American flag. There was a door to the cabin at the front port side. Now. How to draw a guard out.

The flag . . .

Kerebawa rested his bow and arrows. Duck walked over to

the flagpole and used his machete to slice through the nylon rope. Freed the flag, carried it back to a position directly above the cabin door.

He let it dangle half over the window, draping it onto the black glass with a gentle slap. Blown by sporadic winds. Slapped it again. Slid it farther down. Slap. Let it go, to fall to the deck.

Held his machete aloft and waited.

Several moments later he heard the clicking of the door latch. A softly grumbling man opened it, stood just inside the doorway for a few seconds. Out of range. Then he saw the top of the man's head pass beneath him. The man stooped to retrieve the flag, and when he straightened, Kerebawa hooked the machete out and down, then sharply in. It whacked dead-center into the guard's face with the sound of a melon being halved. The blade held fast, anchored into bone, cartilage. He uttered a choked cry, dropped the flag as his hands flailed at the blade sunk into his face.

Kerebawa leaned and reached, pulling him back with the other hand. His right held fast to the back of the blade, directly over the man's split nose, and he seized a fistful of hair with the left. Gave a savage twist that snapped the man's neck; he went limp.

Kerebawa, still looming over the doorway like a gargoyle, pulled him up and onto the roof. Wriggled the blade back and forth to free it from the man's face, now a wet sticky mess.

Kerebawa curled over the roof far enough to peek inside the cabin door, head upside-down. So far, so good. Nothing but the confusing controls that navigated this huge canoe, and beyond that, a large room, full of plush furniture and carpeted and decorated as fine as any building he had ever seen beyond the jungles of home. With a narrow doorway leading down below.

He gathered his belongings and dropped to the deck, slipped through the cabin door. No sound, above or below. He notched an arrow into his bow, held it ready to draw.

And then he went belowdecks.

The narrow twisting stairway led him to a central corridor. Plushly carpeted, paneled, ornate brass light fixtures barely glowing low and warm upon the walls. Several doors branched off from either side.

Including a set of double doors, intricately carved, facing him from the opposite end. Little doubt as to who slept behind them.

Kerebawa eased forward. Some of the stateroom doors were open, and each of these was empty. Behind a closed door he found a sleeping guard, snoring gently into his pillow. He slashed the man's throat in his sleep, clamping a hand over the struggling mouth while his life bled out to be soaked up by the sheets.

In another he found a guard who awakened as soon as the door was opened and the wedge of light fell within the stateroom. Good reflexes. The man groped for a pistol on his nightstand, and Kerebawa loosed an arrow. At less than ten feet, he could not miss. He skewered the guard's skull through an eye socket.

Satisfied that he was now alone with Escobar and his women, Kerebawa set his sights on the carved wooden doors. Three people behind them. Stealth was fine when the enemy were handled one at a time. But this? This was riskier, even if two of the three were his women. Three against one meant confusion, diversion of attention that might be costly. Keep his eye on one, another might find a gun.

There had to be another way. He lingered in the hall. Considered various options, ways to increase the treachery. Discarded most. Then he remembered the sliding glass doors opening onto the lower deck, how they would no doubt lead into this room. A back route escape. He remembered the flag rope he had cut on the roof.

And knew that among the three dead men, he was bound to turn up what Angus had called a cigarette lighter somewhere.

Luis Escobar floated in the arms of Morpheus and the lap of luxury.

Within his darkened stateroom, triple the size of the next largest on the *Estrella*, he slumbered on a king-size waterbed between two of the finest knockout women he'd ever had the pleasure of encountering. Vanessa, the brunette, lay at his right. Redheaded Tracy at his left. They had seventy-four inches of bustline between them, and a pair of mouths that grazed on each other as happily as they did on him. A nice arrangement. Once he drained his scrotum into one or the other and needed a little rest, they could always put on enough of a show that he didn't get bored.

As players went, in the upper echelons, Escobar was one of the more rugged-looking. His heritage reflected more peasant Indian stock than refined Spanish. A wider face, broader nose and cheekbones, thicker hair, though immaculately styled. Just a bit coarser overall, and this was the way he liked it. It instilled more respect and fear than pretty boys—like, say, Antonio Mendoza—were ever likely to command.

It gave him an additional edge too. More people than would care to admit sometimes thought brains the exclusive province of the classy-looking. As if superior intelligence couldn't reside behind more rugged faces. Underestimating was their mistake. And sometimes, their loss.

You had to have brains to move the kind of weight Escobar did. In coke alone he pulled into Miami better than eight hundred keys a month. He did his business on the high seas. Brought on his well-paid captain of the *Estrella* and crew—heavily armed, of course—and out they went to nautical coordinates arranged the day before. Just them and the other ship, or seaplane, or pontooned chopper. Nice and private. The DEA would need a submarine to sneak up on them, and even then, the blow could quickly get turned into fishchow before anyone could board.

Here it was cut and repackaged, and off they sailed for other coordinates, other meets. Move it in, move it out. Or divided up into parcels of varying size so smaller boats could run them to any of several beachfront safe houses. At any rate, its actual time in Escobar's immediate vicinity was minimal. While the rewards went on and on and on.

Rarely was he called upon to make a decision like he had a couple of weeks ago.

Some new product, up from Vasquez in Colombia. Something the old man had brought out of the jungles, theorizing that everybody was up for the idea of a new high now and then. Widen that product line. Tribal rain-forest stuff, visionary. Refined, of course, to winnow out the impurities.

Escobar had been cautious. Vasquez had only managed an initial shipment of six keys, so investment was negligible. He was, however, reluctant to turn it loose within his own area. Should it turn out to be poison, it was best not to foul one's own nest. Exporting it at a distance seemed best. Move it up to Tampa. If soft American somatic systems couldn't handle the stuff, he'd hear about it. And be insulated from the fallout. If it went over as big as crack, fine, he could handle that and pump a lot more into the pipeline.

Where to funnel it—that had been the only real debate. Tampa's kingpin, Rafael Agualar, had been out of the question. Should it turn out to be bad news, future relations with the *Agualares* would be strained, to say the least. Not healthy for business. On the other hand, a midlevel distributor like Mendoza was a calculated risk. If Tony went down for poison stock, Escobar knew he himself would never be implicated. And if everything went smoothly, someone like Mendoza would not be bad to have in the pocket for future consideration. Especially with Agualar snorting his way to an early retirement. Because somebody had to replace him, and while Mendoza was a punk, he was a punk with brains and the real vicious streak so crucial to a rewarding career.

So far there had been no news to indicate anything amiss in Tampa. However, word had it that Hernando Vasquez had messily departed this world, along with a houseful of aides. No more green powder likely to come in, and that was too bad, but hey, it wasn't like there was established demand already. No, he was more concerned with the circumstances behind the Vasquez slaughter.

Fingers down in Medellín had been pointing in lots of directions, while nobody seemed to know a thing. This was strange. The Cartel had eyes and ears and feelers everywhere. Moves just weren't made in that town without *somebody* knowing about it. Bartenders, bellhops, taxi drivers, airline clerks, baggage handlers, hotel desk staff—the network was like a hydra. Cut off one head, and two more would grow in its place.

Some said rival exporters in Cali had done it. Others said

the *Vasquezistas* had been betrayed by one of their own, ready to assume control of the organization; possible, since his woman had disappeared. Still others spouted off about covert DEA raids in tandem with the leftist guerrillas. That a single gunshot had not been fired was most interesting. Poison, machete wounds, and apparent arrow wounds—with the arrows removed, by the way. Escobar himself threw his hands up in surrender. Either a real wild card had been tossed into the game, Or more likely, the real culprits had gone to a lot of trouble to use methods that would confuse the rest and shift blame elsewhere.

Whatever. Medellín was a crazy town. He was glad he lived in the good old U.S. of A. You had rules here.

And as he slept very late on this Sunday night, naked and sated and worn out from the incredible three-way geometrics Vanessa and Tracy had inspired, events in Medellín could not have been farther from mind.

He was awakened by a smell. Faint at first, then growing in strength. Bad stuff. A hot, sweetish, smoky smell. His eyes fluttered, and with greater awareness, his heart skipped a beat. *Smoke.* Why hadn't the bozos he paid to keep an eye out for such things raised some sort of alarm? It was going to take some fancy talking to save somebody from wearing his balls for earrings.

"Hey. Wake up. I think we got some problems."

Escobar put a hand on the girls' shoulders, gave them each a shake. They murmured, they mumbled, they burrowed into the sheets. Lazy bitches. He slapped rumps, and that got them moving. He was up and into his pants before they asked him what was wrong. He clicked on a lamp and told them to shut up.

"I smell something burning," Tracy said. She wrinkled her nose, and the waterbed sloshed beneath her as she reached for panties.

"Yeah, no shit." Escobar glanced at her, shook his head. He grabbed the phone on a bedside table to ring the upper cabin. The phone chirped in his ear three times before he gave up in disgust. Maybe the guy was alow, fighting fires or something.

While at the table, Escobar reached into the drawer to pull

out his weapon of choice. He had a thing for Lugers. Precise German craftsmanship, and the romance of a relic from the world's most kickass army. In their heyday, at least.

"What's wrong? Why do you need *that*?" Vanessa this time. Her eyes had gotten very large.

Escobar ignored her and went striding to the sliding glass doors opening onto the rear deck. Parted the curtains just enough to peek outside and ascertain the deck was empty. Nothing but moonlight on white. Silver night. He unlatched the door lock and tried to open them. They gave maybe a quarter inch. If that.

He rattled them again, this time with more force. No good. He was starting to feel a hammering in his heart that the smoke smell alone had not caused. He looked at the outer handles through the polarized glass—

And saw they had been bound together with nylon rope.

Situation had just been upgraded from serious to critical.

Escobar looked at the carved double doors across the stateroom. Only way out of this place. Because every bit of glass around—sliding doors and side windows alike—was bullet-proof. He couldn't even shoot through them to untie the rope.

He whirled around, and the girls were struggling into their clothes. Designer wrinkles.

"Luis, that smell's getting *worse*." Vanessa again.

She was right. He padded over to the doors, touched a finger to their knobs. Brass. Should conduct the heat quite well if there were a major fire in the hallway. They were faintly warm, but not enough to drive your finger away. Not like touching a hot iron.

This could change, of course. Depending on the fire. And if it grew, they could be trapped. The idea of cooking inside this stateroom was far less attractive than facing whatever lay on the other side.

Vanessa was nearest the stateroom's private bath. He looked at her. "Go soak three hand towels, get 'em nice and soppy."

While she did that, Escobar listened beside the doors. Heard a faint crackle of flames, grew increasingly repelled by that burning stench. All at once it seemed very negligent not to have had a peephole installed in at least one door. He left them long enough to kick his bare feet into a pair of leather deck shoes.

Vanessa came back with the wet towels. He took one, and Tracy took the last, and they put them before their faces to filter out smoke, possible toxic fumes. He tied his like a bandit's mask from an old Western movie.

He wrapped his hands on the knobs, Luger still in his right.

Why the hell hadn't his men raised a fuss? Anybody still sleeping was a dead man. Shark bait, next run out to sea.

Escobar opened the doors, and immediately a nauseating wave of foul smoke was in his face. So was its source.

The short, loud scream that escaped him wasn't the most macho response. But it was involuntary. And very very heartfelt.

Propped against the right door was Jess, one of his men. At least the size indicated Jess. There was a lot wrong with him. The arrow shaft poking out of his eye, for one thing. That he was ablaze was another. A flaming shroud of bedsheets was wrapped around him, and the visible flesh was roasted and blackening. His hair was charred stubble. As soon as the doors opened, his flambé body slid along the carved wood and thudded to the floor at Escobar's madly dancing feet.

Yes, he shouted. Completely blew composure. And let surprise get the best of him, if only for a second or two. Because somebody up the hallway suddenly leaned from a right-side doorway to fire something at him.

And son of a bitch, did it ever connect.

The infiltrator had planned well. With Jess's body at right, Escobar had reflexively jumped left. Opened himself up to more vulnerability to someone in a right-side stateroom. And with the attacker being right-handed, he barely had to lean out the doorway.

The next thing Luis Escobar knew, a monstrous arrow—an *arrow*, of all things—had nailed him in the gun shoulder. The pain was sharp and deep, like a scalpel rammed in to the hilt. His arm spasmed, and he fired a wild shot that cracked into the paneling before him, and then the Luger thumped to the floor.

Escobar grunted and staggered back into the left door,

aware of Vanessa and Tracy shrieking behind him, pain in his ears. He was about to bend over for the Luger when the bastard fired again. At maybe fifteen feet, this was probably point-blank range for arrows. This time he took it in the left side of the gut. No bones here to stop the shaft. Just tight skin, firm muscle, and soft organs. He screamed. And knew before he tried to move that it had gone all the way through.

Not only that.

It had nailed him to his own bedroom door.

This guy—this wild card—knew his business.

Paradise had gone to the province of nightmares in a matter of minutes. Skewered to the door. Jess burning near his feet. The Luger on the floor a maddening three feet before him. He would have to tear his own belly open to bend that far.

And trouble had quickly gotten a whole lot worse. Someone was quickly closing the gap with a machete.

"Get my gun!" he screamed to Vanessa, to Tracy. He didn't care who. *"Get my gun!"*

From the corner of his eye he saw Tracy start for it.

"Don't touch it," the bowman said, and the bitch chose to obey him instead of her meal ticket. If he got out of this alive, she was shark bait too.

Escobar couldn't believe his eyes. This man before him wasn't like any he had ever seen. Especially in *these* parts. South American Indian—he recognized that immediately. Bronze skinned, naked, straight hair still wet. With dark eyes that looked as if they'd never heard the word *mercy.* All at once the news about Vasquez flashed again through his mind, and the gap between Miami and Medellín narrowed to inches. Long-forgotten Catholic prayers and novenas surfaced in memory, all but spilled from his mouth.

He wrapped his hand around the arrow shaft and gave a tug, and all it accomplished was snapping the shaft from the bamboo tip. He looked down, wishing he had taken time to put on a shirt. He could see that razor-sharp arrow tip punching right into his belly. See the puckering wound as it drooled blood down his side to stain his slacks. He started to slide forward on the bamboo, maybe he could free himself that way. Agony, sheer agony. Every fraction of an inch seemed to grate on something inside. Especially deep within his back.

The thing was *barbed.*

No telling what it was hung up on inside.

Escobar, now sweating profusely, looked up in fear into the merciless eyes. They had not changed.

"Money," Escobar rasped. "I have lots of money. I can make you soooo rich—"

The bowman paid him no attention. "You stay inside," he said to the girls. Gesturing to the stateroom. They backed farther in without complaint, and Escobar felt even more alone in a world that had already become too painfully lonely.

The bowman shut the scorched right door. Then gripped the handle of the left and pulled it forward as well. Escobar shrieked. He pedaled with his feet to keep up with it, lest he stumble off balance. Fall. Leave an intestinal ticker tape behind as he fell. The doors latched.

And then, the final insult upon injury—

Vanessa and Tracy locked the doors from the inside.

He danced a careful series of steps. Wasn't enough that he was pinned to the door like a butterfly to a collection board. Now the heat from the burning Jess was getting very uncomfortable. The smoke nauseating. Tears began to leak from the corners of his eyes.

"Money?" he tried again, weakly.

The bowman kicked the Luger behind him, farther up the hall—*no* hope now. He yanked the wet towel from Escobar's face, held the machete along his neck. It was warm, slick. *Already used.*

"Green powder," said the bowman. "A man named Hernando Vasquez gave it to you."

Escobar bobbed his head, eager to please. "Yeah, yeah, that's right."

"You tell me where you have it. And I go."

"Oh, *paisa,* man, I wish I could help you." Breathless, he was panting. Frantic. "You're about two weeks too late. I sent it away. Come on, *paisa,* you don't want to hurt me like this. We got some of the same blood inside, don't you see my face?"

"I'm not your countryman," said the bowman, and Escobar's hopes for appealing to some kindred heritage died.

The Indian grabbed the arrow in his shoulder, gave a wrenching twist. Escobar screamed. He'd rather his arm fall off than go through another one of those.

"Where is the green powder now?"

"I sent it to Tampa! You know where Tampa is, everybody knows where Tampa is!" Escobar felt blisters rising on his sockless ankles.

"Who has it? His name."

"Tony Mendoza. *Tony Mendoza!*" Dear lord, his pant legs were starting to catch fire. He thrashed one leg in the air to try and snuff out the flames.

"Where do I find him?" Another twist of the shoulder arrow.

"I don't know, I swear it!" Wrong answer, he *knew* it.

The bowman sliced a shallow gash down Escobar's left pec, split the nipple dead center. Both hands had been trying to hold his insides together, but he let go with one and flailed at his tormentor. Got a nasty chop across the forearm with the machete.

"Where do I *find him?*"

"I don't know *I don't know!*" Escobar thought he could never die quickly enough. "He's in Tampa, fucking Tampa and please *please put out that fucking fire man* PUT IT OUT PUT IT OOUUUUT!"

With a guttural cry, the bowman wound back with the machete, cocked, ready to fall. Escobar scrunched his eyes shut, didn't want to see the blow. Felt his legs blister, the flames from Jess having crawled all the way up to his knees. Eating toward bone. Toward thighs. Toward genitals.

He waited, welcoming the fall of the blade.

But it didn't come.

And when he opened his eyes again, the bowman was already halfway down the hall. Sitting on his haunches. *Watching me burn.* Greasy smoke wafted up into his face, the sizzle of fat. Escobar drummed his smoldering feet on the floor. Anything to distract from the pain. The fire was feeding on itself now, halfway up his thighs, his slacks charred tatters. Drop and roll—that was all it would take.

Yet he still couldn't work up nerve to tear loose from the arrow.

Flames, broiling his legs into crisped hide. His voice, raw and hoarse by now. Anything was better than roasting alive from the ground up. He braced his palms against the door behind him. Took a deep breath.

And launched himself away from the door.

Well . . .

Most of him, anyway.

Kerebawa was halfway across Miami by dawn. Dressed, once again. Heading northwest. He had looked at the full Florida map opposite the Miami side. Had found Tampa.

The trail of the *hekura-teri* was growing colder. But he knew he should at least try. He had nothing else to do. And so he walked. With his tied cloth roll and bundle of sticks, now three in number, he cut a figure no more imposing than Charlie Chaplin's Little Tramp.

By midafternoon he was free of the city and was in areas less congested. Found himself in a small town called Opa Locka. It was good to have the crushing frenzy of the city behind him, good to feel the open ground beneath his feet more often.

In late afternoon, Kerebawa took respite in a small park area, foliated thickly, plenty of palms towering overhead. Within this emerald theater, he rested. Sniffed some *ebene* in hopes that it might open his eyes, at least in this tiny replica of home. Show him what to do, where to go, what to hunt for.

There were mysteries, still. And his *noreshi,* the hawk, still had not returned. But when he looked in the distance to the northwest, toward Tampa, he saw something else.

An eagle, struggling with broken wings.

And as the heat of the day and the draining effects of the *ebene* sent him seeking a bed of ferns, he smiled. Gave a self-satisfied nod. For at least he had something once again to follow.

13
life goes on

At her tilted drafting table, April poked her tongue out while she worked. Frowning in concentration, working that tongue tip at the corner of her mouth. Justin thought she probably wasn't even aware of doing it. Amazing, all the little habits that characterize us that for years go unrealized. Sometimes even to the grave.

He enjoyed watching her work, tried to be unobtrusive. Just sat in a chair several feet away, a Killian's sweating on the hardwood floor beside his chair leg. *Can't leave the bottles alone, can I?* he thought. *But I'm handling it, it's okay, it's not out of control.* April was doing some cartoonish graphics for a plant rental and maintenance firm. Big business down here, he gathered—expert foliators for office space, for execs too busy to worry about their own green thumbs. Or lack of them. With as many plants as he had sent to an early mulch-grave, Justin figured his own thumb was brown.

April worked in sporadic bursts. A flurry of lines and

strokes, then periods of appraisal and contemplation. Pulling back to view at a distance, leaning close for microscopic scrutiny. Her hair was tied back in a ponytail to keep it from falling onto the paper.

And he watched, committing her movements into an overall gestalt. You never truly know someone until you know how they move. It's not enough to call to mind their face, body. You have to understand the way they move. And with April, he wanted to know it all. Because she, dear young woman, had moved *him.*

At the same time, he had to wonder how long it would have been before they reached this stage had Erik not died. A week ago he hadn't even known her. A week ago she was mere fantasy, an image on Kodak paper. Without Erik's murder, they still would have reached it, probably. After another week, maybe two, perhaps a month. They had been on their way. A moot point, however.

Quantum leaps had been made this past weekend. Heightened emotions squeezed out by a pressure cooker of sorrow, and vulnerabilities so blatant they might as well have had bull's-eyes painted on them. They had turned to each other so quickly it was dizzying. Maybe that was healthy, maybe not. The more cynical of the world might have said they were merely using each other as an antidote for grief. Perhaps they were.

But he refused to believe it.

"So what's it like?" she said, looking up from her table.

"Erik's hometown?"

"Uh-huh."

It was a continuation of a conversation put on hold ten minutes ago, before the graphics had taken over again. He understood perfectly. Even did it himself, back-burner a conversation while in the midst of writing something, expecting it to still be warm when he was ready to pick it up again. The mind in the act of creation bridging the time gap as if it were an eyeblink. It had always bugged Paula. Creative sorts generally belonged together, if for no other reason than they were more apt to put up with one another's quirks.

Erik's hometown. Shepley, Ohio.

"I was there only once, during college."

"Once is enough to know."

Justin shrugged. "It's little. About eight thousand people. Kind of like Garrison Keillor's Lake Wobegon—you get the idea that time sort of forgot it. It's the kind of place you might have expected Norman Rockwell to retire to."

April smiled, rubbed her eyes. A bit red, strained. "He hardly ever talked about it."

Justin drank some beer. "Erik had a love-hate relationship with the place. You know, once he was past a certain age and all, and it just wasn't enough anymore. But still, he grew up there." Justin smiled toward the floor. The ache within—oh, that ache. "He'd gotten too big for the town. Not in an ego sense. Just in what he needed and couldn't get there."

"Will it bother you much going back there again?"

"Probably." He folded arms over chest, shut his eyes a moment. He had spilled many a tear over the past three days, to be dried by April. Just as he had dried hers. "I know his parents want him buried there—but it doesn't seem right, in a way. That place isn't *him* anymore. He didn't much fit in even when we were in college. The gap only got wider after that. He shouldn't have to stay there forever."

She tabled her pen and got up from her chair. Crossed her pleasantly cluttered office and stood behind him. She circled his chest with her arms. Kissed his head, then turned her cheek to rest atop it. She patted a hand over his heart as he gently gripped her forearms. Hand over heart, patting, patting.

"He won't all be there," she whispered.

And he knew it to be so.

April worked another twenty minutes, then checked the time. Nearing four o'clock. She had put in a long day. She clicked off the swivel lamp hanging over her table.

"I need to go to the travel agency for our tickets," she said. "Want to tag along?"

"Sure."

Justin stood up and stretched. Any trip sounded good. He'd not been out of the loft all day. For that matter, he'd spent most of yesterday cooped up too. Had briefly stepped outside yesterday morning for her Sunday *Tribune*.

They put on shoes, and he wondered how long things

would last this way. He could start feeling like a kept man
very quickly. Justin Gray, gigolo for hire. *If she can still walk,
I don't know my business.*

April went through the ritual undergone anytime she left
her office. Weighting down loose papers so stray wind
wouldn't scatter them. Shutting the windows at this end in
case of sudden monsoons. Last, she turned on the answering
machine for her separate business line. All set.

And hand in hand, they left the apartment.

Lupo liked to think of life in terms of boxes.

Packing crates for life's biggies, matchboxes for the little
things. A place for everything, and ideally, everything in its
place. Disorder was his mortal enemy. Of course, when
things began weaseling from their boxes, that was when he
did his best work. Keeping those crates in good repair. He
was, he realized, a stevedore on the S.S. *Mendoza.*

He sat parked in the same nondescript Olds they had used
to snatch Erik Webber. Alone, at curbside. Just as he had been
for many hours, the same weeping-willow branch bobbing
before the windshield. The car's windows were opened up
full, the breezes pleasant today. The weekend's humidity had
dipped to humane.

Behind the wheel, he fingered a box of nine-millimeter
bullets. Not to use, just for fun. He opened the box, slid out
the Styrofoam block. Perfect bullets in perfect regimented
rows, gleaming brass. The Styrofoam a perfect snug fit within
the box. All of life should fit together as nicely.

Things had gotten too loose around the edges lately, as far
as he was concerned. This happened periodically, no way
around it. With Tony running the show, it was inevitable. But
then, nobody made advances in *any* business without occasionally treading over risky ground. It was just that in some
businesses, the consequences were more permanent than in
others. No wonder they paid well.

Skullflush was, he fretted, a potential bastard to keep a lid
on.

Erik Webber dead, now this. Eliminating players in the
thick of the game was one thing. Planning the elimination of

those on the periphery—well, that was when troubles began to rattle at those box lids.

Justin Gray. Tony hadn't been able to turn loose of him. An untidy frayed end that needed clipping. Tony, ever since Erik had bidden a farewell to arms, had run things over in his mind. How and where to find the guy.

Tony had once more plied a girl he knew who jockeyed a computer for GTE. Still no new listing or scheduled hookup for a Justin Gray. Had he gotten his own place, as Erik had said, it seemed unlikely he would ignore a phone. Scratch that off as a lie told to protect a friend.

Then he'd remembered April Kingston. And a slight inconsistency.

Tony had questioned her last week about the guy. She said she didn't know much about him. Okay, fine, he'd had no reason to doubt her at the time. But once Angel had spilled the beans, Tony had to reconsider. Justin and April *had* looked pretty chummy at Apocalips. Now, if Angel had known Justin was Erik's pal and not Trent's, shouldn't April have known too? Sure. Ipso facto, a withholding of information. And she had to have a reason. Maybe even a personal one. Hence Tony's late-Sunday-morning decision that perhaps her apartment should be watched for a while. Just in case.

Well well well. Pay dirt, and this was only Monday afternoon. There they were, hand in hand as they left her building some fifty-odd yards to his left. Going for her car.

April, April. 'Twould appear that she had been less than upfront with Tony. This was not a healthy thing.

Lupo slowly keeled over across the front seat as they left and pulled onto the street. No sense in chancing an unwanted discovery. He straightened up moments later and let them run like rabbits.

He fired up the Olds. Not to follow, but homeward bound. Tony would be most pleased to hear what he had to say.

Justin and April flew out of Tampa late Tuesday morning, packed for a forty-eight-hour layover in Ohio. They touched down in Cleveland, and from there they rented a Capri from Avis and puttered southwest on I-71 some sixty miles to Shepley. It was five miles off the interstate, and they checked into a motel near the turnoff.

They slung clothing onto hangers, divided the shiny silver bar near the bathroom into his and hers sides. Generic motels like this always made him feel a little sad. Forlorn way stations with no souls, when you wished you were somewhere else. April seemed to sense it and stripped the SANITIZED FOR YOUR PROTECTION band from the toilet. She put it on like a sweatband, and this made him laugh.

Shepley was like some overgrown village set in the middle of farm country, sprouting out of land as flat as an ironing board. It was the kind of place Justin could imagine John Cougar Mellencamp singing about, somehow managing to find the heart in this part of the country. This town of white picket fences and White Protestant Values. This town of gossiping phone lines where a good scandal might get years of mileage. This town of teenagers who cruised out of desperate boredom, and of veterans who loved their God, country, children, and beer, not necessarily in that order.

Erik's parents had flown down on Sunday to claim his body, had returned the next day. Tuesday evening after the funeral home visitation, Erik's display with a prosthetic and a glove, the Webber house was like a miniature Grand Central Station. For those who truly cared, and those unable to pass up a chance to show how sympathetic they were. *If there's anything we can do . . .* Justin grew sick of the phrase. Their kitchen swelled with food and drink, and casseroles sprouted like mushrooms.

Justin and April retreated for a while to Erik's bedroom, probably unchanged for years, merely dusted and vacuumed. A shrine to a younger Erik, high school vintage. Pictures on the walls, Erik on a track team, and shooting his camera for the school rag, and looking silly and dated in a leisure suit with some unknown girl the night of a homecoming dance. A whole life lived, however short, before Erik had ever known such a person as Justin existed.

He sat on Erik's bed, and April sat beside him. This was where the whole houseful should be. Out there, with the casseroles from hell and the friends and neighbors playing catch-up with one another's lives, it seemed that Erik was an afterthought.

The funeral was Wednesday afternoon; it pulled a good crowd. A Lutheran church, and it had air-conditioning. The minister possessed some tact and didn't try to schlep it all off as God's will. This Justin appreciated. Maybe if he himself met an early expiration date, they could get this guy to launch him into the hereafter. If, say, cirrhosis caught up with him, or his luck ran out while driving home with a buzz on some night.

Or more likely, if he bit off far more than he could chew once they got back to Tampa.

Burial was on the edge of town, along the same stretch he and April had driven in on. Some small, peaceful cemetery atop the gentlest of rises, with a few desolate trees and a good view of the highway. A scattering of fast-food places on toward Shepley. A Burger King and a cemetery, how quaint. For those who must eat and run, he decided. He had to think of *something* else while acting as pallbearer.

While the minister spoke his final official words on the subject of Erik Webber, Justin scanned the crowd. Lingered on those around Erik's age, possibly former classmates. The difference between him and Erik, and them—it was a subtle thing, but there. Perhaps showing best in the eyes. These people had spent too long playing hangdog in this town where possibilities for the future were as narrow as a strand of vermicelli. He wondered what they thought, having watched this son of Shepley venture forth into the larger world, then watching it send him back literally chewed up and spit out. It confirmed their worst fears.

Ashes to ashes, dust to dust. In dark suits and sober dresses, they stood in concentric rings around Erik's coffin, suspended above its hole by the machine that would lower it. And after it was down, handfuls of dirt were cast in, and individual flowers. This was the only part of it all that felt truly real. The final tribute, the hands-on farewell. The ritual cleansing. He thought about such things as they had been discussed with April that first night at Apocalips. And now, more than ever, they made sense.

Rituals.

Even when they were painful, they were still crucial.

And letting go was easier when you had the format down.

Dawn's early light peeked over the land.

There was something oddly comforting about being in the cemetery so early in the day. When most of the world was, at best, still rubbing the sleep from its eyes. Interruptions were scant, or not at all. Communion between souls seemed to have a better shot at dawn.

Justin had taken the Capri from the motel's lot and driven here alone. April still slept, had no idea he was gone. There was much he wished to share with her, but not all. Never all. All would be forever taboo, and that was as it should be.

He'd had no small amount to drink in the hours following the funeral and burial. As usual, he'd managed little sleep. After a few hours of shallow catnapping at April's side, a trip at dawn seemed as natural as, well, as dying.

Justin left the Capri on the cemetery drive, allowing an ample walk to Erik's grave. There would have seemed something vaguely desecratory about driving any closer. At this hour, at least.

He approached. He sat. This rounded mound of still earth. The newest arrival, festooned with bouquets that were already starting to wilt. No headstone as yet; that would come later. Until then there was just a small flat marker indicating who lay here, metal tracks holding sliding interchangeable letters. Like the price-per-pound sign beside a cut of beef.

Justin had not come empty-handed. He still had a couple beers left over from last night's marathon, had opened one for the short hop to the cemetery. And he drank under the dawning sky, threads of light mingling with darker clouds, blue-gray shadows. Drinking buddies. Bosom buddies. One on the earth, one in it.

"We're leaving this morning," he said to this bulge of earth. "And I just wanted to say good-bye." He smiled ruefully. "We've done plenty of crowd scenes in our day. But yesterday, I just couldn't let that be it for you and me."

He shook his head, self-conscious. Not the kind that comes from embarrassing yourself publicly, realizing you're muttering like a fool to no one but yourself. It was, instead, a sense that somewhere Erik could look down and see him, small and hunched in the dawn, vaguely pitiful in the overall scheme of things. And if Erik could, he'd probably laugh at him and tell him to knock off with the muted histrionics and get on with living, because there were whole giant realms whose magnitudes he had no grasp of. Yet.

But I don't know, I don't know what that's all about, so I guess I'm being selfish here, that this is all for me. So be it. Erik would surely understand.

"I don't know if I'll ever be back here. I don't know if I want to. Or if you'd want me to either. Man, I've got whole photo albums full of better ways to remember you than this place." He drank, shut his eyes, and shook his head, remembering promises made. Promises broken. "I'm sorry you're buried here instead of someplace better. Sorry I let you down. But it just didn't seem my place to say anything. I guess we all have to make those arrangements ourselves if we want them done."

He remembered a distant night, the latter college years. Some night when they should have been studying and weren't. The apartment trashed as usual, a litter of empty bottles. They had watched the late late late show, some forgotten Technicolor epic about Vikings. Hokey, historically inaccurate, and great fun. They cheered and taunted and swashbuckled right along with the Norsemen. But they fell silent at a Viking funeral, watching a longship, timbers blazing, sailing out into a fjord. A sobering moment, in retrospect. They had watched, had held their tongues.

Finally, "If I die first, don't let them bury me." Erik looked very serious. "Especially not in Shepley. Steal me if you have to. And do it just like that." He pointed his long-neck bottle at the screen. "I'd rather go out like that than have people cry over some hole in the ground."

Justin had said he would.

And now, nearly a decade later, he cast his eyes down in shame. Drunken promises, so easily made in those days. But so pure, so heartfelt. Vital. And so easily broken by neglect.

Again, surely Erik would understand. How he hoped.

"April and I are getting along great. You probably knew we would, didn't you? She's special, she really is. And I hope it lasts, I really do. I hope I don't blow this one too." He drank, sighed wetly. "It's like, that was the last great thing you did in this life, you know? Made sure we met each other, forced us on each other for a few hours. You did good. And I thank you for that."

Justin stood, stretched legs that hadn't yet loosened for the day. Birds were joining the chorus of their brethren, more by the minute. Down on the highway, a lone car passed, lights still burning in the gloom. Perhaps someone going to an early shift, or leaving a late one. The noise faded, engine and tires a whispering drone that the town swallowed.

He looked back to the grave.

"You probably wouldn't be here if it weren't for me. Don't think I haven't thought about *that* a lot. I know you'd never blame me—but that doesn't mean I can't blame myself." Now, only now did the tears threaten to start. In the face of guilt. "I'm sorry, Erik. Sorry I screwed up my whole life and dragged you in to help me set it back up again. Because— *look what it cost you.*"

He let the tears burn down his cheeks, pain and shame in equal measures, second and third helpings of each. He twisted off the cap of the second bottle he'd brought, stepped up alongside the mound.

"The cops may not give a damn about anything else but Mendoza's rights, but don't think I'll just let it pass. I don't want this, and maybe it's stupid and maybe it's suicide, but I'm gonna do something about it. April thinks it's a lot of both, but—I can't let it go. My own neck's on the line now, anyway." He tipped a long draught that finished his bottle. "I'm not sure what to do yet, exactly. But I've got a few ideas. April says she knows where Mendoza lives, so that gives me a jump on him, 'cause he doesn't know that about me. I'll figure it out, man. And I hope you're watching. He's gonna go down. I promise you that."

Justin leaned over the earthen mound and scooped away a couple handfuls of soil near the grave's head end. He up-ended the full bottle and jammed it neck-first into the hole he'd made. Letting it gurgle slowly into the ground, the trickle-down effect. He scooped loose soil back over the bottle's base, sealing it in. Out of sight. Their little secret, ties that bind.

Trying to smile, Justin laid both open hands on the grave, as gently as he might a friend's shoulder. And leaving the bottle in place, he turned to walk back to the car.

The ritual completed.

14
punk darwinism

Tony Mendoza managed to stay as busy and enterprising as ever while Justin and April were in Ohio.

Lupo's news lifted his mood considerably early in the week. Just the thing to put those scissors in his hands to trim loose ends. As soon as Lupo came back to the penthouse to report Justin's whereabouts, they had switched cars, back to the Lincoln, and Lupo had cruised him to a nearby shopping center. This in itself was of no interest, but there was a one-story branch bank near the boulevard. Stucco job ringed by palmettos, looked like some sort of Franciscan mission in the tropics. They rolled past the drive-through and got a fat roll of quarters. Then they glided across the lot to a row of drive-up telephone carrels.

This was one call Tony definitely did not want remotely traceable back to his own numbers, or his long-distance-call-

ing credit card. Today it was a cash-only transaction, no electronic footprints to his doors.

He punched in the number, and then on came the operator to tell him how much coinage to turn loose. Moments
later a phone began to ring in Atlanta. Once, twice, answered
on the third ring.

"Wrong number," said a voice, soft as silk and as humorless
as a January gale in Michigan.

"Don't think so," Tony said. "Do you know who this is?"

"I don't forget voices, Mister T. How's the weather down
there?"

"Perfect. Except for a cloud or two I wish would be blown
away. Think you can do anything about that?"

"Everybody talks about the weather, but nobody does anything about it." He chuckled. "Yeah, I think I might."

"How soon?"

"Bad timing for immediate gratification. I have a prior
commitment up north. Maybe the end of the week?"

Tony thought a moment. End of this week, shit. Well, it
wasn't as if he had enough acquaintances of this sort to fill up
a Rolodex. Farm it out to the Weatherman, and he knew it
would be done to perfection. End of the week it would have
to be.

"That'll be fine."

"I'll make travel arrangements and send you my arrival
time. You can send someone to meet me?"

"You won't have to walk."

The line went dead in his ear, and that was that.

As they cruised away, Tony did not relish the need to turn
loose in the neighborhood of ten to fifteen grand.

Nope, life did *not* come cheap.

The next few days he merely wanted to walk through,
business as usual. And true, business got done. There were,
however, distractions.

One was blond, and now unemployed since she had never
returned to a cocktail waitressing job after hooking up with
him. Which was okay, in a sense, because he didn't feel his
woman should have to work. Might reflect bad on him. However. He wasn't sure he wanted Sasha around to assume that

title. She was fun, an interesting diversion. Had come in handy, no doubt about that. But her appeal was limited. He wasn't sure how much longer he would be wanting to plug his prong into the same set of holes.

Couldn't very well just cut her loose. Right now she was on his side, and Torquemada himself probably couldn't get her to talk about Tony's business dealings. She might even *enjoy* such interrogation. But set her forcibly free, and formerly tight lips might get very loose in a hurry. He couldn't have that.

As well, it wasn't a good time to up and off her either. Erik Webber was already kissing dirt. He was planning to do in two more, through the buffer zone of a contract job. Another one that he had ties with suddenly turning up dead, well— bad timing for that sort of thing. Police could be quite determined in hunting for common denominators. Even if they couldn't turn up proof positive on him regarding any of them, he still didn't need the extra attention.

So string her along awhile longer, and an option would arise. Tony was sure of that. Patience was the name of this game.

So much for distraction number one. The blond one. The second was very green, and packaged according to kilogram.

No getting around it, skullflush had thrown a major ripple into his life and career. Six keys, just waiting for . . . something.

What to do with the stuff was a question never far from mind. Annoyingly unanswerable, and that was no good at all. He was used to having control. Tony Mendoza took charge of circumstances, not the other way around.

This was the only time he had allowed a shipment to get through his front door. Except for tiny sample tastes, easily flushable, that came in handy for deals, or coaxing sweeties to bed, like candy to bribable children. Never more than a few grams before. And six keys? Unthinkable.

He was used to very short storage time. Have buyers ready to take a shipment almost as soon as it came in. Of course, he needed time to add his own cut to the mix. But in general, move-it-in-and-move-it-out, that was SOP.

He couldn't very well keep it at any of the safe houses he

used for cutting and temp storage. Not this stuff. No honor among thieves in this business, no way to trust the safe-house guys a hundred percent. They'd fudge from a bag here, a bag there, scooping out their own cut. If you couldn't catch them red-handed, what could you do? Live with it. One more shipment of coke wouldn't cause a second glance among them. Throw the green stuff into the equation, and it could be an engraved invitation for trouble.

So he kept it hidden here at the penthouse. Maybe dangerous, and maybe not. Laws were pretty specific on what constituted an illegal drug. He was willing to bet the U.S. judicial system had never encountered anything like this before. No provisions made, no breakdown of chemical components on their books. For all he knew, skullflush might even be legal. So far.

At any rate, it was probably best to keep it under no one's nose but his own.

What to do, what to do? He'd briefly wondered about trying to move skullflush to the army. They were always in the market for a new weapons angle, something the Reds didn't have in the works. Given the effects, the possibilities were mind-boggling. Battle scenarios. The chips are down, and the platoon whips out concentrated capsulized doses. Breaks them open and pops them under their noses. And in a matter of a minute or two, you've got a platoon of the scariest badass soldiers *any* army has ever sent into battle.

Interesting, and no doubt the army had loads of cash to invest in such projects. Those guys experimented with stuff that would turn the hair of the general populace snow white if it became public knowledge.

There was, however, a big gaping hole in that road. Once army claws were sunk into the project, they would waste no time wasting the middleman. Tony Mendoza would cease to exist. Legally, bodily, spiritually.

So back to square one.

Except a single word continued to nag at him, demanding he give it more attention. *Experimentation.*

Coke he understood, and crack, heroin, crank, and everything else pouring through the pipeline. Just variations on a basic theme. Highs and lows of one sort or another. Didn't take a Ph.D. to figure out their appeal.

But skullflush was one monumentally different can of tuna. It didn't just open your mind or cloud your vision. The stuff drop-kicked you into a brand-new stratosphere. Body, mind, and soul. Sasha had filled in a few blanks, given him glimpses into the effects. But that was like trying to enjoy a Caribbean vacation by listening to someone describe postcards. You had to live it yourself.

I got to know, he thought. *Got to know what that shit's like.*

And this meant compromise. In ethics. In his own loose code of behavior. In the values that had gotten him this far in a very competitive field. In one sense he thought himself nearly as prudish as the temperate bitches during Prohibition: *The lips that touch liquor shall never touch mine.* Update it by a few decades and turn it inside out: *The shit that goes into everybody else's nose shall never hoover into mine.* Same difference.

But when there was progress to be made, one thing was certain. Every scientist in the world knew it—

Rules had to remain flexible.

Wednesday night.

Half a country away, Erik Webber was just hours into his final resting place, and Justin Gray was getting morosely drunk while April Kingston tried futilely to bring him out of his shell.

And on Tampa's home turf, on Westshore Boulevard, Tony was gifted with an evening all by his lonesome. He seized the opportunity when Sasha began to whine about wanting to go out. Dancing, lights, music—she said she was going into withdrawal.

Tony recognized a gift of fate. Gave Lupo a couple hundred in play money and told him to take her out until she got it out of her system. Maybe start her out at Masquerade, the same place she'd been when originally joining their world. Don't bring her back until she's worn herself out.

Lupo didn't like such matchmaking. "She's too close to everything, Tony. Airhead like that, man, you are playing with fire."

"She'll be fine. Trust me on this."

Lupo frowned. He had a fearsome scowl. "It's not you I don't trust." The meaning was implicit.

"Man, what a bitch when your friends don't get along." Tony sighed, looking askance a moment. "Listen, if it'll help thaw the ice between you two, take her somewhere and tear off a piece for yourself." Sometimes his generosity surprised even him.

Lupo looked surprised. Pleasantly, after a moment. "Seriously?"

Tony shrugged. "Ah, why not. No skin off my pecker. Give her a nice change of pace for a night. Make her appreciate the best when she gets back to me."

"Not if I bring her back stretched out."

"I'll take that chance."

Fifteen minutes later they were gone, Sasha decked out in black with her hair teased into a cloud that should come with its own meteorological report. And none too happy about Tony staying behind tonight. She'd forget about it soon enough. Soon as her stilettoed feet hit the dance floor, she wouldn't even remember who she was there with. One blissed-out babe.

Tony was blissed out on his own terms. Locked within his pastel blue and white sanctum sanctorum. Eased back into his recliner surrounded by the horseshoe of softly burbling aquariums, their hoods the only light. He wore jeans only, no shoes, no shirt. The shark's tooth hung against the smooth tan of his chest. And at his side, resting atop the chair's arm . . .

A healthy dose of skullflush.

Six lines were chopped and paralleled on his gold cigarette case. This at his left arm. In his right he held a rolled dollar bill. Tight and ready for duty.

Even before doing line one, he felt a tingling in his belly. Anticipation, nerves. The curdling in the guts of a pioneer ready to step boldly beyond the known. And venture into the unknown, past the edge of a flat earth. To confront Heaven or Hell or whatever else lay in that next realm.

Fish, swimming, circling. Water, soothing as it bubbled. There was nothing else, no other world beyond this room. Only the ones accessed through mind and soul.

He snorted the first two lines, and they slammed his head back against the recliner. Pain, murky green and gold, and a feeling as if he had lit a string of firecrackers in the back of his skull. He moaned aloud. No turning back now. His nose dripped, but he held fast to purpose and lowered for the rest. The next line, and the next, and the next. And the last.

The cigarette case clattered to the tiles. He was glad the penthouse was soundproof. Because he screamed. Oh, how he screamed. Loud enough to wake the dead and send them running for cover.

Not out of pain.

Not out of fear.

But out of head-to-head confrontation with infinity. He found himself standing on the brink of stars, looking down into pits of primordial slime. And here he was, vainglorious adventurer, poised somewhere between the two. At their whim and mercy, for they would send him where they damn well pleased. Everything he had believed, everything he had been taught, everything that had been genetically encoded within his body his bones his blood his cells his nuclei his intertwining dual strands of DNA—it had all been erased.

He was plunging through aeons now as if they were ticks of a clock. There was still self-awareness, but self was no longer the same. Self paled within infinity. Self was scrutinized and blasted with unyielding green light and shown to be the puny thing it was. Self was laughable. Self was humbled. Self was reduced to knee-quaking awe.

No wonder this stuff had seemed to blow the minds of those he had seen take it. Sasha, Justin, Trent Pollard. What they must have seen, experienced, there in his presence—no wonder they had freaked. They had been expecting a coke rush. He had not. He had known so much better what to expect. Even so, it was all he could do to keep from peeling the leather off the chair arms.

For now he was learning by more than mere observation. Now it was strictly hands-on. Scoping out this wondrous new world from the inside.

Falling, cranking back the hands of time . . . *falling* . . .

And only when he hit rock bottom was he able to gather

that nebula of swirling wits. And rise once again. To walk, a
new being.

Alternative evolution.

There was pain now, deeper and more fundamental than
what had come from inhaling the drug. By comparison, that
had been superficial. This ran bone deep. But it was distant,
could've been somebody else's. That was it. Some guy named
Tony Mendoza, back in a mixed ball of past and future. Both
were the same, history spun in circles. Rise and fall of life-
forms, birthed in oceanic stewpot to crawl forth into mud
onto dry land to scale trees to soar through skies to fall, finally,
extinct. Back into the mud, to leach back to the sea. To nur-
ture with rotting bones a new hierarchy destined to rise in its
place.

pain

But he could cope. Rebirth should never be easy.

He could feel the ache and pull of bones in rebellion, the
hardening of the new flesh. The conical head erupting from
his own. An eye on either side, huge, like dark buttons. Jaws
jutting and muscular, rimmed with triangular teeth. A gullet
that craved meat and blood, gulped hot and fresh and kicking, straight from the source. He breathed through his
mouth, still, but bloodless wounds had opened on either side
of his neck, near the ends of the silvery scaled hide.

He lifted his hands. Unchanged, more or less. Although
webbed, translucent membranes between the fingers. As if
they had once been fins and had split to better serve on land.
The best of both worlds.

Tony laughed, an airy wind-gurgling sound. He scrambled
from the recliner to fall before his largest tank, his pride and
joy. A dozen oval shapes glided within. He caught sight of his
reflection in the glass.

He felt no terror.

No disgust.

No worries.

Only the power of exultation, superiority.

And when he rose to plunge his head and shoulders into
the tank, he felt the powerful commingling of brotherhood.
The piranha did not attack. *Would* not attack. Not one of
their own.

He breathed, not through mouth but through gills, sifting oxygen along blood-gorged membranes. And he felt the rhythm and flow of the water, this time from their viewpoint. Sensations like tiny electric currents from receptors within his hide, alert to splashes, temperatures, irregularities, anything that would home him in on prey. He felt the mental singularity linking them all, capable of turning the group into an eating machine. Noise and taste and odor became tactile sensations, something between solid and liquid.

Tony pushed himself up and out, slinging silvery arcs of water to spatter walls and floor. He roared, his throat retaining vestigial traces of human vocalization, his mouth incapable of manipulating them. No matter. Words were of no consequence. Only sensations.

hunger

He fell to his knees, head dripping water to chest and tiles. He reached for a shelf beneath the aquarium adjacent to the piranha tank. Seized the box punched with small round holes. Felt with delight, in a brand-new way, the tiny scramblings within. Smelled wisps of mortal fear emanating from the box—*smelled as never before.*

Tony ripped the lid away, and the high-pitched squeaking was a packet of exquisite needles to his receded ears. He held the box aloft. Opened his jaws wide, his mouth a vast tooth-rimmed pit, all sharp points. Tipped the box . . .

carnivore ecstasy

. . . and let the mice fall.

15
professional courtesies

The Weatherman hit Tampa on Friday afternoon, and Lupo was there to receive him. They knew each other by sight from a previous meeting, which made matters simpler. Nods were exchanged, and that was about it for interpersonal warmth as they traveled to Baggage and then out to the Lincoln. Just a couple of professionals, doing their jobs. No need for trivial chatter.

Once this weekend was over, Lupo was going to breathe one huge sigh of relief. Things would be returning to their boxes, nailed up safe and secure. Two down in one fell swoop.

Leaving one, blond and riskier by the day.

Not that he wouldn't miss Sasha. Tony's generous offer of a couple nights ago had done wonders for bringing them closer. Loads of fun, making her writhe and squeal and kick her stilettos against the back-door glass. It had gotten her very hot to think about slipping Tony the old sexual backstab in the Lincoln's rear seat. Parked at curbside in the heart of downtown, no less. Reflective glass—it didn't matter. The whole scenario hadn't hurt his own ardor as well.

He'd miss her, whenever Tony decided that enough was enough. Couldn't let feelings get in the way though. The cyanide cocktail of vital business mixed with the wrong pleasure had brought down more than its share of great men. He would not join their ranks.

Lupo was a pro, took care of business. He would just as soon Tony delegated to him the responsibility for Justin and April. No sweat, they were anything but hardcases. Just a couple of grief-stricken newfound lovers. Bang-bang, bye-bye. But Tony's logic for subcontracting was hard to argue with. It was going to look mighty suspicious—friends of Erik turning up dead a week after his own murder. Might lend credence to any possible accusatory fingers Justin could have pointed Tony's way. Best, then, to have rock-solid alibis when it went down. They would have one, 125 miles away. It was Fort Myers this weekend.

While the Weatherman brought on the sunshine.

He looked like a real geek, this guy. Every native's tourist of nightmares come true. He wore Bermudas and some yellow short-sleeve shirt with hideous paisley splotches. And some goofy narrow-brimmed hat that might have looked more at home on a fishing charter. He had skinny white legs and a junk-food belly and a roundish face. Very muscular hands and forearms, though, with a gaudy turquoise ring on one finger. He was one of those peculiarities of oddly indeterminate age. Could have been twenty and could have been forty. You took one look at this guy, thought for sure he was some virginal data-processing operator out of Dubuque down for his first vacation.

Until you heard him speak.

Then you thought maybe he was CIA, a killer bureaucrat. A voice like that, with its attendant chill, belonged to someone whose eyes miss little, if anything. Whose brain whirs even in sleep. And whose libido has more twists than a phone cord.

This guy was walking Death.

Tony knew how to pick them, and that was to his credit. Stress might have been weighing a bit too heavily on Tony lately. Yesterday morning's wee hours, for example. Still Wednesday night as far as he and Sasha were concerned. They had found Tony sprawled asleep in the aquarium-room floor. Nothing too serious, he'd had a smile on his face.

And a mouse's tail caught between a couple of teeth. Sasha hadn't seen that; she'd already scooted off to bed. Lupo also found a dusting of green powder on the gold cigarette case, and from that point on, two plus two was easy to sum up.

Tony, man, you psych out on me, and I'll have to kill you myself, he thought at the time. Not entirely serious, not entirely kidding. One thing was certain though: Should Lupo ever go down in the proverbial flames, he wanted his own hand to have struck the match. Not someone else's. Not even Tony's.

Before taking the Weatherman to check into his motel—in whose lot sat parked a drab rental car with dead-end phony ID paperwork—Lupo wheeled him by April's apartment. Same vantage point he had watched from earlier in the week. He parked, killed the engine. Left the power on long enough to whir down the windows. And then, nothing but traffic and birdsongs to keep them company.

"That's where the girl lives," Lupo said, pointing. "Second-floor loft. She's got the lengthwise half facing us, somebody else has the south half. Only entrance is that stairwell at the east end you see there. Goes straight up to a first door, and on the other side there's a little landing, and then the inner door. Both sturdy, and they both got hefty locks. She's got no intercom."

"Peepholes?" asked the Weatherman.

"Yeah. Good thing about the stairway is that it's hers alone, doesn't serve anybody else."

The Weatherman nodded. "Pictures?"

Lupo frowned. "I got one of her. Not him. He's new in town, been here less than two weeks. I'm hoping he'll come out sometime this afternoon so you can see what he looks like. They're probably both up there now. So far as I know, there's just the one car between them." Lupo pointed to the black Fiero parked beside the building.

"Let's see her, at least," said the Weatherman.

Lupo leaned across toward the glove compartment,

opened it. Pulled out a half-size manila envelope. He slid out a single glossy, slightly blurry print.

"Meet April Kingston," he said, and handed the picture over.

The Weatherman regarded it with neither reaction nor emotion. Heart of stone—commendable. It was tough to remain unmoved.

"A body like that in a shot like this," the Weatherman finally said, "you show it to most guys, and they'd never remember the face."

He had a point. The nudity and the graphic sexual content were very definite distractions. He frowned over the face for another ten seconds, then slid the print back inside. Replaced it in the glovebox.

"Don't want to keep it?" Lupo asked.

The Weatherman shook his head. Tapped his temple.

"That picture. Looks like it was taken off a film print. Am I right?"

Lupo nodded. "Yeah."

"Good lighting."

Nodded again. "Yeah."

Apparently the Weatherman had nothing more to add, so they waited in silence. Just a couple of pros. How the cops kept their sanity on stakeouts, Lupo didn't know. Well, given how many ate their guns before retirement, maybe they lost it after all. Brains turning cartwheels onto walls.

Two and a half hours later . . .

"Heads up," Lupo said. "That's him."

The Weatherman whipped up a compact pair of binoculars he'd long since pulled from his single flight bag. Trained them on the lone figure emerging from the stairwell, then heading for April's Fiero. The Weatherman looked like an owl, sighting in on a chipmunk before swooping down with splayed talons. Justin paused at the car door, looking toward a stand of willows and bushes close to the opposite end of the building. Nothing to see from here. Maybe nothing at all. Whatever, his attention was back on the car in two shakes. When he was in, Lupo switched on the power and rolled up the mirrored windows.

"Seen enough?" he asked.

The Weatherman nodded. "I believe you have half the cash up front for me?"

"In the trunk. You'll get it at the motel."

Lupo started up the car. The Weatherman nodded, then turned his roundly cherubic face toward the sky.

"I love this business," he said.

16
FLESHTONES

Justin decided to cut out for a short while around four o'clock. Armed with April's car keys and a general understanding of street layouts, he left the apartment and headed for her Fiero. Paused at the door to unlock it.

For a moment his attention was snagged by a glimpse of someone in the clump of trees ahead. Homeless, by the looks of the guy. Road-worn clothing—olive pants and a pale brown shirt. Definitely foreign, from south of *some* border. Eyes met, and Justin was the first to avert his. To have looked any longer might have been to invite panhandling, maybe worse. There was guilt though. The this-shouldn't-happen-here-and-why-doesn't-somebody-do-something sentiments that fell just short of making him take responsibility himself.

A lot of that going around these days. He wasn't proud. So he hurriedly got in the car and moments later he was on Kennedy and rolling west.

They had been back a little over a day, and now, finally, it was time to set life on track again. Because life goes on. April's career beckoned, needed tending. She had accumulated several messages on her business machine while in Ohio, was taking care of the missed days. Tonight she had a dinner meeting with the owners of the plant rental and maintenance firm to present her layouts and talk about future strategies.

His first night alone since moving in. Distractions were sorely needed.

So were plans for his own life. Justin had thought he'd have a little more time for wit-gathering. Erik wasn't going to push him out the door toward employment until he was ready. April may well have been willing to grant just as many concessions, but he felt it vaguely impudent to expect her to. Because when it came down to it, he had forced himself on her as much as had circumstances.

He needed a car. A job. His own place to live should at least be suggested, and if she honestly vetoed the idea, then fine, his conscience was clear. But the wimpy little nest egg left once belongings had been sold and Paula given her share and lawyers' fees taken care of—it wasn't going to last long. A couple months, at most.

Then there was the whole matter of Tony Mendoza.

So what am I doing going out to rent videos? He needed escape, yeah, that was it. A rationalization that should hold water awhile.

With Erik's lost membership card in his pocket, he wheeled into the lot of Mind's Eye Video. It was a large one-story flat-roofed place that looked as if it might have been a corner market a few dozen years ago. Saved from ruin by the video age.

He joined the other browsers inside. Singles, pairs. Those who spoke did so with the same sort of hush usually reserved for libraries. Justin wandered the aisles, scanning the titles of empty cassette boxes. Skirting the occasional heavy cardboard floor display. Timothy Dalton as the latest James Bond, tuxedoed and pistoleroed. John Candy, capable of blocking an aisle. *Texas Chainsaw Massacre*'s Leatherface, wielding his manicure equipment.

He found a couple of interesting titles to try tonight. Held on to the boxes to trade them for tapes at the counter. Gradually worked his way along until he got to the far side. Didn't want to miss anything, some forgotten nugget of cinematic gold.

On the far side, Mind's Eye had an X-rated section, within its own alcove. Maybe twice the size of the average walk-in closet. Only one customer was in there at the moment. A real nose-picker, he looked like, wearing a T-shirt insufficient to cover his rain-gutter waist or reach the squeezed-down top of his jeans in back. Crescent moon, milky white. The top of his butt-crack periscoped above the beltline.

Justin paused in the doorway. Hesitant. *Remembering.* And decided to go on in.

Lurid boxes greeted him, row upon row of empty passion, frozen moments to tantalize the lonely, the horny, into coughing up four bucks a night for the whole flick. Women, at least eighty percent women on those covers. Every conceivable angle, pose, and orifice, with no standards of censorship imposed on most. They bared pink souls to the camera, or attended living phallic symbols with enthusiasm bordering on worship. If this display of moist overkill wasn't enough to frighten an impressionable young child away from sex, he didn't know what would.

He was no devotee of the great American fuck film. Or Swedish, or whatever else was imported in plain brown wrappers. But he remembered occasional team trips to video outlets with Erik, where they would pop into similar alcoves such as this to simply check out the titles. The titles were always good for a laugh. Especially when they had taken the title of a perfectly innocent, mainstream movie and warped it into perversion.

Hannah Does Her Sisters. Backside to the Future. Great Sexpectations. Beverly Hills Clit. Everywhere you looked, bad puns. Which didn't seem quite so funny alone. He needed the other half of the team. This was like Abbott without Costello. Justin smiled when he remembered Erik's suggestion a few years back that they collaborate on a Japanese horror porno film called *Debbie Does Godzilla.* Now there was a casting coup he would pay to witness.

Justin had seen enough. He turned to leave the nose-picker to his own fantasies over the Marilyn Chambers box he clenched in one plump fist.

And stopped. Frozen.

the shelf by the doorway

It was one of those moments where the relevant leaps right out of a clutter of stimuli to seize your attention. Immediately finding your own name on a page full of names. Your own picture in a group shot.

picture

He reached for the box.

please no please don't let it be

The other pair of movie boxes fell to the floor, and he never heard them hit.

no

But no matter how many times he tried to tell himself the similarity was just an astonishing coincidence, his heart, his gut—newly heaving things that they were—told him it was far more.

Corporate Head, read the title. *Hot Career Women Climb The Ladder of Suck-sess!!! With No Job Too BIG!!!*

He shut his eyes, felt them burn. He was due for another crying jag, wasn't he? Sure. It had been all of one day since he'd let go in a cemetery in Ohio.

When he reopened, the cover shot was still the same. A setting that looked to be some cheesy mock-up of a high-powered office in an ultramodern building. A close shot of male legs, smartly tailored dark gray suit pants.

And the woman he probably loved, hanging out of a disheveled skirt and blouse, getting ready to bury her face where the sun didn't normally shine. Her tongue serpentine.

Justin, hands shaking, turned the box over to scan the cast credits listed on the back. Not that it made any difference. Her name could only confirm the misery. Its absence only meant she was going unlisted.

Names, two lines' worth, mostly female. And toward the end of the list, a compromise of sorts—*April Rose.*

He wanted to be ill. To burn this whole place to the ground. To take her car and leave his belongings behind and hit the open road and find someplace to begin anew, all over again.

Until that dream, too, would end up bleeding and dying by the roadside like a puppy competing with speeding Goodyear rubber. Something was always waiting around the corner to squash dreams.

Always.

Justin left the first two boxes on the floor, forgotten. He flattened the porno box and slipped it inside his shirt and left Mind's Eye Video. Forever. No coming back.

He fished inside his pocket for the yellow card symbolizing Erik's ties to the place. Folded and ripped it, folded and ripped.

And halfway across the lot to her car, he opened his hand and let the tiny ragged squares sift to the asphalt. Wind caught them, scattered them.

Like confetti to celebrate a wake.

He drove blindly for a while, unable to leave, unable to return to the loft. Caught within a limbo of the city's borders. He traveled streets never driven before, new sights falling on eyes that saw them but rarely registered them.

It was before she knew me, he repeatedly told himself. His head was adamant, but his heart would have none of it. His heart felt as if it had met the business end of a medieval lance.

He'd had no silly illusions that he was her first. April was twenty-eight, a contemporary working woman. She'd been engaged. He'd seen the Ortho-Novum prescription in the medicine cabinet. It would be the height of naïveté to think her sexuality had blossomed last Saturday evening. But that was okay, that was expected. No problems there.

But this? *This?*

before she met me

Knowing that still didn't lessen the impact of having it so rudely slap him in the face. He liked to think it would have been far more tolerable learning it from her own lips rather than this way. Anything to rationalize the pain.

Justin drove until he dared keep the car no longer. Running out on this was no defense, but a pipe dream, and a shameful one at that. April had appointments, needed her car. He could not deny her that. She was obviously trying her best to keep the past distant.

But it still didn't soothe the hurt.

She was performing cosmetic ablutions in the bathroom when he got back to the loft. He shuffled in, feeling stunned, a punch-drunk fighter who had lost too many rounds with life lately. He tossed her keys onto the kitchen table with a clatter and aimed himself for the couch.

"I was getting worried," she called out from the bathroom. Over his shoulder, he caught a sliced glimpse of her leaning into the mirror to apply mascara. "I was about ready to call out Crockett and Tubbs to hunt you down."

"Sorry." It was all he could think to say. Two seconds later he was on his side on the couch, facing the back.

"What did you rent?"

"Nothing. I've seen them all."

"Now *there's* a cynic."

Cynics are made, not born, he thought. Kept it to himself. Justin lay there, as if reality could intrude no farther if he did not move, did not open his eyes. As if there were an outside chance it might prove to be a bad dream when he *did* open them. Yes. The movie box still in his shirt would not be there then.

He could still feel it, one crisp corner digging into his stomach. Finally he could tolerate the feel of the thing no longer and yanked it out. Hurriedly shoved it beneath the couch.

Moments later April came in, ready to leave. He'd cut it very close with her car. He rolled over to face her, and it wasn't as difficult as he feared. It was easier to segregate the past when he could see her in the present, know that those eyes, those lips, were focused on him now. Try as he might, though, he could not entirely dissociate them from those in the picture. Wondering what they had been doing ten seconds later. Imagination was torture.

April looked lovely. Business and femininity, she managed to exude both. Her hair was side parted and gathered back to hang down in loose curls between her shoulder blades. Her skirt was navy, her shoes of moderate heel.

She asked if he was all right, and he said not really but that it would pass. Denial would only make things worse. Bringing up the truth, whole truth, and nothing but, could only ruin her evening. Let her think it was due to Erik, to Mendoza, and that would be best. He could hold it in that long, for her sake.

But it would not keep forever.

After she told him good-bye, collected her keys and portfolio, kissed him with tender lingering lips, she was out the door. While he sat up on the edge of the couch, feeling the weight of the past months bearing down all at once. Some people seemed duty bound to attract a screwed-up life. They were magnets.

Justin wondered if Erik had ever stumbled across the video box. Probably so; no reason to think he wouldn't continue checking smut titles, and *Corporate Head* was a title over which he would heartily guffaw—ordinarily. *He probably knew.* Just had the good grace to mentally bury it. But as her friend, platonically so, Erik could have afforded the distance. Love was not so wealthy.

He retrieved the movie box from its temporary stash. Carried it into the kitchen. Paused beside the table, the chairs. *The* chair, site of their first coupling. He rummaged through several drawers before he found a roll of what he was looking for.

Scotch Brand, magic transparent.

And like a parent proud of a child's art-class masterpiece, he taped the box to the refrigerator door.

She returned home somewhere after nine. Justin had accomplished nothing in the interim, hadn't eaten, had thought of little. Time had passed very quickly, and he'd spent most of it rambling about the loft. Upon her arrival, he was leaning back against one of the brick pillars, near her office.

He heard the outer door open and shut, then the inner. Her footsteps. He could not see her; he was facing the wrong way.

"Are you home?" she called out.

"Yeah. Back here."

"How come you're sitting in the dark?"

"Just sitting."

Nothing but moonlight, citylight. There were more footsteps, and then she switched on the light in the kitchen, one in the living room. He was on its fringes, an outsider.

"It went *sooo* great tonight." April's voice was childlike with enthusiasm. "They loved what I've worked up for them. I'll hardly have to make any changes at all. Now that's a rarity."

He lowered his forehead atop crossed arms. Confrontational slime, that's what he was. So unfair to do this to her mood.

Justin still didn't look her way, could only hear sporadic movements. Her heels on the floor, rustles of fabric. He didn't know the precise moment she saw the refrigerator. There was no cry of surprise, of horror at the past boomeranging to haunt her. Justin only realized, eventually, that it had been a very long time since he had heard anything at all.

Dead silence within. From outside, traffic, urban ambience.

He waited. That stubborn idiocy of expecting the other to make the first overtures toward explanations, reconciliation. Fear or pride, he always wondered which was stronger.

Twenty minutes later he finally looked back toward the other end of the loft, and he didn't see her. He got up, walking on stocking feet, silent but for the occasional groan of a board. Not in the bedroom, not in the living room, not in the kitchen. The movie box still clung to the fridge door.

He heard a faint sniffle. The bathroom.

Justin turned on its light from the doorway and found her in the far corner formed by the wall and the shower/tub stall. April was huddled up very small, arms tightly wrapped around drawn-up legs. A mess of mascara runoff peeked above her knees.

"Don't hit me," she whispered with a cracking voice.

He shook his head. Did he look that upset? "I won't hit you."

Her head rose a few degrees. Red eyes, blotchy cheeks. Her hair had come loose and bedraggled. She must have gone to a lot of effort to cry so silently in here.

"Two nights before the wedding, Brad did. That's when *he* found out."

Justin sighed heavily, wandered into the bathroom. Its air was warmer, heavier, weighted with the steam of past showers, smelling of deodorant and toothpaste. The air clung like tears. He took a seat atop the toilet lid.

"Were you ever going to tell me?"

"No," she said without hesitation.

"You didn't think I'd stick around?" He was careful to keep a soft voice. A few too many decibels, and she looked as if she could shatter like crystal.

"I was afraid." April gulped and blew her nose into a smudged wad of tissue. "I thought you'd run too."

"You accepted me after everything I told you I'd done. And you still couldn't trust me to do the same?" His eyes slid shut. "That hurts worse."

April dissolved. He watched it happen. She was facedown on the floor, shoulders wracked with sobs that she would not let escape into sound. She looked as if, were he to pick her up, she would turn to liquid that would stream and puddle out of her skirt, blouse, pantyhose. Finally he reached down to lay a hand upon her shoulder, rubbing gently, and she homed in on it. Crawled miserably across the floor until she could hoist herself up onto one of his legs. And there she clung, wetting it with tears, and he leaned forward to hold her. Stray hairs and bits of lint from the floor adhered to her clothing.

"Do you love me?" he whispered down to her. "Or could you?"

Into his leg, she nodded. Desperately so.

"Then *trust* me."

Justin was astounding himself. He'd been all set to take a hard-line stance. Hadn't rehearsed it, hadn't planned anything to say, but had thought he'd play it cold as ice. Let her suffer the consequences of her actions.

How pathetic on his part. Devoid of forgiveness, understanding. One look at her had destroyed that stance in moments. The realization that she'd forgiven him his own past had buried it.

She looked up, the delicate contours of her face seemingly blurred by loathing that had imploded. Eyes were wet, and nose, and mouth. He pulled fresh tissue from the roll and helped dry her.

"It was just the one movie," she said, and the possibility of more hadn't even entered his mind. "Please don't think it was something I wanted to do. *I didn't.*"

"What happened?"

April squeezed him briefly, then pulled away to sit against the wall. Staring into the floor while she told him a story.

Of a talented artist who, a couple of years ago, left her job in the advertising department of the *Tampa Tribune* in favor of her own free-lance studio. She, like him, did more coke in those days than was advisable. That was before she had wisely curtailed all use of powders and liquids except for the occasional social drink. Unlike his own continual flirtation with ruin.

In the early days of self-employment, she had had to hustle and work to obtain clients. Large, small, it made no difference. Any business needing ad art was fair game. Even a relative giant like a small chain of area department stores who had no in-house agency and broke ties with the full-service agency it had been dealing with. Who planned on getting future adwork on an à la carte basis. And who had lots of income-boosting potential that would last for years. April had targeted them like a heat-seeking missile.

Wining and dining helps win clients. April had a friend in purchasing within the store's hierarchy who had provided her with inside information. That her work was favorably regarded, that they liked her attitudes, her enthusiasm, her specs, and how finally it had come down to her and another artist.

Wining and dining. It was time to invest in herself. April gave a small party and reception for the store's bigwigs, relying on her source that matters might be swayed if she were to ensure their good time by powdering things along for the evening. Just between friends, of course.

Murphy's Law prevailed, however. The account went to the other studio, and April suddenly found herself cast adrift and in debt to the tune of nearly ten grand for party favors. To a young enterprising entrepreneur named Tony Mendoza.

Seems that he'd had his eye on her for some time, and she had continually spurned his advances. The man was, of course, scum. But he'd seemed happy enough to front her the coke when she didn't have the money to pay for it, and she'd been quite proud of manipulating him with feminine wiles.

Only now the bottom had dropped out of everything, and Tony had become a very impatient debt-holder. Business was business, nothing personal. He laughed at her offer to set up some sort of time payment schedule. How terrible it would be, he intimated, if something were to tragically befall her new business. Its location, perhaps.

April spent a week in hell.

Then Tony showed up, knight in shining armor that he was, and offered her a way out of this mess. She pounced on it —anything.

So he told her how he was investing in movie production. The direct-to-video route. Mail-order sales, rental outlets. She could take on a costarring role in his next one and wipe the slate clean. He would even costar with her in one of the scenes. Just so she would feel more comfortable working with someone she knew.

Justin listened. Listened. And as soon as Tony entered the picture—figuratively and literally—it took on entire new dimensions of turmoil. His hold on their lives just did not quit. And it seemed to have come so easily, so seductively. Almost as if by invitation.

He'd met the man but once, and now hated him more than he had hated anyone on the face of the earth. He would hate this man until the day he died.

"So I did it," April said, voice cracking some more. "And he —he didn't care about the money anymore. This was so personal to him. A conquest. Probably the longest he'd ever had to wait for anything."

Justin didn't want to know this, was sorry he'd asked, sorry he'd ever walked into Mind's Eye Video to begin with. He hadn't known how truly blissful ignorance could really be.

April was trembling, locked into the auto-da-fé of memory, of reliving self-betrayal. He could see every tortured fiber within her.

"And damn him to hell, he made sure he enjoyed it. He must have had some deal going with the director. Because *that* son of a bitch made us do our scene—*made us do it five days in a row.*" Only now did her voice rise to a wail. "I was lying on this desk after the last time, under those lights. With his—his—*stuff* splattered all over my face. And I swear, it felt worse than acid. I wanted to die. I came home and I sat in that bathtub for an hour, like some pathetic ritual that might help me feel clean again. But it didn't. The last half of it, I had a razor blade at my wrist. Just trying to work up nerve to do it." She swallowed hard. "And then Erik called. Out of the blue, no reason. I had my machine on and heard his message come in. He just said he missed seeing me at work.

"He probably saved my life. And he never even knew it."

"You never told him?"

April shook her head, pushed hair back from her mouth. "I wanted to. But I couldn't. I would've had to tell him why." She looked up, the first eye contact since beginning the story. "Oh, Jus, I wish I could've told him. I started *so* many times."

He nodded. Erik, saving another life just by being himself. The irony was painfully poetic.

"Do you know what it's like," she said slowly, "living with that in the past? Not that I can't deal with *that*, the actual doing it. But never knowing if I'm going to run into someone who might have seen it? Who might recognize me?" Her voice strained, tightened. "That when a stranger looks at me twice, I never know if it's just because of me—or if he thinks maybe I look familiar. And then maybe he remembers, and that's what he thinks about me. Do you know what that's *like*?"

He gently shook his head. "No. I don't."

"It means I'm never—*never*— far from the worst week of my life. That I probably never will be. Because even if every copy of that tape burned up tonight, someone might still remember."

"Do very many people know already?"

She laughed bitterly, wetly. "How many people does it take before it starts to matter?" She blew her nose again. "Enough do. I told you Brad found out two nights before the wedding. You know *how* he found out?"

Justin shook his head.

"At the stag party. One of the guys rented *Corporate Head* and didn't recognize me from the cover shot. They were having a great time until my part started. Doesn't that sound like something out of a trashy comedy?"

Justin didn't reply. There was no earthly way he could begin to measure the shame and embarrassment she must have felt.

"So they know, all of his friends. I don't see any of them anymore, so that's good. And do you believe it, after Brad broke off the wedding, three of his friends called to ask me out. What did they think I was?"

Justin reached down to hold her moistened hands.

Then pulled her up and held her to him.

"I don't know who else knows," she murmured into his ear. "I don't even want to. Except there's always, *always*, this fear I have inside that something's going to go wrong—and my parents are going to find out. That is my absolute worst fear. Every night when I go to bed I pray to God to keep that from happening the next day. I pray for that like I've never prayed for anything."

He held her, rocked her. Every ache and pain his heart had felt in the store and while driving around had melted, drained, paled into inconsequentiality. He felt like the most selfish person on earth.

"I love you," she whispered, and her mouth sought him, found him. Hungry for something more than contact. Acceptance, maybe.

He had no choice but to give it.

Justin knew that soon, very soon, he would lead her to bed. Maybe even carry her, with April clinging to his body like a koala to a tree. He would lay her down, undress her slowly. Kiss her all over, not missing a single square inch. He would try his very best to give and give and give and this time expect nothing in return. He would become a sponge, trying to soak up the hurt, at least for a while. He would try to make her feel better than she had ever felt before. He would probably fail, but the trying was all. He couldn't heal the scars, but he could love her in spite of them.

April began to laugh into the side of his throat. A strange sound, a mix. Perhaps eighty percent sorrow and twenty percent hope.

"I liked you that first night we met," she said. "But I really started falling for you the next night. When we sat at the edge of Davis Island and you told me what happened in St. Louis. I think I would've done anything for you that night. You know why?"

He shook his head. "Why?"

"Because I was sitting there thinking, here he is, the one I've been waiting for—the one who's just as screwed up as I am."

Justin chuckled softly. Understanding, then, that eighty-twenty mix. He took her comment as no insult.

It was, after all, the truth.

17
STORMY WEATHER

At least half the time when the Weatherman saw a movie featuring a contract killer, he laughed out loud. Seldom did they get it right. Especially when they presented some screwtop who approached death with the mysticism of a Zen master. Thought they were absorbing life essences and whatnot. What a load of bullshit.

Guy like that in the real world wouldn't last any time. Go into it with such personal feelings—especially the deeply weird—and your potential for screw-ups would rocket past the ozone layer.

Fact was, the best in the field were generally the most boring. Total lack of feelings may not translate into high drama, but it definitely makes for cautious business practices.

He allowed himself one luxury of sentimentality: the turquoise ring. Souvenir from the first whackout he'd ever done on a purely professional level, no personal stake other than the half-up-front, half-upon-completion financial terms. Big

Mexican gal in Albuquerque, trying to blackmail the wrong guy. Hefty pair of mitts on that mama; the ring fit his own finger just fine.

Dusk had fallen a half hour ago. Time to get a bit more active instead of sitting and watching the world go by. Saturday night's all right for fighting, Elton John used to sing. It was peachy-keen for dying, as well.

The Weatherman was in his rental, parked in a small business lot across the alley from April Kingston's place. Different vantage point from where he and Lupo had watched yesterday, but equally functional.

He wore a variation on yesterday's attire: tropical geek. Wherever he went to work, if there was a stereotypical tourist look, that's what he adopted. And nobody took a second glance. They had seen it all before. In the West, he wore tight jeans and rhinestone shirts and gaudy boots. In the upper South, he looked like some sort of gentleman fop out of "My Old Kentucky Home." In California, he looked like a novice surfer. Never failed. On the rare occasions he was witnessed, an accurate facial description was nonexistent. They remembered the silly clothes. Which, by the time the witness was dredging his memory for details, had long been doffed. And if need arose, he simply pocketed the ring until on safe ground.

Weapons check: fine and dandy, perfect working order. For this evening's job he was using a Beretta nine-millimeter semiautomatic pistol, silencer equipped. Hollow-point slugs that flattened on impact and tore virtual tunnels of damage within the body and craters upon exit. Tough to salvage the slug for rifling marks, too, an added bonus. In actuality he preferred a revolver with the same sort of bullets. Semiautomatics could jam on occasion, and in a business where second chances were tough at best and more often impossible, a jam was catastrophic. Didn't matter if you had a fifteen-shot clip if that first one jammed; if you couldn't get past it, the rest might as well be suppositories. But hit a misfire with a revolver—just rotate to the next cylinder, and rock and roll.

However. Silence was golden, literally, and silencers did not work on revolvers. No enclosure around the cylinder. Another famous movie fuckup. He always guffawed when he saw that. So he adapted. The Weatherman came fully equipped with his silenced Beretta and a small five-round .32 revolver backup, just in case. Happily, he'd never jammed. But readiness was everything.

Time to do it.

The Weatherman stowed his pistols. Beretta in his waistband beneath an untucked shirt, the .32 in a small holster riding the small of his back. Then he grabbed his ticket to her door.

Last night, he had staked out this place to make sure these two didn't leave long-term. Once the girl had returned from wherever and the loft's lights had gone out an hour later, he returned to his motel and ordered a pizza. He still had the empty box, the strip of adhesive scrawled with his temporary address now removed and burned.

Pizza box in hand, he left the car. A gusty night. His hair swirled in the wind. Damn. He was losing it, that hairline receding higher by the year, and he did his best to comb it to hide the fact.

They were both home. The Fiero was parked by the building, and since nightfall, he had seen a pair of shadows briefly cross the drawn blinds.

He much preferred a double-header like this outside. Both together, side by side, where surprise was optimal and cover minimal. Didn't look to be the case today. These two were the nest-holingest people he'd taken down in a long time. He'd only seen one today, and briefly. The girl, coming down for her morning paper and mail, wearing white shorts and an orange halter top. Not a glimpse the rest of the day.

The Weatherman took stock of logistics halfway to the stairwell. Nearby enough to make a difference, not a creature was stirring. Just the little ole pizza man.

The stairwell. Twenty-five steps, give or take, straight up to a door, blank except for a round peephole eye. Before it, above the narrow landing, a single naked bulb glowed with harsh light. Once he was up that high, no one in the outside world would be able to see him unless they were standing directly at the bottom of the stairs.

He paused halfway up, out of the gusty windflow, and smoothed his hair into place, fretting until it felt just right. Then he covered the rest of the way. A quick over-the-shoulder glance. All clear. He eased out the Beretta with his right hand. In his left he balanced the pizza box like a tray on the palm of a snooty waiter.

He knuckled the bell with his gun hand, dropped it after hearing a buzzer sound within. Held the gun behind his thigh, and with a practiced motion of his thumb, flicked off the safety.

Whoever answered, he'd say the pizza had been ordered in the other's name. Momentary confusion, divide and conquer. Get the second one to the door, with a little luck.

He heard music from inside.

And then the unlatching of the inner door.

Saturday had been as close to a perfect day as April could remember. They could have been anywhere in the world, for absolutely nothing had intruded to remind them where they were. No business calls, no personal calls, nothing. The world was on hold, and they had managed to escape it.

Until the doorbell buzzed.

They were on the couch, the stereo playing as they looked through two albums' worth of her childhood photos. The past he wanted to know more about, and she was happy to pop on the tour guide's hat. Just the fact that he was interested was enough to send her into emotional cartwheels.

Last night, she was sure she'd lost him. Lost another one. One who, faults and all, she had found far more intriguing and deep than Brad had ever thought about being. She was finally starting to feel glad that marriage to Brad had crashed on the rocks two days prior to the event. Better things waiting.

A temporary Black Friday panic, then, finding that movie box on the refrigerator door. A world coming to an end, atomic fury. The difference in her spirits between then and now was like two distinct galaxies.

Because while it had very much mattered to Justin, it had not changed him. He had loved her. Had taken her to bed to prove it. Not in the voyeuristic turn-on way that Brad's friends had seemed to want after the Great Disclosure.

But in a way that healed.

He had kissed her from eyelids to toes. Had ministered to

every sensitive inch of her body with fingers and tongue. He had a wonderful touch, just right. Neither too gropingly rough nor too insubstantially light. It was a rarer happy medium than it seemed it should be. But he had it down right, magic tongue, musician's hands. He had played her like a maestro at a vintage instrument.

And even now, she could catch periodic whiffs of the residue of their mutual orgasms, the blending of their fluids within her into a fragrance at once delicate and musky. She loved it. And him.

He could be the one, maybe. More time would tell. Once lives were back to normal, she wanted to take him over to St. Pete to meet her parents. They would love him too, had to, *just had to*. Their opinions meant everything. For their lifelong love of her, their endless sacrifices—to disappoint them now would be unthinkable. They had loved Brad, his stability, his predictability. Good husband material, father material, son-in-law material. Their silent reproach at the demise of the wedding—whose cause they did not fully understand —was almost more than she could bear back in December. Being unable to explain was the near-last nail in the coffin lid.

That her parents might find Justin a second-rate replacement for Brad was a definite possibility. His were good looks, but not from the clean-cut all-American mold Brad had been cast in. Not anymore, at least. Not since his career derailment. Screw it. She'd make sure he at least shaved on that day to come, and as for the rest, let the chips fall where they may.

The buzzer. Hated intrusion.

"I shall return," she said. Left him grinning over a snapshot of her, gap-toothed and seven years old and holding a squirming cat.

Barefoot, April crossed from living room to kitchen to farright corner. Swung into the little entry hallway and turned left to open the inner door. She stuck an eye to the peephole of the outer.

On the other side was a stranger, round-faced and smiling pleasantly. Hard to tell how old. He didn't look terribly bright, and sometimes the slightly deficient were older than they looked.

"Who is it?" she called through the door.

"Pizza dude." Within the fisheye view, he stepped aside and raised one arm to show her the box.

"We didn't order one. You must have the wrong address."

She saw him frown and read from the edge of his side of the box. "Gray? Justin Gray?" He rattled off the address. "Don't tell me somebody phoned in another joke. Aw, fudge! I'll catch trouble for sure!"

Well, she didn't want that if it could be avoided. Poor guy, he sounded very plaintive about it. Maybe Justin *had* phoned in an order and forgotten to tell her. Less than a half hour ago, she had spent a few minutes in the bathroom. Maybe he had.

"Hang on a second," she said.

hand lingering on the lock

"Hey, Justin, did you order a pizza?" she called, louder.

while the music pounded on

"What?" he yelled back over the stereo.

She sighed. Stepped back far enough so he could see her. "Come here a minute, okay?"

He nodded and stood, came forward. His hair caught a ruffling breeze that rushed in a near window and out a far one. He wore cutoffs, a sleeveless coral shirt. And looked absolutely adorable.

her fingers turning, unbolting the lock

"What's up?"

dropping to the knob

"Did you order a pizza when I was in the bathroom earlier?"

twisting the knob so the poor dim-witted delivery man wouldn't have to keep speaking to a faceless door

Justin frowned, gave his head a little shake. "No." He was eight feet from the door, from her, and closing. . . .

as the door eeaaaased open

And there he stood. The pizza dude. She almost laughed at his clothes.

She should have been expecting it, a blustery day like today. Sometimes that stairwell acted like a giant wind tunnel when her loft windows were open and so were both doors.

One rushing airflow, circuit complete. Her hair flew back from her shoulders.

The pizza guy's box, perched atop his hand, got sucked right out of his grasp. As soon as Justin walked up, suspiciously eyeing the door, the box went spinning into the doorway, as light as a paper airplane. For a second and a half, the bogus delivery man looked at it with utter surprise.

When she looked to Justin, he was already diving toward her. Definitely no pizza in *that* box. She got her hands on the knob to fling the door shut again, only to have it punted back open.

The pizza dude looked anything but dim-witted now.

Justin's arms around her, they went spinning past the doorway toward the floor. She'd seen the long-barreled gun swing up, heard it bark with a soft little cough, and Justin cried out and flecks of blood speckled the inner door behind them.

She screamed once, thinking it would be loud. It wasn't. It was like trying to scream in a nightmare. A weak, anemic warble.

The pizza box went sailing past her face like a hurled Frisbee, this time from the floor up, from Justin's hand. It struck the pizza dude's gun as there came that innocuous coughing sound again and the shot plowed into the wall.

They were rolling, and their bodies were blocking the door from swinging shut, and they were sitting ducks, yes, Romeo and Juliet, they would die together, *together,* and with that as a part of the bargain she didn't find it all a complete loss. . . .

Movement from below, bottom of the stairwell, and she knew if she got out of this she'd never order a pizza ever again.

the silencer's round hole, an unblinking merciless eye

And she saw that this wild card down below was wearing a pale brown shirt and olive pants and her senses were overloading excruciating clarity else why would she be noticing that he had purple socks *purple socks* of all things to notice as he hoisted something that looked like it belonged in the Wild West and something whizzed through the air until she couldn't see it. . . .

And Justin was covering her body with his own now while she felt warm trickles from him that were not sweat not tears *had to be blood* and she found her voice and shrieked a good one now. . . .

And above them the pizza dude's back arced like a sailfish breaking water and he gurgled, and she saw some terribly bloody spike protruding from his lower shoulder by at least a foot, and he stumbled and spasmed and left a crimson smear on her doorway. . . .

And his pistol clattered to the floor of the landing and her hands scrambled for it Justin's hands hers closing first and she pointed into the ugly shirt looming over her and pulled the trigger pulled again again and now *she* was making the tiny cute coughing noises. . . .

And the pizza dude slid down on his rump inside the doorway and his head lolled bonelessly. While she knew that *this* delivery was incomplete.

April gently pushed Justin from atop her. He rolled beside her on his own, and she took that as a good sign. She wriggled on elbows and knees into the doorway, the gun held awkwardly in both hands. Just in case. The bowman was halfway up the stairs by now. An Indian of some sort, though definitely not native American. He watched her with piercing black eyes, and he had not reloaded another arrow.

"What do you want?" April scarcely recognized her own voice. So harsh, so taut, so feral.

"A man named Tony Mendoza," he said. "And his green powder."

She slumped against the floor, energy rapidly scuttling. She lowered the gun. Began to feel very ill at the prospect of having crawled so close to this fresh corpse, corpse of her own making.

Justin sat up behind her. Touched her.

And April knew that within some fifteen seconds, the rules of this game had warped *way* out of shape.

PART III

RITUALS

18

CYPRESS

The night felt like a throwback to the more prodigious days of Justin's former drug use. While he had at least managed to keep a clean nose since Apocalips, he was now having trouble assimilating the whole of reality all at once. At least he'd had a reason in the old days. Not a particularly good one, but a reason nonetheless.

Take them one at a time.

First off, he had goofed. Tony Mendoza had exercised some effort, no doubt, and found him after all. Not surprising, with hindsight. He hadn't exactly crawled into a hole and pulled it in after him.

Next, a dead man was sandwiched between the inner and outer doors. Deceased all of fifteen minutes. Justin had wiped the blood up, had packed the guy's wounds with dish towels and stretchy shipping tape so he wouldn't leak anymore, then retrieved the five spent shell casings. The body would have to be dealt with, the sooner the better, given this heat and humidity.

Probably the most disturbing, at least for the moment, he had nearly had his privates shot away. The bullet had skimmed a shallow trench along his inner thigh a mere inch below the famed family jewels. It probably needed a stitch or three, but that was a luxury they couldn't afford right now. A quick bandage had to suffice.

And now the weirdest, icing on the cake. Some neo-Stone Age guy—who smelled as if his last bath had been during the Carter administration—was claiming to have tracked Tony's green skullflush all the way from Venezuela. Following a vision of an eagle with broken wings. And who was now squatting in the kitchen floor while eating a kiwi. Too too much.

April was in the bathroom getting sick. He figured if he had been the one who'd done the shooting, he wouldn't have lasted all of fifteen minutes before having to clutch the porcelain himself.

Seated at the kitchen table, Justin looked at the two guns before him. Semiautomatic and revolver, the sole items a search of the body had yielded. He groaned. This was precisely the reason he'd not set one step further into the St. Louis trade. This was exactly the sort of thing he had wanted to avoid at all costs.

Now it had come knocking at the door claiming to be a pizza.

April appeared in the bathroom doorway, weak in the knees. "Do you want to call the police, or should I do it?"

He shook his head, tentatively. "Maybe we should leave them out of this."

"I just *killed* somebody! *I* pulled that trigger, and there's no way it was anything else but self-defense." She moved a few steps forward. "They can't ignore this and Tony anymore."

"They did a good job of ignoring Erik, didn't they? And acting like I was the guilty one." He held up a gun in each hand. "These aren't going to register back in Tony's name, I guarantee you that." He let them clunk to the tabletop. "There's still no proof he's done anything at all. Hell, he probably hired this guy to kill us just so he could distance himself from it."

April nodded. Wandered over to collapse into another chair. The Indian—Kerebawa, he had said his name was—looked at her. All told, he appeared the least shaken of them, and here he was the stranger in the strange land.

Justin held up a gun again, said to Kerebawa, "Do you know how to use one of these?"

The Indian smacked down the last of the fruit. "I never have before used one."

Justin looked at the bow, the machete. "You seem to do all right without." He slid the small revolver across the table to April. "You'd better keep this with you."

She looked as if he had asked her to pick up a snake. Not so gung-ho now that the heat of emergency had cooled. But she nodded.

Justin held the silenced semiautomatic, looked at it from various angles. A Beretta, according to the round emblem on the grip. He found the magazine release just behind the trigger guard, ejected the clip to count the remaining bullets. Ten. Plus one in the chamber made eleven. At least they weren't running on empty, in case something else happened tonight. He slid the clip back in.

"Do you need a firearm ID card in Florida to buy ammunition?"

"I don't know," April whispered. "How would I know?"

That question would keep. The dead man?

"I'll tell you what I *do* know," she said. "If we're not calling the police, we have to get rid of that body."

"That's what I was thinking."

"And not just drop him into the bay, like—like they did with Erik. He'd turn up. We've got to make him vanish. And then *we've* got to vanish." Her eyes narrowed with resolve. "If the body's found tonight, tomorrow, Tony'll hear about it. He'll figure out what happened, more or less. And plan accordingly. But. What's the most frustrating thing we could do to him?"

Justin smiled tightly. "Everybody disappears without a trace. You're playing mind games with him, huh?"

"That's part of it. But if he has no idea what's happened, that gives us time to figure things out. It buys us time to think."

Her words hung in the air with the humidity. *Time to think.* His mind needed *something* to aid along those lines. Thirst was raging in his throat, a longing to raid April's liquor cabinet and see what could be found to file down the sharp edges of his nerves. They whipped around inside like the frayed ends of cables snapping under too much strain. Anything would do right about now.

Kerebawa was regarding them both intently. No doubt he'd quickly gotten the idea that the two of them were virginal novices to such a situation. *If I were him, I think I'd pack up and leave us to bungle our way alone.*

Kerebawa began to frown. To shake his head. "No, no, no. You know this Mendoza, we must look for the green powder. That's why I come here. That's what I promised."

"Look, that may be tops on *your* list of things to do, but right now, she and I are a lot more concerned about staying alive. You should be too. You can't take it away from him if you're dead."

Kerebawa proudly thumped his chest. "I will kill him first."

"I hope you do." There, appeal to the Indian's apparently inbred machismo—maybe he would see it their way. "But this place isn't at all like your home. And you don't know a single thing about Mendoza."

This seemed to sink in. "Warriors must know their enemies," he mused, as if reminding himself.

Justin turned his attention to April. "You have anyplace in mind to hide the body?"

She folded her hands before her on the table. "Um, give me a minute."

"Yeah, well, don't be too long about it."

Her hands became fists, and they slammed down onto the table. "It's not like I've done this kind of thing before!"

Temptation got the better of Justin. The liquor cabinet beckoned. He found Jack Daniel's, half full. He didn't bother with a glass. Killers, whether by deed or conspiracy, drank straight from the bottle, didn't they? Sure they did. Direct pipeline to sanding down those nerves.

"Do you have to do that *now*?" April's voice, brittle.

He pulled the bottle from his mouth; caught a whiskey

dribble with his tongue. "You think your way, I'll think mine."

Her flaming eyes, righteous indignation. "It didn't help you think very clearly that night at Apocalips. If it weren't for that . . ."

The implied accusation was as caustic as bile. And irrefutable. "You want to blame me for this, fine. *Fine.* But I don't need you to remind me. You had your chance to cut me loose a week ago, and didn't want it."

They stared across the kitchen, a moment that could have swung either way. Finally she nodded.

"Yeah. You're right. And I still don't want it." A hesitant smile, but hearteningly genuine, and he relaxed. "Sorry."

Justin turned back to Kerebawa. "The powder. Do you know how much you're after?"

Kerebawa hunkered in thought for a moment, as if to find the best words to convey. "If used every day, maybe . . . three weeks' supply for Mabori-teri. It was hard to see how much they carried though."

Three weeks' supply for his village. Meaningless. "I'll tell you how much is around here, at least. Mendoza says he has six kilos."

Equally meaningless. Kerebawa only looked confused. North and south were at definite odds in terms of measurement standards. How to bridge the gap?

Justin started in on her cabinets again. There, next to the sugar and baking soda. He pulled from the shelf an unopened two-pound bag of Pillsbury flour. He tossed it to Kerebawa, who caught it deftly.

"One kilo is a little more than that. And Mendoza's got six."

Kerebawa inspected the package, reverently traced his finger along the image of the Dough Boy. Hefted its weight, then looked up with an air of satisfaction.

"I would say he maybe has it all, then."

At last, a minor breakthrough. Quickly followed by another, when April stood up.

"I think I know," she said, "where we can hide the body."

* * *

Trying to accomplish such a task in April's Fiero was more
than a nerve-wracking inconvenience. It was a logistical
nightmare.

The Fiero was Pontiac's total antithesis of a practical family
car. Two low-riding bucket seats was it. No back seat. The
interior was tight as a cockpit, and directly behind it was the
engine compartment. All except for the radiator, which rode
up front with the spare tire. The only trunk space to speak of
was sandwiched between the taillights and the engine, and it
didn't look much bigger than a rain gutter, even when emptied.

They wrapped the body inside a blanket, and she backed
the car to the bottom of her stairwell while Justin and Kerebawa lugged the body down. April kept watch, forever pacing, fidgeting with her hands. They stuffed the dead hitman
into the little trough of a trunk, bending arms and legs as if he
were some gigantic Gumby doll inside the blanket. His plia-
bility brought on another wave of the queasies. At last they
got him to fit, and slammed the trunk lid. The body was
already emitting a bouquet of unpleasant odors.

They got Kerebawa to stand guard at the door—just in case
of a second-wave attack—while they packed. Hurriedly, a
five-minute job. Justin threw a few changes of clothing and
toiletries into a nylon gym bag. He felt like a Russian peasant,
readying to flee before the German onslaught. With no way
to even leave behind the defiance of scorched earth.

He slowed only when he saw April standing dejectedly in
the midst of her office. A moment later, he realized that tears
brimmed her eyes.

"What is it?" Pointless question, instantly regretted.

She held her palms out toward the office. "I worked so hard
to make a go of this." Voice crackling. "It's not much, but it's
mine. And now—now I don't know if I'll see it again."

He let his bag slip to the floor, stepped forward to hold her.
It would have been the easiest thing in the world to tell her
sure, she'd see it all again, very soon. Promises without guar-
antees were always the easiest to make. He kept his mouth
shut.

They held tight for several moments, then broke the
clinch. April switched on her business answering machine,

said she could at least phone in to check her messages by remote, try to return calls that way. Keep the business from completely stagnating.

Very grim business, this hiding of bodies and going underground.

They grabbed their bags, closed and locked windows, turned out the lights. Locked the inner and outer doors. Down the stairs.

There was but one possible configuration for the three of them to fit in the car. April removed the moonroof and stowed it beside the spare tire under the hood. Then she got into the car first, straddling the console, one leg in Justin's lap as he drove, the other braced against the dash before Kerebawa. Luckily the transmission was automatic; a manual wouldn't have allowed this. Even though she was the smallest, the top of her head still peeked above the gap in the roof, along with the longbow and arrow shafts. Their bags they molded into the floorboard.

This was going to be a long trip. They'd just gotten used to Kerebawa's body odor upstairs. Now it was slapping them in the face all over again. Justin cranked down his window in a hurry. April did the passenger window.

Justin fired the ignition, let it idle. He leaned against the steering wheel, softly swore.

"What's wrong?" April asked.

"We need some way to weight that body down. We can't just have it floating out there."

Really thinking this through, weren't they? A real group of hardcase pros. Might as well cruise on down to Mendoza's place and turn themselves over. Eliminate the suspense.

"Concrete blocks or something," he muttered. "Do you know of any construction sites around here?"

April said she didn't. Figured. Wasn't as if Florida was the real-estate-development-boom capital of the country, oh no. A moment later, though, he sat up, toasted himself with the bottle of Jack snugged between his thighs. He really should pitch that, he knew it as surely as the glass chafed against the bandaged flesh wound. But couldn't yet bring himself to get rid of it.

Maybe Paula had been right all along. Maybe he really did need a reserved seat at AA.

Worry about it later. Those with brainstorms should be allowed an indulgence or two. He had April drop the transmission into drive, and they set off for Davis Island.

He still had Erik's duplicate apartment key, and when they let themselves in, the stuffiness hit them like a blanket. Too many days of direct sun and no ventilation.

Justin clicked on the light, and the three of them stood just inside the doorway. He didn't know how the place felt to April, but to him a world of difference had befallen it. Erik's belongings might still have filled it, but the apartment no longer reeked of him. Sometime between last Saturday, when they had gotten the news, and now, Erik's spirit had seeped away.

"He's really gone now," Justin whispered.

He turned to April, her sorrow tempered with fright. She nodded, nothing more than reflex. Then he looked at Kerebawa, who had no idea where they were, who had lived here, what had drawn Justin here in the first place. Kerebawa knew none of that. And yet looking into the man's black eyes, Justin sensed he understood anyway, on some fundamental level. Here was a place of sorrow.

Justin had never come face-to-face with so different a culture, not like this. The large wad of tobacco, the simple belongings, the bowl-shaped haircut, now unkempt. So much to ask of this strange man who had been deposited on their doorstep like some tribal guardian angel. So much to know before curiosity was satisfied . . .

When there was time. Present tense was more than demanding enough.

Justin walked to Erik's makeshift bookshelves along one wall. Glanced back at the Indian.

"Give me a hand here, okay?"

Kerebawa stood rooted to the spot. A brief flicker of confusion, and he looked at his own hands, then Justin.

Wrong phrase, he thought. *I better watch that.*

"Help me with this, I mean."

The two of them hefted the top strip of plywood, laden

with books, and set it aside. Freeing up the objects of interest: the heavy cinder blocks at either end. Justin hoisted one, Kerebawa the other.

"Get some clothes hangers out of his closet," he told April. "Three or four."

By the time they left the apartment, he was feeling in control again. The jitters were backing down in favor of cool intellect. Maybe they could pull this off after all.

The fit inside the Fiero suffered all the more. The blocks had to be stowed in the floorboard, one before each seat. Good thing they had all they needed, because there wasn't a spare parcel of room to be found.

Justin let April navigate his driving until they were heading north through the center of the city, from bottom to top, on Nebraska. Saturday-night traffic was heavy, but steadily thinned the farther north they drove. They rode in silence, brooding about escalations of disaster, no doubt, and now and again Justin glanced over to see Kerebawa staring transfixed as Tampa flashed past. It wasn't necessarily an awestruck demeanor—look at this great big world I'm missing. More like, look what they've done to their land.

They were well past the city limits when April had him veer left, where Nebraska simply became Highway 41. This they followed through flatland where small forests still flourished, towering pines that grew close to the road. Land that was dotted far and wide with amoeba-shaped lakes, and where the settled areas were fewer, farther between.

They were less than three miles shy of the Hillsborough County Line when April finally directed him off 41. West for nearly a mile, north a few hundred yards. She was telling him to double back east on something called Grandaddy Lane when he stopped the car. Just long enough to jump out and scoop a handful of mud from a ditch of free-standing water and smear it across the license plates. The place wasn't devoid of houses, by any means.

He killed the lights and drove by moonlight back along Grandaddy Lane. Slowing to a crawl, leaving its dead end for open ground. Ahead he could see the shimmering glimmer of moonlight on water, and beyond that, darkly hulking masses of trees, thickly grouped. A relatively small but serviceable cypress swamp.

"How do you know about this place?"

April was riding higher and straighter now, her head nearly all the way out of the moonroof. "See that house back there, with the lights still on?" She jabbed a thumb in its direction. "This guy that works at the *Tribune* rents it with another couple of roommates. Erik and I were out here for parties two or three times." She was still for several moments, then, "Better stop here."

They were drawing close to the water's edge, and he killed the engine. A sudden massive silence descended, unheard since he had come down here. A total nonexistence of all things urban. The houses behind them on Grandaddy Lane? The land merely tolerated them.

He could hear armies of crickets, platoons of frogs. Cicadas. All things wild and untamed. Mosquitoes wasted no time in zeroing in on exposed flesh; he had swatted two before he was four steps from the car. Over the swamp, humidity hung in a gauzy haze, fuzzy in the moonlight.

This seemed a fitting place to hide secrets of life and death.

April stretched her leg muscles, bracing against the car. She groaned. "I can't believe I rode the whole way like that without complaining."

He smiled at her. She seemed a lot more together about things than she had been back at the loft. Maybe all she'd needed was to get set into motion, clear of the place where they had come too close to knocking on Heaven's door.

"Stay here, okay?" she said. "I'll be gone a few minutes."

Before he could question, April took off, running toward the right as softly and gracefully as a deer. Swallowed by shadows before she drew even with the nearest houses behind them.

Justin looked at Kerebawa, who was now squatting comfortably on the ground. He felt as if he'd just been deserted by his best friend and left in charge of some newly met cousin from out of town. *Way* out of town, in this case. Couldn't very well ask him if he'd seen any good movies lately. Just how *did* you small-talk a rain-forest aborigine?

"So. Um." He grimaced. Off to a flying start. "So you found

us because you followed this . . . *vision*? This, um . . . eagle with broken wings?"

"Yes." Kerebawa rose and pulled his cloth roll from the car. Held it up a moment as if for inspection. "I brought a powder from home. We call it *ebene*. It shows to me things. Sometimes things that are important."

Sounded intriguing, if not entirely plausible. Of course, watching Trent Pollard and his floor show at Apocalips hadn't been high on the list of probabilities either.

"What is it, some kind of drug?"

"So *you* call it. To us, it is our way of life."

He nodded. Way of life, right. He'd known a lot of people to whom that phrase applied. "I've taken a lot of powders myself. Or at least, I used to. Never saw much of anything very useful with any of them."

Kerebawa cocked his head, glanced down at his roll. The briefest flicker of a smile. An I-know-something-you-don't smile. Justin found it irritatingly smug and was quickly amused by that.

"Maybe you did not have the right powders."

Justin scuffed at the ground. "Sometimes I looked pretty hard though."

Kerebawa peered at him, long, unflinchingly. It was a vaguely discomforting stare, the scrutiny of culture shock.

"The eagle," he said at last. "That was you."

Justin blinked dumbly. *"Me?"*

A simple nod. "Your *noreshi*. Your spirit animal. You have strength. You have high thoughts, like the eagle flies."

Justin swatted a mosquito, managed to beam with self-satisfied pride for a moment. Then he remembered: *Broken wings though.*

"But," Kerebawa went on, "you are crippled inside."

Lofty self-images plummeted in a deathly spiral. "Thank you, Mister Morale," he muttered. That was the bad thing about listening to someone who could see into you with the clarity of a sixth sense. Brutal honesty, providing you were equally honest with yourself, was often hard to refute.

"You have used the green powder that Tony Mendoza has."

Justin nodded. "Once. I didn't know what it was. He lied to me about it. But yeah, I took it."

"I can feel it about you. You, too, can see important things."

Justin thought it over several moments. Remembering the sole instance when he had transcended the mundane and concrete for pure spiritual dynamite. That flash-in-the-pan linkup with some girl he did not know, whose exquisite fear of the shape-shifting unknown was nevertheless tangible.

"I thought I did. Once."

Kerebawa nodded. "You could maybe see clearer if you were not crippled inside."

They waited without speaking for several more minutes before April returned. Justin was nearly ready to follow her path and look for her when he heard a delicate splishing of water. Soon after, she came into view.

Working both mounted oars of a small rowboat.

Justin and Kerebawa moved over to the shore as she let the boat glide to them, rustling through sawgrass until the prow connected with a gentle thump. She stood, wavered her balance, and then Justin helped her out.

"You're just one surprise after another." The admiration was a hundred percent genuine. "Where did this come from?"

"Some old man in one of those houses back there has a little dock. Erik and I went joyriding in this one night at one of those parties."

They backtracked to the car. And the grislier task at hand. Justin opened the trunk, and he and April stared down at the blanket-cloaked form for several beats. Serenaded by frogs and insects, to which death was an everyday fact of life, an everyday possibility, side-effect of the food chain. Somehow, when elevated to human terms, it often looked far uglier. There was no dignity in this, in being crammed inside a too-small trunk, still wearing the undies that had acted as a catcher's mitt for the last wastes your body would ever void.

Reality was doing far more than slapping them in the face. Reality was rubbing their noses in itself.

Justin nodded at Kerebawa, and the two of them lifted the body free. Carried it to the rowboat and stowed it in the center, where the blanket soaked up stagnant water puddled

in the bottom. Next they loaded the cinder blocks and hangers. April grabbed a small, flat plastic flashlight from the car's
console. Everything the expedition needed.

They boarded one at a time, pushed off. The rowboat rode
considerably lower in the water now. Have to be careful.
Justin didn't relish the idea of tipping it too far and sinking,
dropping in uninvited on a family of water moccasins.

April continued to do duty at the oars, slowly dipping them
in and straining them back. They glided away from shore and
aimed for the treeline, a soft shadow across the face of the
water. Forsaking twentieth-century civilization for a little
microcosm of a world still as primitive as it might have been
long before man had trodden the soil in his present form.

While Justin held the light, she weaved them between the
cypress, the flanged and fluted trunks tapering up and out of
the water to form a canopy overhead. Now and again, the
side of the boat would gently scrape against a cypress knee.
Ephemeral curtains of Spanish moss and spiderwebs brushed
his face, shoulders, and Justin shivered and pushed them
away. While all around, living things seemed to shift, to
scurry, unseen but heard.

"How deep is this water?" Justin asked.

"Oh, four to eight feet, I think they said once. In the spring
and summer at least, with the rains."

He nodded, feeling vaguely shameful, indecent acts under
the cover of darkness. April rowed them in until there was no
more light visible from Grandaddy Lane and they were utterly alone with primordial swamp and their own guilt.

"I suppose," she said slowly, "this is as good as anyplace."

The cypress rose like gray-brown legs around them, their
little floating oasis of light. The air was warm and clinging
with misty haze. Somewhere just within the range of Justin's
vision, he saw a flash of eyes and heard the splash as a rat
tumbled into the water.

He twisted the tops of the clothes hangers, counterclock-
wise, until they came undone and he was left with stout wire.
Shifting in the boat, he bound the corpse's ankles together
with one. Used another to securely lash the ankles to the first
of the concrete blocks. The second he figured he would wire
around the neck.

"I don't suppose you want to keep this blanket," he said, fingering the makeshift shroud.

April shook her head. She was hugging her arms around herself as if cold. "I never want to see that thing again."

He moved to the other end of the body, and the boat rocked precariously. Settled. He fumbled with the limp arms, and one flopped free to rap knuckles against the gunwale. He looked at the curled fingers. . . .

The ugly turquoise ring.

And hated himself a bit for the idea that crept into his mind. This ordeal had really pushed his mind and imagination—and temper—toward the sewer's edge. He pointed at the ring.

"Maybe we should keep a souvenir to let Tony know we came out on top of this one. When the time seems right."

April swallowed thickly. "Then you keep the ring. I don't want to see it anymore either."

He breathed deeply. "Anybody can lose only a ring."

She saw in his face what he meant instead. The realization spread across her face like the dawn of the darkest day.

"You can't—"

"I'm not the one that decided the stakes of this mess we're in. Mendoza did that. I just want to show him we mean to fight."

She turned her head away. "I can't watch this," she said, and a moment later, pressed her palms against her ears.

Mosquitos whined around his face, his heart thundered. Justin looked at Kerebawa, then the machete he had brought. Pointed.

"Can I borrow that?"

He nodded, offered it handle first. Held fast to the blade for a moment after Justin gripped the handle.

"Do you rather me do it?" Kerebawa said.

He considered it. But Kerebawa had saved their lives to begin with, fired the crucial arrow. April had finished the man off, then had gotten them out here. So easy to let others do the dirty work.

"My idea." Justin's throat was abruptly dry and harsh. "I'll do it."

Kerebawa relinquished the machete.

Clenching his jaw tightly, Justin maneuvered the second cinderblock into better position. Chopping block. He draped the corpse's forearm across the flat surface. Positioned it palm down, wrist straight. He passed the flashlight to Kerebawa. "Hold this."

It suddenly seemed very important that the blanket not pull free of the dead man's face. Didn't matter that he had come to kill them—Justin could not do this to someone with a face. He tucked the blanket tightly around the head.

Held the machete in both hands. Waited until it quit quivering.

No matter what it felt like, looked like, sounded like, he promised himself he would not get sick. *Would not.* Not for the entire duration of this whole Mendoza mess.

Justin took a bead on the stilled wrist. Practiced his swing a couple of times. Finally then, sucked in a deep breath and lifted the blade. Tensed his muscles.

And brought it down for real.

19
inside the
NORESHi

When he first awoke, Justin didn't know where he was. There came the heart-prickling attack of nerves, the confusion of an unfamiliar ceiling. Then he remembered. *Motel.* It all came back.

After their swamp excursion, they had driven back into Tampa. Crossed west to the airport and abandoned the tell-tale black Fiero in the long-term lot and rented a Dodge Aries. Very bland, the milk toast of cars. But with room aplenty for three humans and their sundry luggage. They then set off for north Tampa again, a refuge to hole up, after getting a cash advance from an automated teller machine to avoid signing in under genuine names. They settled into a quiet motel off Busch Boulevard, six-lane mecca of more motels and fast food, billboards and tourist traps. Busch Gardens was less than a mile east. Tony might very well think to look for them in this transient part of town, but barring miracles, had little hope of finding them.

Justin rubbed his eyes, found himself alone in bed. The low roar of the air conditioner was all he could hear. He sat up, saw Kerebawa on the floor, sleeping in a corner beneath a blanket. They had rented a two-bed double, but he apparently wanted nothing to do with the other. To each his own.

April was already up, seated at the round table near the curtained window. Sipping from a Styrofoam cup. Another sat capped on the table. Doughnuts too. Glazed.

"I found free coffee in the office." She tipped up the cup. "Want some?"

More acid on top of last night's Jack Daniel's deluge? No thanks. He shook his head. "Maybe just a doughnut."

"In that case you'll still want the coffee. It's the only way to soften them up."

He got out of bed, underwear only, and joined her at the tiny table. Kissed her, hugged her. She held him too long, too fervently, to pretend this was a typical good-morning greeting. The desperation seeped through. She was nailing up a good front though.

Justin realized she was wearing one of his shirts, untucked and rumpled over shorts. No bra. He'd always found it mysterious, this proclivity of women to wear their men's shirts in the morning. An instinct, perhaps, stemming from the male's tendency to shield himself from the female's penetration. If she can't get into his soul, then his shirt is the next best thing.

Coffee, doughnuts, and handguns. Just your average morning. She'd been right about the doughnuts. He got one down with the coffee's help, looked at the remaining one sitting on a napkin.

"Better save one for Bomba the Jungle Boy." He hitched his thumb toward the corner.

"Justin," she said, disapproving, "don't be a weenie."

He smiled. Oh, they were meant for one another, had to be. How many times had he seen the pairing, Mister Rude and Miss Manners? Yin and yang, one an antidote counterbalancing the other.

He pushed aside the curtain to peer outside. A scattering of cars in the parking lot; the Aries blended nicely. The day looked gray, dark, the sun hidden by swollen clouds. Be a nice cozy day, were the air not thick enough to wring water.

He let the curtain fall when he saw a maid's cart a couple of doors down.

"Is the do-not-disturb sign still out?"

April nodded. "I know better than that."

She scooted down in the chair, propped her feet in his lap. He absently massaged the soles, silently played This Little Piggie with her toes. Wondering how long DO NOT DISTURB would need to hang from the doorknob. They weren't about to willingly let a maid in to poke around.

At least, not while the ice bucket was in use. Packed in cubes from the ice machine was the severed hand. They were keeping it in the bathroom, beneath, appropriately enough, a hand towel.

He finished his coffee along with April, bilious sludge that it was. Decided it was worth it when he felt the caffeine kick in. He slipped into a pair of gym shorts to make himself half decent.

Kerebawa awoke soon after. He'd slept in his pants and appeared to suffer the same disorientation that had plagued Justin upon awakening; then the recognition, the remembering. At first, when the vulnerabilities of life and circumstances were stamped plainly across his face, Kerebawa showed little of the resolute fierceness he had periodically exhibited last night. He looked frightened. Worse, he looked sick. Overtired, underfed.

And all we've got to offer him is a stale doughnut.

Greetings were exchanged; grunted, really. And slowly the fire seemed to reignite in his eyes. He ate the doughnut without complaint, and April got him a glass of water from the bathroom.

"We need to talk," she finally said to Kerebawa. "More than we did last night."

Made a lot more sense than kicking back for Sunday-morning cartoons. So many questions. Last night's postshooting cleanup had hardly been the ideal time. And once they had arrived here at the motel, it was nearly four in the morning; they'd all been dead on their feet. Justin had managed to sleep soundly for the first time in quite a while.

"So far," April continued, "we don't understand any of this, why Tony Mendoza wanted us killed. Just that it probably has something to do with this new drug he's turned up with. Whatever *it* is." She was keeping her voice steady, cool, rock solid. "I shot someone last night. And I want to know *why.* And what you're doing all the way up here looking for the stuff."

Kerebawa turned away long enough to retrieve his grubby cloth roll and bring it back. He set it on their bed, sat beside it. He unrolled it, removed a smaller cloth roll. It might have been an ancient handkerchief, or bandanna. This he treated with special reverence, and opened it. Inside, cupped within a secondary layer formed from a leathery leaf, was a stash of powder. Green, familiar.

Kerebawa looked to Justin first.

"This is what I told you of last night. This is *ebene.*"

Justin stared, his hand tensed on April's foot. "And this is what Mendoza has?"

"No. Oh, no." He carefully rolled it back up to put it away, hands moving with the care one might see lavished on a religious icon. When his humble cache of belongings was intact, he appeared to grapple with words. Searching for precisely the right ones.

"Ebene . . . opens doors for us. As you would walk from this room to that"—his finger traced a path to the bathroom —"so *ebene* is for our spirits. We see a—a wider world when we use it. Sometimes it allows us to meet our *hekura.* Personal demons is what you would call them. Sometimes they come to live in our chests. The missionaries all hate *ebene.* Except for one, and he came even to use it himself."

For the next several minutes, Justin and April sat spellbound as he told them of the life and death of an American missionary named Angus Finnegan. Who eventually became far more like the Yanomamö than they became like him.

"Padre Angus came to believe the things about us that the other missionaries laughed at. Or hated and said were lies. He came to believe in the *noreshi.*" He touched Justin and April in turn on the arms, then himself. "You—and you—and me, we each have the *noreshi* inside. Our spirit animal. There are times when I must know something and I am not wise enough to see. With *ebene,* my spirit-hawk and I become one. The hawk is wiser and shows to me the answer."

Justin found himself nodding right along, neither swallowing every line nor disbelieving. Keeping that vital open mind. But this was certainly no more bizarre than the things he *knew* he had seen. Tame stuff, by comparison.

"But your people," he said, pointing to them both, "don't remember about the *noreshi*. They never knew. They have forgotten too much."

This Justin couldn't deny. When you have the memories of generations woven into your heritage, you know where you stand in the scheme of things. Solidly connected to past and future. Sometimes he felt so rootless. Bereft of an unshakable identity.

The eagle. That was you. Kerebawa's words from last night.

Memories of childhood, grade-school Justin. He had doodled a lot, at home and in class. Compelled to keep those little hands busy. He remembered that he had doodled scores of eagles. Legions of them, in flight or perched majestically atop rocky crags. At least to his burgeoning imagination they had looked majestic. He had done some little science project on eagles, magazine pictures cut and pasted into a folder, text carefully hand lettered.

He'd not thought of that fascination for years. Maybe he hadn't forgotten the *noreshi* completely. Maybe he *had* known in some intuitive way. As a child, who seems to accept the hidden relationships between living things as natural, far more readily than adults.

Maybe you drink to remember. April, on Davis Island.

Perhaps she had slammed the truth right on its head. He hoped. It would mean that his life wasn't quite as pointless as he sometimes feared. That he wasn't as rootless as he thought.

"But even when the *noreshi* is forgotten," Kerebawa went on, "it still is there, deep inside. Buried. The other green powder . . ."

"It digs it out."

Justin and April looked at each other. Now they were getting down to the real dirty business.

"At home, the shamans of Iyakei-teri cultivated a new kind of *ebene* with their magic. But it was so different, it was not really *ebene* at all. It came to be known as *hekura-teri* —

village of demons. It made them very fierce and feared, for they had a weapon none of the other villages possessed. Like before I was born, when men first were given shotguns."

Justin frowned. "I'm missing something. What's the difference between *ebene* and the other stuff?"

"It does much more. It takes one back to the days of the first men, before there were such gulfs between men and animals. When there was understanding between both, and spirits freely walked."

Justin's imagination swam with images. Trent gone jaguar. A she-wolf, captive, frightened. Human, animal. The gap bridged.

"Some *hekura*—some jungle demons—hunger to eat the souls of men. The new powder allows them to do that for a time, to come inside and eat the *noreshi*. *Hekura* long to turn men against themselves, so they use the form of a man's spirit animal against him. They can make a good man evil, and an evil man worse." Kerebawa looked at them gravely. *"Ebene* shows to you the demons. *Hekura-teri* allows you to become one."*

The rains came later that morning, and Kerebawa walked beneath them. Trees stood behind the motel, a few sad, stunted palms. He longed to feel the water on his body, the air, the natural cool brought by the rains instead of the artificial cool of the room.

It had been good, finally, to sleep around others once more. Even if the surroundings were completely foreign to what he was used to. Good to feel a part of a tribe, if only a tribe of three.

For he trusted them, these two back in the room. He could smell no deceit about them, no treachery other than that born of their own desperate situation.

He felt pangs of cold sadness for Justin, so lost in this world. Kerebawa too was lost in his own way, but at least he knew where he belonged. Not so with Justin. For a time, though, he had seemed on the verge of remembering forgotten relics of his past. The idea of the *noreshi* had not fallen on deaf ears.

Perhaps he was descended from the Yanomamö after all. Kerebawa recalled the legends from the aeons-distant time of the first beings. There had come a devastating flood in those days, during which many Yanomamö drowned. Some escaped by climbing mountains. Others, though, cut down trees and floated on them to save their lives. They floated away to other lands and became foreigners, and their language changed into unintelligible gibberish. Kerebawa thought it likely that Noah, of Angus's Bible, was one of these.

In the same way, perhaps Justin was descended from one who had floated away. And was unsettled, forever trying to remember Yanomamö roots. Perhaps when there was time, he might help Justin remember.

The woman, April, seemed surer of herself and who she was. Kerebawa had never known a female like her. He'd seen plenty, from his previous trip north with Angus, and along this journey, but he had never come to be around one. So unlike the women of home. She spoke her thoughts, she challenged. At first, last night, Kerebawa had wondered if this boldness didn't anger Justin, if he would hit her to keep her down.

In a way, Kerebawa secretly envied Justin for living in a land where he need not feel compelled to beat his woman. Kerebawa tried not to hit his own wife very often, and never very hard, and took no pleasure in it. But it had to be done, it was expected. It was their way. There was no respect for the man who laid no hands upon his wife, only scorn.

He tipped his face to the rain, let it wash down. Refreshing. Not as tasty as the rains of home though. More bitter, sour.

He wondered where this journey would finally end. From Mabori-teri to Esmerelda, then on to Miami. Only to learn that he would have to continue on to this new land, called Tampa. For a time, it had been a bit like home, as he traveled the roads across the northern reaches of what the map called the Everglades.

The Glades had given him time to think of home, to wonder what life among the Yanomamö would be like if there were roads linking the villages as there were here. How easier the trade would be, and intervillage feasting, and warfare. Given the state of things here, as much as he understood of them, perhaps it was just as well the Yanomamö had no such things as roads.

Which did not mean the jungle remained pristine. Every year it shrank. Literally. The outer world encroaching on their inner one. While the governments of Brazil and Venezuela, as he learned while growing into manhood, made provisions for the natives they displaced, claiming to know what was best. How sad—men who knew nothing of their lives, nor even how many centuries the tribes had lived there, deciding their fates.

A few times, while on the fringes of the Everglades, Kerebawa would stop and watch the horrifying tools of progress wreak havoc upon the land. Monstrous yellow machines, with huge wheels or metal belts upon which they traveled. Scooping out earth, pushing down trees, filling in waterlogged marsh. Stripping the world so that they could plant more buildings, and more, and more. Until the world was as tame as a dog on a rope.

He left the cover of the palms and wandered along the side of the motel toward the front. Rain had plastered his hair to his head. He pushed it off his forehead. Wished he could find some razor grass so he might give it a trimming.

Venezuela. Brazil. America. Perhaps the diseases that got into men's minds and made them unhappy with the way the world grew knew no boundaries. Maybe it infected them no matter where they lived.

And as he looked up and down Busch Boulevard, Kerebawa decided that he was sadly right.

Sunday afternoon was verging on evening, and all three of them were crowded about the round windowside table. The dinner hour; April and Justin had ventured out for a few minutes for food. Chicken, garden salads, and milk for one and all. Kerebawa especially looked to need a well-balanced meal.

The rain had become a soft, ambient patter on the overhanging walkway outside, counterpoint to the TV playing at low volume. Syndicated and local stuff. Kerebawa turned his eye in its direction now and again, half fascinated, half wary. April found his expressions oddly endearing.

"We haven't accomplished much since this morning," she

said. "A lot of talk, but we *have* to settle on something pretty soon. We can't just sit here."

She looked at Justin, and he nodded, almost guiltily. Nerves maybe, inertia born of dread. That hesitancy to make the first move for fear it might be a wrong one.

"Are you scared?" she asked him softly.

He smiled faintly down toward his food. Glanced up. "I guess."

"Me too."

"Fear is not wrong," said Kerebawa. "So long as it does not eat you."

April probed thoughtfully at her salad. "My dad once told me something I've always tried to live by. He said that if you really want to accomplish something, the surest way to do it is take as many risks as you can. Not stupid ones, but calculated risks. It hasn't always worked out for the best—believe me, Justin, we both know that—but I've always tried to live and work that way. I believe in it." A sip of milk. "I'm all for taking some risks."

"Good," Justin said with a decisive nod. It made her feel better. Periodic doubts had wormed inside her since last night. Was he going to have the backbone to stand firm during this? Or was he, while still wobbly from the blows in St. Louis, going to crumble? Had it looked to definitely be the latter, April still wasn't sure how she'd have reacted. Stay or go, not a frivolous decision.

"Let's look at our strengths here." Justin pointed to Kerebawa. "You're a warrior. And you know what we're up against, as far as the drug goes." Then to April and himself. "You know what *we* do best?"

"I draw, you write ads." She rolled her eyes. "Now *that's* pretty intimidating."

He adamantly shook his head. "No. Wrong. Those are just our tools. Between us, you and I have spent probably fifteen years getting inside people's heads to push the right buttons. Make them buy something, or go somewhere, or think a certain way. We're manipulators. This doesn't have to be much different, just the stakes are higher."

She paused in midbite. Intriguing way of looking at themselves.

"Can we fight Tony head-on? No. Can we outgun him? No. But we can damn sure try to outthink him. And the more we can mess with his mind, the better for us."

So Justin's thoughts had been whirring all along. Slightly different direction was all. April regarded herself as a detail-oriented person. Born for commercial art—details, spatial relationships. Practicality. Justin manipulated words. Words were more ethereal, requiring a broader scope, a grasp of concepts. A plus, actually, that they were two sides of the same coin.

"We want different things, but we can get them the same way," Justin said. To Kerebawa: "You want the *hekura-teri.*" To April: "We want Mendoza off our backs." A wry smile, hands spread palms up. "We just have to make sure we do both at the same time."

Kerebawa nodded, eyes shining. Eager to get to the fight, it looked like. "If he was my enemy at home in Mabori-teri, I would attack him first, by surprise."

"I know where he lives." April prodded her last bits of chicken. "But attack how?"

"Break into his condo if we can." No hesitation.

"Enemy camps always can be crept into, if you're wise," said Kerebawa.

"Yeah, but *why*?" Definite unease at the prospect of carrying the fight past Tony's front door. "Not just to show we can, I assume."

Justin drained his milk, crumpled the little carton. "Look at things from Tony's perspective. He's got six kilos of skullflush, *hekura-teri*, call it what you will. He'd be a moron to keep selling it after what happened at Apocalips. But if he's as greedy as any of the distributors I've ever met, he can't bring himself to dump it. He probably can't trust anybody else to store it, because then they might dip into it. So what does that leave?"

April grinned. "Sit on it and pray?"

"And hating every minute of it. You want a calculated risk, there you go." He toasted her with his flattened milk carton.

"He could catch us." There, play the devil's advocate.

"Not if we're smart."

"It's a pretty crowded area, where he lives. It's not like he lives in a cabin in the woods. Somebody else might catch us."

"Maybe. But what if they don't? And what if that stuff's there? We've got some definite leverage on him then." Justin turned to Kerebawa. "What would your people do?"

"Watch and learn"—the answer was instantaneous—"until he would show us his weakness."

Justin nodded, parted the window curtain. Pointed out at the narrow slice of sky, unadulterated by Busch Boulevard glitz.

"There's one weakness, right there," he said. "The guy seems to do most of his outside work at night."

20
dOMESTICATION

Tony loved spy movies. From the fantasy James Bond epics to the real-world scenarios like *Falcon and the Snowman.* He identified. Espionage and the drug trade were not all that different, not when it came down to basics.

You had your clandestine meetings. Your illicit exchanges. A healthy dose of paranoia, don't trust anybody more than absolutely necessary, and even then cover your backside. Above all, the crucial spark plug that kept things moving was communication.

The lack of which was currently giving him fits.

No word from the Weatherman. *Very* distressing.

He'd been looking forward to returning from the weekend down around Fort Myers and hearing good news. The weekend had been pleasant enough, if boring. Lots of pool time, beach time. Sasha had frolicked, reddening her pale skin, and the two of them had had a fun slip-and-slide session on their bed with a tube of aloe gel. Lupo had read most of the time, Sophocles' Theban plays, and had gotten halfway through *Antigone* before it was time to return to Tampa. But for the most part, Tony just sat around anticipating a return to good news. And tipping big so the staff would remember him in case an alibi was needed.

Monday evening now, and he hadn't heard shit.

Nothing in the paper about a double murder, or on the radio, or on TV. Or—and this was most infuriating of all—from the flunky he had hired to take care of things in the first place. This was not the way harmonious business relationships worked.

Tony sat shirtless on his balcony, overlooking the condo complex's courtyard and pool layout. A few people down below, swimming and sunning instead of being good little drones and heading in for the traditional dinner hour. A quartet of big table umbrellas looked like bright, psychedelically painted mushrooms.

He looked beyond the pool, seventy or so yards across to an opposing building. A couple of good little drones grilling on their balconies, guys in barbecue aprons, looking like they needed Chef Boyardee hats. Farther beyond, past a mud flat overgrown with thick underbrush, lapped the Old Bay. A zigzagging boardwalk had been built over the mudflat, running a gauntlet of dense foliage, and it led to a lonely gazebo perched above the water's edge. Sometimes he liked to meander out there, knowing full well that if somebody was out to kill him, it was a perfect spot to catch him alone. But somehow it always seemed so tranquil out there that death was denied admission. He could gaze out over the bay for hours, pretending the water was Bahamian or Jamaican, anything that seemed more exotic than reality. Someday, *someday*, he was going to be wealthy enough to buy his own island.

"Call, you fucker," he muttered to the wireless phone on the table beside him.

He sipped Evian water and watched the phone mock him. Its silence was nearly conspiratorial.

"Hey." A voice behind him. He looked around to see Sasha in the balcony doorway. "You look all stressed out."

Tony shrugged and turned away, heard the screen door slide open and shut. Felt her hands on the back of his neck, tops of his shoulders. She played with his unbound hair. It all felt wonderful. His eyes grew heavier as she lingered, ministering to the knotted muscles. The strength of her hands belied their small size. Jeez, where had she learned to give a rubdown like that?

"Want to talk about it?" she said. Minutes later, must have been.

"You don't need to know. Hell, I've let you see too much already."

"Oh, come on." Rubbing, rubbing. Bribery of the flesh. "Might make you feel better."

"Who do you think you are, a wife or something?" He smiled; it had not come out unkindly. "This is all I need to feel better."

Rubbing, rubbing. Magic hands. He floated, transcendent.

"I never want to be a wife," Sasha said after a while. Almost absently. Regretfully? Maybe so. "All the wives I've ever known all get this same look to them. Like they're trapped animals, and they can't get loose."

"Was your mom like that?" And why was he asking, anyway?

"Yeah, she was." Sasha's hands began to falter, rhythms became choppier. "I had a Barbie Fun House when I was little, can you believe that?"

He laughed. Had this fleeting image of a child in black, poking tiny safety pins through Barbie's underdeveloped nipples.

"Then when Dad left, I burned it. 'Cause it was all just a lie. All of it." She was finding her rhythms again. "I think I'd rather be a mistress all my life. Mistresses seem so much better appreciated." She planted a kiss on his back, between shoulder blades. "Do you appreciate me?"

"Sure." Tony searched his soul for the truth. Assurances were always easy to give. Saying the right words, easy. Did he mean it? Figured he must, to some degree. He at least cared enough to spare her hurt feelings.

Wasn't *that* a kick in the head?

"You don't have to love me," she finally said. "Don't even

have to try." The back rub was over; she eased into the white chair beside him. "I think it's a figment of the imagination, anyway."

He was enjoying this, decided to join in the game. Two could play the cynic as easily as one. "Love is just what you think you feel right before you come. You get over it quick enough."

Tony remembered growing up, the example set by his own parents. Remembered hearing them and their noisy bed-room sessions while he was trying to fall asleep. All the kids did. An apartment that small, you couldn't help it. Their old man was as brutal as a Nazi guard with Mama. Doted like a fool on the kids, then turned around and beat Mama blue half the time. He could still hear his old man gasping how he loved her, bedsprings squeaking through the tissue-thin wall, and then there would be a grunt or two, and then the sound of open-handed slaps. Tony had learned at a very early age how to distinguish passion from pain, and how few the dis-tinctions were for some people.

So he and Sasha kicked the notions around awhile, the death of love and its nonexistence to begin with. Just a case of mistaken identity. They spoke of the balance of cosmic equa-tions: Women got multiple orgasms, if they were lucky; men got backrubs.

Then she asked when she could have more skullflush. After all, he had promised. Tony told her soon, soon. All-purpose answer. Although now, as never before, he understood her deep-rooted desire to immerse herself in that green world once again.

He was feeling the urge to do it himself.

Not tonight though. Tonight he felt like accomplishing something, and if it couldn't be done, then at least he would know he hadn't been sitting around all evening on his thumb.

"Feel like playing a little hide-and-seek tonight?" he asked.

Sasha's eyes sparkled. "Anytime."

He grabbed the wireless and began to phone in reinforce-ments.

Tony called in four guys whom he frequently used for dirty work that required a certain amount of discretion. The more legs, the less time it would take to do legwork. The hired help divided into two teams of two, while he and Lupo and Sasha made the third.

And they searched. Divided up the club scene and prowled anyplace Tony knew April had ever frequented. Not that he expected anyone to find them living footloose and fancy free, but maybe someone would get lucky. Run into someone who knew her or the both of them, same as he'd lucked into learning that Justin was staying with her to begin with. The clubs were all checked thoroughly, and her friends that he knew of were divided among the three teams, addresses looked up so their homes could be scouted.

Tony had Lupo make their own first stop April's apartment. Looked buttoned up and secured, blinds drawn. No sign of her car, mail stuffing the box. Across the alley, they spotted the Weatherman's rental car. A search of its interior turned up nothing more than the set of keys, tucked beneath the seat, along with the motel key. Tony pocketed them. Send one of the flunkies back later for the car, take it back to the agency.

So what did *this* mean, the Weatherman's rental turning up sitting idle? Maybe he'd spooked them, and they ran while he had to give chase some other way.

They took in his motel, and Lupo found some blatantly out-of-town couple inside the room. He called the desk from a pay phone, asked about its weekend occupant, and they didn't know diddly beyond some deadbeat running out on his bill. Shit. Bastard had absconded with $7,500 in front money, maybe. Either that, or some wetback maid had waltzed home with a hell of a tip.

As the evening wore on, Tony's mood grew darker. Periodically his four flunkies would stop at a booth and call in on the Lincoln's cellular. Always with no news he wanted to hear. He had them broaden the search parameters. Maybe they were lying low. He put them to work going down the Yellow Pages, calling motels to ask if anyone was registered under the name of Kingston or Gray.

Keep those eyes peeled. Lupo had his MAC-10, and Tony dearly hoped the big guy would get a chance to use it. Just one glimpse, that's all he wanted of them, it would be enough to lock him onto them for good. *Just one glimpse,* he thought.

Not once considering the possibility that *he* might be the one who was being watched.

21
TURNABOUT

Thank God April had been to a housewarming soirée at Tony's condo a few years ago and had a good memory. Otherwise, Justin reasoned, they might have forever lacked any way to bring the fight to his own doorstep.

Ever since leaving the motel Sunday evening, they had lived to keep an eye on his home, his car. The complex was designed in a healthy sprawl; parking lots, while small, were plentiful. They parked catty-corner across the courtyard and swimming pool and settled in for an uneventful night.

Early Monday they went shopping. Probably the safest time, assuming Tony slept late to compensate for his night-owl hours. April figured somebody should still stay behind to maintain the vigil, and Kerebawa was happy to leave the confines of the car for nearby brush and trees.

Justin and April drove to a large sporting-goods store. The MasterCards were really getting the workout lately. They bought two boxes of bullets, in both nine-millimeter and .32

caliber; no firearm ID required by Florida law, just be twenty-one or older. They also bought a pair of walkie-talkies, good for up to a mile of separation. A thermal jug to keep cool water handy. A small battery-operated fan to keep air circulating in the car once the day really started to heat up. A pair of binoculars. And a present for Kerebawa: a fistful of hunting arrows. He still had three bamboo shafts, but the supply of tips in his quiver was down to two. Those, and a few other odds and ends of convenience, and they drove back to the Westshore Boulevard condos.

When Kerebawa saw the arrows, he laughed. Genuinely amused. Justin couldn't figure it. Heavy dark steel tips, four wicked barbs. Show them to any smart deer, and the thing would probably strap itself to the front of the car just to avoid the additional anguish.

"These tiny things, these are what your hunters use for arrows?" Kerebawa laughed. Held one of his six-foot bamboo shafts, more than twice the length of the new ones. *"Those* are like the toys the children of Mabori-teri use to shoot lizards!" He burst into another fit of healthy laughter.

"Lizards? *Lizards?"* Justin cried. "You could bring down a grizzly bear with one of those!"

The rest of the day passed as uneventfully as the previous night. Though people came and went from the building they were parked beside, no one seemed to pay them any attention. Live and let live; they were bothering nothing.

It was late afternoon before they saw Tony, wandering onto his balcony and sitting shirtless. Top balcony, directly above the three others below it. He looked like some petty dictator overseeing his domain. He had been out fifteen minutes before he was joined by a heretofore unseen blond girl. The two of them looked friendly enough.

"You know her?" Justin passed the binoculars to April.

She stared for several moments, passed them back. "No, I don't think so."

Justin peered more intently, trying to get a sense of the girl. Sometimes he could pick up vibes. A process he had developed as an adman, trying to get into someone's head to see what motivated them. Pick an individual, target them as a typical consumer of some good or service. A worthwhile exercise. Before he had slit the throat of his career, his creative director had been impressed by it.

"What do you think they're talking about?" April tapped the water jug to wet a cloth and dab it across her face. Sweat gleamed.

"Don't know," he murmured. Wasn't easy, trying to suck in vibes through binoculars with nearly a couple hundred yards in between.

He watched. She seemed wistfully sad, someone not very joyous over life as it was but still not clear on what she wanted it to be. He knew the type. Had been that type himself, once upon a time, before settling for the path of success, one more yuppie cranked into permanent acquisition mode. Something about her seemed hazily familiar.

And then it came to him.

"I'll be damned," he mouthed to himself.

He'd never know for sure, not this way, but he would have been willing to lay down cash bets that this was the girl whose eyes he had seen through last week, in a dream that was not a dream. Exactly *why* was slippery to pinpoint. The flash of recognition was like the glimpse of an aura, a nagging question finally answered by the subconscious. Her eyes had grown sensitized to things beyond the rational, as had his; they had, in a way, grown sensitized together. She exuded it, like her melancholy, in vibes in sympathetic resonance with his own. And here she was, like a serving maiden at Tony's side. He shook his head, lowered the binoculars. Couldn't she *see?* Open her eyes?

He'll chew you up and spit you out someday, Justin thought.

Afternoon became evening. Kerebawa was dozing, and April looked ready to do likewise when the most movement they had seen all day began to transpire.

"Heads up," he said, and they all snapped to.

All three were leaving Tony's condo. *Hi ho, hi ho,* Justin thought. *Off to work they go.* Once in the Lincoln, Lupo drove them away.

"We'd better stay put for a while, still," said April.

Justin nodded. "Yeah. Watch them come back in ten minutes with pizzas."

Nightfall came an hour later, without the Lincoln returning. Justin had Kerebawa trek up to knock on Tony's door to make sure that some unseen fourth person wasn't still inside. If someone answered, Kerebawa would simply jabber in his native tongue and kowtow an apologetic retreat. Luckily, he came back to report no answer.

This, however, wasn't even half the headache remedy. When Justin checked the door himself, it looked and felt *very* solid. He was no lock-picker. Could try shooting the locks away, but he didn't much care for that. Even with the silencer, he didn't like leaving blatant signs of his presence visible from the outside. Another two condos were accessed along this open fourth-floor walkway. Hard to predict how long the search would take. One stray flashlight beam from a neighbor was all that would be needed to blow everything; if a shot-up door was noticed, Justin doubted it would be ignored.

So . . .

The balcony? It was the only other alternative. The balconies were aligned in a vertical row. Nothing so handy as a fire ladder clinging down the sides, but it didn't look to be too difficult. They were spaced closely enough that, standing on the ground-floor patio's railing, the climber could reach up to the second floor balcony and pull on up, and so on.

"So who goes?" April asked, once he was back at the car.

Justin looked at Kerebawa. "With some of the things you told us you've had to do, you're definitely the best climber we have."

Kerebawa nodded, then frowned. "But you both know much more of homes like his than do I."

"He's got a point." April looked at them, one to another. "You could both go, while I keep an eye on things down here."

"Okay by me," Justin said. Then, to Kerebawa, "You're probably a lot better fighter than I am, too, if it comes to that. And if something goes wrong, it'll probably happen up there, not down here."

"That's another problem." April, ever the realist. "What about security alarms, something like that? He might have the place wired."

"With the police? He wouldn't be that crazy."

She shook her head. "No. But what about a private security firm? Especially one that's not above looking the other way for some of its shadier customers."

Justin sighed, leaned back against the seat back. Kerebawa regarded him with irritation, as if he were weakening. Maybe he was. The cons of this maneuver suddenly seemed far weightier than the pros. Take, for example—

"The lights," he said. The final straw. "Look at all these damned lights, anyway."

Sodium globe lamps lined various walks and the pool area. More light bled from the condos themselves, balcony doors and bedroom windows. Try to scale that wall up to Tony's, and he and Kerebawa would be picked out by a spotlight like escaping convicts halfway to freedom.

"Is there a switch to turn them off?" Kerebawa asked. Completely serious.

"Get real," Justin said.

"Maybe he's got the right idea," April said.

"How's that?"

"It's kind of drastic."

"At this point, I can live with drastic."

"Maybe"—she was biting her lip, uncertain—"maybe we could knock out a power transformer? We've got a silenced gun, you know."

Wipe out electrical service to the whole complex? Drastic indeed. But nothing would be remotely as effective. Besides taking care of the lights, it would also deactivate any electrical alarms Tony might have rigged to his balcony door.

They wheeled back out to Westshore; traffic was light. Justin headed south, an arbitrary decision. They kept their eyes skyward, both sides of the road, scanning the rows of power poles and their lifelines of cables. They were all the way down near a neighboring apartment complex before spotting one.

"Got to be one closer than this," Justin said, and reversed direction.

They found the likely target about fifty yards north of the turn-in for Tony's complex, hanging on to the pole like a huge gray capsule. He cruised past it, continued north until they could stop for a moment in the parking lot of a 7-Eleven. Had to decide who got the honors. Kerebawa, with no firearm experience, was out of the question. Justin pulled the Beretta from beneath the front seat.

"How much shooting have *you* done?" he asked April.

"Besides a couple nights ago?"

"Yeah."

"I've played Nintendo games. How about you?"

"Few times at a pistol range with a client. He was a real gung-ho NRA type."

April patted him on the thigh. "You're elected." She craned her neck, gazed back down Westshore. "A drive-by shooting?"

He nodded, and they played musical chairs. April slid behind the wheel, Kerebawa rode shotgun. Justin had her slide the seat forward, scrunching their legs, but it gave him more room to lie on his back in the rear floorboard. Not very comfortable, but with luck, this would not take long.

"If there's no traffic, stop alongside the transformer. I'm not good enough to manage this on the roll," Justin said.

He felt the thump as they left the lot for the boulevard. In the floor, every little vibration felt magnified tenfold. Through the open passenger window, Justin watched his slice of skyline traveling past, nothing visible to link it with any landmark. Just the domino row of utility poles, the tops of trees.

He drew his knees together so their curve formed a notch, then steadied his wrist into it. Held the pistol at the ready.

"Almost there," April said. He could barely see the back of her head from this angle. "Wait! Car coming."

They had to make two more passes before it was clear. The Aries braked, sat idling. His slice of skyline froze like a section of a mural.

"Do it," she said.

Knees locked rigid, gun steadied. He brought its sights squarely onto the middle of the transformer. Squeezed the trigger. The gun coughed and bucked in his hand, the ejection port spat a hot shell casing onto the back seat. He squeezed again, again, again, again, swiveling his wrist minutely to cover as much area as possible. The transformer erupted into Fourth of July sparks, streamers of smoke, agitated sizzling. All at once, darkness fell beside them like a partial eclipse.

"Oh, beautiful," April said, and the car started to roll again. "That whole place just went out like a candle."

He raised himself up to peer out. In the beginning was darkness, and it was good. April drove to the south apartment complex again to wait a bit before returning. Hoping that nobody was noticing this same car, however bland, rolling back and forth, back and forth. Justin was getting the necessities together when April ran them back to the condos, now sitting in inky gloom. Even the moon seemed on their side, a mere crescent sliver showing. Their headlights seemed unnaturally bright as she drove them to a different lot from the one they'd used all day. No sense pushing their luck, wearing out their welcome.

Justin took the Beretta and tucked it into his waistband, its safety on. It felt too loose for climbing, so he taped the butt to his bare stomach with a roll of masking tape bought earlier. On the other side of his waistband he clipped a walkie-talkie. The flashlight used two nights ago in the cypress swamp he thrust into a back pocket. Kerebawa did likewise with a second flashlight bought this morning. Justin fit the roll of tape over his wrist like a bracelet. Then he retrieved from a cooler of melted ice in the trunk a surprise package—a plastic sandwich bag. He looked at it a moment, then handed it to Kerebawa.

"Would you mind carrying this?"

He did not, and secured it inside his shirt.

They returned to the car for a few moments, sat there loaded and ready to go, waiting, waiting. Justin's heart and stomach felt quite hollow. He swallowed, and it sounded too loud.

"If the *hekura-teri* is found, this will solve my problem," Kerebawa said softly. "Do you know what would solve yours?"

Neither Justin nor April said anything. Just watched him, waiting for the answer.

"If we waited in his home for his return and killed him at once." A simple solution, even more simply put.

Justin caught April's gaze, held it. Impossible to read her. "It's something to think about, Justin," she finally said.

His eyes slid closed, deliberations of life and death, of morality under fire. Under the circumstances, did morality even matter anymore? He liked to think it did, somewhere deep within. That winning the game was important, but not much more than how it was played. Cold-blooded assassination? He wasn't ready for that.

"I'm sorry." His voice low, measured. "I can't do it. Not like that." He looked at Kerebawa. "And I wouldn't want anybody else doing it for me."

Was April's sigh of relief real or imagined?

"You may be sorry later," said Kerebawa.

Justin nodded. Already sorry. He leaned over the front seat and gave April a quick hug, and she ran a hand along his face. Told them both to be careful. And then they were out their respective doors. Walking briskly, amiably, across the lot and then the courtyard. Just a couple of happy condo owners, out for a stroll the night the lights went out. Justin could hear scattered voices, sometimes see vague moving shadows. From the pool came continued splashing, very feminine giggling. Oh, what acts we perform under cover of darkness.

"Padre Angus taught to me a thing to say at times like this."

Justin glanced over to Kerebawa. "What was it?"

Kerebawa appeared to concentrate, get the words just right. "You watch my back, I watch yours."

They first circled Tony's building instead of walking directly to the row of balconies. Approaching close up on the far side and creeping around the foundation. When they reached the bottom patio, Justin tested the railing. Sturdy. He took a deep breath, checked once more to make sure no one was nearby and watching. The point of no return beckoned.

"I go first?" Kerebawa said, and scarcely waited for Justin's agreeable nod before clambering onto the railing. He secured both feet, then rose. Reached overhead to latch onto the second floor and pushed off with his feet. Kerebawa swung a leg up and caught the edge, and a moment later, the rest of him followed.

"Easy," Kerebawa whispered, waving for Justin to follow.

Justin steadied himself against the outer wall before mounting the patio railing. After holding fast to the second floor, he heaved, hoed, dangled. Kerebawa caught his flailing leg behind the knee and helped him get secured, and that made the rest of the trip easier. Silence, however best he could manage, was primary. Grace was optional. Alongside Kerebawa, finally, he nodded. Wiped sweat.

"Easy," he whispered in echo.

They were just rising on the second-floor railing when, scant feet away, a sliding door unlatched. Justin's every pore seemed to flood, and then the door was opening, and there came the distinctive sound of a champagne bottle popping open, a man and a woman coming outside to enjoy the blackout. Justin and Kerebawa performed arm-straining chin-ups, hauled themselves up quicker than he thought possible. Adrenaline. They clung to the railing, squatting on the edge of the balcony directly over the couple while Justin caught his breath. His heart was in a thunder, and from below sounded the crystal chime of two glasses clinking.

After a couple of minutes, Kerebawa touched Justin's shoulder, pointed up. Justin nodded. Higher, then. The sweat rolled, and his body felt like one giant greased hinge. After a few more silent strains and struggles, they crouched in the midst of Tony's white patio furniture. Justin ran a hand over himself to make sure he'd not lost anything on the trip up. Things may have been twisted around, but they were all there, present, accounted for.

They duck walked directly before the patio door, and Kerebawa tried its handle. Wouldn't budge, just as expected. Kerebawa then rapped his fingertips against the thick plate glass.

"This will cause much noise," he said in earnest concern.

"Don't worry," Justin said. He freed his flashlight, cupped his hand over the end, splayed a couple of fingers until a pencil-thin beam of light shined through. He inspected the glass, the curtain on its other side. Along the glass perimeter ran a thin metallic tape strip. Wired for alarms, just as April had feared.

Justin flicked off the light, and as Kerebawa watched, he slipped the roll of masking tape off his wrist and began to peel strips away. He gridded off an area a foot square beside the door handle, filled it in until the entire portion of glass was taped over. Then he reached beneath his shirt and freed the Beretta. Winced. The tape he'd used to secure it pulled out more than its share of fine hairs. He reversed his hold on it, wrapping his hand around the barrel. He cocked his arm as if holding a hammer, then smacked the pistol grip into the taped glass.

It gave with a muffled crack, buckled inward. He followed with two more, and the section of glass peeled inward, the tape preventing an unnerving and telltale shatter. He pushed it down to the floor, then reached in to unlock the door.

Kerebawa grinned in admiration. "You know ways of treachery too. You may yet be Yanomamö inside."

Justin smiled, feeling an odd sort of warmth. Part of the club. Such compliments surely weren't handed out copiously by those of his homeland. All this for a trick learned in the movies.

When they were inside and the curtain rearranged, Justin brought up the walkie-talkie and whipped out the aerial and flipped the unit on. Thumbed the transmit key.

"We're in," he said.

"That's a relief," April's voice crackled back. "I've been eating my fingernails down here."

"Anything that looks remotely like Tony's car coming back, you sing right out and pick us up at the turnoff onto West-shore."

Justin clipped the unit back to his waistband and left the channel open. A steady pulse of static hissed, and he went for the flashlight again, its beam a welcome ally. Had to be careful where he shined it, keep it from being visible from the outside. He was about to tell Kerebawa to be careful with his own when he discounted that. With the entire complex under blackout, candles and flashlights were going to be the norm for a while.

"What about this?" Kerebawa held the sandwich bag from inside his shirt.

Justin pointed to a coffee table. Deal with it later.

"Come on, let's see how this place is laid out," he then said.

They moved from one end of the condo to the other, Justin sketching a mental map as they walked the darkened hallways and rooms. Kitchen, dining room and bar, living room. Central corridor for bedrooms, baths, closets. The furniture, for the most part, looked glossy and modern. Very slick, very chic. Tony didn't lack for living in style, this was certain.

In one corner of the living room, he found a full bookcase. Lots of classics and arcane modern stuff. Probably Lupo's; earlier, April had mentioned he had a reading list not to be believed. One shelf held a pair of interesting bookends, wedge-shaped blocks of clear Lucite. Embedded inside one was a scorpion; in the other, a tarantula. Charming.

"Let's each take a room to start with," Justin said. "Just look anywhere there's a space big enough to keep a kilo."

Kerebawa disappeared into one of the bedrooms, and Justin could hear him rummaging here, poking there. Justin shined his flashlight on the closed hallway doors, decided instead to start on the closets. He pilfered a linen closet, then one for coats. Midway down the corridor he opened another and found a wall of pitch dark. A room, no windows whatsoever. He shined in the flashlight.

He was momentarily taken aback by the unexpected. Aquariums, nothing but aquariums, and a lounger sitting in the middle of the room. The place resembled some sort of isolation chamber, soothing blues and whites, and all that water. All the more eerie because of its utter silence. No electricity to run motors, pumps, filters.

He entered with the same reverence normally reserved for a chapel. Shined his light from tank to tank, quick flashing glimpses of brilliant color, red and white and blue and black and yellow. They were lovely, and he found it difficult to reconcile the Tony Mendoza he was familiar with to the one who had built this oasis of tranquillity.

On and on, around the room. He stopped when the light fell upon one particular tank that just kept going.

He dropped to his knees. Felt himself tremble.

A dozen piranha, gliding about with the unhurried demeanor of conscienceless killers. The bottom of the tank, the gravel and larger rocks, was littered with tiny bones, tiny fragments of bones. Little rodent skulls, hairless and skinless and lying there with their teeth exposed, teeth that looked ridiculous and puny in contrast with those in the jaws swimming above them.

"Oh, Erik," he whispered, and only when he heard the quavers in his voice did he realize he was in the first throes of crying.

He didn't know how long he had knelt before the tank. Only came to realize that, sometime, Kerebawa had entered and was kneeling behind him. A gentle hand on his shoulder.

"You are troubled inside." Half statement, half question.

Justin nodded. Turned, teary eyed, and nodded more fervently. "Erik, my best friend—this is how they killed him."

Kerebawa rubbed the shoulder, a curiously comforting gesture. His eyes spoke reams, volumes, of understanding the pain of violent loss. Something that transcended culture, time, place. One of the last true universal givens known to man. All men bled the same.

"We must finish the search," said Kerebawa. "The dead hunger for vengeance too."

Justin let his eyes slide closed as he turned away and leaned his forehead against the tank. Inches away, the fish watched him.

"And they'll have it," he whispered. "They'll have it."

They began to move through the condo with a renewed resolve. They searched closets and bureau drawers, under beds and between mattresses. Looked inside covered pots and pans in the kitchen, inspected Tupperware containers and wax-paper-wrapped bundles in the freezer. They ran their hands behind sofa and chair cushions in the living room. Anything that looked as if it might possibly have sufficient space to form a stash, they either looked inside or probed with their hands.

But continually came up with one big zero.

Time had lost meaning. They could have been there an hour or six. Only when Justin was nearing a furious realization that he might have been wrong did he wander back into the aquarium room. As he sank wearily into the soft embrace of the leather recliner, Kerebawa squatted in the floor, idly toying with a butcher knife taken from the kitchen. Maybe he felt more secure with a weapon.

Think, think. Justin massaged his temples; they were flirt-
ing with a headache. He made fists, ground them against the
armrests.

"Would there be someplace not looked in?" Kerebawa
asked.

"I don't know, I don't know," Justin murmured. He looked
at their surroundings, following the light's beam. "He's got to
keep it in here. Got to. It makes a twisted kind of sense."

There, try climbing inside Tony's head for a change. Try
the crafty machismo on for size. Sure, he'd keep the skullflush
in here. As if his pets would guard it.

"In Mabori-teri, we say sometimes the best place to hide
from an enemy is in front of his eyes."

Justin nodded. *In front of our eyes, so where does that put
it?* Wrapped and submerged in the rocks of one or more
tanks? He played his light over them. Doubtful, he decided.
He couldn't see Tony, with a setup like this, risking a rupture
that might poison his fish. Besides, the gravel didn't look deep
enough for kilos.

In front of our eyes—*the recliner?*

Justin hopped out of his seat, borrowed the knife from
Kerebawa. To hell with secrecy. He sliced through the back
of the chair—maybe the stuff was packed inside. But when
the leather back hung in tatters, it revealed only empty
space.

Justin sagged into the floor, leaned against the chair. The
only thing preventing him from conceding defeat was the
look Kerebawa had given him earlier when he was ready to
call off the break-in. He tipped his head back over the arm-
rest so that he was staring up toward the ceiling. He shined
his light overhead, across the white acoustic tile. And
stopped, wondering.

Acoustic tile. False ceiling. Meaning the real, structural
ceiling was hidden, a gap of at least a foot between the two.

Justin scrambled to his feet, tested the sturdiness of the
recliner's armrests. A bit wobbly. He had Kerebawa hold
them steady as he climbed aboard and pushed the section of
tile directly overhead out of its frame. He aimed his light into
the space.

And discovered that pay dirt was green.

He tossed the individually wrapped packages to the floor, five in all. *Only five.* He swept his light all across the false ceiling and found only dust balls. He replaced the tile, then hopped down.

"Where is the sixth?" Kerebawa asked. "There were to be six."

"I don't know. Not there. Maybe Tony's got it someplace else. With him, maybe." Justin gestured impatiently. "Come on, let's find something to carry these out in."

They took the kilos into the kitchen, where Justin rummaged through the pantry and found a cache of grocery sacks. He unfolded one; some supermarket's name and logo were emblazoned across it. And with the skullflush inside, it looked and felt as innocent as if it contained nothing more than a few bags of flour. Getting ready for a marathon baking stint. They could walk right through Tony's front door and waltz downstairs, and no one would think a thing about it.

Justin looked at the sack with a decisively satisfied nod. *"Now* things get personal," he said, and moved for the main hall.

"We go now," said Kerebawa. He stepped forward, far enough to snag Justin's elbow. Urgently. "Justin, we *go* now."

Justin whirled, batted the clinging hand away. For a brief moment, Kerebawa's eyes ignited. There was no other term for it. Burning with the quick temper and hostility that were a part of his birthright, his people. His legacy. An imposing sight, unless you were past the point of caring.

"You got what you wanted out of this." Justin kept his voice low. Unflinching. "Now it's my turn."

"Only fools stay in an enemy village after the work is done."

"It's *not* done, that's the problem. As long as we've been here, a few more minutes won't matter." Justin let that sink in before hitting him with the truly irrefutable argument of his own words. "Remember, the dead hunger for vengeance too."

Kerebawa appeared to resign himself to carrying out the wishes of the dead. Something he was surely no stranger to. And as Justin returned to the aquariums, he put his partner in crime and survival out of mind. Justin was on personal terms now and wanted no help. He was the one who had decreed the need for mind games with Tony.

And there was no better place than here. His refuge. Sanctuary.

From the doorway, Justin shined his light onto the huge piranha tank. At a distance, they looked so innocuous. Then he recalled the condition Erik had been found in. The prosthetic and glove needed for his funereal visitation. He remembered the mound of grave dirt in Ohio. The quiet slumber for the sleeper, in that quiet earth.

Some things just seemed destined to come full circle.

Justin drew the Beretta. Flicked off the safety, sighted in on the tank. Began to squeeze.

And lowered it. No. Not this way. This was too distant, too clean. Pulling a trigger was too easy. He put the gun away and, from the living room, brought back one of the hefty Lucite bookends, the one with the scorpion. Denizen of the desert. The justice factor seemed very poetic. Desert was about to meet deluge.

Kerebawa helped only by holding the flashlights, and this was all he wanted. Justin hefted the bookend in both hands. Gave a pair of practice heaves from the doorway, like a shot-putter before a track meet.

And with a pleasure bordering on the obscene, he let it fly.

The side of the tank staved in with a liquid crunch, and it was as if a dam had burst. Freshwater and foam erupted in torrential violence, gushing across the floor in a wave that reached from wall to wall and even out into the hallway. Justin stepped aside just before it slapped the hallway wall, soaking into the carpet and sloshing halfway up to the ceiling. He laughed. He laughed, and it felt wonderfully invigorating. Nothing he could have done tonight would have felt half as good.

On the hallway carpet flopped a lone piranha, silver with swirls of red-orange around its lower jaw and gills. First-place winner for distance. He took his light from Kerebawa and entered the room, found most of the other fish splashing feebly in water insufficient to cover them. They made low grunting noises in concert, and fascinated, he listened to this eerie cadence of their impending deaths.

Two fish were still in the tank, below its new, drastically lowered waterline. Easy enough to fix. He splashed onward and kicked the massive hole even larger, bringing about a secondary gusher. With it tumbled the two stragglers.

Hell with soggy shoes, he didn't care. All he wanted to do was keep free of snapping jaws, and this wasn't too difficult. He smiled again. The devastation, in just moments' time, was enormous.

Justin squished past Kerebawa, back to the living room, where he retrieved the sandwich bag from the coffee table. Its time had come. Where to leave the contents though? He settled on the kitchen. Inside the refrigerator he found a pitcher of lemonade. Perfect. Guaranteed to kill someone's thirst for a good long time. Once emptied, he pitched the bag in the trash.

While he was in the kitchen, inspiration struck. He gathered cutlery and steak knives until he had collected an even dozen. Then back to Tony's private Sea World.

Kerebawa watched with impassive approval as Justin squatted beside the piranha that had made it all the way to the hall.

"This will bring great fury to Tony Mendoza," he said.

Justin grinned, cold and humorless. "That's the idea."

With that, he gazed down at the piranha. Its tail beat at the soggy carpet; its gills flexed, useless in the air. Gasping its life away. Justin selected a knife, held the point over the thickest part of the fish's middle. And punched through its body.

One by one, he followed suit with the rest, until all twelve were twitching on their own individual blades. He gathered them around Tony's recliner, crippled throne in the center of a waterlogged palace.

Finally, time for the coup de grace.

Justin pinned the first fish to the leather backrest. And the second. And the rest. Not haphazardly, but with symmetry, with precision. Weaving them into a grand design that Tony could not help but perceive. With screaming futility. Justin smiled.

And then stood back to admire his handiwork.

22
MUTILATIONS

The first indication that things were wrong came even before Tony and Lupo and Sasha made it up to the fourth level. His downstairs neighbor had been watching for him. And wasted no time charging out in a thigh-length bathrobe to howl and bitch about water leakage draining into his ceiling.

They left his complaints behind, and Lupo had his MAC-10 drawn and ready to fire as soon as Tony opened the door.

The entire atmosphere felt different. Violated, raped. By that time, the ruined transformer had been taken care of and full power had been restored. They knew nothing of the earlier blackout as Tony hit the lights.

As soon as he saw the sodden carpet, he went running for the aquarium room. When he splashed inside, Tony felt the heavy hand of tragedy as never before. It turned knees to jelly, took stomach and heart with them.

His pride, his joy—*demolished*.

And then he saw the recliner.

His warbling cry of despair brought Lupo in at a run from checking the rest of the penthouse. And all three of them stood in the water, staring. Just staring. It took an extraordinarily pissed-off person to go to all this trouble.

"I don't care what it takes," he said, trying *so hard* to keep his voice from degenerating into a sob, "but I'm gonna kill them myself. I'm gonna tear out their fucking hearts and eat them raw."

He went on and on, and they let him rage, and finally Lupo looked overhead. Tony sputtered into silence and followed his gaze.

"They didn't," he whispered. Blind hope.

"Have to check."

Tony took an automatic step toward the recliner, then stopped. No. Couldn't use it as a stepladder now, not now. It would be too much like wallowing atop a fresh grave.

"Give me a boost."

Lupo wrapped thick arms around his waist and heaved him upward. Tony lifted an acoustic tile, then let it fall back with a strangled cry. When Lupo eased him back to the floor, Tony took two wobbly steps to one side before his knees gave out. Too much grief, too much rage, too much shock. Systems were close to overload. If he had Justin Gray and April Kingston before him now, he knew with complete certainty that he could take them apart with his bare hands.

He sat in the floor like a dejected child, water soaking into his slacks and shirt. Ran a hand through his hair, and water trickled down both sides of his face. He looked up only when Sasha moved toward him with splashing footsteps.

"Get the fuck out of here!" he shouted, and she flinched. "This doesn't concern you, so just get the fuck out of my sight!" She splashed back to the hallway without a word.

Tony uttered a mortal groan. "They took it, man. Every bit of it."

"There's still most of that kilo hidden in the Lincoln."

A singular weak ray of sunshine through this darkest of clouds. "That's right, I—I forgot."

Nearly one kilo left, a gift of fate. He would kill them, oh yes. And knew precisely what form he would take when doing it. One more look at the chair convinced him there was no alternative.

He looked up to seek solace in Lupo's eyes when a scream the equal of his own rang out from the kitchen. Followed by the shattering and splash of what sounded like a pitcher. Full, naturally. Why not, why didn't they just open up the faucets and flood the whole penthouse?

He wearily flipped his hand toward Lupo, toward the door. Sasha was out there somewhere gagging with revulsion.

"Go see what's wrong *now*."

Tony hung his head in his hands. What had happened here, and to life in general? Control was spinning out of his grasp. This night had gone from bad to worse to absolute balls-to-the-wall nightmare. *In my home,* he thought numbly. *They've been in my home!*

He looked around at the other aquariums, undisturbed, and their intact beauty offered shallow comfort. Any one of them would have been painful to lose, but at least tolerable. But *this?* He felt as if he had lost family.

Justin, April—dead. In the most hideous ways he could dream up. He would draw out their agonies for hours and hours and—

Lupo was standing in the doorway. His face was even graver than it had been moments before.

"Well?" Tony said. "What was it?"

Then he saw what Lupo held.

Pale, waxy white, as if all the blood had drained away some time ago. It didn't even look real. Looked like some gag gift you'd buy in a novelty shop and stick inside another kid's lunchbox. Except for the ugly turquoise ring. Only one guy around with enough *huevos* to wear that thing and not care how it looked.

"At least now we know," said Lupo. He threw it down in disgust. The severed hand splatted to the floor and lay there like a dead spider, fingers slightly curled inward. Tony saw the jagged shank of bone protruding through the wrist, and wondered if he might possibly have sadly underestimated Justin and April.

"We'll have to take care of this ourselves now, Tony. Get your head on straight, and we'll take care of this ourselves."

"I wouldn't have it any other way," Tony whispered.

And took one more look at the chair.

It took one sick imagination to do that. Such malevolent glee. Twelve beautiful fish, killed, arranged into a circle, a crescent, and the last two by themselves.

A perfectly rendered smiley face.

She tossed, she turned. Knowing that nothing so simple as a change of positions was going to help. Tonight, for April, sleep was likely to fall under the category of luxury.

Justin slept beside her, apparently soundly. Ironic, his sleeping better these past few nights than he had in quite some time. As if his self-esteem and sense of peace with himself had finally returned under fire.

She loved him; this she knew without question. And therein lay the paradox. He was, in fits and starts, rising to challenges. Yet April had to admit her initial attraction had been, in part, in response to his vulnerability. His teetering balance with pinwheeling arms, near the brink of ruin. Florence Nightingale to the rescue. Only Florence had done some teetering herself.

It had all started with the hands. . . .

April sighed; shouldn't have yelled at Justin quite so virulently in the car. On the ride back to the motel, he had filled her in on everything that had transpired while he and Kerebawa were in the condo. Destroying the aquarium, turning the piranha into a twisted game of Pin the Tail on the Donkey. A nice touch, and it would definitely peel a few layers away from Tony's already questionable sanity. But she had spared few adjectives in telling him just how blindly stupid he'd been in destroying evidence that could link Tony with Erik's death, should the police ever decide to move on him.

As well, Justin had told her of leaving the hired killer's hand in a pitcher, a move Kerebawa especially seemed to enjoy. He told them of some drug lord in Colombia whom he had cornered and whose hand he had amputated when the man went for a weapon. The two of them had laughed over it, some deep-seated bond forming between them that had as its foundation blood and bone and destruction. Savagery for its own psychologically devastating sake. She knew it was absolutely essential in having to fight someone of Tony's ilk, but as Justin and Kerebawa laughed at his story, she had never felt quite so excluded from an inside joke. At that moment, there existed no cultural differences whatsoever between Justin and Kerebawa. Which, brotherhood-of-man rhetoric aside, she found a bit unsettling. It made you wonder if, when the niceties of civilization were scraped away, men were just as primal now as they had been at the dawn of hominids and the opposable thumb.

Another hand-oriented reference. Freudian, no doubt. She was glad to have at least gotten rid of that.

She'd nailed up a good front of nonchalance about it most of the time, just as she could when dealing with someone in the business world she could barely tolerate. But Justin would never know the unease it had caused her. Half out of irrational fear that somehow its owner's purpose would remain a driving force. That she would awaken to find that it had crabwalked across the room and clamped itself around her throat to finish the job begun Saturday night.

The killer's hand. And Erik's, too, she had to admit. It had all begun to mentally fester once they had learned of Erik's fate.

She thought of sitting with Justin a couple nights ago, before their world had convulsed, as she was showing him the photo albums. It had been years since she had rearranged them, removing every photo shot since she was six that showed her father's left hand.

What was left of it, anyway.

The day was etched into memory with vitriolic intensity. Cut into her brain, and the particular fissure would probably be labeled.

Six years old. Summer, home from school all day back in St. Pete and second grade seemed farther away than the stars. Hot all day, like it was getting to be now.

Daddy had been on vacation too, using up one of his two weeks per annum while he puttered around the house doing Dad-things. Stuff that, to six-year-old minds, seemed to serve little purpose. He was turning the carport into a garage, walling it in.

Perfect summer day. She ran amok in the neighborhood,

barefoot in the grass, neat little houses on a neat little street, and no matter where she went, she could hear the sounds of Daddy hammering. Daddy sawing. Daddy ripping boards down to proper size.

April had been in the backyard when a kid from across the street wandered over in the adjacent yard. Patrick, his name was. Patrick used the neighbor's yard as a shortcut to get to some friend who lived the next block over. He was six, maybe seven.

"What are you doing?" he had asked.

"Planting food."

April had some kernels of corn and a buckeye and was digging a small hole behind the bougainvillaea. Patrick watched as she finished the hole and planted them in a row and covered them up. She wondered when they would start growing.

They talked about what they were going to be when they grew up. She was going to be a farmer. Patrick said he was going to be a doctor. Somehow this inspired a discussion of bodies. She no longer remembered the words, only that Patrick had a lot of mistaken ideas about female anatomy. He thought girls peed just like boys, thought they looked the same down below and everything. Not that she knew what boys looked like *down there*, but whatever he was describing didn't sound much like what she had.

So they made a deal.

I'll show you mine if you show me yours. Sounded good. It would clear up a lot of questions. She had always wondered how Daddy could manage to pee standing up without making a mess.

Shorts were lowered. Underwear too. They looked. They touched. Okay, so there were a few differences. Big deal.

And then Mommy was peering over the bougainvillaea, forever on the lookout for new damage done by her tomboy daughter and drawn out to hunt because of a missing shovel. Her eyes widened. Her mouth started to shriek. April and Patrick looked up, raised their underwear and shorts, faces embossed with sudden guilt.

Mommy stormed around the bush and seized a kid in each hand, fingers clamping onto an ear on each head. Screeching about how awful they had been, touching each other's bodies there, *there* of all places, and April was crying because it hurt, her ear would be ripped from her head, and Mommy was dragging them back around front, their six-year-old feet struggling furiously to keep pace because Mommy's legs were so much longer and so were her strides.

The three of them stormed noisily into the carport, now half garage. Sawdust lingered in the air, and she breathed in its hot, dry smell and coughed, tears streaking her cheeks. Daddy had to stop work, looking like some hot, red, wet version of the father she was used to, and as he listened to what Mommy had to say he got even hotter and redder. They sent Patrick bawling across the street with the threat that they would be calling his parents later—oh, the kiss of death.

Daddy was angry but kept his temper from getting the best of him, just kept telling her, "April, I'm disappointed in you, I'm very disappointed in you." His words were lead, huge, crushing her down down down, his disappointment even worse than the three light swats he administered to her bottom. And as she stumbled into a corner, sobbing, she felt overwhelmed by a terrifying witches' brew of love and hate in her heart.

Daddy began to work again.

The gratingly noisy table saw whirred to life once more.

And there came the splintering whine of wood being cleaved in two by its blade.

And then Daddy suddenly lurched away from the table saw with a numb look on his face and his hand *his hand* it couldn't be running like a red faucet couldn't be bleeding that much *couldn't be in two pieces not that no!*

Mommy came running, aid and comfort and emergency medical care, hurriedly wrapping a rag around Daddy's spouting hand as his face paled and drained, and now Mommy's was the red face as she whirled upon her daughter cowering in the corner and shouted, "This is your fault this is all your fault, you distracted him, it's *your fault, April!*"

Through the tears, inside the shrieks, the six-year-old April knew it was true, all horribly true.

Barring her brief stint working for and with Tony Mendoza, it was without doubt the worst incident of her life. But not without positive repercussions, strangely enough. It hadn't really come up until college, when she'd ended up at Student Health Services with a near-terminal case of exhaustion, no small thanks due to a twenty-credit-hour semester. She had consented to a few sessions with a psych counselor, was rewarded with the usual analytical flow chart of cause-and-effect. A relentless desire to succeed because she was forever trying to make that day up to her father. No price too great to avoid his disappointment. Her counselor had even gone so far as to suggest that April made sure to choose pursuits where the results were tangible. Grades could be checked on a semester report. Artwork could be looked at, displayed. Ad infinitum.

She hadn't gone back after that day. Fearful of making too much progress, maybe. She was used to success, lived with it comfortably. The so-called cure might very well undercut the drive.

And what would they think now, her parents? Just how proud and beaming would they be if they knew darling daughter was slumming in the drug milieu, in addition to her erstwhile pornvid feature? Shootings, burglarizing dealers, corpse concealment, while her hard-won business risked suffocation via inattention. She steered her imagination away from it. So. They must never know, *ever,* whatever the cost.

Your fault, April. She could hear it now as easily as when she was six. And now, twenty-some years later, curled onto the bed of a cheap motel beside someone she thought was probably as damaged inside as she, April still couldn't convince herself that it wasn't.

23
pRioRiTies

Come Tuesday morning, it was April's turn to go to the office for the motel's version of a free continental breakfast. More bad coffee, more tough doughnuts. As Justin ate, he thought of the Viet Cong in Nam, squatting in the jungle while eating rice and fish heads. No-frills food to toughen you up. Survive the coffee and doughnuts, and their abuse to kidneys and jaw muscles, and the rest of the day seemed more palatable. *Eating to Win, Part Two.*

The adrenaline boost of last night's strikeback had carried over to this morning. His system still surged, in spite of April's justifiably angry response to his destruction of the piranha tank. Her good morning kiss had been warm enough, so he'd apparently been forgiven. Buggering possible evidence, though, he couldn't much blame her being angry. Yet everything was a tradeoff. Tony was probably giving himself ulcers by now.

Too hotheaded, I was too reckless, he thought. *I've got to*

watch that. Because things were finally moving along, by
their hands this time.

Justin looked across the little round table at Kerebawa,
who was licking flakes of glaze from his fingers with loud,
smacking gusto.

"I've been meaning to ask you something for a couple of
days," Justin said. "How do you plan on getting home once all
this is over?"

Kerebawa glanced up from wet, sticky fingers. "I hoped I
would meet someone who would take me back to Miami-teri
and help me find the skymen. Barrows and Matteson."

"You've got that," said April. "You've earned all the rides
you need."

Justin tipped his cup, and the coffee was history. "It might
be better to take you down there right away. We've got most
of the *hekura-teri* now anyway."

"But not all." He was shaking his head, no no no, fiercely
stubborn. "I would never know about the rest."

All because of a promise to a dead man. This guy's sense of
honor and duty was something out of a medieval code.

"I will destroy the *hekura-teri* we took last night," Kerebawa went on. "I will destroy it this day. But I will not
return to home until I destroy the last."

Justin glanced sidelong at April. A sudden tightening of
both their mouths. *Trouble brewing* was the unspoken trans-
lation.

"Kerebawa," said April, her voice soft, placating, "we can't
destroy the powder. Not while Tony Mendoza is free."

He peered up from his fingers again. His whole face sharp-
ening. More trouble brewing.

"We might need it, either to try and get him in jail, or at
least to have some control over him."

Justin nodded. "Destroying the powder, that's like throwing away the biggest weapon we've got against him."

Kerebawa was back to shaking his head, even more fervently than before. "No! This was my promise to Padre
Angus, to find the *hekura-teri* and destroy it! It has no place in
your world. It has no place even in mine."

"But it *is* here, and we're in trouble because of it." April
the diplomat, unruffled and earnest. "If we need it to help

ourselves, and it's gone . . ." She held up her palms, implied defenselessness.

"Yeah, you're not the only one around here who's in a mess because of that stuff," Justin said. "Most of your problems are taken care of. Five out of six. But ours? We haven't managed to do much of *anything* about them." He paused, looking for some sign, however small, of Kerebawa's wavering. Like trying to read the thoughts of a brick wall. "Before we got up I was lying there awake, and I had this idea, how we might use the powder—"

"No. *No!*" Kerebawa rose from the table, legs widely stanced, hands curled into fists, knuckles braced against the tabletop. "You will need to find other ways."

With that, he moved swiftly away from the table along the side of the unused bed. Knelt on the floor long enough to pull out the kilos of skullflush still in the grocery bag. His eyes were chips of onyx, his jaw granite. Justin rose, moved for the bag, feeling oddly that this seemed as ridiculous as some petty playground squabble among fourth graders. Stay away from my toys, or else.

Two steps closer, and Kerebawa knelt to his pile of belongings.

And reared back up with his machete. Arm cocked, ready to swing.

Justin froze. *I don't believe this don't believe he's pulling that blade on me.* More disbelief than fear, on April's face as well as his own. Which doubled when Justin found himself reaching for the Beretta atop the dresser and holding it at Kerebawa's chest. At ten feet, there was little doubt of accuracy.

"Would you guys knock this *off*!" April shot to her feet, spoke sternly, but the unease was evident. Justin thought it probable that she knew he wouldn't fire. Kerebawa, though, was a less definitive story; less apt to bluff. More apt to be like the countless tales of canines, gentle as lambs for years, who suddenly tear into the family child for reasons known only to primal instinct.

Seconds ticked by, metronomed by the bleedthrough voices of a TV in another room, muffled through the walls. Five, ten . . . they seemed far longer with a gun in hand.

Finally Justin looked at it. Tossed it onto the bed, midway between himself and Kerebawa.

"You too," April said to the Indian. Then to both: "This macho chest-pounding isn't going to solve anything. Now put that machete *down*."

It didn't waver. Nor did his eyes.

"He's not going to use it." *Maybe in his own home he would, but not here. Not with us. Not with what he's learned over the years about our civilization.* At least, that was what Justin was betting on. He looked straight at Kerebawa. "We owe you our lives. We'd be dead if it weren't for you, we're not forgetting that. But you wouldn't have gotten back those five bags of *hekura-teri* if it hadn't been for us. We need each other."

Another several seconds. Sounded like a game show worming through the walls. At last, the blade was lowered. Tossed toward the bed to clank against gunmetal.

No apologies though. Neither in voice, nor in demeanor. Rather refreshing, in a way. No chance for anything phony.

"We can talk," Kerebawa said, and sat on the bed.

Justin took the floor, leaning back against the dresser. April returned to her seat at the table, like a mediator between the two. Justin frowned, composing his thoughts for a moment. Had to put everything in a context Kerebawa would best relate to.

"First off, I promise you—*promise* you—that we won't do anything with the *hekura-teri* that would risk getting it back to Mendoza. But this land is our home, and we need to defend it from him."

So far, so good. No recurring flashes of temper.

"You want the last kilo, we want Mendoza in jail. Jail is something your people don't have, so we have to do things a bit different here. Not that your way is wrong. It just won't always work to get you what you want in this land. Do you see that?"

A hesitant nod. Oh, he was on a roll here.

And then, inspiration. "Suppose your village is at war with another village twice as big as yours. For every one of your warriors, they have two. Now, suppose they have something you want to get back. You can't find out where it is, so you can't steal it. Would you charge right over and attack them?"

Kerebawa shook his head fiercely. "We would not be fools. We would first seek the help of allies. Another village who is their enemy too."

Justin smiled, relaxation washing him like spring rains. "That's all I think we should do."

That afternoon, Justin arrived at the meeting first. Not liking the way this was going already. Seemed that if things boded well for cooperation, there wouldn't have been any problem meeting at the police station.

April had driven him here and was staying behind in the car with Kerebawa, keeping watch. He was at some little patch of greenery called H.B. Plant Park, beside the University of Tampa. Its centerpiece was a bizarre metal sculpture growing out of tiered brick planters: a ring of seven tall, tapered steel spires, straight until the top ends hooked. They looked like a Stonehenge of giant dental picks.

Justin sat on a nearby bench beneath a Spanish moss–infested oak. Cooler under here, shady and lazy, the sky as blue as virgin summer should be.

Justin fingered the vial in his shirt pocket, a bulge he felt a touch of paranoia about. The vial had previously housed aspirin, apportioned into April's travel kit from an econo-drum of a thousand; no longer though. *Yes, I'm carrying drugs*, it seemed to shout. To passing students in shorts and T-shirts, to office workers from the nearby downtown towers, immersing themselves in a tiny oasis of nature while taking a late lunch. One glance and they would know it couldn't possibly be anything like allergy pills or Primatine Mist.

It was the only trace of last night's thievery left in easy reach. This morning, after convincing Kerebawa that the skullflush was best left intact and sharing his idea with Kerebawa and April, they had decided to hide the stuff. Justin bought a roll of aluminum foil and a ball of twine at a walking-distance convenience store.

Back in the room, he had repackaged the five kilos within the foil, rolling each into a longer, thinner shape. He tied the ends together with twine until they resembled metallic sausage links.

The stash was April's idea, born of intimate familiarity with her car. They ran a quick trip to the airport's long-term lot and her Fiero. While keeping a watch for security sweeps, they got into the Fiero's engine through the trunk, disconnected the air hose, whose opposite end sat just inside the intake port behind the driver's door. They fed the sausages in, one at a time, then reconnected the hose. A far better stash than the stereotypical spare tire. Justin had retained only enough for a sample.

He fingered the vial again. Eyes distracted by a co-ed in cutoffs until his reason for being here was almost upon him. Rene Espinoza, the only marginally tolerable aspect of his experience with Tampa homicide.

"I'm a little late," she said. "I'm sorry."

He nodded, waited until she took the other end of the bench. "Why the hell wouldn't you meet with me at the station? All I hear in the media from cops is how they need public cooperation. I'm trying to cooperate, and you don't even want me setting foot inside the door."

"I can't get into that, Justin. But I'm here. And I *will* listen to what you have to say, so don't start on me."

He'd been watching her face, her eyes. While with the agency in St. Louis, he'd often done that with clients. Sometimes they hedged. The maker of a new mouthwash fails to tell you that initial test sampling has found that a majority regard the product as tasty as mule piss. There were usually signs when someone was bugged over a situation they were keeping mum about.

And a couple of tics seemed to creep through Espinoza's facade.

He decided to begin with more comfortable territory. For her, anyway. For himself, the wounds were still nearly raw.

"Has—has anything turned up yet about Erik's death? Anything about Tony Mendoza?"

"He had an alibi for the night. It wasn't shaky." She reeled it off with all the ease of a prepared answer, as if the question had been anticipated. Very smooth.

Justin nodded, neither believing nor disbelieving. Only

knowing that unsubstantiated accusations of a lie or laziness on the police's part would be counterproductive.

"Do you have any pull with the narcotics department?" he asked.

"I know people. We don't work in a vacuum."

"Has anybody been talking about some new drug on the street, something called skullflush?"

Espinoza gave it a few moments of thought, then shook her head. He thought it wholly honest. "Doesn't ring a bell."

"Well, believe me, there is such an animal"—he winced inwardly at the unintentional pun—"and it's bad news. Mendoza brought it in, I guess. Only he's lost most of it, all but one kilo."

"How do you *know* this?"

"Because I took it away from him myself, five kilos."

It was always a perverse pleasure to reveal the unexpected, the look of surprise being its own reward. Then her large brown eyes narrowed again, all-seeing and every bit as watchful as his own.

"So in other words, now *you* could be busted for possession with intent to sell," she said. "You're on thin ice here. Your background isn't exactly squeaky clean in this area."

"Oh, please." He huffed in exasperation. "If I had any intention of dealing, do you think I'd call you up to brag about ripping off another dealer?"

"What I think doesn't mean a thing. I'm telling you how it looks."

Couldn't fault her there, he decided. Imagine the scrutiny of an outsider—a judge, say, or a prosecutor—looking at his past and present, should he and April trip up and be found with five kilos of a new drug. Not a rosy picture. Be that as it may, however . . .

"You didn't leave me with much choice. Mendoza wants me dead, and I didn't see much help from you. I'm just trying to keep afloat, is all." He realized he was, maybe unconsciously, referring solely to *me*, to *I*. No *us*, no *we*. Protecting the others, he supposed, by refusing to drag their names in without need. "Now, I know you're in homicide, that you don't represent the narcs. But you're the only one there I know who treated me civilly. So I'd like to bounce an idea off you, if I could."

She said nothing, simply nodded once. The palest of green lights.

"Suppose I try to work out a deal with Mendoza where I sell the five keys back to him. Whether or not he believes I'm stupid enough to think he'd actually cooperate is irrelevant. I'm pretty sure he'd go for it, just because his macho pride won't allow me to get away with ripping him off. He won't pay, he'll want to kill me. But if I'm there, he's there, and you people are there—you should have a good solid place to start digging away at him. He wouldn't be there alone, either, so maybe you could lean on one of his own people enough to divide and conquer, get somebody to implicate him in Erik's death."

She pondered things a moment, then shrugged. "It's not my decision, you know that." She frowned. "And skullflush. What is it exactly? Some new form of coke?"

"This is where it gets tricky. I brought a sample."

Justin two-fingered the vial from his shirt pocket, discreetly palmed it to her. Almost sleight-of-hand, it had come automatically. A move developed and honed to perfection in earlier days. Must be like riding a bicycle; once learned, never forgotten.

The vial was in her purse before she spared it a good look. A frown. "I've never seen anything like this before." She snapped the purse shut. "First, I'll have to get this analyzed and find out what you've got. There's no sense in planning anything else until that's done."

"And then?"

"We'll see."

Frustration at this lukewarm reception was reaching beyond tolerance levels. *We'll see.* It had been spoken in the same tone of voice every guy in Western civilization has heard from female lips. *I had a great time tonight; when can we go out again?* An uncomfortable pause, lasting geological aeons, then: *We'll see.* A noncommittal response with all the finality of a slamming door.

"What the hell *is* it with you?" His voice was finally rising. "This guy is trying to kill me. Maybe I'd have better luck talking to somebody else in the department, take my chances that way."

"No. You won't. I *guarantee* you that." Espinoza was getting a bit heated, as well. "Just stay out of our faces, Justin. You have no idea what all this involves, and if you step on the wrong toes, you *will* get bulldozed. That's a fact."

He let the light of realization dawn in his face. See if he could push the envelope a bit more, the master manipulator. "Are you people on Mendoza's payroll, is that it? Bought and paid for?"

The anger contained behind her face suddenly snapped. If she could've gotten away with punching him, he believed she'd have tried.

"You asshole, I already went to bat for you. I met you here because I can't risk being seen talking to you. So don't feed me *that* shit." She fumed and stewed for several moments. Finally, in her eyes, a conflict wearily laid halfway to rest. "You *do* deserve an explanation. And I wish I could give it, completely, but I can't. But. My . . . superiors . . . decided that moving against Mendoza at the present time could jeopardize another ongoing investigation. Which could break any day now, it's possible, so if you could just stay low until it's safer for us to move on Mendoza . . ."

He gazed at her, watching her mouth move, the sound seeming to come from increasingly farther away. Feeling his eyes blank out into stupid disbelief.

"You stonewalled us." His voice had dropped to a whisper. "You stonewalled me, and someone I love, because—because our lives weren't as *important*?" His voice, on the rise. "We weren't high up enough on the fucking *priority list*?"

"It wasn't a matter of priorities—"

"The hell it wasn't!" He leaned away from her, raised his arms in futility. Politics, everything was politics, from sex to career to happiness to life and death. "Damn you to hell."

"Why can't you just leave town?" she asked. "Mendoza's arms can't reach across the country."

Justin rose from the bench, thrust hands into pockets, and wandered a few steps away. All around, students and denizens of the business world whose lives he envied—their security, their relative simplicity. He'd gladly trade problems with any of them.

"Why don't we leave?" He laughed without humor. He felt broken, suddenly, disconnected, as if now discussing someone else. "I'm almost bankrupt. April? Her family's here. And everything she ever worked for and invested in, it's right here. She goes away, it falls apart." Justin shook his head, recalling the sight of her earlier today, taking care of business. Retrieving the messages from her answering machine. Making calls to clients, making excuses. Trying to hold it all together.

Justin turned back to Espinoza, finally. " 'To protect and serve.' What a crock."

She didn't blink, didn't even seem to breathe. "Whether you believe it or not, I *am* on your side. I just can't make you any promises." She patted her purse, the vial. "We've got this. And it's a start."

"Whoopee," he said flatly. But still clung to hope.

24
THE GREEN AND
DISTANT VOYAGE

"Come here," he said, and she came.

Sasha moved across the bedroom, a seductive wraith, smooth ivory skin strategically draped in black silk and lace. Blond hair wisping past her shoulders. Victory and hunger, blended until they were one, swimming in her eyes. She knew she had won.

Sasha stood at the foot of the waterbed, lingering as the material whispered down her sylphlike body to puddle at her feet. She kicked them free, and then was on the bed, naked, moving on hands and knees to where Tony sat against the headboard. Also naked.

She had won, yes, and taken him with her. Victory was not total though. Could it truly be surrender when you wanted to fall? He didn't know, didn't care. All that mattered was that he had come to stand on the brink, had looked over, and decided that jumping wasn't such a bad idea after all. Hand in hand.

Lovers' Leap.

Tony, smiling as Sasha crawled inch by inch along his legs to his lap, reached over to a tabletop for a flat, rectangular mirror. Chopped and paralleled across its surface, sixteen lines of fertile green. And two straws, as if they were a pair of carefree teenagers ready to share a malt in the fifties.

Grief had driven him to this, grief and thwarted rage. Today he had taken his deceased piranha and lovingly placed their punctured bodies in a plastic bag, then had taken them along the boardwalk to the edge of the bay. Alone, refusing Lupo's company, Sasha's comforts. He had leaped over one side of the gazebo to the mudflat below, landing with a squishy thud. He shed his shirt, the shark's tooth already glued to his chest with a film of sweat. And while the sun beat down, while the surf lapped yards away in a perpetual bid to reclaim all that had risen from its depths, Tony dropped to his knees and dug. With his hands. Until the grave was ready.

He had buried more than pets. He had buried brethren.

Only fitting, then, that he now honor them. In form if nothing else.

As well, he was fundamentally curious. What would happen if two of them took skullflush at the same time?

The Lincoln was equipped with a few custom-installed stashes, invisible to the eye and nearly impossible to blunder into unless you knew where to look. In one of these a kilo had remained since his initial test on Sasha nearly two weeks ago. He praised his reluctance to take it from the car and store it back with the rest as foresight bordering on sixth sense. Because, oh, the wonders he could wreak with this last of such a precious commodity, not the least of which would be figuring some way to regain the rest.

Sasha was even with him now, rolled back against the other pillow. Tony reached toward the table, its lamp. Flicked off one bulb, the regular one, then switched on the mood bulb. Where matters of sensuality were concerned, he much preferred this one. Whitewash disappeared and rinsed everything within reach a vibrant red.

Where even green became crimson.

He rested the mirror between them. Straws dipped to glass, noses dipped to straws. She at one side of the mirror, he at the other. Like the malt-sipping lovers from the fifties, they would meet halfway, when the well ran dry.

There was pain, that golden-green glow bursting in the backs of their skulls. But with his second primal voyage under way, he was beginning to regard it less as mere pain and more an exquisitely intense prelude. Ride it out, ride it out. He relished the opportunity to prove himself the master of his own senses. Wondered if she felt anything remotely similar.

Sasha slid the mirror across the satin covering the waterbed, and Tony heard it thump to the carpet. Hunger augmented, turned in on itself, twisted its head around into passion.

Their limbs entwined, and their mouths lapped at each other's, and they rode it out. It was wet, it was messy, it was orgasmic.

Pain. Oh yes. *Yes* . . .

The wickedly spiritual cousin of childbirth.

"Come," said Kerebawa, and Justin moved across the motel room. He had to admit, his curiosity was piqued.

April had scooted out for a while minutes ago, using the cover of new-fallen dusk to head for the post office. Things she had to mail for work, clinging by desperate fingertips to normal life, normal routines. Rituals of the late twentieth century. He wondered if she needed them more than he. Perhaps, if anything he'd built had survived, he'd be doing the same.

"Justin, you and I—we will chant to the *hekura* together?" There was an eagerness to Kerebawa's manner that he'd not exhibited before. An excited child on show-and-tell day. Perhaps, as well, it was his way of eradicating the last of this morning's tension.

Justin nodded, couldn't refuse this gesture. "You'll have to teach me."

He grinned slyly. Placed a fist over his own heart. "You know inside. You know."

Perhaps it was for the better that April had gone. Her approval would be questionable. Perhaps the Indian had been waiting for this moment for days: female gone, two men left alone with idle time.

Kerebawa reached under a bed to withdraw one of his bamboo arrow shafts, held it lengthwise toward the light and peered into one end. He drew an experimental breath and heaved it into the end, like a blowgun. Seemed satisfied.

"Won't the *hekura* be dangerous?" Justin said.

"Not with *ebene*." Kerebawa unrolled his cloth pack for the powder. "If we are lucky, we will meet them. We will see them. They may come to live in our chests. But they will not rule us."

Justin felt scant reassurance, and then Kerebawa began to strip away the clothes that, even to Justin's thoroughly Western-acculturated eye, looked out of place on the man. Finally he was naked, save for the thin cord encircling his waist like a G-string, to which his foreskin was tied. Justin shrugged, stripped down to his shorts.

"Are there paints here?" Kerebawa asked.

"Paints?"

Kerebawa nodded. "Paints. Yes." He held his fingers toward his face and moved them in circular patterns. "So we may decorate ourselves and become more beautiful for the *hekura*."

Paints. Justin shook his head. Ceremonial pigments hadn't ranked very high on the list of necessities. They would have to do without. Go before the *hekura* ugly.

But wait; he reconsidered. Went to the bathroom and returned with a small plastic case. April's eye makeup.

Kerebawa nodded when Justin opened it, showing shallow wells of blues and greens and browns. They squatted on the floor, and Kerebawa decorated himself first, then turned his fingers onto Justin. Rough fingertips, but gentle in their strength, sure and deft as they stroked squiggly brown patterns up and down his torso, lines on his face. With every stroke, as the pattern gained definition, Justin felt the differences between them eroding that much more.

Kerebawa took his bundle of *ebene* and began to carefully load the bamboo tube. Pouring a bit into one end, tapping so as to distribute it along the length. Finally he set the bundle aside and reversed the tube, held it before Justin's face.

"I hold it in front of my nose?" From Justin's vantage point, as the two of them squatted a few feet apart, it looked as if Kerebawa was holding a gun barrel toward his head.

"Yes. One side, then the other. There will be pain."

Deep breath. Release. His heart had speed-shifted into high gear. Fear of the unknown. "I'm ready."

"If you have strength left, then you do me."

Justin nodded. And shifted the bamboo in line with a nostril.

Squatting on his haunches, Kerebawa drew a massive breath, held it within a puffed-out chest. Placed his lips to the tube. And with a blast of air that sounded deceptively gentle, propelled his breath through the tube.

The pain was staggering, an invasion of his skull by both solid and gas. Justin tumbled backward onto his rump, his head feeling clubbed by a hickory stick. He looped his arm around the small waste basket provided for the room and retched into it, then wearily resumed his squat.

"Bei!" said Kerebawa. *Again.*

They did the other nostril, and if the pain was less, it was only marginally so. Justin leaned groaning against the bed while mucus dribbled from his nostrils. When he wiped it away, he marveled at the vivid green tint. Memories swirled, kaleidoscopic. Trent, at Apocalips, his running nose. But while the pain of insufflation may have been similar, he knew instinctively that he was on a completely different journey. And as its cocoon began to draw tighter, there was no fear. Only the dawn of wonder.

"Are you able?" came Kerebawa's voice. Justin was dimly cognizant of him reversing the tube.

He nodded. This ceremony was for his benefit, so that he might better understand his newfound ally, no, more than that, newfound friend. Understand him, the world he had come from, the fates that had bound them together. And perhaps, in the doing, understand himself a little better. Pain and disorientation could be mastered; he would not fail in his half of the exchange.

Justin squatted again, balancing with knees gone to rubber. Breath came easily, powerfully, and he released it in a sharp blast that Kerebawa signified was well done by a flicker of his eyes.

"*Ai!*" said Kerebawa, and Justin complied with more.

They set the tube aside and let the *ebene* work its wonders, and readied to travel to the edge of the universe.

The change came upon him, upon them both, bringing with it the power, and Tony reveled in it. This time he knew precisely what to expect, and welcomed it with open arms.

Limbs entwined around Sasha, hers around him, they undulated together and weathered the backfall, that dizzying plunge toward a world of alternatives and possibilities undreamed of. Until each's new form began to take shape, substance. Groans of ecstasy and anguish shed humanity, fell toward bestial, hung suspended somewhere between the two. Every nerve burned, every fiber. He bellowed, not caring how much noise they generated. Lupo and a couple others from last night's fruitless hunt were pulling covert guard duty outside. The penthouse was their own private jungle.

Red fog diffused the room, and within the glow, Sasha returned to the blond-pelted, hybrid she-wolf he had seen two weeks ago. Animal from the shoulders up, forearms down, wispy fur elsewhere. He could smell the primal musk, sense the quickening heart. She writhed atop satin, and he heard it rip under her nails, did not care. Satin could be replaced. Experiences such as this were priceless.

For with them came knowledge. The power flushed all the flotsam and jetsam from your head, left only what was important. He saw his future destiny spread out as clearly as a gameboard. All he had to do was move the right pieces.

He could see his rise within the Tampa hierarchy, a takeover by blood and powder. Rafael Agualar had had his day in the sun, and was now as fat and lazy as a lizard at midday. It could be simple, *so simple.*

Gills flexing, useless in the air, Tony leaned back in rapture as Sasha squirmed across him, canine tongue lolling out to slither wet tracks across his chest, stomach, groin. Where his had gone, he had no idea. Receded far down his throat, maybe, or become something else in his gullet entirely. He could not return the favor to her.

Instead, he tilted her atop him, her ivory flesh glowing red. He opened her gently with his newly webbed hands and rubbed the armorlike plating of his blunted snout between her thighs. The smell of her was ravening, and she tipped her head up from him long enough to howl.

Purpose, individuality—he had retained both. This stuff was absolutely amazing. *Retention.* His mind had often turned to business during heated sex, and even within this new shell, he was no different. Scratch that. He *was* different. He was *better.*

He charted his meteoric rise, unstoppable because he had something no one else did, had the market cornered on feral and would exploit it of every viable ounce of self-interest it held. He had truly not lived until skullflush had opened his eyes.

And this woman with him could be a part of it, he could use her, exploit her as easily as the drug. Expansion meant acquisition and investment, and it was not good to leave a trail of receipts leading to your door. He had done it before, could do it again, use a woman as a front for purchases. The penthouse had been bought through the name of a former ladyfriend, as had the Lincoln, and even public utilities.

Sasha would pull her weight, a leech no longer. So long as he could tempt her with nights like this, where the two of them could truly let the beasts loose, she would remain forever his.

His teeth, now triangular and sharp as razors, clicked in the air. His breath was a roaring cyclone. Close, he was very close. . . .

While three words longed to climb up and out of a throat that could no longer give them form.

Justin followed Kerebawa's lead and had never felt freer in his life. They rose from the pain of the air blasts, put it behind them, moved on to the infinitely more important business of living.

It felt as if great weights had lifted from his body. Arms undulated in imitation of Kerebawa's, and it no longer mattered that they were in a motel room, surrounded by accoutrements of the modern world, for they pranced together in ceremonial dance as old as a civilization.

They moved with graceful abandon. Justin realized that he loved to dance after all. For it *meant something,* and anything he had seen or attempted on a nightclub floor was but pale imitation of the origins of dance.

Spots of light flashed before his eyes, and he heard Kerebawa raise his voice in tuneless song. The words, the meaning, the motivation—they were everything. Justin sang with him, at first attempting to follow, parrot fashion, then finally letting go to allow it to come instinctively. As if something buried for aeons had broken free.

Together they danced, they sang. They shared. Whatever passed between them was more than the sum of its parts, for while they hailed from two different worlds, Justin knew that some common middle ground had been achieved. And crossed as equals.

He understood, then, why he and so many contemporaries had so earnestly sniffed and snorted and smoked and injected themselves ever closer to early and sordid graves. *This* was what they had been seeking—the grail of altered realities. A quest as old as humanity, that spread even beyond humanity.

He understood why bighorn sheep in the Canadian Rockies climb dangerous ledges solely to eat a narcotic lichen. Why cows and horses in the West eat the hallucinogenic locoweed. Why Andean natives have chewed coca leaves for millennia. Why species beyond number seek out hallucinogenic mushrooms. Why even children whirl themselves into stupors, or hold their breath until their perceptions *shift.*

We are born to it.

He understood the futility of the ways he had tried before and now knew he would never try again. Only those living so harmoniously with nature could manage the trick of deriving only benefits. The animals didn't become addicts. Generations of aborigines the world over lived long, healthy lives. It was surely the hallmark of advanced civilization to misplace the simplistic beauties of primal philosophies. To bastardize the earth's gifts and mutate them to poison, while ignoring the fact that spiritual transcendence could just as easily come from art, music, religion, emotional bonding. *Achievement.*

Justin soared within, borne on wings of joy that came from knowing such heights were attainable—always had been—without the accompanying shackles of dependence, addiction, bodily ruin.

Tapestries of music wove through his mind. Primal rhythms, then lofty celestial grandeur, Beethoven's Ninth Symphony.

He gyrated, looked up, past roof, past sky. . . .

Looked, and saw the eagle. . . .

And followed as it led him away.

Three words. They choked and gargled as Tony's throat and mouth wrestled pointlessly with them. At last he surrendered, and the phrase *I love you* died somewhere between heart and brain.

He grunted as Sasha's lupine tongue finished its task and coaxed him to the edge and past it, as seed mingled with blond fur. And with it came the death of love, the dropping of the veil, realizing that he had allowed himself to be misled by the confusion of sensuality.

Animal instincts, however, were less easily fooled.

His heart was betraying him; he had let Sasha get too close to his own soul. A man in his position could ill afford that. First comes love, then comes downfall.

He spun her around toward the headboard once more, her sides heaving with excitement and her muzzle panting hot musky breath, and he held her by the shoulders. Seeking points of contact that went far beyond physical, buried somewhere within spirit.

And somehow the drug acted as the bridge.

Her essence, his will. They interlocked like the fingers of lovers' hands. Only love was illusory, he had forgotten that most important of lessons.

He caressed his own inner core—muscular, sleek, predatory. Touched hers. Skittish, whimpering in the dark. No comparison.

No contest.

And so he pressed.

Will to will . . .

Soul to soul . . .

Core to core . . .

And like the good little she-wolf that she was, Sasha let primal instincts surface, willingly rolled belly-up and stretched back her head. Baring her throat, submitting to the dominant. A lupine mechanism of surrender that would defuse the dominant animal's aggression as soon as his muzzle touched exposed throat.

Only Tony cared nothing for the ways of the wolf.

And he let his *own* instincts rise . . .

. . . while Justin hurtled through forests seen best when glimpsed from the corner of the mind's eye. Primeval awe and wonder—flying, he was flying. The air was murky, as if never kissed by sunlight, and from the branches and canopies of foliage hung suspended not-quite-human figures that dissolved the more closely he looked at them. Ravenous beings, hungry to eat the souls of enemies, *hungry.*

Onward he soared, until he saw a red glow emanating from the dark emerald depths of a distant tree. Closer, drawn half by his own will and half by another's, unknowingly, because the road had already been paved that night he half-slept on Erik's couch.

Closer.

And he looked, and this time the images held form—

And Tony opened wide his jaws . . .

. . . while Justin saw wolf and piranha on a bed of red light. *Tony.* The face was unrecognizable, but this could be no other. Obviously experienced in the ways of *hekura-teri.* Why had he felt only the she-wolf's previous foray not Tony's? Perhaps with hers, as now, his twentieth-century guard had been down, doors of perception opened during half-sleep and leftover powder in his system.

And as Justin hurtled in with the speed of a comet and the reactive impotence of a dying breeze, he watched Tony lunge . . .

. . . and bite through the center of her throat, encountering no more resistance than if chomping into a piece of ripe fruit. Even before teeth pierced hide, he knew there was no

turning back, not even if he wanted to, for he could smell the
pulse of blood beneath the surface.

Sasha managed a strangled yelp, exhaling a glittering mist
that washed over him and fanned the flames of hunger even
as the slab from her throat was gulped down whole. Her core
screamed within his own, locked in futile subjugation.

Forepaws slashed out in a frenzy, and he dodged, and her
nails ripped open the mattress. Arcs of water splashed them,
shimmering rainbows tinted red. Followed by arcs of blood,
so dark and rich in the haze they looked black, liquid velvet.

She thrashed, and Tony drove into the cratered ruin of her
throat with hunger and thirst which knew no abatement. She
flailed and rocked from side to side, shredding the top of the
mattress. Satin drenched through; bright moist fans spattered the wall and ran together into runelike tracings.

The waterbed's frame contained the outflow, and the mattress parted to receive them both. Tony bore down on her
from above, her legs splayed to his either side as she kicked
with steadily waning efforts. Sinking, sinking . . .

Her head, then shoulders, slipped beneath the water, his
own following immediately after. Gusts of air bubbled from
her mouth, her throat, and the water the blood the foam the
churning melded into an orgiastic stew. *This* was what he was
meant for.

He feasted. He gorged. With no need to come up for air.

When she no longer kicked, and his snout was buried into
her midsection, he paused. Senses aflame, the smell of rich
life flickering madly within her. A mingling of scents. Hers, of
course. And another, even more familiar: his own. Coalesced
into one tiny mass, growing. Souvenir of their first night of
intimacy nearly two weeks ago.

Huh. She'd said she was on the Pill.

The pause gifted him with other thoughts, other senses.
The fibrous hold on her core, now like cold mist, became a
window of sensations. Another presence, voyeuristic, receding, its link to host extinguished.

He knew who it would be, and if Tony could have, he
would have grinned. Give the peeper one last parting view.

Tony slammed into her with renewed hunger, crunching

the tiny cellular spark of life before it could wink out on its own.

   After all . . .

   Fish often eat their young.

25

THE
MISSING LINKS

Under a sky beginning to tint in the east with muddy shades of rose, the Lincoln ate up the miles. Lupo held it steady, as firmly on track as a slot car. None of this meandering around within his own lane—he couldn't stand drivers who did that. You had to keep the focus tight.

"Traffic'll be picking up before long," said the guy in the passenger seat. One of the hired help from the past couple of nights, one of two brothers named Barrington. This one was Bruce; everybody called him BB for short. Neither particularly big nor menacing in appearance, but looks were deceiving. BB had been into the martial arts ever since he was seven. Got hooked on Bruce Lee movies at an early age, partially because of the draw of identical first names.

"Don't worry about traffic." Behind the wheel, Lupo was steady as Scylla, beast of rock from Homer's *The Odyssey*. "We'll be on the bridge before long."

BB looked down in faint distaste at the garbage-bag bundle at his feet. It looked weighty, shapeless. Lupo knew he would just as soon be rid of it.

"What happened to the rest of the body, man? That's the lightest corpse *I* ever lugged around."

"It's been disposed of," Lupo said. Voice very cool, very even.

But his nonchalance was a mask, if an effective one, covering the sliver of doubts and disturbances pulsing beneath. He thought he'd seen it all, death in all forms that mattered. Torture. Murder. Brutal interrogation. Had a crinkly white scar across his own gut guaranteeing that he had endured some heavy-duty abuse of his own. Thought he'd seen it all, no more surprises left.

And then Tony had to go throw a new one in on him.

A couple hours earlier, he had walked into the condo—alone, as the Barringtons remained outside—and was almost immediately slapped in the face by the rich, coppery odor of a recent kill. A messy one. He had rapped on Tony's door. Waited. Rapped again.

"Yeah. Okay. Yeah. Come in." Tony's voice was ragged.

What Lupo had found inside had given even his own battle-tested gorge a run for its money.

Tony, sitting in his waterbed. Not on it, *in* it. As if it had been hurriedly converted into an aquarium to replace the one he had lost. Tony had been leaning back against the headboard. An absolute mess, blood caking his mouth, face. Streaking the wall behind him. And in the water, floated, well . . .

Things.

Things that had once been joined, parts of a whole. And were now apart. The most recognizable of which had been a foot and lower leg, rising from the water to drape over the bed frame.

Tony had sighed heavily. Finally met Lupo's astonished gaze.

"Don't we do a lot of bizarre things out of love?" he had said.

Lupo's mind had spun frantically to grasp it all. Not entirely sad to see their association with Sasha come to an end.

Not entirely relieved to see it come about *this* way. It was the last thing he'd expected, because for the past few days Tony had actually seemed to be falling for the girl. Falling, and fighting it, maybe even subconsciously.

Tony had likely snapped back to his right mind. But was it possible to snap back too far in the right direction? To go beyond?

Then he saw the mirror on the floor. The straws. Recalled finding Tony last week after his earlier experiment with skull-flush. He wasn't sure he wanted to learn anything more of what had gone on in this room than absolutely necessary.

"Need to get rid of this mess." Tony held up a second foot and let it go to splash back into the water. Too far apart from the other one, the angle all wrong. "And then we've got a lot of things to plan out."

Sometimes, over the past couple of hours, Lupo had wondered why he was going along with this, as if it was par for the course. This was careless, sloppy, needlessly risky. Tony had been taking more risks, calculated and otherwise, the past two-plus weeks than he had in the past two years. Why stick with that, given the consequences?

And then he knew.

That was the way it had always been.

Childhood friends, from the same neighborhood. Tony had always been the outgoing one, Lupo reserved, preferring the company of books to that of other kids. They were an escape from decay, the stink, the rats. He'd earned no small number of beatings and torment because of it. Until he began to grow. And grow. And beat the hell out of Tony Mendoza, who had made the mistake of picking on him one too many times.

But instead of now fearing him, like all the rest, Tony had said he was impressed. Glad to see him standing up for himself for a change. Lupo still remembered looking down at him with those split lips, puffy eye, scraped forehead and cheekbones. Watching him laugh. Not believing it when this early teenage Tony Mendoza had said he'd been looking for someone with *cojones* like that.

Man, you gotta be crazy, Lupo had thought. His knuckles ached from Tony's face, and here the bloodied kid was acting as if Lupo had passed some sort of audition.

You had to listen to a guy like that.

Crazy; now *that* was par for the course. Seemed like every time he fought a little harder and higher up the powder heap, Tony got a little crazier for it. For that was the way to pull it off. The meek may have been penciled in to inherit the earth, but not in *their* time.

He had told himself before, on occasion, that whenever it appeared that Tony had finally twisted his mind to the point where it might snap for good, he would cut his losses and bail out. Maybe that time had come. Probably.

Yet here he was lapdogging same as before. No real intention of leaving, just curious as to how crazy Tony could get and hold it all together. He *had* talked a frightening kind of logic up in his bedroom—especially since taking that surprise call from the accountant.

So he'd hang tough with Tony awhile longer, see where it led. Had to know how it would all turn out. From a ringside seat. Face it—what else did he have going to fall back on?

So. *Drive.*

The Lincoln left land behind them as I-275 cut southwest from Tampa over the Old Bay toward St. Pete and Clearwater. The Howard Frankland Bridge spanned better than five miles of water, and once on, you could soon see neither the land you had left nor the land you were heading for. Midway to the west you picked up a whiplike spur jutting from the mainland, just barely wide enough to provide bedrock for the bridge, but that was it for solid ground.

Lupo began slowing the Lincoln after the first couple of miles. Looking ahead, behind. Across the low concrete divider, in the two northeast-bound lanes, a pair of cars passed in tandem, and the next headlights were hundreds of yards away. Behind them, beneath the pink ridge of dawning sky, the nearest headlights were pinpricks. The time was right.

"Let's lose her," Lupo said.

He was in the outside lane and hit the brakes to bring the car to a halt just shy of a skid. Nothing but dawn and vast plains of water for company. BB had one hand on the doorlatch, dropped the other to the sturdily wrapped and weighted garbage bag.

Just as well this one was going to sink to the bottom with

precious little chance of floating and discovery. Packing up the pieces had shown him some bizarre things about this particular corpse, things that would attract all manner of attention. Try getting fingerprints from paws, for one thing.

Dead stop. BB flung the door open, lugged the bag of bones out behind him. Sent it whirling out over the retaining wall, against the northern horizon, out of view.

Just before BB hopped back into the car for quick takeoff, Lupo could barely hear the splash.

With every tick of the clock, Tony felt himself gaining momentum. A sluggish start in the wee hours of this morning, though, waking up wet and bloody with recollections of the night that seemed more like dreams than anything.

He had been sleeping underwater. Awoke when the change reversed and sent him back to reclaim full humanity. Gills sealed, and his sleeping body had no option other than to begin sucking water into his lungs. He erupted from the water in a choking flurry, coughed it back up.

Only then did he realize what he was sleeping *with*.

For a short while, tears had wanted to flow as memories settled into focus. No more Sasha and her horizontal dance of delights. No more Sasha, period. The death of an impending fatherhood he'd not even known about, nor she. Tears. Had he let them, they could've come.

But then came the resurgence of feelings more instinctual than emotional. Predators had no time to waste mourning dead mates they themselves have brought down.

Besides, she was still with him in a sense. You are what you eat, and all. He could feel bits of her essence within, food completely unrelated to physical sustenance. He had eaten bits of her soul and felt all the stronger for it. Fragments of silently screaming distress that fueled him like a battery. He would drain them until there was nothing left but anemic flickers.

Meanwhile, the future beckoned. Its possibilities to be plucked like ripe fruit from trees. Now that he had unlocked this green Pandora's box of secrets, he was limitless. Not the least of which had begun with that early-morning phone call.

It led them downtown around noon to pick up their rider, a

guy named Santos. A thin, nervous sort of twit, one little speck among the glass and steel towers. The Lincoln swallowed him whole, then cruised back into traffic.

Tony was wearing one of his finest white suits, but even that didn't stave off a sense of coming in second on a comparative basis. Santos wore basic Wall Street gray, Savile Row all the way. Looked as if he'd been born in that suit. Tony smirked inside though. Above the neck, seemed like nine out of every ten accountants looked alike. Some kind of international law, maybe.

They shared the back seat, stretched out on the leather with plenty of legroom. Tony fixed him a drink out of a portable bar, which Santos accepted gratefully. Not once did he move toward doffing his sunglasses. He was fooling no one. The rich bruises around the left eye socket needed far more than shades to screen them from sight.

"You're doing the right thing," Tony said. "I personally guarantee you will *never* have cause to regret it. Never."

Santos nodded his battered head. "I swore to myself, this is the last time that *hijo de puta* does this to me. Thinks I'm skimming off the top? If I'd done that, he'd never know. Paranoid *cabrón.*"

Tony nodded, sympathetic. You bet, pal, life's tough enough, and you've already been dished out more than your share of shit. "That's what happens when you mix business and pleasure."

On the outside he was calm, easy diplomacy. Inside, he was turning orgasmic cartwheels. The timing on this was incredible. Life was grand, life was charmed. He had been subtly working this guy for nearly a year. Agualar's primary accountant, increasingly dissatisfied in his present position. The money was prime, but even that wore thin after a while when Agualar put you on the brunt end of his greaseball temper. Waltz you around the office with his fists, no matter how much he was paying, you still felt like some kind of kinky whore. Pride rebelled eventually.

Santos could take him places. Oh, yes. Guy was a money-laundering wizard, all kinds of connections with cooperative Bahamian and Panamanian banks, plus a network of bogus brokerage houses and furriers and jewelers acting as legit fronts nationwide. As it was, Tony currently belonged to a loose financial coalition that pooled resources for laundering purposes and doled out eight percent cuts of the gross as commission. Santos had promised he need never pay anything more than six and a half ever again.

So long as he was successful in his bid for coup d'état. Tony was willing to take that risk. Now more than ever.

He snapped his fingers. "Let's see what you got."

Santos unlocked his briefcase and flipped through an immaculate array of files, folders, and sheafs of paper. He withdrew a sealed envelope, passed it over. Tony ripped it open and unfolded papers that appeared to be overhead maps of a highly upscale residence.

"The electronic security is based in a second-floor room in this part of the house." Santos aimed one manicured fingernail. "Two men are on the console, with eight monitors in all. The cameras are programmed into the monitors on a rotational basis, with each one changing images every five seconds. Any one of which they can lock-in permanently."

Tony nodded, watched as the fingernail began to tap various little blue dots labeled with *C*s.

"Cameras here, and here," Santos said, "and here, and here. . . ."

And on he went, that most dangerous of spies: the one with a personal grudge. Tony loved it. He watched, listened. Learned. The seeds of revolution already sprouting in his mind.

Midafternoon.

Santos had long since been deposited back where they'd found him. An hour later, they linked up with the Barrington brothers, who followed in a second car as they drove to Kennedy, turned off onto Magnolia.

The Barringtons parked first. Bruce's brother, Ivan, was no slouch when it came to locks. He and BB headed for April's second-story loft while Lupo circled the block an extra time. Wait until Ivan was in and things looked kosher. After the first lap of the holding pattern, Tony saw that BB was leaning against the building, and gave them a slight nod. Lupo parked, and up they went.

Tony didn't know what he was looking for. Something, anything, to give them a clue as to where he might find Justin and April. One solitary fact they were overlooking or were not yet privileged to know.

"Look," said Lupo, just past the threshold. He pointed with one shoetip toward the wall beside the inner door. A bullet hole. Angled downward, as if it had come from someone firing down from the outer doorway.

"The Weatherman," Tony said flatly. "Fuck. I'd give just about anything to know the story behind that."

He wandered in, Lupo and the Barringtons in tow, stood at this end of the loft and stared down its length. Stuffy and stale and overbearingly warm in here, closed up for days. Dim, too, all the blinds drawn. Shafts of sunlight slanted through the narrow gaps between the Levolors and the tops of the window frames. Dust motes swam in the air.

Tony had had people continuing the phone campaign to area motels and hotels, still hoping to uncover a likely registration. About ready to give that tactic up. If they were taking the motel route, they weren't using their own names. Of course, they couldn't manage that indefinitely; April wasn't rich, and he was willing to bet that Justin wasn't either. Plus, April worked right here at home and couldn't survive away for very long. He could wait them out, let them deplete their cash reserves, but that could take too long.

Had to be another way to smoke them out.

"Start running this place through a fine-tooth comb," he told his men. "Go through everything. Every drawer, every cabinet, every shelf."

The guys divided it up by room assignments, or what passed for rooms in her home. Lupo took the kitchen and dining area. BB the living room, Ivan her bedroom. All wore skintight surgical gloves to avoid fingerprints.

Tony began in the bathroom. He went through the medicine cabinet, then the vanity, then the narrow linen closet. Didn't take long; not much he could learn from soap and towels and Tampax.

Gleefully, then, he emptied the nooks and crannies of their contents. Jars and bottles he hurled into the tub, where they shattered, contents mingling into sickly splashes of color. He jammed the toilet full of tampons and sanitary napkins, gave it a flush, then had all her towels strewn across the floor to soak up the overflow. Lastly, he found a curling iron and fired it into the mirror, watched his sneering reflection burst into a radius of a thousand fragments.

It was a slim fraction of the rage boiling inside over his piranha. He'd let it all out, in time.

While combing her belongings, the boys eyed him surreptitiously as he stalked through the loft with a mounting sense of vengeance. He slipped a butcher knife from the cutlery block and reduced the cushions and backrest of her sofa to ribbons. Carried the knife with him into her walk-in closet and slashed every dress, every blouse, every pair of slacks and jeans. Men's clothing hung in here, too, from one bar, and he took unbridled delight in ripping it and pretending that Justin was wearing each piece.

Of course, when the *real* time came, their hides would not be cleaved by anything so mundane as a simple knife.

An address book was uncovered in a living room end table, and this Tony perused, found a few names to check into. Nothing so definitively ripe with possibility as a map for a remote family cabin, but a valuable find nonetheless.

Tony bulldozed along toward her office, pausing in the bedroom to slash her mattress and bedsheets, then smash a freestanding antique full-length mirror and overturn it in a clamor of shattering fragments. Into its rubble he added a ceramic bowl and pitcher from atop her dresser. Framed pictures hanging on the loft's inner wall and brick pillars he plucked from their supports and clashed together like cymbals. Everywhere, broken glass and torn fabric.

Her office.

Drafting table, desk, file cabinets, desktop copier—he could have boundless fun in here once it was searched. He could cripple her business as effectively as a torpedo in the hull of a ship. Maybe let her live after all, let her come home from a dead lover to find this place in shambles. Let her die a slow death of business strangulation. Let her sit amid the sackcloth of shredded financial documents and contracts, the ashes of all her files. Let her know what it feels like to come home and find a piece of your life ripped out by the roots.

He was about to seize her business telephone and plunge it through the glass of her copier when he froze. Stared at where it sat on a deskside tabletop, beside an answering machine. With both its ON and CALLS status lights glowing red.

It had the calming effect of a sedative.

Tony rewound the tape counter down to zero, hit PLAY-BACK to listen. Several calls, clients yammering for one thing and another like petulant children. He shook his head, thought he'd likely go bugnuts having to spend his life answering to people like that.

"April, this is Marian again," came one voice near the end of the string of messages. "In regards to our conversation earlier this morning, I decided we can probably wait until the middle of next week on those proofsheets. No later than that though. Call me if you get this message before five-thirty today, okay? This is Wednesday, by the way, that I'm calling. Um . . . I really do hope you get your family problems ironed out soon. We need you here."

Another message followed, but Tony scarcely registered it. His mind was racing, trying puzzle pieces together and finding that some were starting to fit. Smart girl, she was keeping tabs on business by checking calls. Daily, at the very least.

Tony set the machine back to ANSWER CALLS. Looked at her business line long enough to commit its number to very short-term memory.

And walked to the other end of the loft to her personal line hanging on the kitchen wall.

26
SETBACK

 The bubble, fragile as it was, burst on Thursday morning.

Justin had tried phoning Rene Espinoza a few times on Wednesday afternoon and evening, hoping to get news of the lab results and how they would subsequently proceed. She was always out, though, and he would talk to no one else, wouldn't leave his name. He finally caught her Thursday morning.

As soon as he heard the shift in her voice when he identified himself, his heart stuttered with a downward lurch. Hers was not the voice of triumph incarnate.

"The stuff you gave me?" she said. "It tests out as a hallucinogen, really potent. The lab said they'd never seen anything like it."

"And?"

"And it's legal."

His heart deflated. Every hope nailed on using the skull-flush against Tony blew away in the breeze.

"Legal?" he whispered. "How can that *be*?"

"Because it's not *il*legal. The law's pretty clear-cut when it comes to things like this, the chemical makeup of the drug." He heard papers rustling over the phone. "I've got a full readout here that looks like a chemistry textbook. It probably wouldn't mean any more to you than it does to me. But the fact is, it's never been seen here before, nobody even knew it existed. So it's just one of those drugs that manages to slip through the cracks in the law, like some of the designer synthetics managed to do." She sighed, a wearisome sound. The sound of someone who had climbed too many paper mountains. "Mendoza could be sitting on a dump truck full of the stuff, and there's nothing anybody could do about it."

Justin had been slumped onto the bed, and now he lay back a moment to stare at the ceiling. *I suppose I could tell her he's killed somebody else,* he thought. Of course, she would wonder how he knew. *I saw it in a vision induced by another tribal drug,* he could tell her. That would go over big. Iron-clad testimony. Despite all the benefits from his experience with *ebene,* he still felt heartsick over what it had ultimately shown him.

"So where does this leave us?" he finally asked.

"Did you have any backup ideas?"

A frantic mental scramble, then, "No." Barely a word, barely a noise.

"Then my advice from two days ago still holds. Lie as low as you possibly can until something blows over."

He barked an embittered little laugh. "For how long? You said something could break any day, but be honest. You don't know, do you? You don't honestly know. It could take another month, or six months, for all you know. *Couldn't it?*"

Another weary sigh. "I'd be lying if I said that was out of the question." They shared silence for a few moments, and when she spoke again, her voice was lower. An almost conspiratorial hush meant for his ears only. "I'm not going to tell you what to do, one way or another. Just what *I'd* do, if it was me. And if you *ever* tell anyone I said this, I'll deny it. To your face, in court, in church, wherever—I'll deny it."

"Let's hear it." Although he suspected what it would be.

"I'd kill him. Flat out kill him. I don't know if you're up to something like that."

"I—I don't either."

"But you ripped him off to the tune of five keys, so you've got something in the way of a pair of stones. At least you can be sure of two things: If he turned up dead, I don't know of anyone who'd shed a tear. And the natural assumption is that it would've been one of his business associates. If you get my drift."

"Yeah. I do." Another whisper.

"That's all I'm going to say on the subject. Ever."

Kill him. She was probably right. And while Justin had passed on that option a few nights ago, now he wasn't so sure it wasn't the best one after all. In no small way due to what the *ebene* had shown. A man who slaughtered like that didn't merely deserve to be locked up, the key melted down into something useful. No, he deserved to die. But to have no qualms over decreeing such a fate and acting as executioner —a veritable gorge separated the two.

"It'll be taken under consideration," he said, and after she wished him luck, the connection was broken. He sat on the bed holding the receiver a moment, then cradled it gently when he instead felt like pulverizing it to plastic chips and dead circuitry.

"What's wrong?" April, at the round breakfast table. Kerebawa sat across from her. Optimism was not showing its sunny face.

He told them of the lab results, watched shaky hope lose all ground and become lost hope. And then offered the partial redemption of Espinoza's suggestion, the apparently last-ditch chance among their rapidly depleted roster of options. Sad, in a way, to watch morality become the next casualty when the situation looked this desperate. He put it to an informal vote.

"I say we do it," was April's.

"We already should have." Kerebawa had probably never heard the phrase, but his expression plainly said *I told you so.*

Justin rose from the bed and paced toward them. "Can you do it?" he directed to April. *"Can* you? Because I'm not so sure I can, to be honest. When it comes right down to sticking a gun in his face and pulling the trigger."

Kerebawa tapped his chest. "*I* can."

"Mentally, okay, I believe that. But you've never even used a gun! And believe me, he and his people will have them, too, and machetes and bows and arrows aren't going to be any match. It might have been close when you had the curare arrows, but you said those got washed clean in the rains before you even got to Tampa." Justin sunk onto the bed beside them. "It wouldn't be as easy as that, anyway, just walking up into his face. We'd never get that close."

"So we do it from farther away," April said.

"A firefight against people who've got us outnumbered, outgunned, and outexperienced." He reached over to rest a hand on her knee, hoping she would join his with her own. She didn't. "Plus, no matter what Espinoza says, it's still murder, it's still illegal. Even if we stay alive, we could still be caught with the smoking gun."

April snatched her knee from his touch. "Do you want to do this, or don't you?" An angry demand. "Because what else are we gonna do, huh? *What else?* Look at us! Do you want to live like this forever!"

Justin looked at Kerebawa. No words needed; the set of his face indicated that he was siding wholly with April.

Some change in life he had managed to fashion for himself. At least back in St. Louis he had had identifiable hallmarks to dread, court dates and meetings with lawyers and cops. None of whom were out to kill him, but who drained him of lifeblood just the same. This wasn't much different; the main distinction was not knowing when the hammer would fall, or if the blow would be fatal.

"I never said I didn't want to try," he finally told her. "Just trying to be realistic. Nothing wrong with being realistic."

April nodded, swirled the last swallow of coffee in her cup. "No. And you weren't wrong about anything." She finished the coffee. "I'll tell you what our problem is. Tony's got too much control. We don't have any leverage to get him to behave like we want."

"We have the *hekura-teri*," said Kerebawa. "He wants this."

Justin shook his head. "That's not good enough. Sure, that was a blow to his pride when we took that, but it didn't hurt him much. He couldn't sell it anyway. He'd probably already gotten used to the idea of eating the financial loss." He smiled thinly, an idea starting to gel. "What motivates Tony? More than pride, more than ego or sex drive or power. What does that leave?"

"Money," April said immediately.

"Exactly. And if we want more leverage to bargain with him to maybe get the last of the skullflush, and to get him into a position of maximum risk to himself at minimum risk to ourselves, we've got to hurt him through his cash flow."

Kerebawa had been following carefully, new terms and concepts alien to his home. He seemed a quick study. "I have seen many men die from their greed."

Justin nodded eagerly. Amazing, how the strength of one idea could take root, fill you full of steam again. "If he thinks we're stupid enough to try bargaining with him, he just might let down his guard enough so we can finish it all."

"So what's the bargaining chip you've got in mind?"

"Rip him off again."

April looked as if her night's sleep had been negated. "Justin, the dumbest bank robbers in the world are the ones who go back to the same place two or three times, just because it worked the first time."

He held up a hand, like a teacher confronting a pupil's objections. "I don't mean his condo. Look, this is a little more my area than yours. There's got to be a drop point somewhere we can find. Either get away clean, or rob one of his mules." He spread his hands. "It's the only way we'll ever be able to maneuver him."

April appeared to weigh it, mental scales tipping to and fro. Finally settling on agreement.

"This just doesn't end, does it? All this scurrying around?"

He didn't know what to tell her. What to do. Pat her hands, babble empty promises? Offer a little comfort in a blatant lie of total confidence? No. She would see through it, anyway.

He crossed around behind her, kissed her atop the head, and leaned down to squeeze her around the shoulders. She felt stiff against him, but a moment later he felt her lips press to his arm.

"I just want my life back, Justin." Her voice sounded flat, as cheery as a dying balloon. "That's all. I just want my life back like it was before last Saturday night."

"I know. And you'll get it," he whispered. Then grabbed his half-cup of coffee. "I'm gonna step outside, get some fresh air. Too stuffy in here. I'll be back in a few minutes."

She nodded, and he straightened, wandered out the door. He wore jeans only, no shirt, barefoot. Morning sun and humidity, a potent mix. He faced the parking lot, watched a family of out-of-towners load into their minivan. Shorts, T-shirts, visors, a bag of camera gear. Maybe going to Busch Gardens, photograph the kids at the petting zoo. He watched them roll out to the boulevard.

I just want my life back.

It didn't seem too much to ask for. For any of them.

She watched his bare back disappear out the door. And once the door had shut, watched where his back had been. Maybe she should have gone along; two could get fresh air as easily as one.

"He will be back," said Kerebawa, simple comfort in his voice.

She smiled and nodded, didn't bother to correct him that he had misread her concerns. Where he came from, men probably weren't used to dealing with many women's concerns beyond worrying over children and hut and missing their men. *Whole new world up here, my friend.*

"He admires you," April told Kerebawa after several moments. "A great deal, I think."

The Indian cocked his head for a moment, an oddly childlike gesture, then smiled. Broadly, as if pleasantly delighted.

"Justin would seem to have much to be proud of," he said. "I have little that matters in his world."

"It's the difference in worlds that's important. The difference in purity. Yours? The—the absolutes—they're clearer there."

Now the cocked head meant confusion. He frowned, perplexed.

"You don't understand, do you?"

"Absolutes, I don't know what you mean, absolutes."

She held a breath, let it out thoughtfully. How could she make him understand the gray areas of American life, how black and white varied with every viewpoint? How could he understand the compromises required in nearly every facet of life if you were to survive it with both sanity and bank balance intact? It'd be pointless to try.

"The absolutes," she finally said, "are what's right and what's wrong. What's allowed, and what's forbidden. You understand them a lot better in your world than we do in ours. And I think that's what he admires so much."

She watched the smile reappear on his face, but this time it was tainted by sadness. The bittersweet taste of loss. April then recalled the depressing tales of South America's cannibalization of its rain forests—along with the people who lived there—and feared she had spoken far beyond her due.

"My world has grown more confused," Kerebawa said. "What saves most of us—who want to be saved—is remembering the past."

How sad, she thought. *Someday they'll be as extinct as the dinosaurs.*

"At least," she said, "your people have a past they *can* remember. That's worth remembering."

She felt a stab of hypocritical guilt. Even she wasn't above occasional horror at the alien nature of his world. As evidenced a couple nights ago when she had walked in from her mail trip and found Kerebawa and Justin languishing in a stupor of green mucus and voided stomachs. Her first thought had been utter revulsion. Her second had been of running for good. That Justin had finally caved in from the pressure. It had taken a good long while to get over that one.

For that thought meant that the fear had undeniably been lurking within all along. Fear of his unreliability, just waiting for sufficient reason to pop into view like a malevolent jack-in-the-box.

She wanted to believe in him. Badly. So badly.

The thought brought her up short. How long had Justin been outside, anyway? Ten minutes? More? She looked at Kerebawa.

"Maybe you'd better go see where he's gotten off to."

Kerebawa nodded, vacated as readily as had Justin. And there she sat. Prisoner of fate and circumstance. *I want my life back.*

She realized what she probably needed more than anything was to return to the security of simply doing her job. Occupational therapy. For now, though, she'd do what she could. Check her messages.

Sanity was hard bought these days.

Justin had continued on around to the back of the motel, to the small patch of palms, their pathetic attempt at maintaining a touch of nature amid the tacky glitz. He had sat atop one of two picnic tables, sipping coffee, his feet slick with morning dew.

He found himself strangely reconciled to the possibility that he might not be breathing after the next few days. Precious little fear was left, only weary resolve to see everything through to the end, cut the maddening day-to-day uncertainties. And the regret over the lives he had hopelessly entangled into his excuse for one. He missed Paula, bone deep for the first time in months, wished for one last chance to apologize for wrecking their marriage. Sorry, hon, I just woke up brain-dead one day and never got better.

Justin had heard nothing behind him, was aware of Kerebawa only when he too slid onto the table. He wore a pair of Justin's gym shorts, and his ribs looked like washboards.

Minutes passed. Silent communion, long monologues spoken through the occasional locking of eyes alone. Listening to traffic pick up on the boulevard. Justin knew he should be moving.

"The eagle," said Kerebawa. "It no longer suffers broken wings."

Justin smiled, crumpled the Styrofoam cup. Then stood and clapped Kerebawa on the shoulder. "Come on. Let's go hunting."

As soon as he set foot inside the motel room, he could tell that April had been crying. Red eyes, red nose, soggy tissue on the table. It set off low-grade alarms inside, which abated when she didn't say anything. Tears on general principles.

He felt guilty for leaving her so long to cry alone. Maybe it was something she needed, though, to flush the poisons from body and mind.

April rose from the chair, met him halfway across the room. They hugged, held it. Her arms drawing him tight, tighter, seeking to make one body from two.

"Whatever happens," she said, her voice choked with warbles, "please remember that I love you. *Please* remember that."

He murmured that he would, and held her tighter than before. Their arms like nothing so much as a pair of nooses, till death do us part.

Staking out Tony's had proved beneficial before, so they decided to stick with the tried and true. They sweltered in the car for the rest of the morning, then adopted a change in tactics when Lupo went out alone in the Lincoln shortly before one o'clock. He wasn't empty-handed; the binoculars showed a sturdy attaché case in one hand. If, like most dealers, Tony buffered himself against needlessly dirtying his hands, then this was the man to follow.

Justin gave him a head start of two hundred yards, then followed him onto Westshore. Midday traffic gave him ample opportunity to blend into the background. The only worry was losing him when it got a little too heavy for comfort. He hung onto the wheel and felt his stomach clench as tight as his hands.

They tailed the Lincoln onto South Dale Mabry, an endless thoroughfare of strip malls, one- and two-level successions of relatively new buildings sharing adjacent walls. Dominos of the consumer economy. Clothing stores, home entertainment centers, yogurt vendors, video outlets, shoe stores—they just didn't end. He had noticed the repetitiveness before, with Erik. You traveled onward with a snowballing sense of déjà vu.

The Lincoln pulled off into one of the mall's parking lots, and Justin hung back after following. He watched the Lincoln turn down a row of parking places, then nose into the empty space alongside a sleek Dodge Daytona already there. A lone figure sat in the Daytona, and Justin's last glimpse of

Lupo before passing the same row was of him leaving the
Lincoln, attaché case in hand.

"What'd he do?" he asked April, who was craning her neck
to look back.

"He got into the other car." She was squinting against the
glare of sun on windshields.

"I feel like we're driving around in one giant sore thumb,"
Justin grumbled.

From the back seat, Kerebawa uttered a sound of confusion.

"A dumb American expression," said Justin, and that
seemed to satisfy him.

Justin turned the same direction as the Lincoln three rows
later, found a vacant space that gave them a reasonably unobstructed angle on the Daytona. He geared into park, let it
idle.

The Daytona was white with red trim. Probably showed
dust like crazy. He lifted the binoculars and trained them in;
the conversation they zoomed in on, while silent, appeared
neither too casual nor too heated. Very businesslike.

While looks may have been a poor judge of character,
Justin decided he liked those of Lupo's contact far better
than those of Lupo himself. Lupo was probably fearsome in
his sleep. This new guy? A receding chin inspired superiority
every time. One good punch, and it looked as if the guy's
lower jaw would slot all the way back to his Adam's apple. Big
deal, though, in a vocation where Uzis acted as the great
equalizer.

"What do you think?" Justin passed the binoculars to April.
"Guy mean anything to you, ever see him before?"

She watched, tongue tip working nervously at the corner
of her mouth. Then nodded and passed the binoculars back.
"I don't know him, never saw him before. He looks fine to
me."

Ah, a green light. They could ditch the Lincoln and set
their sights on a new target. Better still, a target to whom
their faces were unknown.

Now, if only educated guesswork would hold water. Justin
was betting that Lupo hadn't come out of Tony's with a case
full of kilos. Cash, more likely. Leave it off with the mule—or

mules, if he should make subsequent stops—give a time and place to exchange it for product in the next day or two, and a drop site to leave it for the next link in the chain. Dealer, subdealer, whatever.

One gigantic *if*, on which everything hinged. It was enough to bring on a migraine.

Lupo vacated the Daytona for the Lincoln. Across the rows, Justin watched them back out of their parking places and head their separate ways.

Moments later, he did likewise. This time, taking the path whose end he did not know.

27
COUP d ÉTAT

Dusk was deepening over Tampa as the Lincoln cruised south along Bayshore Drive. Tony loved this jaunt at night, gorgeous view. It was better when you were in the northbound lanes and downtown lay ahead like a promise, but he could always turn around. See the lights, the skyline in retreat. And all that water to the east, rippling black and silver beneath the rising moon. What secrets it must hold.

Lupo continually checked the rearview mirror, once every several seconds. He seemed satisfied.

"Okay back there?" Tony asked.

Lupo nodded. "If we had a tail, I would've spotted them by now. I'm taking it like a maze tonight."

Standard precaution for business trips that fell a bit beyond the realm of ordinary. Not like this afternoon, when Lupo had grown a tail, knew it, and didn't mind one tiny bit.

That too was business a bit beyond the ordinary.

Tony felt as if he were fighting a low-grade war, on two fronts. Justin and April, on the one hand. And on the other, Tampa's big cheese himself.

Rafael Agualar lived far south on Bayshore in one of the city's most exclusive neighborhoods. Perched on the edge of the bay, these homes demanded substantial dollar investment, but Agualar could surely afford it. Directly or indirectly, he controlled a full eighty percent of the cocaine flow into the area.

His house was new, modern, its architecture composed of intersecting and overlapping cubes, all a pristine white. In emulation of Hugh Hefner's hedonistic tendencies, Agualar had constructed his own open-air grotto, gardens and pathways that converged upon a man-made pond, complete with low rock cliffs and a waterfall at one end. A splendid place for entertaining of all orientations, the playground was shielded from neighbors' curious eyes by a surrounding thicket of palms and banyans. Security was further enhanced by a nine-foot brick wall circling the estate, its top ledge studded with broken glass embedded in poured concrete. According to Santos, photoelectric eyes were spaced at intervals along the walls. If a beam between them was broken, the security staff inside knew where and could zoom in with a closed-circuit camera to cover the breach in an instant, while at the same time drenching the area with floodlights.

The Lincoln stopped at the front gate, overseen by two guards in suits. No problems, he was expected. The steel latticework gate swung open at the middle, and they were in.

Agualar's drive was heavily tree-lined, a curving affair designed to prevent a straight open view of his house from the gate and street. That passion for privacy. Tony compared the layout from the map with the real thing as the Lincoln rolled in. One camera on the drive from up at the gate. Gradual curve to the left, then a straightaway toward the house. One more camera mounted near the house to cover the straightaway. Tony called the overhead diagram to mind—angles, curves, areas of visible coverage. On the inside of the curve, there should be a crescent of roughly fifteen feet that was pure blind spot. Covered by neither camera.

He had just pinpointed Agualar's Achilles heel.

Lupo parked on an asphalt oval before the house, and they were admitted by a goon who was every bit Lupo's equal in size. Must have had his suits custom tailored. Tony and Lupo submitted to the indignity of a quick frisk and had had the foresight to leave weapons in the car. Tony wondered if, in their absence, guards would emerge from hiding to search the car. Depended on how paranoid Agualar was today. Cocaine could bring it on, make you fear enemies that weren't there. And on the bright side, fuck up with enemies that were.

Even if the car was searched, they wouldn't find anything to worry them. Lupo's MAC-10 and straight razor, a Browning automatic Tony often carried. No heavy firepower, just tools of the trade. Just those—

And a four-foot coil of nylon rope in the glove compartment. Innocent enough, just simple rope.

"You can wait here," the doorman told Lupo, and his voice was a rumbling bass from a tomb.

Tony nodded to Lupo, let yet another guy who materialized lead him deeper into the house. How Agualar kept them all straight Tony didn't know. Guys all looked alike—short hair and suits, most of them looking to have steroid dependencies.

Whatever you could say about Agualar—greedy, a stubby obese pig of a man, paranoid—he lived in fine style. Tony was led from the entry hall through a large arched portal. Past an open, airy sprawl looking up two stories to the ceiling. A curving balcony ran along one wall, and the first floor was built on two different levels linked here and there by four-step stairways. The walls and balcony and its railing were eggshell, the carpet and walkway tile were pale gray. Most of the furniture was a darker gray, and in one corner sat a gleaming white Bosendorfer grand piano.

Style. What a waste, considering the owner.

The aide led Tony into a branching hallway, down to one end, and stopped before a closed door. He rapped twice.

"Come," said a voice from the other side.

The aide poked his head in. "Tony Mendoza. Still wanna see him?"

"Yeah."

The aide fell behind Tony as they entered Agualar's den. More eggshell and grays, even a smooth gray desk made of some plastic polymer. The wall behind Agualar held huge windows of thick cubes of translucent glass, now shiny black with the new-fallen night.

Another wall held a seven-foot tarpon, mounted. Those fish were fighters like Ali was a boxer. Tony had heard Agualar's version of the catch, also knew the real story. The fishing charter in the gulf where Agualar had hooked it and then let one of his steroid monsters wrestle the thing all afternoon, until it had about two minutes of fight left inside those silver scales. He'd pulled it on board and posed for pictures like he was sweating testosterone. Just looking at the thing made Tony want to vomit.

"You want me to stay?" asked the aide.

Agualar gave a curt shake of his cannonball head. "Outside the door."

Tony heard the door latch behind him, waited for Agualar to tell him to sit. Fat bastard. Still, best to keep on his good side at this crucial stage. Tony fought the urge to laugh. In the man's presence, he felt especially dark and sleek in black slacks, black shirt. Agualar, on the other hand, was taking this Hefner crap too far. Sitting behind his desk in silk pajamas. All he needed was a pipe.

At least Hef managed to project something of the debonair. Agualar looked more like a child molester. Sawed-off porker with thick fingers and lips, a hairline receded back to the crown of his head. He grew it long on one side, combed it over the sweaty gleaming dome, thought no one noticed.

"Go on, go on, take a load off." He jabbed one thick finger at the chairs before his desk.

Tony sat while Agualar studied him with beady pig eyes. Tony noticed white flecks beneath his nose. Still dipping into his stockpile too much for his own good.

Achilles heel number two.

"Thank you for seeing me," Tony said, smooth as butter.

Agualar sniffed. "I figured, if nothing else, it might be good for a laugh. I'm not used to guys way down in your little sewer wanting a meet. I hear, hey, he's asking around to my guys about a meet, what the fuck does *he* want?"

Tony smiled. Harvard M.B.A., a real charmer. "I have a present. A token of appreciation."

Suspicion and delight filled the man's eyes in equal measures. Schizoid. Tony reached into a shirt pocket and withdrew a clear glass vial, set it on his desk, then folded his hands.

Agualar frowned. Checked the light. Bent in closer to peer at the thing. "What the hell?" He picked it up, turned it this way and that.

"Pretty, isn't it?" Tony said. "You act like you never saw the stuff before."

"Don't be a dickbrain. Where the hell did you get this? And what the hell is it?"

Tony feigned the look of a man suspecting he had heard a joke and wasn't sure it was funny. "Are you serious? You were supposed to know all about this a few weeks ago."

Agualar stared at the vial, then popped it down onto the desktop. Drummed his fist beside it for a moment. Hurriedly reached into a desk drawer and pulled out a nickel-plated revolver, ivory grips with scrimshaw inlay. Tony didn't bat an eyelash as Agualar waved the gun at him.

"Yeah? *Yeah?* Well, I don't." Fat man was sweating more, his nose twitchy as a rabbit's. "Why don't you educate me."

Placatingly, Tony spread his hands. Kept his voice soft, hypnotically smooth. Here sits a reasonable man. "I got six keys of that a few weeks ago. Directly from Luis Escobar."

Agualar perked up further at Escobar's name. His death early last week had been big news statewide, although everybody on both sides of the law still seemed to be scratching their heads over it. His bookend bimbos hadn't been much help in figuring it out. A wet man with golden brown skin and black hair—that was all they could agree on. Great, detain Latin America for questioning. A real pro job, though, and the hitter had a twisted passion for novel ways of whacking people. Some rival importer's doing, no doubt. Competition for Escobar's throne had been a hard, fast, and bloody scramble. Dade County was in definite turmoil.

"Escobar said you weren't interested in handling this stuff. Skullflush, it's called." Tony shrugged. "I know, I know, I thought it was screwy myself. But what, I'm gonna call him a liar?"

Agualar's jaw was clenched as he stared at his desktop. He began spinning the revolver's cylinder while shaking his head. "That dead fuck, Escobar. That dead fuck. Didn't say dick to me about this, didn't say *dick*!"

"My source for it has dried up," Tony continued, "and so naturally I turn to you. I was hoping to find someone with longer arms than I've got, help keep my customers happy."

Agualar was nodding, sweat glazing his skull, beading over his upper lip to make a watery paste of the residual coke smeared there. From another drawer he pulled a larger vial of his own and a tiny gold spoon. He loaded each nostril twice and shut his eyes and groaned. Rolled his eyes open again. Watery, bleary, bloodshot.

"I'll check into this," he said.

"At least I brought you a token taste." Tony nodded toward the vial of green. "Enjoy."

Agualar's eyes narrowed. Ever suspicious, poisoners in my midst. "You first."

"You know I never touch the stuff."

"Make an exception."

Tony had fully expected this. He held out his hand for, and received, the gold spoon. Snorted a load into each nostril and shuddered distastefully for image's sake. His mind was momentarily swimming by the time he recapped the vial. The dosage hadn't been enough to bring on the change, just a heady light show.

Agualar nodded, nonplussed. "I'll see what I can do."

"Careful with that stuff. Very pure—it's uncut." He rubbed the bridge of his nose. "Packs a punch at first, but worth it, I suppose." He paused. "*If* you're into that sort of thing. Not my cup of tea, personally."

Agualar sniggered wetly.

"My gratitude," said Tony.

"Andy? *Andy!*" Agualar bellowed, and the guy outside the door reappeared. "See Tony out. And leave me the fuck alone tonight. Anybody bothers me, I'll have his balls for paperweights."

Tony bade the pig good night and dutifully fell in step with

Andy as they retraced their steps. He would have given anything to read Agualar's thoughts right now, seeds of panic sprouting in the muddle of his mind. Groping for reasons as to why Escobar had shut him out on skullflush distribution. He had to be wondering if he was ready to be set up for the high and mighty plunge because of his own addictions. So the Medellín cartel had dealt with one of its own, Carlos Lehder. Set him up for capture when his head got too full. Quickly extradited, and now doing life at a U.S. federal prison.

Things would surely look bleak to Agualar, at the moment. And no better way to perk up sagging spirits than chemically. With whatever happened to be at hand.

Tony collected Lupo at the door, and they were ushered out. Night had become complete. They got into the Lincoln, Lupo fired the ignition, and they were slowly rolling to loop around and head back out the drive.

"Did he buy it?" Lupo asked.

"Oh yeah." Tony laughed, going for the rope in the glove compartment. "I bet his shorts are full of bricks by now."

One end of the nylon rope had already been tied into a tight loop, and this he slipped over the handle of the passenger door. Fed the other end into Lupo's right hand. Should be just enough slack.

Their headlights cut twin cones of brightness through the drive, already dimly lit by a gauntlet of small sodium globes. All the better for the cameras. Lupo kept the speed down, a steady six miles per hour. As they neared the curve, he hung as far inside as he could without it looking overdone.

Tony unlatched the door, held it ready. Before leaving the penthouse this evening, he had taped the little button down to prevent the inner light from winking on and the buzzer from going off.

Into the curve . . .

Into the blind spot . . .

"Banzai," said Tony, and pushed the door open far enough to slip out and tumble to the ground beside the asphalt. While Lupo gave a yank on the rope to swing the door shut again. Its clunk was scarcely audible over the engine. No way could the pair of guards at the gate have heard.

Just as surely as they would never know that only one man now sat behind the mirrored windows.

Tony hung in beside the trees while the Lincoln continued its slow, steady trek to the gate. Saw the glow of the brake lights, heard the opening, then the closing, of the gate.

Alone, then, night, and shadows.

According to Santos, the bulk of Agualar's closed-circuit cameras on the grounds were mounted to keep watch on the walls. The house was covered as well, but less thoroughly, mostly the entrances and ground-floor windows. Couldn't have *too* many cameras going at once, or the guys on monitor duty inside could never keep track of them all.

Tony didn't need doors, didn't need windows. Just shadows, and occasional ground cover. His maps of the grounds had been committed to painstaking memory, his route worked out in advance. And he hadn't chosen black clothing tonight as a fashion statement.

He took his time, worked his way back toward the house, then made a wide sweep around it. Tree by tree, shadow by shadow. In view of Agualar's den near the back of the house, Tony could see his distorted image through the thick cubes of glass. Bloated and wavy, multiple Agualars still sitting at his desk.

Tony crept all the way into Agualar's hedonistic playground of gardens and pathways, deck and waterfall and pond. These too were softly lit, and beneath the night sky, both water and grounds became a dreamy tropical oasis.

He pressed on until he came to the farthest reaches of the screen of trees, then doubled back through thick-trunked palms, ferns, palmettos, banyans. As he neared the perfect man-made rocky bluff, the noise of the turbine-driven waterfall drowned out whatever faint rustling noises he made.

The rocks, finally. Safety, shelter, and water.

Tony crouched between the sinewy multiple trunks of a twisting banyan and the water's edge, and there he shed his clothes. Everything went into a neat pile. He reached into a shirt pocket and pulled out another vial. Substantially larger than what he'd given Agualar.

While bringing himself to the brink of change and beyond, he remembered the effects the drug had brought about when he and Sasha had taken it together. The meshing of mind and spirit in some higher plane of existence, the union allowing him to subjugate her will, make it bend to his own. He was born for this. The game was his to win.

And so in the midst of artificial paradise, he became new. The remolding of his head and shoulders into a sleek, scaled bullet. The cavernous mouth rimmed with carnivore teeth. The coarse, webbed hands. Far more effective for certain situations than the old Tony could ever have been.

The water was cool, as inviting as a silken featherbed. He slipped in and beneath its surface with barely a ripple. Free at last to swim and take full advantage of what the gifts of nature redefined had bestowed. Freshwater flowed past gills, infusing them with oxygen richer than he had ever known with lungs. No orgasm could ever have felt as intense or lasted as long.

Within his soul, his spirit searched the inner planes for another nearby spark of life. Nothing yet. He was content to wait.

The amount he had left with Agualar would never be enough to bring on the change, even if the man had known of it and willed it. Just enough to open his mind.

And leave exposed its vulnerable white underbelly.

Tony dove, he swam. He explored the bottom of the pond, its sand and rocks. He glided beneath the waterfall, heard and felt the pounding roar overhead. Farther in, behind the falls, he found a grate recessed into the rocks where water was sucked in and recycled for the spillway. He swam away, skimming bottom . . .

. . . and soon sensed that feather-tickle of a new window opening near his soul. The first terrifying and awe-inspiring steps down someone else's road, illuminated by green powder.

contact

He stroked, he soothed frayed nerves into submission, as gentle and unobtrusive as a guardian angel. Even from out here, Tony could sense Agualar's quickened heartbeat, then its slowing as he ministered to the fear. Nothing to be afraid of, nothing at all.

With any luck, Agualar would think the thoughts were his and his alone. Never suspecting them of being spoon-fed.

Soothing . . .

Calm . . .

Tranquil . . .

Nothing but bliss, soft and loving.

Come on in, the water's fine. . . .

Tony swam in broad circles at the bottom of dark, dark water. And oh, what secrets it held.

While above, there came footsteps. A shedding of clothes. Low groans of someone in the throes of never-ending wonder. Finally, a tremendous splash.

Tony felt the shock waves from above, minute ripples reaching all the way down, tingling along nerve receptors across his new hide. He didn't even need sight to pinpoint direction.

He flashed up from the depths, jaws opening, the shark's-tooth necklace trailing down against his chest.

Contact.

Hard. Fast. Bloody.

Thrashing, flailing. A flurry of jaws and pyramid-shaped teeth like razors. Screams that gargled in a throat choking with water.

Tony dragged him all the way under, no longer disgusted by the man's bulk. Not in the least, the more the merrier. He burrowed into gushing warmth, drove the struggling body into the rocks. Nowhere left to go. Agualar's fingers clutched weakly at the grate.

And moments later, the waterfall began to run red.

28
THE JUDAS kiss

Justin sat half awake, half asleep, while the hours they had spent in the car hung over him like swollen clouds. Swabbed with moonlight, April was curled in the seat beside him, in deeper sleep. The first several times she whimpered, he couldn't place the sound. Tiny high-pitched moans, weaving in and out of stray thoughts trying to become dreams. They tugged him awake, and for a moment he blinked and watched the turmoil rippling across her sleeping face.

No peace, even in slumber. He gently shook her by the shoulder.

April awoke with a start, a soft cry. She clutched at his hand. Seconds later, she was leaning into him, embracing with heat, fear, desperation. Her cheeks felt damp against his throat.

"You were having bad dreams," he whispered.

She nodded.

"Want to tell me about them?"

"Huh-uh." A quick shake of her head. "Just hold me."

Whether it was late Thursday night or early Friday morning, Justin did not know. Darkness hung poised somewhere between fading dusk and coming dawn. As much one as the other.

They had followed their mark in the white Daytona, northeast across Tampa, until he arrived at what was presumably his home. A shabby two-story house in a block full of similarly humble dwellings, not far east of the University of South Florida. April had said the general area had been coined Suitcase City, so named for the transient population.

At first they'd parked along with other cars out on the street, a block away but in view of his car in the driveway. But after darkness fell, they knew they had to get closer. Easier said than done; the only available places were too close for anonymity. Justin had turned their car onto an intersecting street, around the corner from the guy's house. Out of sight as well, as they found what was undeniably an unoccupied house with a badly overgrown lawn and boarded windows. He parked in its driveway. Kerebawa solved the visibility problem by leaving the car and finding a bushy vantage point from which to keep an eye on things. Anything happened, he promised to be back in a flash to let them know. Justin had told him to come back for a shift change when he felt tired.

Hours ago, that had been. Kerebawa seemed adamant about pulling his weight. The only time they had seen him since was after April had hiked off on an expedition for fast food, and they sneaked him some chicken.

Justin keyed the ignition to auxiliary power to check the time. Blue-green digitals, almost two o'clock. From somewhere in the neighborhood he could hear a stereo, through open windows, but it sounded small, far away. A distant lullaby when he didn't feel much able to sleep at the moment.

He kissed April on wet cheeks. Salty. Nuzzled at her forlorn attempt at a smile.

"What do you want to do to celebrate when all this is over?"

She pulled her hair free where it clung damply to her neck.

"I want to go someplace where it's cold. I want to feel cold outside."

A worthy goal. They had spent too much time sweating in cramped cars, sweating out hopeless situations. Somewhere cold in May, June. Far far north. Sometimes it felt as if he would never know cold again.

"Make love with me," she said softly. "Please."

"Right here? Now?"

She nodded. Clutched at him. "I need to feel you with me."

He stroked her hair, traced a finger along her cheek, jawline. "What if Kerebawa comes back?"

"Then he comes back." She lifted fingers to her blouse and slowly began to unbutton. In the moonlight, her hand was a sensual ghost. "As close together as they live in his home, you don't think he's used to that by now?"

"Probably." It was the last thing he needed to say for a while.

Justin slipped his jeans down as she wriggled out of hers and let them lie in the floor atop accumulated trash. He scooted out from behind the wheel, slumped a fraction to let her turn her back to the windshield and ease down onto him. She gasped, leaned in, and hung on to his shoulder, then swayed back.

Moonlight burned through her hair, turning it platinum, and as she began to ride him with a frantic urgency, he felt on his chest the splash of a single tear.

Late Friday morning, Tony tried on Agualar's office throne, just for size. It felt a little sprung out by the ample butt of the late, unlamented kingpin, but still, not bad. Not bad at all.

He got up, strolled out from behind the polymer desk, crossed the room to a mirrored mosaic on the far wall. Nine separate square mirrors in all, etched with a pattern that looked vaguely oriental. Tony stared past the pattern, checking his reflection. A far cry from last evening. Now he sported one of his two-grand white suits. Freshly showered and shaved up in one of Agualar's sumptuous bathrooms, with his hair skinned back from his forehead into an immaculate ponytail. He was the resplendent picture of success.

A grand morning, absolutely. Tony had company, inside

himself. Chunks of the essence of Rafael Agualar, held eternally in a prison of flesh, locked into a soundless scream. Until he, like Sasha, would be drained into a negated existence. Food for the soul. Tony had never felt as nourished, neither physically nor spiritually.

A knock at the door.

"Yo," Tony called out.

The door swung half-open and Lupo popped his head in, much as Agualar's boy Andy had done last night.

"First car just came up out on the drive," Lupo said.

"You know who it is?"

"Guys at the gate radioed back, said they thought it was Rojas."

Tony nodded. "Keep everybody waiting out in the front room until they're *all* here."

Lupo said he would, and that was that.

The takeover of Rafael Agualar's stronghold of a home had been accomplished with military precision. After dispatching Lord High Agualar himself, Tony had waited out the skull-flush regression in the pond, flexing muscles and psyche alike. Working off the lethargic bloat of his meal. A couple hours before dawn, he climbed painfully out of the water as he became himself again. No worries about the staff raising an eventual alarm over the boss's absence; Agualar had signed that particular clause of the death warrant by his own hand— had told Andy in no uncertain terms that he should be left alone all night.

Tony had waited for dawn, and by the time the first blue and pink smudges kissed the eastern sky, he was dressed back in black. When coming out for the moonlight swim, Agualar had left his office exit unlocked; another subconscious suggestion Tony had planted while tiptoeing through the man's mind. Tony had crouched just beyond the range of the camera covering the unlocked door. Timing was vital here. He knew from Santos's briefings that he would have a three-second window of opportunity to get inside unseen moments after the camera had finished a thirty-degree pivot, due to the rotation of monitor images in the security room.

Once inside, Tony had retrieved the pistol from Agualar's office desk, then stalked the plush world of eggshell and gray, up to the second floor. Burst into the security room like a nightmare. He'd just as soon have dropped both guys on the monitors right where they sat. One shot, two shots, wipe the brains up later. But Agualar's gun was a revolver, not prone to silencing. A pair of shots would rouse the rest of the house and sleeping staff.

So he improvised. Held the gun on them while he entered, and in that moment of terminal surprise and its attendant paralysis, they offered precious little fight before he clubbed both their skulls. And as he watched them slide unconscious to the carpet, Tony knew he had chosen the moment of attack with a strategist's eye. Dawn. Favored by the military for launching offensives against the enemy. Dawn found an enemy encampment in its most psychologically vulnerable state, he had heard. The night had been survived, the greater security of daylight lay ahead, reprieve and finish line all in one. Mental safeguards relaxed. For a wise attacker, then, dawn was when your punches packed the most.

Tony stripped the fallen security men, bound them with their own shirts, stuffed their mouths with their own underwear, and dragged them into a closet. Then he turned attentively to the matt black console of closed-circuit video monitors and computer grid showing a graphic overhead map of the entire estate. After scanning the control panels for a few moments, he found the in-house remote controlling the front gate. And kept his eyes glued to the gate monitor, showing two guards with far too little to do.

Four minutes later, the monitor's static image showed the Lincoln easing to a halt before the gate. Lupo got out, sipping from a large cup of steaming coffee. *Fingers crossed.* The pair of guards spoke with him through the gate a moment; Tony had granted him carte blanche on whatever lie he wanted to feed them as an opener. Then in a wink: The scalding coffee was pitched into the face of the nearer guard. Next thing they knew, Lupo had produced a very business-oriented silenced automatic and had clipped them down.

At which point Tony happily pecked the switch to open the gate. The barbarians had just breached the city walls.

Lupo cruised the Lincoln in, the Barrington brothers hidden behind its mirrored glass. A minute behind were another two cars filled with reliable soldiers recruited from street operations, each one rabid for an upgrade in salary and choice of assignment.

Tony closed the gate, watched the silent black-and-white screens as the trio of cars rolled up the drive to the house. By the time they were at the front door, Tony was down to meet them, greet them, open up, and let them inside.

Soon followed by a quick, efficient mop-up operation of off-duty sleeping staff. Divide and conquer, search and destroy. A few prisoners, a few casualties. And a few immediate defections by some wise souls whose ties to Agualar were solely a matter of employment without sentiment. Tony and Santos had gone over the roster one by one the day before, separating wheat from chaff. Likely candidates for conversion, guys with enough brain wattage to recognize a silver opportunity. And guys whose pigheaded allegiance to an outmoded regime made it pointless to offer them anything other than lead.

Never let it be said that Tony Mendoza killed indiscriminately.

Satisfied with his reflection in the mirror, Tony paced back to the desk. A bit nervously, he had to admit. Nothing wrong with that. Nerves were good, kept you alert. Nerves kept you thinking and watching, so long as you didn't let them snowball into panic.

He reached to the floor beneath the desk—ample legroom down there—and brought up a vinyl bag. A softshell camera case; he had found it upstairs earlier in the morning. He plopped it to the desktop at his left elbow as he sat waiting for the final act of the coup d'état to play itself out.

It began ten minutes later. A half-dozen guys whose shiny cars lined the drive, summoned earlier by one of the defectors under admittedly false pretenses. Rojas, a walking display of jewelry-store gold. Henderson, fair and vaguely Nordic and wearing light workout clothes. Fernandez, a cherub-faced guy who favored open collars. Others; Riva, Diaz, and Monroe. Agualar's lieutenants one and all. The next set of links in the chain of command, the men who legged the orders out into the streets, who got things done or delegated responsibility and puppeteered life and death and dealings from a comfortably insular distance. In purely conventional white-collar terms, middle management.

The wary confusion was in their eyes, ushered into Agualar's inner sanctum by enough familiar faces to make things seem normal enough. But plenty of new faces, too, who made no effort to conceal just how well-armed they were. All told, fifteen guys in this office. With more to come when the time was right.

"Mendoza, what the fuck you doing here?" Fernandez didn't try to disguise the contempt in his voice as he took a seat before the massive desk.

Tony smiled tightly. "Mister Agualar has finally taken me under his wing. He and I—well, we've come to a business arrangement that should interest all of you. He'll be down in a few minutes." A big grin. "He had a rough night."

"Rafe's gonna have your balls, he comes in and finds you in his chair," said Monroe.

A knowing titter rippled among them. Let them laugh, Tony did not care. He'd have their undivided attention—and respect—soon enough.

Tony glanced back to the doorway, caught Lupo's eye, and gave a terse nod. Lupo disappeared for a moment, then came back in escorting Santos. The accountant turned Judas. He had doffed the sunglasses today, although the bruises inflicted from Agualar's fists had faded only minimally. Other than that, he looked as cool and collected as a grand-an-hour lawyer.

Tony rose and met Santos at the edge of the desk, drew a comradely arm around the man's narrow shoulders. Ushered him to his own reserved seat behind the desk. A move that brought no small degree of interest from the lieutenants. Legitimacy.

Tony opted to remain standing as he addressed his guests.

"Ours is a business no different from any other," he said. "You want to know who the movers and the shakers are in the game, all you need to do is follow the money. Money doesn't lie."

Let it sink in a moment, make sure they were all on the right track.

"Mister Santos here"—a friendly clap on the accountant's

shoulder—"with all his financial savvy, has decided to side with me. And this is one smart man, by anybody's standards."

Financial savvy. Now *there* was the understatement of the day. While he didn't know the combination—that was likely lost with Agualar's last breath—Santos had assured him that an upstairs wall safe was stocked with roughly five million in emergency cash. No matter; the safe could be blown. Of considerably greater significance, Santos had access to another fifty-five mil in bank accounts and holdings as far west as Dallas and as far east as Zurich. And sixty million in play money was nothing to take lightly. Sixty mil could sling around vast tonnages of weight.

Especially when considered as a mere seed for greater fortunes.

Tony realized he was letting the thought of all that cash distract him. He barely caught it, somebody bitching about his boast of Santos shifting allegiance. It would be weak to ask the whiner to repeat. No real need though. He'd caught the gist of it: Agualar would most definitely have something to say about *that.* Hell to pay.

Tony merely smiled and unzipped the camera bag. "I'm glad you brought him up, I was about to forget him." He reached into the bag. "Why don't you ask him to his face if he minds."

Tony grabbed a fistful of matted hair and yanked. Like hefting a melon by the vine. He let the vinyl bag fall to the floor and in the same fluid move plunked Agualar's head onto the desktop. The ragged stump of his neck made a wet slap and dribbled pinkish water, the last drainage of what he'd soaked up in his pond. Tony took care that the ghastly gray face was staring out at the lieutenants, no mistake in the identity.

"Makes a good paperweight, don't you think?" said Tony.

He couldn't have snared their wholehearted attention any better if he'd snorted skullflush and changed right before them. Controlled pandemonium. You could chart it in their eyes, a comfy complacency over what they thought would be another routine meeting veered 180 degrees away from the norm. Bedlam, babble, and uproar.

At all times, Tony had been keeping one eye on Riva. One

of the younger lieutenants, good-looking chisel-faced guy. Looked like he should do shaving ads. Santos had filled him in that Agualar and Riva had almost some sort of father-son rapport. Not the choice of background that would allow him to take this type of news with an amiable shrug. Tony watched Riva regain his fragmented composure, then plunge a hand beneath his jacket. Tony had seen enough custom-tailoring jobs to know what hung beneath Riva's left armpit.

He had had a few custom-tailoring jobs himself.

This time, though, the gun was resting in an open desk drawer. Almost immediately in hand, and silenced to save a lot of grief on all their ears in the room's enclosure. He fired twice into Riva's chest, sent him tumbling backward to overturn his chair atop himself.

"Sit down!" Tony shouted to the rest. He held the pistol with a rigid arm, bent at the elbow so he aimed at the ceiling. A very James Bond pose; he wished he could see himself in the mirrors. Should have assigned somebody to do photodocumentation of the event. *"Sit down and shut up!"*

He waited a few more beats, and when the silence fell, it was thick with tension that bordered on electric.

"Anybody else?" he asked them. "Anybody else stupid enough to let sentiment get in the way of profit motive?"

It was a moment of nervously roving eyes, twitches, and tics. Of dawning realization of being players in a brand-new ball game.

"Let me tell you something." With equal halves amusement and amazement, he realized he was sporting, at desk level, one impressive erection. Not that anybody was keeping their eyes lowered to half-mast. "Let me tell you something. You think Agualar was gonna keep his fucking head together for much longer? *Think again.* Every one of you that used to work for him, I just saved you prison time."

This was always a grabber. Talk of rehab and restitution and making little ones out of big ones was no topic for idle chatter.

"You know what kind of man he'd become. Every one of you. He was paranoid. He was hooked on his own supply. His judgment wasn't worth shit anymore." Tony shook his head, then took a gentle swipe at Agualar's. It toppled over with a thump and performed a languid roll, like a jack-o'-lantern nudged by a careless foot. "It was just a matter of time before he went down, and I promise you, if he'd gone down for the DEA or somebody, he would've taken others right here in this room with him. Shit rolls downhill, you know."

Now, at last, a few murmurs of agreement, and Tony bulldozed right ahead, keep the show moving. He flicked another glance back to Lupo and snapped his fingers. Lupo ducked out for another several moments.

A few months back, Lupo had read a biography and insisted Tony read it as soon as he was finished. The book was about Vlad Dracula, the Transylvania-born fifteenth-century prince of Wallachia. Tony had balked at first, but once into it could hardly put the thing down. Forget Lee Iacocca and Donald Trump; now *there* was a guy who knew how to rule an empire. Vlad the Impaler, as he had come to be known, had been the real-life inspiration for the fictional vampire. That they had managed to water him down into limp-wristed, swishing Bela Lugosi was a travesty. Lugosi couldn't frighten his way out of a wet paper bag. The genuine Vlad, though—one scary monarch. He surrounded his capital with a virtual forest of corpses impaled on huge wooden stakes to warn off marauding armies. When meeting with visiting dignitaries who refused to remove their hats in his presence, Vlad said more power to them and had the hats nailed to their heads. For all his bloodlust, though, he had been an incredibly successful ruler and defender of his country.

The book's lessons were not lost on Tony. In a world where you lived by your balls as well as your brains, you could never overemphasize the importance of driving home your point with a good Technicolor display of carnage. Just to demonstrate that you meant business.

Agualar's death? A necessity. Shooting down Riva? Self-defense.

Next on the agenda though . . .

Lupo and a couple of other soldiers marched in seven guys with the efficiently brisk stride of guards in a POW camp. Former Agualar employees, hands bound with nylon cord behind their backs, mouths sealed over with two-inch tape. Above the tape, their eyes were huge and luminous white, endlessly roving for escape or salvation, they didn't look picky. But the sawed-off shotguns carried by their escorts were all the incentive needed to kneel when told. Before the desk, facing the audience. Pretty maids all in a row.

"I *do* respect loyalty. These men were loyal to Agualar, and I can respect that. Can't understand it, but I can respect it." Tony spoke while pacing out from behind the desk into a pathway between the desk and the kneeling men. When he came to a pair in the middle, bruised and lumpen headed, he cuffed them with open-handed slaps, one each. "And *these* two geniuses, they're the ones let me walk right in here in the first place. I can't function with fuckups like that around me."

He was at one end of the lineup by now. He turned smartly on his heel, military crisp. And shot the first of the seven in the back of the head. Was already behind number two when the first went pitching to the floor like a sledgehammered steer. Number two followed suit. A couple of the others whose turn was rapidly coming tried squirming to safety, wobbling frantically on their knees, and were kicked back into place by the soldiers.

"Look at you!" Tony screamed at the lieutenants, Fernandez, Rojas, Henderson, Diaz, and Monroe, whose reactions were ranging from paralytic fear to utter nonchalance.

Number four had his eyes clenched tighter than fists, and from behind the tape came what sounded like garbled prayers. Hail Mary, full of grace, pray for us sinners now and at the hour of our deaths. Tony let her kill two birds with one stone and dropped him spasming to the floor. Then continued on his merry way, administering the final coup de grace to men who had been dead since dawn and simply hadn't had the foresight to cease breathing. Borrowed time was now being recalled with a vengeance.

"Look at you!" he screamed again. His voice had grown tight and husky with passion, a hoarse roar. "You can't tell me that a single one of you didn't look at Agualar and think of a moment like this. You saw it, *you tasted it!* But you didn't have the brains or the balls."

Number six dropped with a strangled bleat, and the stink of blood and cordite perfumed the air. Wisps of gunsmoke wreathed Tony's head, an ephemeral victory laurel sweeter than any olive branch. He could scarcely sense his feet touching the floor, swept away in a blissful angry whirlwind of Grand Guignol theater and allusions of deity. He was gliding, the angel of death.

Tony looked down at his suit, the pristine white now the canvas for a splotchy expressionist painting. Head wounds were a bitch when it came to blood. He felt another drop rolling down his cheek, as if he had wept blood. Tasted it when it rolled into the corner of his mouth. Salty, thicker than any tear. He shivered with delight . . .

And felt the familiar swirling sensation. The start of the plummet through aeons whose journey began with a single step of daring. Flesh and bone began to tingle, the ache in his jaws a sweet masochistic daydream. Loss of control, a fistful of sand.

The stunned eyes of his audience, the inner landscape of timeless possibilities—he felt poised between the two. Mind a cloud of wonder and fear, yes, fear, but shouldn't he have expected something like this? Three heavy skullflush trips in just a matter of days. Residual powder chugging through his system, the possibilities more lethal than nuclear half-life, just waiting for a trigger.

The smells, oh *the smells*, overpowering, he wanted it so much, *so much*, fighting to keep a rein on his runaway mind and body while hunger burst into a ball of ferocious instinct while he watched from the inside and paled before its intensity.

"You wanna know why nobody had the brains or the balls to do this before?" he shouted, and curled a trembling fist into the seventh man's collar. Ah. Andy, the steroid king of Agualar's elite corps. He hoisted Andy halfway up with one arm, muscles infused with strength gone primal, and it was either keep going and prove himself the master of body and soul, or stop and let it all pound him under like a tidal wave. *I'll tell you why—*"

Four rapid shots into the back and side of Andy's head, shearing away a bowl of skull, and Tony realized he was salivating, his chin slick and wet.

"I'll tell you why, nobody's hungry anymore NOBODY'S FUCKING HUNGRY LIKE THEY USED TO BE!"

He lunged forward like a striking cobra, drove his mouth into the red-gray ruins. Gnashed with teeth still human, then yanked back and felt the fresh warmth streaming down his chin. Felt the beast, now sated, crawl back into the past. And swallowed.

He let Andy's body collapse at his feet, faced the room with fists on hips. Lieutenants and soldiers, all his. Too scared to move, too scared to even wet their pants. Even Lupo looked wide-eyed, chalky, blown away. Vlad the Impaler had had the right idea.

Tony's breath panted as he stared them down.

"Hunger makes all the difference in the world," he said. "Any questions?"

Tony greeted Friday's nightfall from his condo complex's Olympic-size swimming pool. It had been a taxing day; a respite was mandatory. So fast, things were moving so fast. The mind swam, success triggering vertigo. And fearful awe at the uncharted territories the skullflush was lighting within him.

He backstroked while gazing overhead and watching the sky deepen to blues and violets more perfect than dreams. Maybe skullflush *did* strap you into a roller-coaster, but admittedly, he had never lived as richly, never tasted such depth in his senses. He wished he could bring down some more powder and get into its world right here and now.

He broke water at one end, slung his hair back from his eyes, and let it bunch down against his shoulders. Smiled up at a trio of girls sitting around an umbrella table, iced highball glasses before them, a cooler at their feet. They smiled right back, all dimples and bedroom eyes.

"Thirsty?" one asked him, a blonde with a pneumatic chest.

"Got any Bloody Mary mix?"

They chatted awhile longer, and soon he looked up to see Lupo standing on the penthouse balcony. Leaning on the railing, gazing down with expectation. Tony nodded up to him, lifted a hand full of splayed fingers. *Five minutes.* He bade the ladies a fine evening and splashed away from the side. Wordlessly stroked past BB and Ivan Barrington as they made sure nothing happened to him. A few more laps ought to finish his workout in prime form.

Lupo. He was starting to worry about the guy. Just a whisper. Sometimes he sensed that Lupo was going soft over the latest developments in the powder world. Not that they didn't take some getting used to, even for this line of work. And so far, so good. But now and then, a sidelong glance at Lupo's expression showed a wane in that old enthusiasm.

Be a shame to have to retire him. Not something Tony wanted to do unless it became unavoidable.

But the opportunities offered by skullflush were too broad and limitless to turn your back on. High-premium rocket fuel. The possibilities for the future, with its judicious use, were legion.

But his one kilo, minus what had already been used, was not going to last forever. While neither would the additional five, they were a far healthier stock than one. Getting them back was paramount, every bit as important as corking the gap left by Agualar's swift departure.

The latter had already been accomplished, the former soon to commence. Yesterday's phone call had changed everything.

Tony surged up and out of the water at the end opposite the girls. Rested his forearms against the tiles. Floating a few feet away, bundled into a tiny life vest, was a dry-haired little boy. He kicked and paddled and bobbed without making much headway, then looked over at Tony with a huge grin.

"Hi, mister," he said. Cute as hell. "You sure can hold your breath underwater a long time."

Tony patted his head and smiled.

Justin felt as limp and wrung out as an old dishrag by the time the white Daytona gave them cause to move. It had sat idle until eleven Friday night, and he was ready to tear his hair out from the inside. Too much monotony, too little food, too long doing a slow baste inside the car. April looked just as bad. Kerebawa wore the strain the best. Getting to push the car up near seventy and stir up a brisk airflow was like a smile from heaven.

"I feel like hanging my head out the window and letting

my tongue flap," he told them. "A billion dogs can't be wrong."

Anything to keep the mood a little buoyant. Seemed that every avenue of diverting small talk had been explored in this pressure cooker of the past thirty-some hours.

The Daytona led them south down Tampa's middle along I-275, then exited to the west for a neighborhood near the airport. A definite step up from what it had just left. Justin, from a block away, saw it turn into a driveway; he cut onto a cross street and circled this adjacent block and came back around to park and watch and wait. His eye sockets left oily smears on the binoculars.

"I can't believe he's doing this alone," Justin said. "If that was me, I'd for sure be bringing some backup along."

They watched. Waited. After ten minutes' time . . .

"And here's our boy now," Justin murmured. The binoculars felt like an outgrowth of his face. "And he's *not* empty-handed."

"What's he got?" April asked.

"Looks like a nylon jock bag. It's bowed in the middle, got some weight to it." He lowered the binoculars. "One wimpy-looking guy, he shouldn't be any problem at all."

After the Daytona started to roll again, Justin felt profoundly grateful that their rental looked just like a dozen other nondescript breeds on the road. They played hound and hare south, then east as the courier led them back toward the city's heart. Through it. Past it.

They eventually picked up a street named East Platt, below downtown, one of the southernmost streets of this portion of Tampa, apex of the inlet formed by Hillsborough Bay. Across the channels from Davis and Harbour Islands. East Platt was dismal by day, no better by night, an industrial and shipping district resembling several such port cities along the upper eastern seaboard. Railroad tracks crosshatched paths between and alongside streets. Beyond the dim buildings lurked still caravans of boxcars.

Traffic had thinned considerably, and by now it was well after midnight. East Platt was little better than a ghost town, and Justin began to sense a creeping feeling in his gut that the end of the line was very close indeed. He killed his headlights, drove by following the taillights ahead. With no more headlights to blend into as part of the background, darkness was the only alternative.

One hundred and fifty yards ahead, the Daytona's brake lights flared. After passing a grimy warehouse, it turned right onto the grounds, disappearing from sight a moment later. Justin drifted farther to the right, hoping the warehouse would keep them shielded. When he drew alongside, just past the near end, he stopped and killed the engine and hopped out with the silenced Beretta in hand.

"Be right back," he whispered. "I want to take a quick peek, see what he's doing."

Justin went sprinting around the end of the warehouse, bent low and trying to keep his running shoes from doing more than whispering on the asphalt. He was wearing a cut-down T-shirt, now smelly and vile, and its oversize armholes flapped in the breeze he made. He passed loading docks and dumpsters, hugged their shadows.

The corner. Justin let the Beretta lead the way as he eased around. There were more loading docks at intervals along the back, and across the lot was scattered a loose collection of truck trailers. Some in fair shape, others rusted and skeletal. Overhead, the moon played games with clouds, sometimes there, sometimes not.

Near the far end, he saw a quick flash of backup lights as a transmission shifted to park. The Daytona sat near a haphazard group of other cars near a chain link fence. While the driver got out, Justin dropped lower and scooted along the base of the nearest loading dock, elbows and knees. Get a little closer.

From forty yards he watched the mule take the nylon bag and carry it to the back of one of the other cars. Corroded hinges squalled as a trunk lid was raised; a moment later, it slammed. The courier was a vague silhouette as he returned to the Daytona empty-handed. Justin lay prone as the mule geared his car, popped his headlights on, and backtracked for the exit. A moment later, the car disappeared around the warehouse's far end. He listened to the motor fade until it became one with the city's ambience. Forever lost. Fabulous. Wouldn't even have to rob the mule directly.

Justin rose to his knees, swept his gaze over the grounds. Truck trailers to the right, warehouse bulking over his left. Its multipaned windows were as dark as dead eyes. Spooky place. Any security, night watchmen? Apparently not, if Tony's network used the grounds for a drop point. Or maybe security was bribed to look the other way. Have to take that chance. He stared at the cars near the fence. From here, they looked like junkers. Six or seven, a couple sitting at a slant with flat tires. Overall, the place was cluttered with hiding places. But—nothing ventured, nothing gained.

He returned to their rental, told April and Kerebawa what he'd seen. Then tugged the keys from the ignition and motioned for Kerebawa to follow him to the trunk. A car cruised past on East Platt, and he suddenly felt very conspicuous. Get this over with. He opened the trunk.

"Just in case we have trouble down there," he said, "you think you can go in from this end and work a path around to watch out for us?" Justin swept an arc with his hand.

Kerebawa nodded. "I can."

Justin took the longbow and a clutch of hunting arrows from the trunk. Noticed that Kerebawa was already carrying the machete. Thinking ahead. Kerebawa relieved him of the bow and arrows, then slung on the bow with the string crossing his chest.

"When you see us get the bag and drive away without any problems, come back here and we will too, pick you up here at the same place."

Justin bent into the trunk to pull out a tire tool with a beveled prybar at one end. He softly shut the lid, looked over to tell Kerebawa good luck, something, anything.

But he was already gone. No sight. No sound.

Justin brought the tool with him as he got behind the wheel and started the car. April glanced over her shoulder.

"Where's Kerebawa?" she asked.

"He's going to play our guardian angel."

"*Justin.*" She looked close to panic. "Do you think it's very smart to split us up this way?"

"Yeah, I do. Come on, relax." He frowned, rested a reassuring hand on her shoulder. It was trembling. "Don't worry, this'll be the easiest thing we've done all along. A couple minutes' work, and then we can head for the motel to sleep for real."

Justin followed the Daytona's earlier path in. When his lights caught the menagerie of cars, he saw he was right. Ready for the scrap heap. Several of the windshields were nothing more than jagged fragments stuck in the frames. Rust had eaten into bodywork like cancer, while weather and salt air had aged them. The mule appeared to have dropped the stash in the trunk of a car near the far left, and there Justin parked. Killed the engine.

He got out, took the tire tool along. The Beretta he slid inside his waistband. The silencer probed uncomfortably into his crotch. April followed him to the car.

He looked down at the trunk lid. Broad thing, the car was once an LTD. He tested the lid. Solidly locked. At least something still worked.

"Keep watch, okay?" he said to April. "This'll take all of my attention for a minute."

He widened his stance and dug in his heels, jamming the chiseled end of the tire tool up under the trunk lip, beneath the lock. The muscles in his arms corded, biceps balled up as he strained. He shifted for leverage, felt sweat drip from his face. It already felt coated with greasepaint, a little more wouldn't matter. He heaved several times, and at last the lock gave with a satisfying pop. He raised the lid and knew he had the right one as soon as he heard the hinges.

The trunk, full of night.

"Let me see the flashlight," he said.

April gave it to him, and as it passed from hand to hand, he could feel her shaking. His own sense that this was a cakewalk began to ooze away. *Something's wrong here, she feels it I feel it . . .*

He aimed the flashlight into the trunk, flicked on the beam, starting to dread what he would find. Wild imagination got the better of him, and he knew he would find Erik folded inside, no, that was ludicrous, Erik was safely buried, beyond their reach and infliction of pain forever, and he held his breath and saw—

The bag. The whole bag, and nothing but.

Sigh of relief.

He yanked down the zipper, parted the nylon opening, and shined the beam inside.

And felt suddenly very ill when he saw that all it contained was clear plastic bags full of sand.

Kerebawa had gone farther back than had Justin before heading to the opposite end of the warehouse. He crossed the asphalt lot entirely, then a narrow stretch of ground overgrown with waist-high weeds, and came upon the railroad tracks before turning east.

The tracks were on a slight rise overlooking the back lot, a definite advantage over staying below. Too many bulky objects scattered about. If he needed to loose an arrow, he might not always have a clear shot unless out in the open. And to do any good for Justin, he had to stay hidden.

Kerebawa bent low and followed a string of boxcars. Ugly things, but strong, and big as houses. He kept to their shadows, while ahead and to the left came the sounds of Justin attacking the drop point. Metal squealed.

Kerebawa knew nothing of trains, of boxcars. Seeing something ahead of him, thin and poking horizontal from one's doorway, seemed no stranger than the idea of boxcars to begin with.

Until it shifted.

He froze.

He began to feel panic when he realized he could not read this situation as one like Justin could. Justin *knew* these lands, these structures, what they were like inside and out.

He inspected the boxcar to his right. Saw how its door slid back and forth instead of swinging open and shut on hinges. This particular door hung half open, and he looked through it to see how they had doors on the other side, as well.

Clamping the machete between his teeth, Kerebawa dropped to hands and feet and scuttled directly beneath the boxcar and moved forward. Counting off one car, then two, until he was under the suspicious one. He eased out from beneath on its far side, drawing near to the doorway, machete cocked and ready to swing.

Inside, he could see little more than dusky brown shadows, but once his eyes grew accustomed he made out, from behind, a man lying prone on the boxcar floor. A rifle notched against his shoulder.

Kerebawa ducked back from the doorway. The man was too low, spread out flat, a poor target for an arrow. And with the floor itself nearly chest high, he doubted he could climb up in perfect silence.

From above, then?

Kerebawa backtracked along the boxcar's frame, found the coupling hitch. A starting boost, at least. Then he looked up and saw the ladder. He set the machete down, all but one arrow.

And began to climb.

Sand. All this exhausting time and turmoil for bags full of *sand? Sand?*

Justin slammed down the trunk lid, didn't know whether to laugh, cry, or scream.

Seconds later, he could scratch laughter from the list; someone else had beaten him to it. His shoulders slumped even before he turned and saw Tony and his Goliath of a friend and bodyguard. Where they had come from he couldn't tell, maybe from behind one of the nearby truck trailers. Didn't really matter. What did was that they were there, not ten feet away, and looked very pleased with themselves, and that Lupo held a small submachine gun on him.

Justin rested his right hand against his hip. Inches from the Beretta. Half a chance, given half a chance . . .

"Ah ah ah. Naughty, naughty." Lupo jiggled his gun. "Hand away from that bulge under your shirt."

Dead hope was plummeting beyond the reach of light when he heard another squeal of hinges. He looked back to see a door opening on the very car he'd just jimmied, and a third man came out.

"Make sure Mister Barrington gets that gun in your pants," Tony said. "Just ease it out with your thumb and your pinkie."

He obeyed, looked over at April. She stood with eyes downcast, and he noticed she was no longer trembling. Barrington took the pistol, and Justin tightened his hold on the tire tool held alongside his leg. Barrington was in reach. He started to bring it around in a whistling sidewinder.

Barrington must have read his mind. The guy's body was incredibly lithe, and he spun into a wheelkick, his foot connecting solidly with the right side of Justin's face. He might as well have been swatted with a board. He flopped back onto the trunk lid, tasting blood inside his cheek. He dropped the tire tool, and it was scooped up before he even saw where it landed.

Kerebawa —where is *he?*

Lying back against the trunk, Justin rolled his eyes toward April. Statue-still. Eye contact at last, though, and she looked haunted with hollow resignation. He held out his hand, mumbled her name, now wanted only to die with the touch of her on his fingers.

But she didn't reach out.

Didn't move.

And finally averted her eyes.

"I'm sorry, Justin," she whispered. "I'm so sorry."

He blinked at her. Stupidly, blankly. Sensing the birth of the blackest notion he had ever come to know.

Tony began to applaud. "Good job, April," he said. Laughed again. "You did perfect."

Justin shook his head to clear the numb ringing. Couldn't believe he was hearing this right.

But when she looked his way again, smothered with guilt, and their eyes met—he knew it was true. Suicidally true.

"You set me up." His voice sounded far away.

"I'm sorry."

"You set me up?"

"You don't understand!" she shrieked. "He said if I didn't do this, he was going to send a copy of that movie to my parents! It would *kill* them, Justin. My dad—my daddy—he . . . it would . . ." She shrank into herself and was silent.

How? When? was all Justin could wonder. Monumental questions. Then it clicked. Morning rituals, April checking her answering machine. Thursday morning, when he had gone outside after getting the bad news about skullflush, soon followed by Kerebawa. Leaving her alone. Tony must have put a message on her answering machine. April's mood had gone into a morose nosedive ever since.

If he'd had anything in his stomach, he'd have lost it. The

way he had lost everything else he was clinging to in this last-ditch attempt at a new life.

Tony was laughing grandly. "Fuck a duck, man, I wish I had all *this* on film!" He danced an impromptu softshoe a few steps in April's direction, then began to sing. " *'You oughta be in pictures'!*"

Even hate was beyond Justin now. Couldn't love her, couldn't hate her, couldn't even hate Tony. Nothing was left, he was empty. Emotion was alien, in a heart that was cauterized shut. He lay on the trunk lid, a Julius Caesar to April's Brutus, bleeding from that unkindest cut of all.

His eyes flicked from one to another, Tony to Lupo to Barrington. Settled on Tony, obviously calling the shots. He watched Tony end his jig, and with it his exuberance chilled horribly. Celebration was apparently short-lived. Justin feared he was too.

"You know what I want from you," Tony said. "You took two things from me. One of them you can give back. The other—you're gonna pay, and pay, and pay."

Justin refused to blink, for fear he might miss something. Tony had become a live wire. With a queasy sense of his own vulnerability, Justin felt the cut across his cheek from Barrington's kick. The trickle of blood working its way toward his chin, jawline.

Saw Tony stare at it.

Sniff the air, intently.

And lick his lips.

"I don't need you," Tony said abruptly, and his voice had grown huskier. "I can get the skullflush back from her." A nod to April.

Watching the blood . . .

Tony produced a large plastic packet. Moonlight distorted color, but Justin knew what it would be. Tony's nose dipped low, and there came a snuffling sound. He jerked his head back, shivered, returned for more, and more.

"I was gonna save this for later," he said, his voice sprouting fearsome rough edges, "but I just can't wait."

And the change descended with the fury of a storm.

* * *

The first thing Kerebawa did after reaching the top of the boxcar was remove his shoes. Better for silence. He was half-way to a perch above the doorway when he saw that the situation over by the junked cars had fallen to pieces.

Crossroads. He weighed options and alternatives with the speed of a striking snake and decided it best to eliminate the man in the boxcar before anything else.

Why does he not shoot? Kerebawa wondered while getting into position. As silent as a panther. Then: *His job is maybe the same as mine.* Someone to act only in case of trouble.

He heard April's voice, could not make out what she was shouting. Only knew that accuracy and timing were more crucial now than ever.

He notched the arrow he'd brought into the bowstring, frowned at the way it felt, so different from the bamboo he was used to. He drew the arrow back nearly to the head, steeled his arm against the tension, and clamped the index and middle fingers of his bow hand against the arrow shaft. He could hold it this way, but not for long. He dropped his other hand away and, poised over the doorway, held fast to one of the metal ribs spanning the roof.

He leaned out, held the bow downward. Fixed his gaze on a pale arc of the man's neck, between his neatly trimmed hair and shirt collar.

Adjusted the aim . . .

And let his aching fingers spring open.

The feathers burned as they whickered past his fingers, but the arrow dropped straight and true, bursting through the man's neck just beneath the base of his skull. Kerebawa saw him jitter for a moment and hoped the gun wouldn't clatter to the ground. It didn't, was too far inside.

He looked back to Justin and the rest. And saw a sight that froze him in place.

The *hekura* . . . It wasn't supposed to happen like this tonight, not like this.

Out of arrows, he'd brought only the one. It would be quicker to jump to the ground, but at this height, with rocky ground below, he'd likely cripple himself. He scuttled back across the roof and slid down the ladder, seized his arrows and then the machete. Ran along the boxcar to the doorway.

The dead man had been nailed completely through the neck to the car's wooden floor. Kerebawa lifted the rifle from his limp hands.

Shotguns he had fired. This was something else entirely. A grip that stuck down from the stock, like a pistol's. A long, curved metal box sticking down from the center. This was like one of the wasp-guns that Padre Angus's enemies had brought to the jungles back home. He knew he dared not try to work it. But took it anyway.

Kerebawa crouched and began to cross the space between the tracks and the chain-link fence separating him from the others. Twenty yards, fifteen. He kept low inside the thicket of dry weeds choking the ground.

Close enough.

He notched another arrow, and when he looked up he saw someone ahead with the body of a man and the face of a demon, newly emerging from the contortions of the change.

Kerebawa hated these new arrows. Too short, too light, the balance all wrong, all wrong. As soon as he let it fly, he knew that the aim was off and saw it sail over the heads of their enemies to ping into the side of a truck trailer.

At least it got their attention.

There came shouting, and then angry starbursts of a wasp-gun, and Kerebawa dropped to the ground while above him, the weeds disintegrated as if hacked with a scythe. And fell like dry rain.

Justin was ready to shut his eyes and surrender to the inevitable. Tony had finished his contortions and was ready to leave Lupo's side, and the Barrington guy was looking at Tony as if *he* had been the one to drop hallucinogens.

Then the unmistakable twang of a bowstring.

A wild shot, but priceless in its reprieve. Tony, or whatever he had disintegrated into, froze. Lupo was on top of it in a microsecond, raking a line of fire through the fence.

Justin dropped beside the LTD and watched April cry out in anguish and reach into her own waistband. He had forgotten all about it, the hitman's other gun. The .32 revolver. She held it out crookedly, and it jumped three times in her hand, and the night was full of fire and thunder, and Lupo's throat burst with a shower of blood that glistened black in the moonlight.

Spraying in a beautiful arc . . .

Splattering onto the brand-new Tony Mendoza.

"Justin!"

He heard his name screamed from behind, and when he looked back he saw Kerebawa running hell-bent for the fence. Hurling something dark and sleek into the air. Some of it was shiny, some not.

Then he recognized the shape.

It slammed onto the hood of the LTD, clattering across sheet metal and then through the gap where once had been a windshield and now was open space.

Lupo was firing haphazardly, as if his trigger finger were spasming. Bullets sprayed in one direction, then another, in a random waste. When Justin looked back, he saw why.

And what fate had befallen him.

April had dropped to the ground and scrambled for cover behind another of the junkers, and now Barrington had regained some of his mind-blown senses and was swinging the silenced Beretta around to fire. The sound was deceptively gentle, delicate, and Justin went diving headlong across the LTD's ruined trunk, through the empty back window frame, falling into a back seat littered with crystalline safety glass, and soggy and mildewed from a thousand rains.

Just as the bullets began to chop out the last of the side windows, bringing them in on him like hailstones.

The hunger had begun even before the change. As soon as Tony had noticed the blood on Justin's face, smelled it on the salt air. Residual effects of the drug must have included heightened senses, because from that point on, his urges were not his own. Just like this morning at Agualar's. Then the change, against his own better judgment, like an alcoholic grasping for the lethal bottle. Finally the faceful of Lupo's blood. Hot. Rich. Potent.

Instincts surged, ancient and primordial, powerful enough to have insured the survival of a species for millennia. He could not fight them. There was no resisting them. Only bending before them, paying the homage that was their due. He was no longer their master.

He dropped the package of skullflush to follow the spouting blood back to its source. Bathed in it. Watched the insane horror shatter in Lupo's eyes as Tony brought him down to the asphalt with a roar and let the morbidly efficient jaws go to work.

Oblivious, while all around, the battle raged.

With Barrington firing blindly into the car, Justin slithered to the floorboard and reached around the front seat. Groped with one splayed hand through grit and dirt and rotten upholstery and slime until his fingers touched metal. They closed, and he maneuvered it back with him, paused a moment to see what he had.

The shape was familiar to anyone who had watched the news of ghetto violence and schoolyard massacres. An AK-47.

Justin popped up in the back seat while snapping the assault rifle to his shoulder. Hazily wondering where it had come from, if Kerebawa had disarmed some fourth member of the welcoming committee. Had to be it. He didn't know where the particulars of this weapon were situated, could only trust that if a sniper was ready to fire if needed, the safety would be disengaged.

He slammed the gun onto the back window deck, swiveled it with a loud cry. Amazing, the way a shift in the balance of power could infuse a dead soul with fresh hatred. He boiled, he raged. The magnitude was ungodly. He brought the muzzle onto Barrington and squeezed the trigger as fast as he could, for the sniper had it set on semi instead of full auto.

Fans of white fire spat from the muzzle, four times, six, ten, and he screamed the whole time while watching the karate kid disintegrate into wet fragments. The AK-47 put out a solid meaty roar that made all the others sound anemic by comparison. Barrington was dead on the ground and twitching, and still Justin didn't trust him, kept firing even as he pushed himself through the window and across the trunk. Even as he slid to set foot on solid ground once more. Until there was barely enough left to bury.

Then he turned his attention to Tony Mendoza. Grand

architect of all misery in the known world. Survival instincts must have taken precedence over hunger, for Tony rose dripping black blood from the mangle of Lupo's throat. Grappled for the fallen submachine gun.

"Don't kill him, Justin!" he heard from somewhere behind him. Kerebawa's voice barely registered. "Don't kill him *DON'T KILL HIM!*"

"Fuck that," Justin whispered, and squeezed the trigger.

Blood and tissue flew from Tony's shoulder, knocked him back and sprawling across asphalt. Justin took the time to carefully sight in while behind him, Kerebawa screamed and clambered up the fence. Again, fire. Dark blood splotched on Tony's shirt, just left of center chest, and coughed out through the exit wound. Raise the gun, fire again. Stalk this tumbling body across the asphalt like some dark avenging angel, watch organic shrapnel pinwheeling from the side of Tony's leviathan head.

Fire again, and again, and again, the banana clip in the AK-47 bottomless. Sometimes he missed, sometimes he grazed, sometimes he plowed home with deadly accuracy, and beneath the crackling rumble of the gun he began to hear a new sound, something completely out of place.

Tony was laughing.

Laughing like a man who understands the funniest, most ironic joke ever conceived, to your exclusion. Justin stilled his trigger finger, stood wreathed in the war zone stink of smoke and cordite—and watched him sit up. *Laughing.* His ruined features began to melt and flow beneath moonlight, achieving some ghastly netherworld state between his two polarities.

"Nice try," he rasped, and rose halfway to his feet.

Justin stood rooted to the asphalt. Nothing could have survived that kind of gunfire. *Nothing.* Barrington lay deader than a roadside animal. His finger twitched on the trigger twice more, blew Tony back another six feet, but it only seemed to help him along. He lurched, hobbled back toward the warehouse, and Justin could do nothing more than watch wide-eyed as this darkly spattered figure made his retreat.

Kerebawa came running up to his side, scooped up the

fallen packet of the green drug. "Do you know what you've done?" he cried. *"Do you know what you've done!"*

Justin could only stare.

"We must go."

Justin nodded. Heard the muffled sound of an engine roaring to mighty life. A moment later, one of the loading bay doors exploded into curled panels of metal and flying glass. A pale Olds sedan bulldozed out, tires squealing, and hooked sharply to its left and careened for the exit. There was no choice but to let it.

"We must go," Kerebawa repeated. *"Now."*

He was right; the police would be converging on this scene like flies. Justin hung on to the assault rifle, snatched up the fallen pistol from beside Barrington's body. The rented Dodge—he spun in circles, disoriented, probably couldn't find his own feet.

Only then did April emerge from behind her own shelter. Hate may have been out of the question before. Not now.

He looked at the guns in his hands. Then the one in hers; so far as he knew, she still had two shots left. He was sure she had gotten the same idea at the same time. *Who's first?* he wondered. Finger tightening all over again, nauseous fright.

April let the .32 fall to the ground. She walked closer, eyes empty, mouth downturned in sorrow. She looked half dead already. Then she stopped. Yanked open her blouse hard enough to pop a button free and expose more chest. Like a target.

"If you're going to do it," she said, *"do it."*

Justin shut his eyes, felt his own tears burn. Caesar and Brutus, betrayer and betrayed. Bestower and recipient of Judas' kiss. He actually felt his finger put more pressure on that trigger before he shook his head.

"Live with it," he said, anything but forgiveness in his voice. Nor was it in his heart.

But there was necessity.

"Come on."

He grabbed her wrist, yanked her along to follow. Kerebawa was already at their car. And sirens wailed in the distance.

29
FRAGMENTATION

Most of all, Tony remembered the light. Or rather, *lights.*

Those supernova blasts before him from Ivan's AK—how had Justin ended up with it?—that tore pain through his shoulder and then skewered him through the chest and soaked both sides of his shirt with dark cardiac blood. The killing light. Followed by darkness.

And there was where the gaps in memory began.

There came more light, he recalled, at some point—but from the inside. Drenched with it, he knew that in its presence a moment could seem a thousand years just as easily as the reverse could hold true. It could have lasted no more than a few seconds, given that the next thing his eyes registered was the same as the last before the blackout: Justin, closing in.

Tony stumbled up stairway after stairway to get to his penthouse, clinging to the rail as if it were a lifeline. Past two in the morning; he was the only thing moving, which was for the best. His features had oozed back to full humanity while he was behind the wheel. But before ditching the dirty-work Olds for good, Tony had inspected his damage in its mirror and knew he would give anyone, bar none, a sphincter-loosening fright.

Lights before him, lights inside. And then he had snapped rudely back to gritty reality, and the lights were before him again, Justin pumping round after round, and there had been no more pain, only annoying tugging sensations through his body.

Gaps plagued his memory, like alcoholic blackout; he wasn't sure how he had found his way home. It was as if some autopilot had taken over, leaving his own cognizance to drift without anchor.

No longer the master of his own mind; he'd grown frightfully aware that he had signed over the title papers at Agualar's. The hunger born of smelling Justin's blood underscored it. First the mind, now the body was relinquished. And the soul? A toss-up, anyone's guess.

It felt as if the being known to himself and others as Antonio Mendoza were nothing more than a figurehead. Ceremonial head of state for public appearances and the sake of continuity. While the deeper, more elemental decisions were made by something else, from the deeper levels where it preferred to hide.

Pushing buttons. Pulling strings. Routing switches . . .

And speaking to him in a language understood on the inside when it would fall on uncomprehending ears if coming from without. *We are one now,* it seemed to say. *And we are hungry.*

It told him so very many things, and each one gave him the strength to go on. Step after step, stairway after stairway. It would tolerate no disagreements. For the *hekura* were wise beyond the reaches of time.

Tony lurched through the penthouse door and quadruple-locked it behind him, reeled along until he could hit the bathroom lights and prop himself against the sink before the mirror.

The old Tony was strong inside, of stomach and heart, with

no low tolerance for things gruesome. Even so, the old Tony couldn't have seen himself in this condition without dancing on the rim of madness. His skull was wreckage. He peeled away his shirt and saw that his torso fared no better. Hamburger.

But the new Tony stared with detachment and fascination. To shriek would have been to risk the rebuke of the master. From somewhere behind his eyes, Tony peered out at a ravaged body he could no longer conceive of as being wholly his own.

Left of the breastbone, a hole, red-rimmed. He ran a finger around the ragged edges, then sank the finger in. Probed with the nail through a scabrous crust. Up to the first knuckle. Then the second. Deeper still. Alongside his finger, he felt the clenching beat of his heart. Weak, arrhythmic—but on the mend.

He popped the finger out with a wet sucking sound. Watched the unplugged hole drool a few trickles of blood before the flow turned sluggish, ceased altogether.

Tony gulped. But then smiled like a child taking his first few unaided steps. *Gonna be all right, gonna be all right.* He just needed a little sack-time, time to heal.

He shuffled over to the sunken tub and turned the faucet on full blast, watched water splash cool and inviting. The sound was sweeter than Brahms, than the voice of a lover. The chlorine though. It had burned a bit before, nothing he couldn't handle, but now it would likely be excruciating.

Tony wobbled into the aquarium room and listened to the hiss and gurgle of the homes of kindred souls. He rummaged through supplies until he found what he needed: the bottle of dechlorinator.

Soon he shed the rest of his tattered clothes. Eased the equally tattered body into the tub, nearly a three-foot depth waiting to engulf him.

He had but to think of it, and the change came over him, and while the pain was greater this time by far, given the wounds, it was better this way. A few bloodied scales slipped from his neck to the water.

No more need of the powder. For himself, at least. He

would still need it for others, and there *would* be others. A good man tries to find homes for homeless friends.

Sleepily, Tony slipped beneath the water, curled onto the bottom of the tub, the change complete.

And let the *hekura* work healing wonders.

Most of all, Justin remembered the blood. So much, so copiously splashed about.

With every passing mile back to the motel, he tried to force it from his mind. No crying over spilt milk, nor over shed blood. That he had been shoved face-to-face with the one thing that he had always wanted most to avoid in the drug world —violent physical confrontation—and that he had coped somehow, tended to foster new self-respect.

But what the hell had *happened* with Tony? The big question. He tried to impose calm on himself, wait until he and Kerebawa could talk without shouting back and forth across the seat, volume driven by sheer intensity. Wait until he could think again.

They dragged themselves through the doorway into their room, now stale and as cloying as a prison-camp sweatbox. April took it upon herself to turn on the air conditioner, and once it had rumbled to life, she sank onto the bed with her head in her hands. Apparently none too inclined to look at Justin or Kerebawa.

Justin took a step closer to her, without knowing why. And now she looked.

"If you lay a hand on me, you'll lose it," she said.

The temptation was there; perhaps she had sensed it from the wounded fury of his eyes. It had been strongest in the car, while she sat silently in back, while the enormity of being sold out washed over him stronger than a monsoon. Taken all the love, the intimacy, the passion, and kicked them into his face like sand. He actively hated her then, for being so willing to trade his life in on whatever pathological hang-up she had about disappointing her parents. The temptation to lash out in retaliation, to reach back and blacken an eye or bloody a nose, had been a tangible urge.

But he knew he could never succumb. Knew how horrible it would make him feel the instant after fist met flesh. He had killed one man, tried to kill another, and maybe someday the gravity of that would be hard to live with. Now, though, he was tolerating it just fine, jazzed on adrenaline and righteous rage. But turning the anger on April and imprinting it in blood and bruises—he found it oddly intolerable.

Maybe it was the benign sadist in him instead. Hitting April might make her feel the peace of absolution, an evening of their scores. It should never be that easy.

"She should be killed," Kerebawa said with contempt. "In my home, she would be killed for her treachery."

"Yeah, well, we're *not* in your home, so get that idea out of your head." A little of Justin's anger went deflecting toward Kerebawa, who did not pursue the matter and sat across the room with a disgusted huff. Justin turned back to April. "Answer me one thing."

She nodded, but he had to prod her shoulder to get her to face him again. Her eyes were bloodshot, purgatorial in their misery.

"Why the hell didn't you *tell* me about that message from Tony as soon as you got it? We could have figured something out." He stalked back and forth, burning nervous energy. *"How the hell could you do that to me!"*

"I didn't think we would've . . . had a chance." She wrestled mightily with something inside, and finally wrenched it free. "I was starting to lose faith, Justin! I was losing faith!"

That one nailed him where he stood. "In me, you mean."

"In you." Her eyes pleaded for some sort of warped understanding she knew could never be granted. "You don't understand about my father, if he finds out about that movie something'll happen to him, I know it will, he'll be crushed, *please*, Justin, please see that."

He stared as if seeing her for the first time, his face a shaky balance between repugnance and astonishment. "You're a head case. You really are. Hasn't anybody ever told you to get some kind of therapy?"

She hunched her shoulders, and he shook his head wearily, you never know, you just never know.

"Remember what I told you last week, why I first liked you?" Her voice was meeker. He fleetingly wondered if the shift was as calculated to manipulate as her betrayal.

He tried to remember, but too much in the interim clamored for attention. Trivia was not a strong point at present. "Why?"

"I said I liked you because you were the only guy I'd met lately who was as screwed up as I am."

Justin gave a derisive snort. "Huh. Keep looking."

He moved before the air conditioner, let the output wash over him and chill the sweat into a sticky coating. It felt as thick as caramel by now.

He badly wanted a drink. Whiskey, gin, beer, rotgut moonshine, anything would do. Blame it on dehydration. He couldn't remember the last time he had urinated. He ran water from the bathroom into one of the chintzy plastic cups, gulped it down, refilled. Came out and stared at Kerebawa, who sat on the floor beside the recovered packet of skullflush.

"And *you*," he said. "What was all that about back there? *Why wouldn't he die?*"

Kerebawa's dark eyes brimmed with knowledge, mystery. Almost otherworldly. For the first time, it looked to be a burden.

"He did."

Justin stared as blankly as when he'd first heard Mendoza compliment April on a job well done. "He did," he echoed.

"He died. And the *hekura* was able to fill him completely, then, and bring him back as its slave."

Justin hurled the half-filled plastic cup into the wall. "Why didn't you *tell* me about this? This isn't the kind of thing you just forget about!"

Kerebawa reared up from the floor. "*I* told you! I told you not to kill him!"

"*I mean before!*" Justin screamed.

"*I did!*" he screamed right back.

From somewhere on the other side of the beds' headboards came a pounding fist, a muffled shout for them to shut up, keep the noise down, people were trying to sleep. Justin stomped over and pounded in reply, both fists, hard enough to dent the plasterboard. Shouted inarticulate threats, then whirled around to snatch up his water glass. He refilled it, then slammed it down and fell into a chair at the round breakfast table. Tired, so tired. While his mind raced like a hamster on its wheel, getting nowhere fast, just burning out.

He had to calm down. Knew that if the light sleeper on the other side of the wall started to whine again, he was nearly crazed enough to grab the AK-47 from the bed and begin firing sedatives through the wall. Breathe deeply, count to ten. Make it twenty.

"You told me?" he finally said. "When?"

"When I told you how I first came to be here. I thought you understood from when I told you of how Padre Angus died. When he was taken by the *iwä*—the alligator—and would rather die than risk us killing it. Because of how the *iwä* would return."

Justin paled, now remembering the tale. At the time, he had dismissed it as so much rain-forest superstition. Filed it away.

"I didn't believe you." His voice was a raw whisper. "I didn't know . . . didn't know it would end up like that." He slowly pointed at the assault rifle. "Didn't think anything could survive *that*, I—I—" He dropped his hand and reeled back any more excuses. He had no one to blame but himself for this outcome. "I sure have fucked us."

He looked over at April; she had keeled over on the far bed, her back to him, drawn into a fetal position. Useless—for now, at least.

Finally, "Let me get this straight: Tony's dead, right?"

Kerebawa seemed to hedge against a definite answer. "Yes, no. He died for a time, but the *hekura* brought him back. They both share his body now, with no need of the *hekura-teri* powder."

"You mean he can change into that ugly fucker anytime he wants to?"

Kerebawa nodded. "Whenever the *hekura* wills it."

Justin threw his glass into the air in exasperation, let it fall to the carpet. "Then this is worse than what we started with."

"And it will heal his body."

"Sure. Why not," he muttered. Justin pushed off his shoes. The stink was offensive even to his own nostrils. "Isn't there any way to kill him now?"

"It will be difficult."

Justin brightened. "But possible?"

"Yes." As it sometimes had during their stay together, Kerebawa's face reflected the search for words to explain concepts understood intuitively in his world. "The *hekura* and the *hekura-teri*— they are born of jungle. Not born of man. So its slaves cannot die by a man's hand. Your guns, your bullets —they are not from that world, they have no results that will last. If your machines pull down a tree in the jungle, a new tree will grow, in time. The jungle heals itself, if allowed. The *hekura* are no different. He is theirs now."

Justin was beginning to see this reasoning. Primitive, the key was primitive. "Okay. Okay. What about your bow and arrows? You've still got a couple of those bamboo tips left. Why not use them?"

Kerebawa was shaking his head even before Justin finished. "No, no, no. They are no different than guns, they are made by men. *Hekura-teri* is born of jungle, and its slaves must die by jungle."

Justin nodded. Kerebawa had explained as best as he could, and the case appeared to be closed. Here it was, take it or leave it.

Options, what were his options? They had, with tonight's recovery, taken ownership of the entire load of *hekura-teri*. One victory, at least. Destroy it all, and Kerebawa's duty was fulfilled. Run him back to Miami, try to link him up with his smugglers, and that would be that. And then keep going. Maybe south, down into the Keys, where life was as lazy as waves splashing on coral beaches and the languid winds in palm fronds. Feel it, taste it, live it. Hemingway's ghost beckoned. Or head back north, look for someplace new to settle and call home. An entire nation was at his disposal. Hurl a dart at a map and head for the point. He had always liked Boston, and Boulder, Colorado.

He could start the trip tomorrow, once sleep had buffered him against the violence and horrors of this night. He could be on the road in hours.

But he knew he wouldn't be.

Ultimately, Mendoza had been the responsibility of the police. Rene Espinoza and her guarded assurances. Now, though, the burden had surely shifted, the moment he had pulled that trigger on Tony. And then there was the matter of a graveside promise to Erik.

"Jungle," he murmured. "Where are we gonna find a jungle in the middle of Tampa?"

The only thing to answer was the chug of the air conditioner.

After another couple of minutes, Justin could tolerate the feel of his skin no longer. He dragged his waning body into the bathroom, cranked the tub water to maximum intensity. The nervous wired energy of the firefight was starting to neutralize. Soak it out, wash it down the drain.

He stripped, let the vile clothes lie where they fell. He inspected his body. Several cuts, nicks, and scrapes sustained from crawling back and forth through the windshield frame. Tiny smears of blood and scabs dotting his torso, arms, knees. He looked at his face in the mirror for the first time. More dried blood, plus the bruised swelling from Barrington's foot. Not too horrendous; he might have been able to get away with a lie about dental work if not for the cut on his cheek.

While the tub filled, he wrapped a towel around his waist and left the room long enough to hotfoot down to the ice machine and fill the plastic bucket. Back in the bathroom, he dumped the ice into a hand towel, bundled it up, soaked it in cold water in the sink. A crude but effective ice pack.

Justin eased into the tub, leaned back with a warm wet washcloth draped over his eyes and the ice pack pressed to his cheek. Club Med couldn't have felt any better. Water and porcelain became as rich as silk. He could open the drain and risk oozing away with the water.

He floated in a timeless limbo in which the world outside could not penetrate past the washcloth, the ice pack. Sleep came to flirt with him, an elusive tease. He had no idea how long he'd been in the tub when light footsteps sounded on the tile floor. He pulled the washcloth away and blinked into focus.

April.

She cracked open a can of Busch beer, set it on the rim of the tub. Blue sky, white mountains. His hand crawled for it with a will of its own. Good, oh, very very good.

"I went out a few minutes. That convenience store down the street," she said.

He nodded.

"Can we talk? Please talk to me."

He looked at her sideways, evenly. Betraying nothing within. "You should have thought of that earlier."

She sat atop the toilet lid, each hand cupping the opposite elbow, resting down upon her legs, knees pressed together. No more tears, of which he was glad, but their legacy remained. He idly wondered what the convenience-store clerk must have thought of the sight of her. She looked as if one sharp word would draw blood.

"Why did you bring me back?" she asked. "Why didn't you just leave me behind at the warehouse?"

Justin drank, worked his tongue in the cut on the inside of his cheek. The beer seemed to anesthetize it.

"I don't really know," he finally said. "Cover my tracks, I guess. If you'd been around when the police got there, how long would it have taken before you'd have given them this room number?"

She said nothing.

"Maybe I can't trust you, but I can at least keep an eye on you until it's over." He shook his head. "I'm curious about something. You obviously didn't tell Tony about Kerebawa. He wasn't prepared for that at all. The guy with the assault rifle was there in case *we* got out of hand. So why didn't you serve *him* up on a silver platter like you did me?"

"I'm not sure. I guess . . . I was hoping he might get away, and—and I wouldn't have to live with the idea of him too."

"Nice of you to take him into consideration, at least." His voice was cobra venom.

"You don't understand."

How many times had he heard that? Ten? Twelve? Justin shook his head slowly. Stared at her, the low cold throbbing in his face, the trickle of water crawling along his scalp. She squirmed under the scrutiny, and as the seconds wormed by, he could almost grasp some sense of the depth of whatever she had suffered in an unfathomable past. Somewhere so deep and so tangled in the roots of her life that it might never be extricated, could be brought to the surface only by hacking and mangling those roots beyond repair. Never understand? He might at that, if only he knew. But understanding did not mean forgiveness. That legendary unkindest cut of all was a wound like no other, and oh, such scars it left behind.

Justin wiped across his eyes with the washcloth. He could feel his own tears starting to form, did not want her to see them. Although she would likely detect their presence in his voice.

"I loved you," he whispered raggedly. "I believed in you. I would've trusted my life with you." He swallowed. Anybody who said that emotion was not a tangible solid had never had to deal with the kind of lump he had in his throat. "What a fucking moron I was."

He'd thought her crying was over. He was wrong.

Justin felt as if he were on some accelerated reactory cycle of loss. Same pattern as dealing with a loved one's death. First denial, then fury. Then real grief, ravenous and all-consuming. He had sped through the first two, was now on the nauseating spiral down to the third. But in some ways, this was worse than death. It was like watching a loved one rot before your eyes, by choice, knowing you were helpless to stop it. At least the dead leave behind memories, pristine, unspoiled by time. This? This was like watching all the memories, one by one, sprout thorns, turn to poison.

"Just leave me alone," he said. "Just walk out that door and shut it, like you found it."

April nodded, rose from her seat. She was halfway out the door when she lingered, one hand wrapped around its edge, and turned to look back. Red eyes looking hopelessly for chinks in that tarnished armor he wore.

"No matter what you think about me now, please remember a couple of things. I loved you too. And—and between the two of us tonight, *I* was the first one to start shooting."

She did as asked then, and the door latched softly. Leaving him to his water, his steam, his soap, his life. Solitude, hovering over the tub like a ghost. He took a long pull at the beer, tried to soak the solitude away with everything else. Strange. Far more stubborn and clinging than blood, sweat, tears.

So try harder, later. He had the rest of his life to fret about lost loves, which wouldn't be a very long time span at all if he didn't get some priorities straight.

He drank the Busch, thought about jungles.

And then realized that the answer had been in his hand ever since April had stepped in.

30
ASSIMILATION

There is nothing worse than the scream of a friend. Only degrees of how long it lasts, how deeply it pierces. When *it will not end for hours* and comes from within, then it borders on the seventh level of hell.

Tony could hear Lupo screaming on the inside. Couldn't turn it off, couldn't sick it up like a bad meal. Had it done any good, he would have raged a tormented path through the penthouse, battering his head against walls and furniture and floors, but the *hekura* would not let him. Its vessel had sustained enough damage lately. On which it had worked long and hard.

When Tony reclaimed humanity and rose dripping from the sunken tub a couple of hours past dawn that Saturday morning, he walked to the mirror in a gait owing its shuffle more to trepidation than to bullet wounds. Risen from a watery grave, he bore only faint scars to mark the night before. A round, puckered depression beside his breastbone, more scattered elsewhere. Lumpy skin on his shoulder. He finger-parted his sodden hair and found bare little patches of scalp, but these could be hidden easily enough.

Inside his head, though, it was anything but the picture of health. Snippets of hoarse masculine cries, redolent with the stink of blood and confusion and betrayal. They rose and fell like a whining wind in the eaves on chilly nights of isolation.

He toweled himself dry, then dressed in black leather slacks and tank top, the actions automatic. He wandered about the penthouse, slowly realizing that it was beginning to seem alien. Someone else's to do with as they pleased. Smash it to bits, burn it to cinders, while he couldn't do a thing. Watch, maybe, if allowed.

In the living room, he stood before a multishelf bookcase and ran someone else's fingertip along the spines. Lupo's books, every single one. Mocking him, like patient friends that were not his to share, and who now pointed fingers of accusation.

"Get out of me!" he shrieked, not sure to whom it was directed. *"Get oouuut!"* He wrenched the bookcase over, and it crashed to the floor in a cascade of volumes. Tony dropped to his knees and tore through them, ripping the thinner ones in half and hurling them up until pages drifted about him like autumn leaves.

Energy spent, he sagged down to elbows, breathing harshly. He was on center stage, it felt, watched as a child throwing a tantrum is watched in silent reproach by a wise guardian who knows there is all the time in the world for the petulance to burn itself out. He rolled onto his side, small and insignificant beneath its gaze.

We are one . . .

and we are hungry.

And there in the floor, he surrendered. Wholly. For fear that he too would be devoured, then find himself in that worst of hells. An equal with Sasha and Agualar and now Lupo, surrounded as they ravaged him out of vengeance.

Surrender was a matter of survival as much as anything, and goals to be accomplished in vivid splashes of emerald and crimson. Too much weakness in him that had to be purged. Time to learn the basics. Again.

He went to the aquarium room, flipped on the lights. Knelt before a fifty-gallon tank with four oscars inside, striped gray and orange. Aggressive, hungry, and whose concept of mercy meant only that they toyed with food awhile rather than dining immediately.

Tony netted several feeder goldfish from their own small tank, dumped them into the larger aquarium. Then settled back in his brand-new recliner to watch the show. Strong consuming weak, the large consuming the small. Back to basics.

How primal.

How fundamentally right.

The sight was a soothing balm. He began to regard the strange dynamics within himself as a kind of seesaw. The ancient presence rising up to seize control in matters of danger, instinct, and fury—then dropping down to let the old Tony rise and carry them safe and undetected through the crafty ways of the modern world. A perfect symbiosis, and oh, such a team they made.

When the telephone rang, he was ready. Almost expecting it. He whipped up the aerial on the remote receiver. Knew it was Justin from the first word out of his mouth.

"I'm calling to see just how smart a businessman you are," his voice said. Far calmer than the last time Tony had heard it. "So far I haven't been very impressed."

Tony smiled, mildly amused. Not quite the tune he was expecting. "Sometimes business sense has to be sacrificed for personal gain."

"Yeah, and that's why you blew yourself out of the water. By the way, very impressive comeback last night. I haven't seen anything like that since the time I dropped acid." Tony couldn't believe this was the same guy close to pissing his pants last night. "Now, I don't know what kind of bogeyman that green stuff has turned you into, but I figure there's got to be at least something inside that shot-up head of yours that'll listen to reason. And will agree that it makes good business sense."

Was Justin really this naïve? Thinking he could just call up, appeal to logic? Guy had rocks in his skull. So play along, see where this infantile game led.

"I'm all ears. You got thirty seconds to interest me before I just decide to sniff you out and tear you open."

"You want the skullflush back? You can have it. It's more trouble than it's worth, considering what you've pulled to try and get it back. But I want something in return."

"My promise to leave you alone?" A malicious grin in Tony's voice.

"Yeah. Right. I'd trust you there about as well as your former bodyguard can do his job now."

Tony winced. *That* one stung.

"I'm thinking more in terms of cash. Twenty thousand for the load. If it's wholesale priced about like coke, that's not much more than you'd have paid for one kilo. A bargain, considering what you've put me through. And in return, you get your stock back, and you never see or hear about me again. Call the twenty thousand stake money to get me someplace way the hell away from here. Now, I *know* you got this big hard-on to see me dead, but just look at it with a business head for a minute."

"Twenty grand for you. Hm. What about April?" His tongue caressed her name, twist that knife a little deeper.

"Far as I know, she'll be sticking around here, 'cause she's sure not coming with me. Do what you want with her. I feel like cutting her up and feeding her to you myself. Maybe you'd choke on her."

"Not likely," Tony said. Then he mused, "So sad when love dies. If you believe in that sort of thing."

"Right now I believe in cash. What do *you* believe in?"

"Mutual trust," Tony said, then roared laughter. Oh, this was getting jollier by the moment. He tried to keep his dark delight from betraying the fact that he had no intention of shelling out one cent for what was rightfully his or letting Justin walk away with it. He agreed to the terms, none too readily, a little complaining so as not to arouse suspicion.

And then Justin laid down the particulars. The when and where.

Definitely an unexpected choice.

Justin had hung up before Tony got a chance to question. Why there? Chalk it up to his fruitcake sense of drama. What a numbnuts.

It had crossed his mind that Justin and April might be working with the police by now, that they were merely the bait for a much larger trap. At least until Justin rattled off the swap point. Way too many people for the police to feel comfy any shooting, and a fatality or two among innocent bystanders was not only possible, but likely. Hot damn, then. A genuine offer from a witless amateur.

Tony compressed the phone's aerial, feeling the hunger flood him, fresh and raw. The change was already starting to ripple across his features from excitement.

Hours to wait, though. Sadly. At least there was one consolation.

Plenty of time to work up an even greater appetite.

April watched Justin stare at the phone for several moments after cradling the receiver. The bravado may have registered well in his voice, but less so in his face. Finally he looked up.

"He bought it, I think," Justin said. So he'd been right after all. Earlier, April had feared the offer might not work, since Mendoza no longer needed the skullflush to change. Justin had said it didn't matter. Tony's pride and fury would make him seize any opportunity to get in close to them. Of secondary value was the likelihood that Mendoza would long to exploit skullflush's mindfuck potential for his own gain.

Kerebawa had been listening to the conversation from the floor, leaning against a wall. He nodded, eyes darkly set in anticipation. He spared no looks for her; she might as well not even exist, so far as he was concerned. Which was preferable, she supposed, to bearing the brunt of the ill will he professed last night.

She sat at the breakfast table, sharing it with no one but herself. The survivor who was now caught between the most rocks and hard places of all. Wishing as never before for some way to spin back clocks and calendars, to retroactively derail stupid trains of thought. The aftermath of her decisions ached like a rotten tooth.

"It made me uncomfortable hearing my fate talked about that way," she said.

Justin gave her one of the no-humor looks she had become

intimately familiar with since last night. "You don't have much room to complain."

She nodded, the responsibility leaden. "No." And turned away.

April heard him moving closer, around the bed. The bed that had been unused until last night. Her exile to it had been unspoken, but no less expected, no less absolute. Justin settled a couple of feet from her chair. He took her chin between thumb and forefinger, tilted her head around to look him straight on. Not roughly. Just sternly.

"I don't know if I can trust you on this today. Especially when you'll be out of my sight. But I've got no choice. We need three people to make this work. So if you tip off Tony in any way, or do one little thing to blow this for us, I'll figure that's it, I'm dead. So I won't care anymore. And I promise: I *will* kill you."

She reached up to curl her fingers around his own, and he pulled away.

"No, you won't," she said quietly. Not hating him for the threat, just aching for having pushed him to it. "Maybe you can bluff Tony, but don't try bluffing me. I know you better than that."

He stared, worlds apart. "I never dreamed I'd need leverage over you."

"You don't." While sleep had enabled them all to greet the world with clearer eyes and heads, for her it had only served to shine more light on the ugly truth of betrayal. Guilt, the master crippler. But she stood firm against it, refused to fall. Survival by atonement. "I can't change what I did. All I can do is try to help undo the harm. If I do one thing, I want to show you that."

Justin got up, and she could tell he remained unconvinced.

"Then you'd better do a good job. Because Tony can still send out that videotape. If he hasn't already."

There. Whether Justin realized it or not—and he most likely did—*there* was the leverage. She decided he was far more effective at manipulation when he was subtle.

"If that happens, I'll deal with it however I can." A thought that still set her insides on a ten-point quake. "So my best bet . . . is making sure he never gets another chance."

* * *

Homicide was buzzing Saturday morning. A domestic tiff on the north side had turned fatal for the husband after an upgrade from dinner plates to kitchen cutlery. Tame stuff, though, in comparison to what had gone down just off East Platt.

At first glance, Rene Espinoza thought it looked like a standard dope-deal-gone-sour slaughterfest. Of particular interest was that all three of the DOAs were ranked as known associates in the file of the one, the only, Tony Mendoza. You had your basic shot-up body, shell casings of various calibers strewn everywhere, a couple fallen guns. But closer looks showed wild deviations from that typical scenario.

Anyone could see that Eduardo Lupo's throat had been torn away to the extent that his head wobbled atop a fragile stalk of spine. But forensics said that the bulk of the damage had been caused by as-yet-unclassifiable teeth. Not human. Even so, a single bullet had been dug out of the ruins, having lodged in the spinal column.

Then there was Ivan Barrington, in the boxcar. A hunting arrow?

Nothing settled comfortably into place. And upon leaving the scene, well before dawn, the dismal night lit with swirling beacons and the entire area roped off like a grisly museum exhibit, her first stray thought had been, *Justin Gray? No. Couldn't be.* For even if it were, that still wouldn't explain everything.

Midmorning in the homicide bullpen. Rene and Nate Harris were poring over the dead men's files and logging paperwork time. Nate's metronomic two-finger hunt-and-peck keyboard prowess always grew irksome after five minutes. Her ashtray was loaded with enough butts to resemble a jumble of dry bones. She had started in on her fifth cup of coffee when Lieutenant Chadwick materialized. He wore the look of a terrier who'd just been tossed a particularly tasty scrap.

"I want you down on the lot in twenty minutes. We just got the go-ahead to move on Mendoza."

She let the sheaf of papers she'd been holding slap the desk blotter. Typing halted in midpeck. "Something must've broken on Agualar."

Chadwick nodded, fluorescent lights gleaming a nimbus around his balding pate. "Agualar's dead."

"Pity," Harris said. No mourning and a cockeyed smile.

"I just left the captain. Oh, this is rich. Turns out the DEA had a man inside on Agualar even higher up than we did. Guy's cover was the name of Diaz or something, one of Agualar's newer lieutenants. We never knew. Shit, don't you just love interagency communication?" He bummed one of Rene's cigarettes from the pack on her desk. "It's still kind of sketchy, but Thursday night Mendoza did the job on Agualar. Don't ask me how. Then, yesterday morning, he calls the lieutenants together to show off Agualar's head and announce a change in management. He lines a bunch of Agualar's goons together and pops them in the head, one by one. Diaz saw the whole thing, said it was like something out of the St. Valentine's Day Massacre. He also popped one of the lieutenants."

"How come we're just finding out about this now?" Rene asked.

"Diaz—whatever his real name is—he didn't get a chance to come out of cover until late last night. Probably about the same time you were out scraping up what was left of Mendoza's boys."

"So maybe that was a retaliation move?" Harris hunched his shoulders, spitballing.

"Who knows? All I know is, we got fresh warrants on eight counts of murder. Probably more'll turn up too."

Rene frowned. "If Mendoza falls on straight murder, the DEA won't get a thing out of it. How come they're being so generous?"

Chadwick blew smoke and shook his head with haunted eyes. "Diaz doesn't want to go back, not after what he saw. Says Mendoza's the most unstable guy he ever saw, he's wired tighter than a drum. The last guy he shot? Diaz says he cannibalized the guy right there in front of everybody."

"Oh, *that's* a cute wrinkle. Just when we thought these guys can't get any sicker." Harris threw down a bottle of white-out in disgust. "So where are these bodies now, anyway?"

"This is the sweet part. After he shot them, Mendoza picked a cleanup crew to get them out of Agualar's place and lose them. He picked Diaz. Low man on Agualar's totem pole and all, he got the shit detail. Diaz says they loaded up these eight guys and some other stiffs, and Mendoza had them drive this panel truck down into the Glades and dump the entire load. Diaz is heading back down there right now with a couple of meat wagons so they can pull the bodies back out of the swamp."

Rene held up crossed fingers. "Let's hope the gators left enough for us."

"Amen," Chadwick said. "We got two teams going after Mendoza. One at Agualar's place, in case he's still there, and one at Mendoza's condo. I want you with that team."

"If we pull him in, I want you to push for two things," Rene said.

"What are they?"

"No bond. I don't want this guy out in time for lunch."

Chadwick nodded. "Way ahead of you on that one. What else?"

"I'd like some damned loud press releases."

"What for? What's it to you?"

"Are you forgetting two weeks ago? How we stonewalled that Justin Gray character, after the Webber killing? Gray's holed up just trying to stay alive. I don't know where to find him offhand, so I want to make sure he knows it's safe for him and his girlfriend to crawl out again. We owe him that much."

Chadwick flipped a dismissive wave, cigarette clamped between two fingers. "Not my call, but I'll try." He checked his watch. "Fifteen minutes."

And then he was gone.

Rene reached into her purse, checked the load in her service revolver. Prebust ritual, obsession-compulsion masquerading as better-safe-than-sorry precaution.

She looked at the telephone and bit her lip in frustration. *He didn't even trust me enough to give me a phone number.*

Satisfied with her revolver, she thrust it back into her purse.

So keep sitting tight, Justin. And I hope like hell you're not planning to try anything else on your own.

Tony's day began to develop serious kinks by late morning.

He'd begun to feel some concern over how the mass grave down in the Everglades had gone. No word yet. Of course, it was his inner staff who generally followed up on piddly little details, then reported back to him. And his inner staff had, overnight, been decimated.

He briefly considered tapping a couple new up-and-comers who had performed well at Agualar's. Get them to back him up in secret at the late-afternoon meeting with Justin and company. New faces—the anonymity would serve well. But. It would be downright embarrassing to have to admit he'd been unable to handle witless amateurs, that they'd gotten lucky. Letting new guys in on this, it might be a tough call keeping the truth secret about what had happened to Lupo and BB and Ivan. Which translated into a serious loss of respect, negating yesterday's show of strength.

So nip this one last problem in the bud today solo, then bulldoze on ahead afterward with new business. No looking back.

Tony couldn't say precisely what prompted him to wander to the balcony doors and peer out at the virgin day. Some protective guardian looking down upon him, perhaps. The *hekura* watching out for its vessel. Whatever. Tony knew only that he should take a peek.

And didn't like what he saw.

Saturday mornings were always prime pool time. Sun and water worshippers by the dozen. But a couple guys in suits were down there evicting the whole crowd. Swimmers, sunbathers, towels, tanning oil, air mattresses—*everything* was going inside.

If the suits weren't cops, Tony was the Pope.

His breath hitched in his throat. He looked at the condos directly across the parking lots. A starburst of sunlight glimmered off polarized sunglasses, just above the edge of the roof. Some guy wearing a dark cap. No, two guys, different locations. Snipers. No doubt one or two raiders were perched on his own roof, ready to drop straight down onto his balcony and blast right through the doors.

A low growl rumbled in his throat, unintentional and ferocious. He felt his mortal self tipping low, lower, countered by the rise of the primal, whose sole instinct was survival. At all costs.

Tony went sprinting down the main hallway, slammed open a closet door, and tore through the detritus until he could reach a hidden panel. He ripped it out of its brackets and plucked up a pair of objects just behind it. Serious firepower. A Browning Automatic Rifle, World War II ordnance. And an Israeli-made Uzi. The best of yesterday and today.

Heightened senses were almost excruciating in sensitivity. He felt, heard, sensed the multiple footsteps clicking up the outside stairs. The scent of his guns' oil was as potent as an aphrodisiac.

He slung the Uzi around his neck and held the massive BAR in both hands, then went charging back to the living room. Careful to avoid direct lineup with the balcony doors.

His breath panted, a husky grunt. It wasn't the change, but he was nevertheless packing a lot more beneath his scarred hide than before. Some hybrid state, the seesaw balanced with equal weights at both ends.

Motherfuckers. They tried to take him, wouldn't *they* be in for a big wet surprise? Absorbing a few shots from them didn't mean squat. He'd take a licking and keep on ticking. Firing away the whole time. Their safety-in-numbers machismo would wilt soon enough, once they understood that he wasn't going to roll over and play dead. Ever. He wondered who held the world record for copkill.

Tony bared his teeth, jacked shells into the chambers of both weapons. It sounded very loud, metallic adrenaline. He could smell the advancing fearsweat, at least six or seven sources coming close, closer. Could even distinguish one female in the group.

He took aim at the door . . .

And reconsidered.

Why be hasty? There *were* other ways.

Like giving them the totally unexpected.

He remembered childhood, Mama dragging him to Mass

and Sunday school. Remembered the lessons. Jesus—now, *there* was a guy Tony could respect. Because He knew how to take people by surprise. Tony couldn't see much use for that turn-the-other-cheek rhetoric, but hey, go please the world, right? He remembered a snippet from some prayer all the little tykes said: *Gentle Jesus, meek and mild* . . .

Yes. Yes! He loved it. Besides, he had a meeting in a few hours. It wouldn't do to show up full of holes, even if they were halfway healed.

Tony was guessing the cops were on the third floor by now. Barely enough time. He chugged for the closet and stashed the guns again. Ran for the door and unlocked it. Swung it wide open and lifted his smiling face to the warm winds lapping in. In the entry hall behind him, a hanging fern swayed, fronds rustling.

He took a seat in the hall floor, and the *hekura* submerged. For it respected treachery, above all things.

Gentle Tony, meek and mild.

And when the attack squad showed up on the landing and before his door, Tony gave them the biggest bright-eyed smile he could muster. Plainclothes detectives, uniformed guys, a few shock troops in the lead with AR-15s and bulky tactical vests. All staring down their gun barrels at a smiling childlike man in the lotus position.

"Hi, guys!" he said eagerly, then noted the sole puzzled woman. "And ma'am."

They would have none of his good cheer. The tide surged in, surrounded him, and he offered no fuss. Next thing he knew, he'd been rolled facedown and somebody had a heavy knee at the base of his skull, and the floor didn't taste all that great. His arms became pretzels, his wrists home to a pair of handcuffs. The really inconvenient kind, the bracelets linked by a rigid steel bar instead of a chain.

Once they were secured, one of the tactical guys, built like an NFL linebacker, hauled him to his feet.

"Thank you."

"Shut up," the guy said.

And then the policewoman was in his face. Nice-looking, but too serious. A few more years, and worry lines would carve into the smoothness of her dusky skin. He smelled too many cigarettes too.

"You have the right to remain silent," she said. "Anything you say can and will be used against you in a court of law . . ."

"Yeah, yeah." Tony nodded sheepishly. "So what else is new?"

He watched the world go by from the northbound lanes of Westshore Boulevard. To his left, the silver-gray plains of the bay helped lull him into the proper frame of mind. The language of water.

They had thrown him into the back of a patrol cruiser, one of the bland white sedans with a blue stripe down each side and a municipal shield on each front door. Altogether uncharming. No handles on the inner back doors and a wire mesh, like chain link fence, separating him from the pair of uniforms up front.

"Hey," Tony piped up. Practically forced to sit on his hands. Undignified. "You guys get very good gas mileage in these things?"

The cop in the passenger seat swiveled around, looking irritated to no end. His trim little moustache twitched indignantly and looked ridiculous on a face much too broad for it. Earlier, Tony had heard the driver call him Alvie.

"What do you care?" Alvie said. "You'll be lucky to worry about mileage when all you can do is push the gas pedal with a cane."

The driver chuckled and drummed big hands on the wheel like a snare rimshot.

"Just curious," Tony said. He was leaning forward, pressing his forehead to the wire mesh. Testing its tensile strength. "I was just sitting here wondering if they were very fuel efficient. How much gas a big caravan of these things burns on the way to a funeral—for, like, cops who *die* in the line of *duty.*"

Alvie had been smirking, but smoldering anger wiped it away. He cracked his knuckles. "Better watch your step when we let you out. Be a shame if you slipped and banged your face on the roof—broke your fucking nose."

Tony leaned back. The wire mesh hadn't flexed much, but enough to leave him reasonably optimistic. He charted their route to the police station in his mind. They could hang on Westshore all the way up to I-275, then cut east. A straight shot from there all the way to the station, which was cradled in the crescent formed where the elevated 275 curved to the north.

Soon, however, it appeared that they were taking a less distant route. The convoy of police vehicles veered northeast onto Henderson, which slashed diagonally across the north-south/east-west street grid. Tony began to smile. Henderson linked with Kennedy, which they would probably take until after they'd crossed the Hillsborough River. Then turn north and run him up to the station through downtown.

Or so they thought, anyway.

He kept his mouth shut until they hit Kennedy, then:

"You guys mind if I lie down? I had a long night."

"Go ahead," the driver said.

"Yeah, I don't think *too* many people's pissed on that seat."

Two miles to the river. Tony lowered himself on his side, folded his legs onto the seat. It wasn't likely they'd be rubbernecking around to check on him. So far as they knew, what was to see?

And so, turning his face down toward the seat, which exuded the pungent whiff of a public urinal, Tony willed the change. It was already champing at the bit like a winning racehorse. He trembled with the exertion of keeping it a silent process. Head elongating, flesh thickening, scaling over. New teeth bursting from hiding.

He exploited the increased elasticity of bones and joints by stretching his handcuffed arms, nearly wrenching his shoulders loose at their sockets. *Stretch.* He bucked his arms down once, twice, a third time—shoulders flaming and molten—and managed to slip his wrists beneath his rump. Slowly wriggled them forward beneath his thighs. And finally, one by one, working each lower leg and foot back through the loop of his arms.

Cuffed in front now. Which opened up worlds of possibilities.

He lifted his wrists to his mouth, fit the manacle bar into his protruding jaw. Chomped down. It parted like soft lead. He drew his wrists apart, free at last. The bracelets he could worry about later. For now, time was growing short. The Hillsborough was less than a mile distant.

And the zero hour had drawn nigh.

Tony popped up in the seat, all savagery and instinct now, and hurled himself at the tiny chain link fence. Jaws open wide, he hit like a torpedo. Even the burliest of felons could shake the fence all they wanted to no avail, but piranha jaws are among the the most powerful in the whole of nature, and Tony's were considerably larger than what nature allowed her own. The partition was no match for several tons per square inch of rending pressure. He sheared through it as easily as he might a lace curtain.

At the moment of impact, both cops swiveled their heads about, to check the commotion. The driver was secondary in Tony's mind. Take out the unoccupied man first. Alvie's irritable expression melted into unglued fear, and by the time his hand unsnapped his service .38 free of its holster, Tony was halfway through the fence.

Exceedingly upset.

And the screams were exceedingly loud.

Tony took out Alvie's throat with a single lunge of beartrap jaws. Black slacks and blue uniform went red. The driver bellowed and pressed against the door, too little too late. Draped over the seat back, Tony squirmed through another foot, rocking as the cruiser weaved beyond control.

Another lunge, and Tony clipped off half the driver's right ear and gulped it down whole. Through the windshield, Kennedy Boulevard tilted across like a crazed mural. Tony seized the wheel with one webbed hand and hauled himself further, more room to maneuver. Room to kill. Blood sprayed the dome light.

With his left hand, Tony shoved the dying driver's leg forward. Push the gas pedal with a cane, like hell. He jockeyed the foot into place and powered it down. The driver gurgled, tried to fight. Tony wrested the wheel away from him.

The radio had erupted with a barrage of static, distress calls from the other cars, shouts and panic and entropy. Music to his ears.

Tony had the cruiser up to sixty as he neared the University of Tampa on the left, the main building that was once a luxury hotel topped with onion-shaped minarets. Saturday drivers were sent into panicked skids, or looping out of the way as he barreled through like a runaway train that had jumped its tracks. Sirens from the escort cars wailed all around, while in their midst, he raged. An unmarked car drew along the right side, trying to box him in and bring him to a grinding halt. Tony jammed the twitching leg all the way down, his nails piercing the regulation black slacks until they drew blood; the V-8 engine roared. He yanked the wheel and broadsided into the unmarked, sent it ricocheting away.

Sixty-five and climbing. While sweet chaos reigned.

Past the university. Past the park and its sculpture, bent steeples erupting from the earth. The cruiser began to crest the rise leading to the bridge spanning the Hillsborough. A drawbridge affair, built to split in the middle for approaching boats. The center section was forged into a vast steel grate, with railings along either side. No concrete retaining walls, no curbs—just an unobstructed path into the rails.

Tony twisted the wheel and aimed. Tires screamed, and so did the driver. The radio caterwauled into fever pitch.

Tony released the wheel, snatched up the fallen .38 in Alvie's lap. He aimed at the windshield and jerked the trigger as quickly as he could, unleashing a deafening volley within the tight interior and etching a pattern of starbursts across the glass, side to side.

Let the bullets pave the way.

An oncoming car in the westbound lane locked into a skid as the cruiser rocketed past its nose. And Tony braced.

Impact.

Grillwork mashed into steel like aluminum against a sieve, the back end wrenching a yard off the bridge. The driver screeched his last and took out the pile-driver steering wheel with his chest.

Poised over the seat, Tony was catapulted straight at the windshield. He roared triumph, crossed his forearms before his head, and exploded through the weakened glass. Bursting free, free, sailing out over the hood and beyond in a blizzard of crystalline glass, a hailstorm of flying metal.

He straightened his body, curving into a graceful arc against blue, blue sky. Arms thrust before him, fingers straining for distance.

The glitter of glass, the heat of the sun, wind in his face. Life was grand.

Free fall.

Twenty-five feet down, the glimmering surface of the Hillsborough River beckoned. He dropped, as pure a missile as a falling arrow, and splashed down. Water enveloped him, cocooned him, nourished him, protected him.

With no need whatsoever to return topside.

He skimmed the silt of the bottom, dazed and shocky but his head clearing by the moment. Exchanging one world for a completely new one was always disorienting. Water rippled past gills, and he was ecstatic. He swam north, upstream, and the current was no great foe. The sunlight through water was comfortingly murky.

Flitting images, plans for the next hour, two, three. With any luck, back on the bridge they'd think him dead. Never surfaced once, drowned for certain if not killed by the impact. For the next few hours, the absence of a corpse wouldn't be terribly unusual. The river's current could have sucked it down into the channels, then out to Hillsborough Bay.

Swim, then. The river would eventually put him less than a mile from the safe house near the airport, where they had suckered Justin into thinking the mule was picking up a load of coke.

Perfect. There he could rest up, dry off. Exchange the glass-tattered shirt he wore for a new one. Lie low for a while. Make a phone call or two to put together the twenty grand in flash money he'd need. Then commandeer a car, or grab the Lincoln. It was still in the downtown parking garage where Lupo had switched it for the dirty-work Olds last night. He could switch the plates on it, just to be safe. He always carried a spare set of tags, registered in the name of a time-tested lady friend, in its trunk for emergencies.

And then he could be his usual punctual self.

And by tomorrow, the world would truly be his.

31
the dark continent, revisited

Justin and Kerebawa and April arrived far earlier than needed, at Justin's insistence. Busch Gardens, three hundred acres of theme-park Africa, simmered in heat sufficiently wicked for the real thing. He didn't know which was worse: walking in the open beneath the sun and its negligible mercy, or keeping to shaded walkways where the vegetation wove a blanket for humidity.

Go early, get a renewed feel for the place. They had parked east across Malcolm McKinley Drive after turning north off Busch Boulevard. Left the car in one of the auxiliary lots and caught a tram on one of its endless circuits. Twenty-two and a half dollars a head got them through the main gates, and as with his previous visit, some employee in Indiana Jones clothing snapped their picture together—all a part of your day at Busch Gardens. A claim receipt was thrust into his free hand—the one that wasn't carrying a gym bag—and he was told he could pick up the print later that afternoon. Only five additional dollars.

Bad memories, he didn't need this. He wished he'd sprung the few extra bucks for the picture of himself and Erik. One final memory, assurance that once upon a time, life had promise.

Justin looked around at the other park visitors. Families, couples, groups of friends, all of whom seemed determined to have a fine time despite the sweltering heat. He felt like a mutant in their midst.

Check the time; four o'clock. Two and a half hours to show-time, so to speak. Here in late May, Busch Gardens was on a nine-thirty-to-seven-thirty schedule. Hopefully the place would be a bit more thinned out by six-thirty.

Didn't want to traumatize any more kids than necessary.

After the rigors of last night, the day already felt long and wearying. A trip to a sporting-goods store to buy the gym bag, plus a box of 7.62mm cartridges for the AK-47—which would hopefully be unnecessary. Then the airport's long-term parking lot to recover the five kilos. Finally, hardware and drug stores for the last few odds and ends. Ready, set. The rest was up to sheer dumb luck.

"When you meet Tony here inside the main entrance," Justin said to April, nodding at the rough desert-hued portals, "take the lead. Bring him on through the park to meet us. Soon as you can get off by yourselves, get a little privacy, make him show you the cash. You don't do that, he'll know something else is going on."

She squirmed, uneasy, but nodded as he unfolded the brochure map given to him by a parking-lot attendant along with their permit. The graphics were cartoonish and very simplified, but the overhead layout was all he needed. His finger pinpointed their own location, then traveled a gradual path to the northwest.

"Now, we've got to get him up here in this corner, but if you walk it the whole way, it'll be tough getting him around to that rock hill without him realizing what's on the other side." He flicked his finger near the center of the map. "Take him to the Nairobi Station and get on the train there."

He followed the tracks' path to the east, then as it curved

north, and finally back to the west along the top of the park. Most of the route looped what was dubbed the Serengeti Plain, a large preserve of free-roaming animals. Zebras, giraffes, impala, gazelles, water buffalo, more. His finger lit in the northwest.

"Take him off the train here at the Congo Station. Then all you do is bring him down this little path, and to the rocks the back way. We'll run the course just to make sure, but you got all that?"

April nodded. "What if he's not alone? He might have someone following."

"That's a chance we'll have to take. But I'm betting he'll be alone. I mean, why bring backup when you can do what *he* can do?"

"Watch his eyes," Kerebawa offered. Half grudgingly, but a marked improvement. It was the first thing he had said to her since last night. "Watch who he watches, where he watches. The eyes will tell you if he comes alone."

Justin led them through the entire circuit, from entrance to train to disembarking to the spot where Tony had to be brought. They moved in somber contrast to everyone else around them, no joy, no delight, no interest in rides or gift shops or animals.

An hour had passed by the time they strolled south along the middle of the park and left April near the entrance. She waited beside a fountain, and Justin felt unexpectedly cold upon leaving her there. He felt her eyes at his back while he and Kerebawa set off the same way they'd come from. He would not turn around, *could* not.

You brought this on yourself.

Soon they were out of sight, and he decided the two of them should take a little time trying to enjoy some sights. Justin led Kerebawa to a shallow fenced pond stocked with alligators. Most lazed like olive green statues; a few glided through the water, prehistoric tails slowly whipping side to side.

"The *iwä*," Kerebawa said softly as they stood over the pond on a wooden platform. He shook his head in mild disbelief, as if things had come ironically full circle.

They moved along, Kerebawa's head a perpetual swivel as

they passed rides, festive buildings, contained animals. Justin wondered how pointless it all looked to him. Bulldozing nature to recreate it in some other foreign image.

At last they neared their destination. To their left, a glimpse of a vast skewed crater in the ground. A flash of blue water, a series of observation posts around the perimeter, gray rock bluffs at the north end. Justin and Kerebawa held their path until they moved in behind the bluffs, topped with foliage, and halfheartedly fenced off from the walkway. At one end, a small orange, brown, and white plaque read DANGEROUS ANIMALS—PLEASE DO NOT CLIMB ON ROCKS.

Justin leaned against one of three planters at the base of the rocks. Made from tiers of weathered wood, each sprouted a twisting banyan tree. Nice and shady back here. From somewhere up on the rocks, hidden speakers droned a constant ambience of animal cries and native drums. Muzak, Congo style.

Justin rested the nylon bag at his elbow atop the planter. Looked at the side he planned on keeping away from Mendoza the whole time they were dealing with him. Unless you were looking for it, the narrow slit cut along the bottom was invisible. And the red spur protruding from it resembled a loose thread, if a thick one.

"You are hungry?" Kerebawa asked when he heard Justin's stomach growl.

"I don't know. Maybe. Guess I haven't felt much like eating the past couple of days."

"There is time." Kerebawa pointed west along the curving path, bordered across from them by a stockade-type wall constructed of round vertical logs. Justin followed his finger until he saw a food stand far down along the path.

Justin shook his head. "Later. And listen—after all this is over? I'm buying you the biggest meal you've ever seen."

Kerebawa stretched and patted his stomach with a grin. He looked very young all at once, very innocent. "I have seen some *big* feasts in my time."

"I'll bet you have."

It was a pleasant moment, cutting the tension as easily as a knife. Pleasant, but all too short-lived. They were left looking at each other with no more self-delusion over their chances to sustain them through the duration.

At ten minutes until the meeting time, Justin pushed the bag closer to Kerebawa. "You still got that lighter I gave you?"

Kerebawa fished it from his pocket. A brand new butane.

"Still remember how to use it?"

Kerebawa gave him what he had once taught Justin as the Yanomamö version of the bird finger: an eyeball bared by tugging down the lower lid. Holding his eyelid, he lifted the lighter and flicked the flame, waved it for inspection. Smartass.

Justin returned the gesture with a wry grin, then glanced around. A momentary lull in foot traffic back here, might as well take advantage of it now, while it lasted.

"You better get up into those rocks and find someplace to hide yourself."

Kerebawa put the lighter away, deep into a pocket. He rested a hand on the bag, full of that elusive green cargo he had chased for more than two thousand miles.

"As soon as you see us get to these trees and planters," Justin said, "you know what to do."

"I know."

Eyes met, the great moment of frozen dread. Time to separate, leave behind the courage bolstered by proximity, side by side in the hot water. He wondered if April had felt this hollow in the pit of her stomach.

"Friend," said Kerebawa, and each met the other halfway in a brief, fierce hug. Justin smelled the sharp tang of his heat and sweat, and it meant as much as a lover's perfume.

They broke. And while Kerebawa slipped up the rocks, graceful as a cat, Justin crossed the walkway to stand against the stockade wall. To wait, alone.

Hating every minute of it.

Especially when he looked to the sky.

Tony was on time, and April found herself disheartened by his punctuality. Life and business go on, without hindrance.

As soon as she saw him crossing through one of the vast portal gates carrying a canvas satchel, she feared she was hallucinating. Too much stress, too much guilt, chemical malfunctions in her brain. This could *not* be the same man she had seen gunned down last night, half human and half devil. He had run away in a shambles of a body. Whatever he was, April had been expecting bandages at least, maybe a limp or some other sign of convalescence.

Instead, he was as robust as she had ever seen him.

Only when he came closer—smiling behind a pair of mirrored shades, hair drawn back into a careful ponytail, tight and lean in his leather and tank top—did she see the scars. At least the visible ones on his bare shoulders. Pale striations and faint puckers against the dusky brown of his skin. He blew her a kiss.

"You look like you've seen a ghost," he said. Never lost the predator grin.

She swallowed hard. Be strong, be tough, or he would be gaining the upper hand before she knew it. Didn't matter if it was only psychologically; that first wedge would make the next all the easier. Here was the chance for redemption; lose it, and living with herself would be tough, if she lived at all. For if guilt was anything, it was corrosive, slow death while eaten alive from the conscience outward.

"So you're back on Justin's team again, huh?" he said with an amused smirk. "Really playing both ends against the middle, aren't you?"

"I figured I'd try doing the right thing again."

"Right thing. Huh. That's in the eye of the beholder."

April stepped forward and placed her hands on his sides, ran them along his hips. Then swallowed her revulsion and skimmed them along the insides of his thighs.

"I'm not carrying a weapon. I look like I could fit one in these clothes?" He huffed indignantly. "You wouldn't believe the day I've had already."

She ignored him, continued to pat him down as subtly as she could. A sun-wrinkled woman with dyed red hair walked by, and her expression soured with distaste.

"Get a motel, why don't you?" she said down her nose.

April glared back. "Mind your own business, you prune-faced bitch."

The woman huffed, stomped away. Tony burst into laugh-

ter, high and delighted. Grabbed her behind and was still
laughing when she shoved him away. He patted the bulge of
his crotch.

"You act like you still remember your way around down
there."

She flushed with barely restrained anger. Wisps of hair
clung to sweat newly broken on her cheeks. She pushed them
free.

"Take off your boots, let me see in each one."

Tony perched the shades atop his head so she could see him
roll his eyes. "Knock it off, this is stupid."

"You do it, or this whole thing is off."

"And you're dead, babe."

April stood her ground. "I'll take that chance. Maybe I
wouldn't have before, but I will now. Believe it."

This time she chalked up a minor triumph for herself. He
looked visibly irritable as he complied, first one boot, then
the other. Nothing tucked inside, he was clean. That left only
the bag.

"Okay," she said. "This way."

Side by side, they moved deeper into the park. He slipped
back into cool composure a few steps later, dropped the
shades down again. Through the simulated Moroccan street,
into a shaded area designated as Nairobi. April eyed a spot
beside some caged parrots that looked private enough, for
the moment, and motioned him to follow. So far as she could
observe, he had come alone.

"Open the bag."

Tony sighed and unzipped the canvas satchel, held the
opening wide. Money, bundled and green. Lots of it, more
than she had ever seen at once. Twenty bundles of one thousand each—or so it looked, without occasion to count each
stack—jumbled loose inside. No weapons either. The bag was
the type with a hard, flat bottom. She rapped her knuckles a
few places. Solid, no hidden compartments.

"Happy now?" Once more with the irksome smile. "Where
to now, boss?"

"Just up ahead."

They joined a flow of others who looked to be having a far
better time, followed a row of fan palms, then veered

through the turnstiles of the train depot. Had to mill about the platform for another five minutes before the next one came along.

The train was built solely for sight-seeing—an engine, followed by a string of several cars with open sides and flat roofs. A flood of people got off, others remained in the rows of molded bench seats facing the front of the train. They boarded, settled down for the ride. As soon as the platform had emptied, the train started off with a lurch, and a girl near the front in one of the safari outfits began her tour-guide spiel. The family on the bench behind them were camera freaks, and she heard the constant clicking of shutters and whirring of motor drive units.

Tony propped a brown arm onto the seat beside her, leaned in with a conspiratorial light to his face.

"You know," he said, "looks like Justin's gonna be taking his earnings from today and, well—he's just gonna be kissing you off for good, you know, suck the fat one, honey. Not that I blame him. Bitch like you, you fuck a guy over like that the first time, how's he ever gonna trust you again? I don't blame him one bit, taking this wad and blowing town."

"Shut up," she whispered.

"I guess he knows I'm planning on taking *real* good care of you. I should think that goes without saying. Don't you?"

"Shut *up.*"

He smiled, very broadly, flicked his tongue in the air before her nose. She could smell his breath, hot, heavy, a thick meaty scent. She wanted to gag.

"Mmm-*hmmm.* Good care of you. Be ready to spread those thighs tonight. Tomorrow night. The next night. Whenever I catch up with you." He ran his tongue over his teeth and leaned within a couple of inches of her face. "Because I'm gonna eat you out like you've never been eaten before."

The train ride went on, and every minute at Tony's side was an hour, a day, a week. On flat and rolling plains, the displaced animals walked, ran, or stood and stared at this strange processional in their midst. The engineer had to stop once for a zebra that wandered onto the track and stood there, glaring in equine defiance.

"Who was your friend last night?" Tony asked later.

"Friend?"

"Yeah. Guy over by the railroad tracks."

April saw no point in denying Kerebawa's existence. It wouldn't wash, not with Tony. "It's a long story. He's from Venezuela."

Tony frowned, genuinely puzzled. "Arrows? Bow and arrows? I bet he had something to do with Escobar." He shrugged, chuckled. "No way to smuggle *those* into this place. They'd think he was here to hunt the animals. Too bad about one thing though. Can't surprise me twice with this guy."

Tony thoughtfully stroked the side of his mouth. Smiled.

"Maybe we'll have a chance for a proper introduction this time."

April watched him from the corner of her eye, feeling as though she were treading the razor's edge. No trust anywhere, with any of them, only suspicion, paranoia, hate. And still Tony seemed so calm. She saw his lips protrude for a moment, thought he was working his tongue around inside his mouth.

She was wrong.

He smiled at her, tightly, briefly. But the glimpse was eternal, enough for her to see every new tooth in his skull, evolved in just moments. Triangular, sharp, uppers perfectly meshed with lowers like the cogs of highly efficient gears. She shut her eyes and turned aside, remembering how well they could strip away flesh, without restraint. He chuckled at her side and stretched a taut muscled arm around her shoulders, pulled her close. She resisted, but couldn't fight, couldn't make a scene. Not here, not now, not this close.

Her stomach rolled again as he leaned in to nuzzle her hair, two sweethearts on a quaint train ride, and the carrion breath washed sweet and fetid past her face. Piranha teeth clicked in her ear, close, closer—and then his lips were at her earlobe and she could *hear* that breath. A brittle whine began in her throat as she felt his teeth open, brush her earlobe, and then nip down, and pain pricked her, hot and sharp. Anyone else would have mistaken the whine for delight, but no, he'd bitten a nick out of her earlobe. She felt the tiny beads of blood welling up to drip to her neck, hidden by hair. April trembled, feeling his tongue lap at the blood, once, twice, remembering all too well the electric effect blood had had on him last night. It took a staggering amount of self-control to keep from leaping off the train, running away to seek refuge among the giraffes, gazelles.

"I'm learning self-control," he whispered in her ear. "But you better still keep me calm. You know how excited that smell can make me. And you know if it goes too far, I just. Can't. Stop myself."

His tongue squirmed against her earlobe once again, while time dragged eternal. He pulled back, finally, smiled to show her that his teeth were back to normal. While she felt her blood dripping, dripping.

"I owe you for Lupo." The smile vanished. "That was just the beginning. Oh, we'll have time later, plenty of time."

While the train clattered on, April looked to the sky. Felt fresh heartbreak when she realized that none of them had thought to check a simple weather forecast today. Sunny this morning, sunny early this afternoon, so it should have remained all day. But the clouds had come, low and dark and sullen. Traitorous, conspirators.

The first fat raindrops panged down onto the train car's roof, harbingers of a coming downpour on their heels. *No, please, it's too late to stop everything now too late TOO LATE!*

Their guide on the microphone announced that the Congo Station was coming up on their left. The last thing she wanted to hear all of a sudden . . .

cloudburst

. . . because she sinkingly knew that this flat-out changed everything.

Before the rain began, Kerebawa had been crouching half in and half behind a creeping tangle of bush atop the rocks. Hugging low to the massive formation, that was the key to not being seen. Justin had made it very clear that being up here was taboo.

There was little to do during the anticipation but think, and his mind went in directions unbefitting a warrior. He was dirty within, his soul filthy. He had still not been able to perform the ritual of *unokaimou*, that week-long purification for having taken lives in warfare. They had started all the way back in Medellín, those dead men behind him who had stacked up like plantains for a feast. Their blood was an anchor on his soul.

Distracted by these thoughts of the recent past, he didn't foresee it as he should have. He smelled it only a couple of minutes before it came, read it in the thickening of the sky . . .

Rain. Tentative drops at first, soon a torrent that drenched to the skin, and suddenly he bore a fresh set of worries. From around him and below came the sounds of people fretting and scurrying for the cover of these strange buildings that were supposed to look as though they belonged in a jungle and truthfully looked anything but. Rain pelted him, darkened the rocks and drummed off them in a fine spray, ran across them in rivulets.

Rain. The very worst thing they could have hoped for.

Kerebawa raised his head to look for Justin, see what he would do. Call this off? He squinted against the rain, couldn't see Justin through the screen formed by the tops of the banyan trees.

Kerebawa's heart began to pound as it never had before a raid. This was punishment for his impurities, for straying so far, so long, without cleansing his soul. *He* had brought this down upon their heads. So he must not fail them, *must not fail.*

He laid his body across the nylon bag, anything to keep it dry. Then he remembered the little blue firestick Justin had given him. Surely it too must be kept dry. He wiggled it from his pocket and held it clenched inside his fist, trapped the fist between his body and the bag.

Waiting for hell, enduring high water.

If anything stands out as a symbol of Busch Gardens with all its diversity, it is surely the tigers. Not just any tigers, but the white Bengal tigers, of which a scant fifty or so are known to exist in the world, all descending from a single white (though not albino) male captured in India in 1951.

Busch Gardens owns a male and female pair, both born in

1981. Also living with the pair is a second female of normal orange coloring, but carrying white genes in addition to the orange.

The tigers are kept in an area called Claw Island, a misnomer, since it is not an island but a peninsula. Set in a vast hole of geometric oddities, it is separated from the park's visitors by a moat of water. A series of fenced observation posts rings the outside, some open to the sky, others roofed and rustic. Anything remotely close to the tigers' land is screened by a tightly woven net of stout ropes, easy to see through, but nearly impossible to climb over.

The land itself is of a skewed hourglass shape, bulbous at both ends and tapered in the middle. It is dotted with palms and small shade trees, a few stumps and logs, and most of the land's outer edge is lined with rock to prevent erosion into the water. The southern end borders the moat. The northern borders the curving formation of elephantine rocks built into a bluff some twenty-odd feet high, sloped down and in to prevent even the most dextrous tiger from climbing up. Wholly inaccessible.

That is, unless one were to try from the other side of the rocks. Where the only thing preventing access to Claw Island is a three-and-a-half-foot fence, a small plaque warning against climbing, and common sense. If you can overcome the latter, the former two are no great obstacles.

Just don't get caught by park personnel, that was Justin's main worry, and so far, so good. Kerebawa had remained undetected. Justin was beginning to think they had a chance of pulling this off, damn the consequences to be faced later.

That is, until the rain.

It seemed to come out of nowhere, one of those sudden Florida gulf storms, clouds cruising in and darkening the day in a matter of minutes. Pressed against the stockade wall, he felt it wash him from top to bottom, and fumed with panic bordering on paralysis. What an absolute idiot he had been, hadn't even considered this possibility.

On the walkway, parkgoers scurried with frantic urgency, tenting brochures and maps over their heads. Probably packing under the roofed observation posts, joining those already there, watching the tigers or grazing from the various food stands nearby. Waiting out this humid steambath of a rainstorm.

When Kerebawa didn't come down from the rocks, Justin knew the call was up to him. Every fiber in his being that was remotely vindictive said to grab Kerebawa and stage one final retreat, leave the traitorous April to whatever fate Tony had a whim for. Sure, and spend the rest of his life—far, far away—knowing he had lapsed to her level of betrayal.

No option, he couldn't do it. And by now, he couldn't pull her away because she would already be with Tony. The convergent meltdown of fate and destiny was minutes away.

He curled his lower lip in over his teeth, bit down to the point of pain. Slammed both fists back against the wall. *Hell with it.* They were committed.

Justin moved over to the end of the wall, beside the branch for the path leading north to the train station. He looked down along his body. The rain had soaked through the yellow and green surfing shirt he wore loose and untucked; it now clung revealingly over the Beretta tucked into his jeans. Although he didn't know what good it would be, since not even an assault rifle would stop the guy.

He was pushing sodden hair back from his forehead when April and Tony rounded the corner. They saw him, stopped. Drowned rats, the both of them. His heart lurched when he saw just how wet Tony's clothing was. This situation was steadily approaching lost cause.

"You're empty-handed," Tony said. Behind rain-beaded shades, he smirked. Looked back and forth. "Let me guess: It's with the other guy. Wooo, clever. I can tell, you've done this before."

Justin wanted to haul off and smack him. Probably lose a hand in the process. Then he noticed threads of blood stringing from April's ear, rinsing in rain down the curve of her neck. It was almost a shock to realize that, despite everything, he could still feel pity for her.

Get on with it.

Tony glanced about, craning his neck in exaggeration. "Where is he? Mmmm? Down there in the bathrooms? Hmmm. Maybe in that trash can over there. No? Don't tell me we have to ride the little choo-choo again. Oh *my*, anything but that." He shuddered theatrically.

Justin did some looking about as well. They were completely alone back here, thanks to the rain. It was good for that, at least. He pulled out the Beretta, held it in close to his body while training it on Tony. Who didn't even flinch. Instead, he looked bored.

"You're incredible," he said. "You just don't learn, do you? You got some kind of disability? That's no good to you anymore."

Justin shrugged. "May not kill you, but it'll still trash you over for a while." He nodded toward the canvas bag, looked at April. "Is it all there?"

She nodded. "I think. I didn't have time to count it."

"What's the use, anyway?" Tony said to her. "Why count his money for him, huh? *You* won't be seeing dime one."

Trying to divide and conquer, Justin thought. Be a smart move, if the situation were as it appeared on the surface. He reached for the canvas bag and Tony swatted his hand away, held the bag out of reach. Justin was glad he couldn't see the eyes behind those shades.

"Not yet, don't even think it," Tony said. "Try that again, I'll bite. Just ask her."

He looked at April, her bleeding ear. And believed.

Justin wiggled the gun barrel. "Come on. This way."

Tony eyed him, statue-still for a long moment. Sizing the situation, one hand wrapped around the bag's handle, the other resting against its bottom edge. A very defensive pose. At last he began to move, step for step with Justin, while April hung behind.

Across the walkway . . .

Toward the banyans, beyond them, the rocks . . .

Eye contact with Kerebawa, peering over a bush . . .

And Justin began to count seconds. *One . . . two . . . three . . .*

They came to the fence, Justin trusting that Tony was paying too much attention to him to bother looking at the little plaque at the west end of the rocks. They eyed one another like a pair of duelists awaiting a vulnerable opening, thrust and parry.

six . . . seven . . .

"Up the rocks," Justin said.

Tony narrowed his eyes, watchful, ever suspicious. He flipped his hand in an *after you* gesture. "Age before beauty."

Bastard. "Same time."

Agreed. Justin slid the Beretta back into his waistband. They skirted the end of the fence, then moved along to a spot that looked easiest for climbing. A better slope, a few more hand- and footholds. The rain drummed down, stinging, washing off the rocks and turning them slippery.

twenty . . . twenty-one . . .

A mere eight feet of quick freestyle, and they were on top. Justin crouched beside Kerebawa and the bush on a narrow plateau. He'd beaten Tony by several seconds, since the guy was slowed by his canvas bag. Justin looked at Kerebawa, saw him wink. A curious gesture; he'd never seen him do that before.

thirty-three . . . thirty-four . . .

Justin's heart began to quicken as he looked down from this new vantage point. He could see all but the northernmost reaches of Claw Island stretching away down below, surrounded by the dimpled surface of the moat. One of the sleekest, most muscular animals he had ever seen padded along its domain toward the rocks, perhaps seeking shelter from the rain. The alien nature of its coloring made it seem almost spirit. He then looked up and out, saw crowds packed beneath the roofed posts along the west side. Felt as if he were onstage. And sure enough, one or two people under the roofs began to point.

forty . . . forty-one . . .

Tony was up, his footing solid, six feet away. Had to distract him, keep him from idly looking down. Justin unzipped the nylon bag, reached in to hold up one of the kilos of skullflush. Another. Another. Just to show he was an honorable guy.

And to check something else, as well. Kerebawa had not let him down. For there it burned, along the inside of the bag where it was taped on a path rimming the bottom edge . . .

A construction-grade fuse. No worries about the rain dampening this part of the plan. The stuff would burn even underwater. Six inches every fifteen seconds. A magnesium-white ball of sparks crawled along the stout red cord, and the first foot-and-a-half was a track of crusted ash. He zipped back up.

fifty-three . . .

"So. What next, chief?" Tony stood with one hip cocked holding the bag in the same way he had below, one hand on its bottom edge.

All at once, Justin didn't like that pose. At all.

fifty-five . . .

It came as suddenly as a jet screaming overhead. A tiger giving a shattering roar at them. Tony yanked his head around at the sound, with such force that his shades went spinning away in the rain. His hand arced away from the bottom of the bag, holding some sort of knife. The blade no thicker than a credit card, the hilt no thicker than the blade. So very sleek, perfectly balanced, and Justin figured he must have cut a concealing gap in the middle of the bag's base, like an envelope. He was dropping the bag, whipping his arm back to throw.

fifty-seven . . .

"Eat it!" Justin screamed, and hurled the nylon bag with as much force as he could muster. He went dropping down to the scrawny bush with Kerebawa, drawing the silenced Beretta when he saw a startled Tony catch the bag one-handed. He aimed while on the roll along wet brush and unyielding rock, squeezed the trigger. The bullet popped Tony in the forehead as he staggered back with the bag clenched to his chest. Justin rared up to fire again, and then Tony's cobra arm flicked the knife, and it was a whickering silver blur that punched into his right shoulder. Justin went down again, the blade buried halfway in, and the gun clattered down the rocks. He cried out, heard April do likewise, and the sentiment was echoed by more than a few people in the roofed pavilions.

All drowned out, though, when the bag erupted.

One simple plastic bottle of isopropyl alcohol, very combustible and available in every drugstore in the country.

The colors were almost beautiful. The bag detonated into blooms of blue and orange fire, launching streamers of powder every which way, and they became a nebulous green

loud that hovered in the air for no more than a second
before dissipating into the rain, washed along the rocks,
gone, gone.

Tony.

He was staggered. But not fallen.

He roared, and from where Justin had toppled down the
rocks, he wondered if Mendoza might have been temporarily
blinded. Tony was blackened, eyebrows crisped away, his
tank top shirt in ragged tatters that looked streaked with
charbroiled blood. If it hadn't been raining, he would by now
have been flambé, a barbecued treat for tigers. But the fire
died almost as soon as it had been born.

All this had truly accomplished was pissing him off.

Struggling on the rocks, rain beating down, Justin
wrenched the knife free of his shoulder with a hoarse shriek,
and Kerebawa helped him to his feet just as Tony charged.

Mendoza was beginning to unleash the *hekura*, homing in
on the blood pulsing down Justin's arm. He was halfway into
the change when he swatted Justin with a backhand across
the face. Same spot Barrington had kicked, and it knocked off
last night's scab. It was like taking a fastball to the head, and
as the knife went flying, Justin flopped back to the rocks,
rainwater mingling with hazy spots swimming before his
eyes.

Kerebawa went on a weapon-free attack, crouching forward and ramming a shoulder into Tony's broiled midsection. From where he had rolled into a shallow crevice between two adjoining boulders, Justin watched as they spun
across the rocks, saw blood fly with rain.

And then saw them *both* go dropping over the edge of the
bluff.

Kerebawa watched the ground spin better than twenty
feet below, and even though he pinwheeled his arms, he
knew balance could never be regained. The only consolation
was that Mendoza was faring no better.

They dropped, and Kerebawa lashed out blindly with frantic arms.

The bluff was built so that a stone lip overhung it at the top.
One hand caught, and he clawed peeling fingernails into

rock. Swaying, dangling. He sensed the tigers pacing below two whites and an orange, heard the rumbling of their prima throats. Heard the cries of the watchers somewhere behind him. His free arm flailed to stabilize him, sought to grip the overhang.

He then dared to look beyond his own predicament, saw Tony hanging two-handed, not four feet away. Grinning like the demon he was. The raw, blackened face, further erupting into the image of his *noreshi*, the blunted snout pushing out out. The wound Justin had fired into his head had already quit bleeding. Razor teeth snapped at the air, and he lunged for Kerebawa's shoulder. Missed by a foot.

Webbing began to sprout between the man's fingers, the change near completion, and he raked out an arm to seize a fistful of Kerebawa's shirt. Next time, those teeth would not miss.

Kerebawa recalled so many vastly different things in those fractions of the next second. His wife Kashimi, the son she bore him who still nursed at her breast. The son he had someday hoped to teach to fire an arrow straight and true into food and enemies alike. He remembered Angus, the man who had opened his eyes to a world never before dreamed of. And Justin, even April—with whom he would likely never make peace—who had become his only friends in this world of far greater peril than any rain forest.

But the perils of home could sometimes not be escaped even in the heart of a city.

Piranha teeth, parting wide as Tony readied to strike . . .

Kerebawa knew the mythology, the legends. *Hekura* who ate the souls of men, kept them in turmoil, kept them from ascending to that next layer of the sky. God-teri.

It would have no piece of his.

His soul felt the wintery cold of sorrow as never before. Tony lunged . . .

And Kerebawa shut his eyes as he released his hold on the rock. He dropped with a tearing of shirtsleeve. Free, eternally free, as he fell toward white fur, white claws, white teeth.

* * *

Justin crawled painfully across the rock, on hands and knees, out of the crevice and toward the edge. There was a chance, always a chance. His shoulder throbbed, his cheek throbbed. Behind him he heard a scrape, and turned. April was coming up, draped over the lip of the slippery rocks. She'd found the Beretta, held it clenched by the barrel in one hand.

His arm buckled. He coughed, breathed rain. Ran prayers through his head in one endless sentence. And then heard the horrified outcry from spectators who were getting more theme-park show than they had ever expected, followed immediately by a renewed roar of beasts that rocked the evening air.

He knew precisely what had happened. The only question was *who*.

Kneeling, bloody and spent. Close to the edge. Drenched in the downpour that had sent everything to the brink of ruin and beyond.

He watched the arms of the sole survivor as they hurriedly clawed up and over the edge, saw the rising head. And cried out, half mourning, half mortal dread.

Justin toppled backward, in no shape to fight, not now, not with *that*. Not when the scent of his blood would send the thing into a frenzy that would end only when its hunger was sated.

They'd lost. Life. Hope. Everything.

Justin tumbled back, past April as she pedaled her feet against the incline. He fell down the curving slope, thudding into the gravel at the rocks' base, just inside the fence. He heard the crunch of April's shoes as she dropped back down, and then she was kneeling, helping to pull him up and over the fence, just as Tony reached full height on the plateau overhead.

Justin reeled backward, halfway supported against April as she aimed into the risen Tony's midsection. She fired. Again. Again. Again. Tony jerked, was knocked off his feet. Mere inconveniences.

Justin wavered, feeling steady enough to run, and locked hands with her. He heard the wet spatter of approaching footsteps along the walkway, on the run. He wheeled around and saw a trio of soggy guys in the Indiana Jones outfits, quickly ascertained they did not carry guns. April wasted no time in letting them know she did.

"Back off!" she shouted, and they froze. *"Damn you, just back off!"*

They shifted into slow motion, raising empty hands and backstepping out of the way. And did not interfere as he and April rushed past them. They would find plenty of cause to move in a few moments. Tony was struggling to his feet atop the rocks, dragging that canvas bag of money.

So they ran, he and April. Determined not to look back.

32
FROM CRADLE
TO GRAVE

The rain was beginning to ebb, and the more
adventurous were leaving their shelter. Busch
Gardens steamed, worked its way inside clothes. You got wet
no matter what, but at least rain was cooler than sweat. The
walkways were beginning to fill with life once more. Parting
like the Red Sea when Justin and April came charging along
the paths.

The inconvenienced were irritable, or curious, or just plain
did not know what to think at all, this bruised and bleeding
man rushing past in headlong stumblebum gait, the woman
beside him with a gun.

Wait a minute or two, he thought sourly. *Then you'll really
be curious.*

They lurched past rides and animals, gift shops and food
stands, along wide thoroughfares and narrow curving paths.
Everywhere, trees dripped the sky's burden. He could hear
distant sirens by the time they reached the main entrance,

voices in the early-evening gray that he knew would prove no help. Where understanding was limited, reliance could be suicidal.

A parking-lot tram was loading just outside the main gates, but they bypassed it. They'd move faster on foot. They had a death-grip on each other's hands as they pounded onward, beneath a sky whose indifference was etched into every rolling cloud. They were halfway across the entry drives when Justin broke his new cardinal rule and looked behind. Tony was wheeling through one of the desert-toned portals. From this distance, he appeared to have reverted back to the old Tony they knew and loved so well.

They sprinted across McKinley Drive, playing a dangerous game of chicken with hydroplaning cars that skidded and fishtailed and blew angry horns. Into the auxiliary parking lots, row upon row, so many cars. For a moment he blanked, could not remember. It came to him a few seconds later, and he twisted them on course for the rented Aries.

Mendoza was relentless, all the worse for his concentrated silence, total bloodlust focus breathing steadily closer down their necks. And then he branched, going his way while they went theirs. A reprieve was too blindly naive to expect; it was a race to get to a car first. And Justin knew Tony could cover far more ground and do a lot more damage in something the size of the Lincoln than they could in their little rolling box.

Justin was wheezing by the time they got to the Aries, fumbling with the key while April slipped and slid around to the other side. He fell behind the wheel, let her in. Threw his head back in pain and clamped a hand over his bleeding shoulder while jamming the key home. Let it rev, throw it into gear. They kicked up a plume of spray in their wake across the asphalt.

"Justin!" April cried out, pointing.

Tony was paralleling their path one row over, fenced onto the other side by parked cars. The separation wouldn't last long though.

Thanking the deities of Detroit for power steering, Justin spun the wheel right when they came to the lot's main drive. They skidded, spun halfway beyond control, and he battled to bring it under rein while shooting for the exit. Behind them, Tony had just careened out of his own row.

Justin gunned for the exit, the lines of cars already waiting to turn onto McKinley. Tony's grillwork loomed steadily closer in the rearview mirror, and Justin knew if they had to wait in line, they might as well roll belly-up here and now.

He saw his chance. Went for it.

He threaded the needle between the two rows of exiting cars, the right- and left-turn lanes. The fit was tight as a wedge; sheet metal flexed and scraped paint and primer down to bare steel. More horns, more angry faces. He stomped the gas and shot out across the northbound lanes, realizing if he stayed there a couple more seconds, devastating collisions with oncoming cars were inevitable. Once he swung left into the clear southbound lanes, he let out a breath he'd been holding for what must have been minutes.

Behind them, they heard a grinding crash as Tony tried to bull the Lincoln through. Justin looked back, saw the cars ahead of Tony furiously maneuvering out of his way rather than sustain more damage. Their lead on him was minimal; he was out of the exit and after them a lot sooner than anticipated.

Justin gunned it south, hung a screeching right onto Busch Boulevard. Veering from one lane to another and back like a stock-car driver jockeying for the winner's slot. April leaned over to buckle him into the seat belt and shoulder harness, then secured herself afterward.

He raged and pounded the wheel when they reached their first traffic light intersection. Red light, and too clogged to do anything but wait. He brought the Aries to a skidding fishtail stop, two cars between them and Tony.

"You're bleeding," April said, and he looked at his arm. The drops pattering to the seat. He had a crazy fleeting thought that it was good they'd taken the insurance option when renting the car.

April hunted for a cloth, found nothing, ended up ripping her shirt bottom into a long strip. She wound it around his shoulder, knotted it snug. Not perfect, but better than leaking.

"Does it hurt bad?"

"It was worse earlier." He spared the bandage a second look, then one for her. Gave her a softly grudging "Thanks."

The sirens he had heard minutes before grew as loud as an air raid; police cars in the eastbound lanes, rocketing toward Busch Gardens. The timing couldn't have been better, for they at least inspired Tony to keep his cool during the rest of the red light. While sidearms and shotguns may have been limited in effectiveness, they could still introduce him to new realms of inconvenience.

The police rolled past just after the light turned green, and Justin wasted no time exploiting the compact size of the Aries to thread back and forth through every gap opening ahead of them. The Lincoln may have had momentum on its side, and sheer V-8 battering-ram power, but no way could it boast the same maneuverability.

"I did something I didn't tell you about," Justin said. He took a hand off the steering wheel long enough to reach beneath his seat, pull out a familiar shape, and rest it on the dashboard. April blinked at it. One last kilo of skullflush.

"I thought you blew it all up."

He shook his head. "I held out on him. Just in case. So think fast. Come up with a way to use that against him, sing right out."

If his years in the ad game had taught him anything, it was to never, but *never*, go into a potentially hairy situation with only one idea to pitch. The more you had up your sleeve, the better off you would be, and the people at the top had the roomiest sleeves of all. Not that he had any idea how to turn one final kilo to an advantage, but better a little leverage than none.

Option number two lay in the rear floorboard beneath a blanket swiped from the motel. Fully loaded and ready to roar. A minute later, when the motel flicked past, he felt a kind of passing nostalgia. It had served its purpose well. We who are about to die salute you.

I-275 was less than two miles from Busch Gardens, and Justin breathed easier once they reached it. No more red lights to blow, no more intersections where disaster could be courted. He veered onto the circular on-ramp and let it slingshot him around into the southbound lanes. Tony followed fifty yards behind and closing.

Justin kicked the speed higher, saw Tony do likewise. No way to peer through that reflective glass. It was as impassive and impenetrable as the shades he wore earlier. And as they both pressed south, they played deadly games of hound-and-hare, wolf-and-stag among the traffic. The highway led them steadily closer to the towers of downtown, past exit turnoffs for quiet suburban neighborhoods, the likes of which Justin feared he would never know. He remembered them from the previous trip with Erik. He got a lump in his throat when shooting past a billboard for a radio station promoting its traffic reports. A yellow monoplane sat atop the sign, angled as if on crash course for the highway, and Erik had told him it was responsible for a lot of stained underwear in those seeing it for the first time.

The Lincoln gained, even got close enough to crimp its front fender against their rear. The Aries wavered, glass and plastic littering the pavement like confetti. It was coming back for a second taste when Justin cut left around a bus with curious faces pressed against the glass, looking down in restrained panic.

April sat rigid in her seat. He had a momentary thought that he would prefer to be doing this alone, not for her safety, just that he no longer cared to have her around. It was emotionally safer that way. He uneasily began to realize that she was becoming the receptacle for every free-floating bit of fury boiling inside. He wanted to blame her for the rain, for Kerebawa's death. Wanted to blame her because Tony was as tenacious as a pit bull on the attack, would not give it up even though common sense screamed for it. Wanted to blame her for things he'd not even thought of yet. Wanted to lean over into her face and yell until his lungs were raw, that none of this would have happened had she just had the courage to live up to the consequences of her past and not knuckled under to Mendoza.

But the road rolled on, and so did they, in tortured silence more corrosive than bile. Had Saturday evening traffic not been so plentiful, Tony would more than likely have already borne down on them and ground them into an end-over-end junkpile.

Nearer to the heart of the city, I-275 made its curve to the southwest, toward St. Pete and the bay. He had no choice but to follow, did not want to coax Tony into a chase through the city's streets. As recklessly as he was barreling along after them, drop him into inner-city traffic with that juggernaut and watch the casualties mount up in his wake. So southwest, then.

"Justin, where are you going?" April, tight and wired.

"I don't know." An honest answer, wearily offered.

"We can't keep this up, Justin. Pretty soon we'll run out of heavy traffic, and *then* do you know what he can do to us?"

"Hey, I'm trying, all right?" He glared at her, a gaze to wilt flowers. "You got any better ideas? I'm all ears!"

He sagged against the door. Hated this, hated everything, hated the speed, the tropical landscape, the other vehicles he dodged with no more concern than if this were a giant game of bumper cars. Hated himself for falling in with psychos and head-case bitches who masked their neuroses until they already had their claws sunk into your heart. Hated himself some more, on general principles.

The highway was an endless flatland, arrow straight. Open fields with gauntlets of palms on both sides. Stretches of glass office buildings and multistory hotels alternating with suburban tracts encroaching upon the highway. Billboards like widely spaced dominos. Justin had the Dodge opened up as wide out as its engine would chug.

At last they rolled through the succession of gentle curves that he remembered from his previous trip to St. Pete, the perfect night with April when she had shown him where she'd grown up. The curves that sucked them toward the Old Bay and the Howard Frankland Bridge spanning it.

Justin gripped the wheel and fumed, high-octane adrenaline burning through veins and arteries. He felt like a machine whirling toward inevitable breakdown, an explosion of parts that would rain shrapnel for yards in every direction. Couldn't remember the last time he had eaten, his belly an empty sack caving in on itself. Cannibalizing himself inside to keep it going, keep it all together.

He jogged around a pickup and thumped onto the bridge, shocks flexing, and in the mirror, the Lincoln followed his lead. Traffic, finally, had thinned enough to grant Tony his wish. He was on their tail, grinding bumper to bumper as Justin veered back and forth across both lanes. He turned the Dodge's fenders to junk on both sides. First the right, on the outer retaining wall, then throwing a slipstream of sparks from the left as it raked along the center divider. Tony pounded them again from behind, and the jolt was enough to cause whiplash.

Too many more like that, and the Aries would be a rolling junkpile.

"Get the rifle out of the back," he said.

April leaned over the seat and brought it up front, blanket and all. Unwrapped it. She had one hand on it when Tony came bashing forward yet again, and he heard the bumper dropping to the bridge.

Justin fought around another car, then had April take the wheel. She leaned across and gripped it with white-knuckled hands, and Justin pivoted in his seat, foot still jamming the gas, and propped the AK-47 across the seatback. No single-shot action this time; he switched it for full automatic.

The gunfire was agony on the ears inside the tight interior, and the first volley chewed the back window into crystal that avalanched from the frame. The second he centered on the Lincoln's windshield; Tony got the idea and cut sharply to the side and dropped back. Justin squeezed off anyway, aimed lower at the engine. Sparks pinwheeled off the hood and front quarter panel, and Tony dropped back another twenty yards.

Justin turned to face front again, regained the wheel. Rested the AK-47 beside his leg, muzzle pointing at the roof. It had bought them time, nothing more.

Rolling, rolling. The land disappeared behind them, the last of Tampa. Miles ahead, St. Pete. In between, only this ribbon of bridge. Justin wiped blood and chillsweat from his face.

Overhead, the sky had turned schizophrenic. To the north, day's last light was breaking through a caul of clouds, a horizon smeared with pink and tainted by an eerie yellow haze.

To the south, it was apocalyptic with clouds as dark as betrayal, and far far away, a jagged trident of lightning speared the sea. A sky at war with itself. He entertained the crazy notion that the eventual outcome would hinge entirely on his own victory or defeat.

Another mile later, he had the sense that his thoughts were not entirely secret. Privy to another.

He locked onto the wheel, wide-eyed, while he found himself experiencing that dizzying plummet through aeons. Began to shake his head, *No, no, no, I can't be feeling this again, not now, NOT NOW!* But protest as he might, he fell prey all over again. His mind swam, his soul reeled. And he recalled Erik's explanation for the first flashback. The hallucinogen gets into your system, lies dormant in fat cells, can be released later when the cells are broken down. Rationality still held a finger on him, and he knew that with no more than he had eaten lately, little wonder it hadn't already happened.

Ride it out, ride it out. . . .

The Dodge, hurtling toward destinations he could no longer clearly see. Blind instinct, dumb luck, sheer terror.

April was forgotten, yet he was not alone, in a manner that she had nothing to do with. He was open to some desperate soul clawing pitifully for companionship, and through a green soulstorm he recognized her. . . .

The same one as before, who had pulled him across the city to watch as she fell victim to Tony's experimentation in some sordid dungeon. And later, as Tony's twisted love turned to hunger. He felt the anguish of her self-loathing, realized she was incomplete, in fragments. And when he began to wonder where she was coming from, he received a claustrophobic image-sensation of sleeping at the bottom of the sea, where anything with a taste for your waterlogged flesh—or what remained of it—could come in for a nibble.

She's . . . she's right under *us.*

Erik had been found floating south of here. Justin felt sick with the realization that this was Mendoza's watery graveyard for those whom he chewed up and spat out.

Whatever was left of the girl clung to his soul with the frantic urgency of an abandoned child seeking comfort and assurances that she was not alone after all. Confessions, remorse. All at once he understood that she too had played a part in Erik's final night. She too bore the guilt, and it was digesting what remained of her. Seeking forgiveness and absolution, before nothing was left to burn.

How to finish Tony, it was all he wanted. If she could help, he would light a candle for her wayward soul every day that remained of his life. She did not turn him away.

She filled his head then, so much in so little time. Wherever she was now, in some transcendent Yanomamö realm, or a hell of her own making, she at least was privy to the laws of nature that those who traveled above her overlooked.

The sea. The answer had surged beneath them all along.

For a moment, all too brief, his mind floated with an image of her as she had been in life; blond, the face of a wanton child. And if two souls can kiss, they did. Just before she said good-bye, for he could divide himself no longer.

And when the green haze cleared, he could see as never before.

They were nearing the three-mile point where the microthin spur of land from the west jutted out to underpin the bridge. Its rocky shoreline was in sight ahead. Behind, Tony was regaining nerve enough to creep closer.

"Okay, son of a bitch," he muttered out the window, "let's see what you're *really* made of." Then, to April, "Hang on."

The Dodge was in the inside lane, and he wrenched the wheel to put it in the outside. Jammed both feet on the brakes, and as the Lincoln came squealing alongside to mash doors, Justin one-handed the AK-47 up and out the window. Held the trigger for a burst of fire that ripped through the Lincoln's fender and engine compartment and coughed out spumes of smoke and steam.

Tony lost control of the Lincoln, and as it lurched back and forth, it squashed the Dodge against the outer retaining wall. Justin slammed the transmission straight into park, brought mechanical anguish from his own engine, and then both cars were spinning into blurs that sent them bowling along the bridge in loops that reduced knees and stomachs to jelly. Justin wrestled the wheel, saw pavement and sea and sky whirl interchangeably. The world was motion gone insane, and shrieks of tires twisted beyond endurance as rubber sprayed into the air. And then . . .

Stillness. Can't spin forever.

Equilibrium was trapped in a slowing whirlpool. As the two cars sat cockeyed across the bridge in an effective barricade, Justin tried his door, found it wouldn't open. April wrenched hers open with a metallic groan, and once he'd undone his seat belt, Justin crawled after her and they both spilled onto the bridge. The stink of burnt rubber and antifreeze and hot metal reeked in the air. He stood, shakily, momentarily using the AK-47 like a crutch, and propped himself against a crumpled fender. Saw Tony emerging from the Lincoln some thirty feet back.

Beyond, the cars that had trailed them were slowing, stopping, giving them plenty of distance. Horns were starting to blow already, out here in the middle of the sea, of all places for a traffic jam. In the greater distance, sirens, and the telltale red wash of their beacons. Good luck to the boys in blue, then, because there was no longer room enough to bring up their cars.

"End of the line, numbnuts!" Tony yelled. The victorious glee in his voice was richly unmistakable.

Movement beyond Tony, furtive, the approaching clatter of shoes on pavement. Justin saw blue shirts and badges and a shotgun and figured a couple of the earliest arrivals had abandoned their car to sprint the rest of the way on foot. Passengers in civilian cars ducked into seats, and the cops were planting themselves behind the cover of fenders. Yelling orders. Throw down weapons, faces down on the bridge, all that.

Suicide, Justin thought.

They opened fire on Tony before he'd gotten all the way back into the Lincoln. He was hit at least twice, then popped back out with something lethal of his own, firing full automatic. The firefight was brief but intense, and glass flew all around the cops, and Justin saw a revolver twirling in the air from a dead hand. Mendoza was shouting, no, *laughing*, laughing as he stalked across open space with a rain of shell casings at his feet, and Justin dared not fire yet for fear the surviving cop deem him as unfriendly as Mendoza. And not nearly as resilient. A moot point, however, as the next of Tampa's finest was blown back onto the hood of a sedan missing half its windshield.

Tony turned, charged, leaped atop the Lincoln's ruined hood, and jumped down on their side, narrowing the gap.

"Now!" Tony called. "Where were we?"

The skullflush. *Where was it?* He'd meant to bring it—

Still on the dashboard. Miracles do happen.

Justin socked the assault rifle into his good shoulder, twitched the trigger enough to blow out the Dodge's windshield. He reached in and plucked the kilo from a litter of safety glass. The fragments sprinkled away like cheap jewels.

He held the kilo aloft at arm's length. And Tony stopped, frozen, homing in on it as sharply as a bird dog onto a pheasant.

"Last one in the free white world!" Justin cried. "What's it worth to you?"

The peal of Tony's laughter could probably be heard on both shores. He tossed the submachine gun to the bridge, and it clattered behind him as he passed it by. Bloody and utterly unfazed.

"I can be a sport," Tony said. "Fight you for it!"

"Justin!" April cried, tugging at his arm. "You can't make deals with him!"

"Go with it, I know what I'm doing," he whispered to her. Then, to Tony, "Come on, last one! What's it worth?"

Mendoza was all forward motion, confidence, and hunger. Burning. You could read it in his eyes from twenty feet, eighteen . . .

"Better believe her on this one," he called. "Guess what. I think you just played your last ace in the hole." Closer still.

Justin brandished the rifle, aimed it along the bridge. Tony stopped. Smiled, his burned and battered face still handsome in its own demented way. There was no denying the charisma. The *hekura* living inside him was probably the greatest single asset to ever agree so totally with him.

Smiling at the muzzle, Tony lifted both hands, displayed the webbing beginning to fill in between his fingers. He

ripped apart the remains of his tank top, stood at a cocky
pose. Black folds of fabric, tearing over his already-perfo-
rated chest. He puffed it out, slapped it with both hands in
open display of a perfect target.

"Be my guest." His voice was starting to roughen.

Justin backed over to the retaining wall, leaned his hip
against it. Watched Tony let the *hekura* out, and then April
fairly snarled and tried to wrench the AK-47 away, sweaty
hair swinging in her face. He twisted the rifle from her grasp,
pushed her behind him. Waited until the change was complete, and Tony was ready for hunting.

Justin gripped the assault rifle by the barrel, spun his body
like a discus thrower. And with a grunt and a heave, he sent
the gun hurling out over the bay. Far as he could throw. It
dropped, and they all heard the splash.

"You bastard, you just killed us," April said bitterly.

Tony was surprised, so far as Justin could tell. It didn't do
much to slow him though. The gap, smaller by the second.

Justin hopped onto the retaining wall, balanced on the top
with the kilo still in hand. He looked down at the choppy gray
water, foaming and sudsing against the bridge's supports fifteen or twenty feet below. The schizophrenic sky above, a
riot of contrasting colors. In between, the earth burned,
steamed, Justin suspended in the midst of it all.

"Justin, don't, the water!" April cried. *"The water, it's what
he wants, he'll kill you down there!"*

He ignored her. And from his perch, gazed down at Tony,
now coming in for the final charge. The kill. Twin rows of
teeth looking like the world's most formidable weapons.

Justin held the kilo high, totemistic.

"Follow your dreams," he said.

And jumped.

He curved his body into a dive more functional than graceful. Let go of the skullflush as soon as he began to drop,
plastic-wrapped green falling alongside him. His eyes were
open, and he watched the water swell and roll beneath him.
Shut his eyes, hoped for the best. Entered the water like a
dull knife.

A slap of water, crisp at first, then muffled as it sealed over him. All was dark, cool and wet, and the salt water wasted no time in playing havoc with the raw wounds on his cheek and shoulder. They burned, the cleansing salt scouring them, a harsh astringent that swallowed him whole.

He was thrashing in darkness to reverse his sinking when he heard the second muffled splash from above. Just as he knew he would. He felt Tony atop him like a living shadow, the grappling of hands and feet, and for one terrible lung-bursting moment he wondered what if he was wrong.

But he wasn't.

He knew it as soon as he heard the gushing bubbles of a warbling roar so tormented, it couldn't possibly be human. Half human, he'd give it that benefit of the doubt.

The feet, the webbed hands—they felt very feeble all of a sudden. No trouble to push away. The struggling body beside him grew weaker by the second, and when a single triangular tooth grazed his arm, it made nothing more than a small scratch. The saltwater sting almost felt good.

He kicked to the surface, broke water with a choking cough. Burned his nose. Well, he'd live.

Not so, Tony. Justin knew it the moment Mendoza bobbed up beside him. Head canted to one side, limp and boneless. Justin saw a blood-dappled gill.

The salt stung his own wounds, he couldn't deny it was unpleasant. But how much more magnified must it have been for Tony? A hundredfold? A thousand? *Salt.* Cleansing, cauterizing, abrasive. Freshwater gills just weren't meant to deal with it. Almost instantaneous death, painfully so. At least he hoped it was painful.

Oh, how he hoped.

Justin kicked for the rocky shoreline a few dozen yards to the west, his shoulder aching to the bone. Overhead, the sky darkened toward night, and he contemplated this entire liquid world he had immersed himself in. This part of that three-quarters of the earth's surface.

Maybe Tony hadn't died by jungle, by rain-forest justice, or restored balance of all things natural from that world. Born of primal, die by primal though? Okay, that much he *had* managed. For what was more primal than the sea? This vast, dark cradle that gave spawn to *everything*—land, plant, and, eventually, animal.

There could be no more fitting grave.

He kicked the last few yards, and finally pulled himself onto the rocks, salt water bubbling down his face, streaming from his hair, its taste upon his lips. Soaking his clothes from top to bottom. He sloshed up to his feet, rose beneath a sky whose crimson nodded its quiet approval.

Rebirth.

April had somehow climbed down from the bridge, perhaps over the retaining wall to lower herself from the outer lip. The drop would have been reduced to a few feet then. She stood on the rocks near one of the concrete pillars. From above and behind, the air was filled with the sound of a city of idling engines, blaring horns from nameless strangers who had places to go, things to do, people to see. Let them wait. Their lives would not self-destruct.

And the sirens, always the sirens. This time coming from St. Petersburg, the traffic lanes clear and unblocked across the bridge.

Justin moved carefully along the rough rocks, most at least the size of his head or larger. He turned around without knowing why, just in time to see Tony's lifeless form slip beneath the water. Almost as if it were sucked down by something that craved it, craved it badly. For whatever reasons. Sometimes the universe dispensed fitting justice after all.

April didn't say a word. And when they came face-to-face, at last, neither did he. Five seconds, ten. Finally, he walked past her. St. Pete was miles ahead, but it was no impossible goal. If he kept under the bridge, maybe he could even make it without encountering the police. Behold, the fugitive. When he reached into his pocket, he almost laughed when he felt his wallet still there. Another miracle. Green currency may have suffered from the plunge, but plastic was always intact.

He gave momentary thought to their cars, up topside. What they held. The Beretta in the Aries. And the Lincoln, that bag stuffed with twenty grand. Blood money. Probably be kicking himself tomorrow for not trying, at least—but leave it. Leave it all. He didn't want any part of that anymore.

St. Pete. His shoulder needed stitching, but maybe that could wait, he wouldn't bleed to death. He hadn't endured all this to run dry. No. Sleep, then. Sounded like the best medicine of all. Find some dirtbag motel where his appearance would not be questioned. Hole up, sleep forever. Hope like hell the police would not come knocking at the door until he was at least rested. What to tell them, what to tell them? Start with Rene Espinoza, get her in on the aftermath. He'd work it out, somehow.

Justin must have gotten a good twenty yards past April when she called out his name. He shrugged it off. But couldn't do it a second time. Had to turn back to at least acknowledge that voice. But was two weeks of love enough to undo that knife from his back?

He wasn't sure he could ever answer that one.

"I'm sorry," she cried out, and he watched her drop to her knees. Ritual posture of atonement. "Sorry I didn't . . . didn't *believe* . . ."

Crossroads.

He searched his soul, open wound that it had become, found the file marked forgiveness. A good deal fuller than it had once been. He'd finally learned to forgive himself for the mistakes that had sent his life on its downward spiral. Maybe it was time to branch out.

Maybe.

The sea, at the rocks near his feet. Splashing, eternal and constant and utterly without constraint. He watched it for a long long while.

Forgiveness was such a chancy proposition. And it wasn't fair to nail someone into a position where your resentment of their mistakes could eat you both alive. For the wounds ran so very deep.

He felt a trickle of salt water from his eye, and this time it had not come from the sea.

Justin took that first step toward her, and when it went okay, another. Scales were tilting inside him, one way, then the other. Maybe he couldn't do it. Maybe he wasn't that healthy yet.

But maybe he could. Taking it one day—and one sin—at a time.

Maybe . . .

Nineteen yards and counting.

He'd know when he got there.